jackie cassada

the toybox

a
changeling: the dreaming
novel

WHITE WOLF
PUBLISHING

the toybox	jackie cassada
cover illustration	joshua gabriel timbrook
cover design & layout	larry friedman

White Wolf Publishing
780 Park North Boulevard
Suite 100
Clarkston, GA 30021

Dedication:

For Nicky, Jim, and Sam, whose constant and abiding friendship and counsel means more than I can ever say.

Special thanks to Mark Rein•Hagen, Sam Chupp, Ian Lemke and Josh Timbrook, whose dreams became the heart of this story; to Carla Hollar, for her support and encouragement; to Erin Kelly, for her editorial skill; to Rich Dansky for the sparkling wit which helped me through the frantic final stages; to Stewart Wieck and Staley Krause for giving me the opportunity to tell this story; to Susan Adams for eleventh hour heroics; and to my family, for believing and helping me to believe in my dreams.

> When we are young
> Wandering the face of the earth
> Wondering what our dreams might be worth
> Learning that we're only immortal —
> *For a limited time.*
>
> — Rush, "Dreamline"

chapter

one

4

"Tell me more about the faeries." Dr. Adrienne Walters gave her warmest smile to the child seated across from her in the brightly decorated playroom that served as her office. Morgan Daniels was one of her most endearing patients, and the hour each week that she spent exploring the child's relatively harmless delusion more than made up for her more depressing cases. She settled back, her notebook open on the table in front of her, ready to hear the latest episode in Morgan's remarkably imaginative fantasy life.

Morgan brushed her long black curls away from her face and composed her features into what she hoped was an expression of sincerity. She had been giving serious thought to her visits to the child psychologist, visits her father had insisted on ever since the first time she had tried to tell him about herself, about who she really was. Her father thought she was crazy. Her mother insisted she was merely "gifted." The Lady Alyssa, Morgan's mentor in the duke's court, advised her to stop trying to convince her family that she was anything other than a normal child.

"There aren't any faeries," Morgan said. She sighed. "It was all just a story I was telling myself." She tried to sound disappointed.

"Oh?" Dr. Walters arched an eyebrow. She looked puzzled. She flipped through her notes, trying to appear casual. Her eyes scanned the transcript of last week's session with Morgan and found the passage she wanted.

"Last week you said that San Francisco was full of faeries — only you called them something else." She

the

paused, inviting Morgan to fill in the missing word. When the child remained silent, she continued. "Changelings, you said. Faeries who wrapped themselves up in mortal bodies. Now, why would they want to do that, do you suppose?"

Morgan sat up straight and folded her hands in her lap. She stared directly into the doctor's eyes. Lady Alyssa said that royalty always sat up straight and met the gaze of the people they addressed.

"I can't tell you that," Morgan said. "It's a story, and stories don't always give reasons for why things happen."

Dr. Walters stared thoughtfully at the child, noting her apparent calm and the sincerity that saturated her soft, musical voice. Apparent calm, she thought, because the girl's left foot tapped out a steady, muted rhythm on the plush carpet. She hides her nervousness well, the doctor surmised. She turned a page in Morgan's file, read over her notes carefully, and then closed the folder.

"You talked of something you called Banality," she said, "that makes it hard for these changelings to keep hold of their magic. If a faerie is touched by this Banality, she disintegrates forever."

"That's not what I said," Morgan corrected her. "You've got it all wrong. They don't disintegrate, they...in my story, I mean..." Morgan's voice trailed off as she realized that Dr. Walters was nodding her head, almost imperceptibly, at Morgan's words. She pressed her lips together and sighed. This was going to be harder than she thought.

"Go on, please," the doctor urged. "I may have misheard you last week, and I don't want to do that." She reopened the file, flipped to the page where Morgan had talked about the changelings' protections against Banality, and made a show of lining out a phrase with her pen.

"It's just a story," Morgan said, struggling between the desire to sound casual and the impulse to burst into tears. She could hear Lady Alyssa admonishing her, as if she were inside her mind. *"Ladies of the court do their crying in private, where they can indulge themselves in the luxury of their emotions. Tears weaken an argument, unless one is arguing with one's lover."* Morgan wasn't quite sure what a lover was, but she understood the first part. Dr. Walters must not see her cry.

"I'd still like to get the story right," said Dr. Walters, smiling faintly. "Even if it is just a lovely fantasy. Wouldn't you like to help me do that, Morgan?" she asked.

Sudden inspiration struck Morgan. "I can't," she said. "I promised myself that I would stop making things up in my head and pretending things were different from the way they are. You wouldn't want me to break a promise, would you?"

"Then why don't I just repeat to you some of the things you've told me over the last few months? You can correct me if I get anything wrong." She paused as Morgan's brows creased. "You look dubious," she said. "It won't be breaking a promise if you simply help me review what you've already said. It's very important that my records be absolutely accurate. Otherwise, I'm not a very good doctor."

Morgan thought carefully before answering. "Does this mean you believe me?" she asked, trying not to appear too anxious.

"Yes," Dr. Walters said. "I believe you when you tell me you made a promise to yourself that you don't want to break. And I believe that you want to convince me that you understand that your stories of changelings are just that — stories. That's the first step toward emotional growth, Morgan, understanding yourself. And you understand yourself by identifying your fantasies as fantasies, which you say you have done, and then by looking at those fantasies again, to see them for what they really are." She took a deep breath, let it out slowly, while she watched Morgan closely to see if the child grasped the logic behind her words. When Morgan's face continued to register only her usual sweet composure, she leaned forward across the table that separated her and the child. It was important to create a sense of intimacy between them if she was to continue to draw Morgan out. Lessening the physical distance between them would help. "Do you understand what I just said?" she asked.

Morgan nodded. "You're saying that now that I know I've been telling stories to myself, I need to look at those stories and see what I've been trying to tell myself."

"Exactly," said Dr. Walters. "Do you feel uncomfortable with that?" Sometimes the clarity with which Morgan grasped certain concepts made her feel less comfortable than she usually did around children. Despite her proclivity for elaborate fantasy worlds, Morgan often seemed wise beyond her years.

Morgan shifted a little in her chair. Sitting up straight was harder than she had expected. Lady Alyssa must have a much stronger backbone than she did. She tried to decide whether going along with Dr. Walters' idea would help convince the psychologist that she was normal. If she refused, she might just arouse the doctor's suspicions that she was lying to her, but if she agreed, the doctor might think she was falling back into her "made-up" world.

"Morgan?" She heard the doctor's voice calling her back to the present. She decided to compromise — a word the nobles of the Seelie Court insisted was important in matters of intrigue and social affairs.

"Okay," she said. "But just so long as we realize that what I said before was just pretend. That I really don't believe in faeries or anything like that."

"Let's start by talking about some of the people you've told me about, the ones who are really faeries in disguise," Dr. Walters said. "You mentioned something about a pooka who masquerades as a street corner poet. You say that when your own faerie self looks at him, you see a young man with rabbit ears. Aren't pookas associated with horses?" she asked.

Morgan shook her head vehemently. "Not just horses," she said. "They can be other animals too, especially if they're city pookas like Ras — like the one I told you about in my story." A thrill of fear ran through Morgan as she realized how close she had come to actually putting a name to one of the changelings she had so carefully tried to keep anonymous. "Besides, he's more like a hare than a rabbit. Rabbits are fluffy and cute, but this particular pooka is much longer and leaner, and when he actually becomes a rabbit — I mean a hare he's sort of a golden brown. You'd never mistake him for an ordinary rabbit." Morgan paused suddenly, aware that Dr. Walters was furiously making notes.

"This isn't new stuff," Morgan said quickly," and I told you I don't believe it anymore." She wished that she had Rasputin's easy ability to lie, but she wasn't a pooka. It just didn't come naturally. "I was just imagining what this person would be like if he were in one of my faerie stories."

"I understand," Dr. Walters said reassuringly. "I'm just making a few notes. There was also a storyteller, you called him a name I was unfamiliar with. Eshu." She found the word in her notes and marked it with her finger. "What's that? I just have the word here with no explanation. Is that his name, Eshu?"

"No," said Morgan. "The eshu came from Africa a long time ago. They like to tell stories and they roam around a lot, sort of like Gypsies. And this — person — he spends a lot of time on the street talking to people and trying to sell them things he convinces them they want. He's sort of like a used car salesman, only he doesn't sell cars. At least, I don't think he does."

Dr. Walters put her folder aside and folded her hands on the table. "Morgan," she said, and her voice was filled with concern. "Where have you been seeing these people?" She was appalled that she had become so caught up in the details of the child's fantasies that she had been blind to some very real potential dangers those fantasies posed, dangers not to Morgan's sanity, but to her safety. "Surely a street corner poet and a sales shark don't spend their time in your neighborhood?" The Daniels family lived in Pacific Heights, one of San Francisco's best residential areas. The people Morgan was describing sounded more like they occupied the lower rungs of the city's nearly imperceptible but no less stratified social ladder.

"Oh, I've just seen them around town," Morgan said, trying to sound nonchalant. How could she explain to the doctor about her secret trips away from her parents' house, usually with a changeling escort? So far, she had been able to avoid talking about that part of her other life. She chewed on her lower lip until she came up with an explanation she thought the doctor might accept. It was also partly true. "I saw them once or twice when I went with my mother to buy art supplies. Mother's an artist, you know."

"Yes, Morgan, I know that," Dr. Walters said, "and a very good one too. Your mother's illustrations for children's books are very good examples of how to use imagination to support, not substitute for, reality. You don't think that she believes that the unicorns and goblins and elves she paints are real, do you?"

Morgan stood by her mother's side, watching in fascination as the painting emerged from what was once a white canvas. Two trolls were arguing over a large sack of gold. In the background a pair of small, wizened men in pointed caps snickered as they crept toward the booty, ropes in hand, with the obvious intent of making off with the treasure while the fearsome creatures were occupied.

"They look real," Morgan said, restraining herself from reaching out to touch the still-glistening surface of the painting. Her mother laughed. "Sometimes," she said, "I think they are real. At any rate, there are people just like them everywhere you look. Big bullies who spend their time fighting over the spoils and not noticing when someone takes their prize right out from under their noses."

"I never asked her," Morgan said. "I think she'd like to believe, though." Her voice sounded wistful.

"We'd all like to believe in such things, Morgan." Dr. Walters got up from her chair and walked over to the large window of her office. She looked out at the vast metropolis that lay beneath her, stretching outwards to engulf the patch of ocean that was San Francisco Bay. Her eyes took in the sprawl of buildings, so crisp and eyecatching when viewed from a distance, but which could not stand up to close examination. A picturesque city, yes. A tourists' mecca, certainly. A sordid collection pool for wastrels and criminals and the self-serving, soulless masses who made up the bulk of humanity, most definitely. A thin layer of smog floated across the city. She turned back to Morgan, her face set in a hard line.

"It would be nice to believe that there existed a world free of the troubles and problems of the world you and I live in." She returned to her seat, but remained standing behind it, resting her hands on the polished leather upholstery. "But this is the world we're stuck with, and parts of it are very nice, almost as nice as the worlds of your imagination."

Morgan wondered if the doctor expected her to reply. She wanted to tell Dr. Walters that the world she really belonged to, the world of the Dreaming, was much more beautiful than the dreary world that surrounded her most of the time, but she didn't think it would be wise. So she just nodded her head.

That seemed to satisfy the doctor, because she sat down again and smiled at Morgan. "I'm sorry," she said. "We were still talking about your pretend stories." She looked at her watch. "Your hour is almost over," she continued, "but we still have a little time and I'd like to hear some more about these changeling friends of yours and where they spend their time. You said they had a...freehold...was that what you called it?"

Morgan nodded again. "I'm not sure why it's called that," she said, "but I think it's because it's a place that's free from Banality."

"The word 'freehold' is a medieval term," said Dr. Walters. "Your changeling world sounds very much like a world of knights and dragons and castles. Don't you think that in some way one of the things you are trying to express in your fantasy is a desire to live in a world where knights ride about on prancing horses and save maidens in distress?"

"I don't know," said Morgan truthfully. "I don't have any dragons in my imagination, and there aren't very many knights...only a few. Most changelings are commoners, because they are the ones who stayed behind when the noble faeries left the world a long time ago."

"I see," murmured the doctor. She had Morgan's file open again and was perusing its contents. "That was when the gates to Arcadia were closed? Is that the time you're talking about? I thought you said the faeries came back from Arcadia, though."

"I wish I could have seen it," Morgan said, and her green eyes sparkled as she tried to visualize what she had only heard about from her friends and from Lady Alyssa. "It was when the moon landing brought wonder back into the world. The faeries in Arcadia thought that there was enough Glamour on earth again to keep them alive, so they opened the gates and came back through." She heard her words and stopped herself from going on. "I mean, in my story, they came back through," she said, hoping that she had made what Valmont called a "good save." The look on Dr. Walters' face wasn't reassuring.

The doctor made another note in her file and closed the folder. "Your session is over, Morgan," she said, rising from her chair and walking past the desk to stand near her patient. She smiled down at Morgan. "I think you truly want to let go of your fantasies, but you still haven't shown me that you can keep from slipping back into them."

Morgan bit her lip hard this time to keep her eyes from filling up with tears. She had really hoped that she could convince the doctor that she no longer needed to come to these sessions.

"I'm trying, Dr. Walters," she said, her voice strained because of the hard lump that was forming in her throat and making her jaw ache.

The doctor stroked Morgan's curls once, soothingly. "It's all right, Morgan," she said softly. "These things take time. You've spent many years building up a perfect world to run away to when you're unhappy with the real one, and you can't just leave it behind you by making one promise to yourself. You have to work at it, and that's what you're coming here to do. I'll help you work at it."

Dr. Walters' phone chimed once, followed by the disembodied voice of her secretary, announcing that Morgan's father had arrived. Morgan got up from her chair and straightened her skirt. She blinked several times to clear her eyes of the moisture that was threatening to trickle down her cheek, and tried to smile. "I'll see you next week, Dr. Walters," she said as clearly as she could.

Lady Alyssa would be disappointed, she was sure, but even she couldn't expect overnight success. She retrieved her sweater from the hook by the door and went into the doctor's outer office to greet her father.

On the drive back to Pacific Heights, Gordon Daniels studied his daughter with an investor's keen eye. Morgan would have her mother's dark beauty when she grew up, but he was determined that she would inherit his own practical assessment of the world. His wife Alicia was everything he could ask for and a talented artist besides, but he felt the constant need to protect her from life's more brutal realities. If it hadn't been for his direction, he felt sure she would be selling her whimsical illustrations on some street corner for less than a tenth of their worth. If he had anything to do with it, Morgan would be able to face the world squarely and beat it at its own game. But first he had to make certain that she learned, and learned early, that frivolous dreams and sugar-coated fantasies had no place in her life.

"Did you and Dr. Walters have a good talk?" he asked his daughter.

Morgan turned her gaze away from the street scenes that trundled past her window and looked up at her father. She had been trying to see if, even within the closed confines of her father's Lincoln, she could catch even the faintest trace of faerie Glamour that sometimes emanated from the many shops that populated the Haight-Ashbury. Her father frequently took a route that passed through some of the city's less reputable areas for what he called "object lessons," pointing out various losers and derelicts to her as a warning of what she might become without a firm grounding in the real world. Morgan giggled to herself as he drove right by places she knew were shelters for the city's changelings.

"It was all right, I suppose," Morgan said, still trying hard not to laugh at the antics of a pair of street performers she knew to be pookas. She tried to summon forth her faerie sight to see if they were just mimicking a battle or if they were actually fighting chimerical monsters, creatures of dreams and Glamour that were invisible to mortal eyes, but the Banality that poured from her father made it impossible to do more than perceive the houndlike nose of one mime and the tufted ears of the other.

"What's so funny?" Gordon asked. "You should pity those poor clowns, not laugh at them. They're probably on welfare, you know."

Morgan nodded solemnly. She caught a fleeting glimpse of a familiar figure disappearing into the door of the Toybox Coffee Shop, at the corner of Haight and Ashbury. She had the impulse to unsnap her safety belt and jump out of the car as her father stopped at a red light. Her hand was poised to open the door when she heard the lock click into place.

"What on earth do you think you're doing?" Gordon's voice held not only anger but a tinge of fear. "This is a dangerous part of town, Morgan Daniels. Get your hand away from the door."

"I thought I saw Grandpa," Morgan blurted out before she could stop herself. Her father muttered something under his breath that Morgan knew she wasn't supposed to hear. As soon as the light changed, he pressed his foot to the floor and left the district as quickly as possible, cutting short his normal routine.

"I want you to forget about him, Morgan," he said harshly. "Your mother and I have agreed that he's given up his place in the family. He knows that he's not to see you under any circumstances."

"But why?" Morgan had asked this question many times before and never really understood the answer. "He's Mother's father, just like you're mine. Doesn't she love him anymore?"

"I'm sure she does, sweetheart," her father said, relaxing a little as they left the Haight and climbed the steep streets that led to Pacific Heights. "But sometimes people have to make hard decisions in their lives. Your grandfather came home from Vietnam a different person than he left. He was...disturbed...mentally disturbed and both of us were afraid he might do something irresponsible."

"That's not fair," Morgan said hotly. "Tor would never hurt anyone he was sworn to pro—" She put a hand to her mouth, and felt a blush rise to her cheeks. Of all the secrets she needed to keep from her father, her grandfather's true identity was the most important. Once she had thought that if her father knew that Tor was really a changeling like she was, he would change his mind about letting Morgan see him. That was before she realized that her father would never understand anything, and before Lady Alyssa made it clear that changelings were a secret that mortals like her father must never uncover.

"Where did you get that name?" her father wanted to know. They were nearing Morgan's house now and she was desperate to escape a situation that was getting out of control.

"Mother said his name was Torvald," she said. "Torvald Larssen, and he got a medal for bravery in the war. I just shortened it a little to Tor." Morgan closed her eyes and braced herself for the lecture she knew would follow her next statement, but it was better than pursuing the matter of her grandfather. "I was just imagining that he was a great warrior...."

Her father's lecture started on schedule and didn't stop until the car was in the garage and her mother came down from her studio to greet her husband and daughter.

Adrienne Walters sat in her office pondering her notes on Morgan Daniels. In more than ten years as a practicing child psychologist, she had come across many cases of disturbed children whose fantasies often horrified her with their dark imaginings. Usually those children came from dysfunctional or abusive families and their inner worlds were attempts to escape from the miserable circumstances of their lives. Morgan's parents obviously loved and cherished their daughter, and the child showed no signs of physical or emotional abuse. Yet Morgan had evolved one of the most vividly detailed personal fantasies in her professional experience.

From her first insistence, in her initial session, that she was not making things up, that she was really a faerie creature disguised as a little girl and that the city was full of many other "changelings," as Morgan called them, the child's fantasies demonstrated an internal consistency and logic that made them difficult to penetrate except through absolute denial of their objective reality. Gordon Daniels' intentions had been plain.

"I want my daughter to live in the real world," he had stated during the parental interview Dr. Walters always insisted on before accepting any new patient. Alicia Daniels had sat quietly throughout most of the interview, speaking only now and then to soften some pronouncement her husband made about their daughter's future. Dr. Walters was familiar with the children's stories

Morgan's mother wrote and illustrated, and suspected that mother and daughter shared a common interest in fantasy and whimsy. It was not her business to question Mrs. Daniels' grasp on reality — adult delusions were outside her area of specialization — but she wondered how successful her weekly sessions with Morgan could be if the child's mother continually reinforced her fantasies.

She had once recommended that Morgan spend some time in a children's institute in Colorado, where more intensive therapies might serve to ground her in the real world. Mr. Daniels had been adamantly opposed to any sort of institutionalization. He was equally against administering pharmaceutical treatments, claiming that he wanted a normal daughter, not a drug-dependent zombie. Privately, Dr. Walters agreed with him, but she also realized that in some cases, where fantasies were so ingrained that they threatened to replace reality, drastic measures were often necessary. Morgan was not, in her opinion, severely disturbed — at least not yet. So far her fantasies were for the most part benign, and her schoolwork did not seem to suffer because of them.

And the stories inside Morgan's head were intriguing in and of themselves. According to her, faeries had once lived with humans in an idyllic time before time. When logic and rationality began to replace superstition and myth, the faeries deserted the planet for their own dreamlike realm, leaving a few of their kind behind them. These faeries found humanity's general disbelief harmful to their survival and in order to protect themselves took on the appearance of humans to hide their faerie natures. They called themselves changelings, and spent their lives trying to keep in touch with their true selves. They did this by harvesting something called Glamour, which was provided by human inspiration, and it was this Glamour that not only powered their magical abilities but also kept them from forgetting they were more than the mortals they pretended to be. Morgan said that sometimes changelings forgot who they were altogether, and only a massive amount of Glamour could save them from being forever trapped in Banality, the child's name for the real world.

Dr. Walters read and re-read the Daniels file. Each time her eyes encountered the words *Banality* and *Glamour* she paused, as something struggled to emerge from her memory. She had seen those words used together before, but the context in which they appeared eluded her. In and of themselves, the words were not unusual, but the meanings which Morgan gave them were. She mentally referenced some recent professional journals, trying to identify the source of the strange sense of familiarity she felt when reading her notes on Morgan's delusions.

The beginnings of a migraine teased at the back of her head when she finally put her notes aside. She would find the time tomorrow to consult her references in an attempt to track down something that might help Morgan's progress toward normalcy. If a colleague had had previous experience with the same or a similar fantasy, she was curious to see how someone else's approach differed from her own. Meanwhile, her long work day was over and she anticipated another quiet evening spent nursing her aching head in a darkened apartment.

After dinner, during which she was very careful to keep her conversation confined to her schoolmates and other safe topics, Morgan went upstairs to do her homework. Her parents remained downstairs, watching a documentary on wilderness preserves on public television.

When she was certain that she would not be disturbed, Morgan closed her geography book and tiptoed into her mother's studio. She shut the door softly behind her and flipped on the lights. The paintings for her mother's latest project, a story called "The Flower Princess," stood propped against the walls of the airy room. Morgan went from one to another of the delicate paintings, drinking in the Glamour that poured off them from the abundance of her mother's talent. The same pictures, reduced to prints and transferred onto the pages of a book, were simply pretty illustrations, devoid of their ability to inspire Morgan's changeling nature.

After a while, Morgan felt sated. The ravages of contact with Dr. Walters and her forced denial of her true self had nearly depleted her of her connection to the Dreaming. She sometimes regretted her decision to remain with her parents instead of going to live full-time at the duke's court on Nob Hill, but she couldn't imagine just abandoning her mother and father. They would assume she had run away or been kidnapped, and the pain that would cause them was more than Morgan could bear.

Tomorrow night, her parents had tickets to the symphony. It shouldn't be hard to work an enchantment on Mrs. Goherty, her regular babysitter, so that she wouldn't notice the absence of her charge for a few hours. Morgan looked forward to trying out the results of her latest lessons with Lady Alyssa. In the meantime, she would have to content herself with conjuring up something to play with.

In their enjoyment of a rare moment of shared companionship, Gordon and Alicia Daniels failed to hear the delighted laughter that came from their daughter's room as Morgan played pillow tag with a pair of winged lion cubs that flew and pounced noiselessly above their heads.

chapter

two

Day or night, San Francisco's Haight-Ashbury presented a visual cornucopia of sensual delights. Although places like the I-Thou Coffeehouse and the Psychedelic Shop, bastions of those halcyon years when the area reigned as the capital of the Love Generation, had long fallen to the passage of time, other quaint and picturesque shops had taken their places as witnesses to the profligate variety of lifestyles and cultures that met and jostled each other along Haight Street and its environs. Near the intersection of Haight and Ashbury Streets, the Toybox Coffee Shop presented a mild front in comparison with its wilder neighbors. Unlike the tattoo parlors which specialized in body piercing, the goth boutiques and nostalgia vendors, the modest cafe attracted few customers.

Those individuals who passed through its frosted glass door, however, formed a special subclass in a city composed largely of societal subgroups. To the unpracticed eye, the patrons of the Toybox seemed to have little in common with one another. A pack of street urchins shoved their way inside past a well-dressed young couple who seemed to be slumming, while a tall, dark-skinned man from the pages of GQ held the door open for a slender, mousy looking woman who clutched a dog-eared paperback under one scrawny arm.

Inside, the coffee shop radiated an aura of cozy comfort. Dark, hand-carved furniture — including a massive mahogany bar in the rear of the main room — lent a timeless feeling to the interior, while soft lighting from a twin pair of hanging chandeliers encouraged a sense of privacy as well as conviviality among its customers. A row of booths lined one wall, while the center of the shop held enough tables and chairs to seat twenty people. Here, the changeling community of Haight-Ashbury found a shelter from the harsh world of Banality that assaulted them outside its confines. Here the pookas, eshu, nockers, redcaps, trolls and a few of the noble sidhe came to enjoy the freedom to be themselves.

Chip Fizzlewig stood in his usual place behind the bar of the Toybox and surveyed his domain. His dark, curly hair, thinning a little around the edges, framed his round face like a chaotic halo, giving his otherwise conservative appearance a look of wildness. He scowled as the room began filling up with the usual crowd of wilders and a few childlings — younger changelings, all of them — and began to make a mental list of the broken mugs and soiled napery he would have to contend with by closing time. He hoped the redcap population of the area would give the place a miss for a change; what was broken or dirtied could be mended or cleaned. He had a knack for doing that. But redcaps tended to eat anything they could get their hands on, including the silverware. He had no skill which could deal with that.

Since the coffee shop's opening, more than twenty years ago when the Accordance Wars ended and the fiefs and holdings of the Kingdom of Pacifica were established, Fizzlewig, or "Sir Charles," as Lady Zoe had dubbed him after he rescued her from assault by a group of redcaps, had held the Toybox and the building which housed it in fief to his liege. So far as he was concerned, his duty to the Seelie Court and to the nobles ended there. Within the freehold, the politics of nobles and commoners, Seelie and Unseelie, held no sway.

Changelings of all kinds were welcome in the Toybox so long as they minded their manners, paid their bills, and didn't rag him about being "promoted" from commoner to noble.

He finished his survey of the room with his customary, appraising glance at the coffee shop's "centerpiece," even though it stood well away from the center of the room. A large, ornate steamer trunk, it rested on a low, sturdy table against the wall opposite the booths. The fanciful carvings that decorated the trunk made it look more like a chest for storing toys, and its presence in the coffee shop gave the place its name — The Toybox.

It had been discovered, along with other relics from the last century, in the basement of the building soon after Fizzlewig had taken charge of the freehold. He had fallen in love with the trunk's delicate craftsmanship and with the intricate wooden puzzle built into its lid. He hadn't even noticed, until much later, so absorbed was he in its externals, that the chest fairly exuded Glamour from within. By all rights, some would say, the steamer trunk should have been turned over to Duke Aeon where it could reside within the security of his stronghold. But Fizzlewig, loath to surrender such a fine piece of artistry, had wrested a binding promise from Lady Zoe, his liege, that both building and contents should come under his rulership. By the time she discovered that "contents" included a probable faerie treasure, it was too late. Being a lady of her word, she accepted her loss with good grace, though she in turn charged "Sir Charles" with its protection.

It had been his idea to display the chest in the coffee shop rather than hide it, and it soon became a matter of pride for the local changelings, who considered it to be their collective treasure. That in itself served to guard the chest far better than Fizzlewig's own vigilance.

the

His sharp eyes detected movement in the rear booth. Tor was waking from his afternoon nap, he surmised, and a cursory look at the blond troll confirmed his thought. More than once, the boggan proprietor found himself ruing the mortal world's corruption of the word for those of Tor's kith. More like the giants of Norse myth than the grotesquely repulsive creatures of mundane folklore, trolls were once the most well-regarded of faerie races. Only the Unseelie trolls — the ogres — bore any resemblance to the monsters of false myth. His own boggan kith, as well, had suffered serious image problems, converted in the minds of dreamless humans into brownies. Both he and Tor labored under a further onus. Like himself, Tor had passed beyond his wilder years and was advancing into the twilight of changeling existence. The world's harshness had taken a larger chunk out of Tor, however, and it was all the aging troll could do to hold onto enough Glamour to retain his faerie sight. Fizzlewig sighed as he headed for the coffee maker. His friend could probably use a cup of cinnamon coffee right about now.

"All I want tonight is a small cup of cappuccino, thanks."

Fizzlewig turned at the sound of the familiar voice and eyed the speaker skeptically. "No baked apples and brie? No ginger pears? No seven-grain sandwich? What's the matter, Rasputin? Gettin' fat around the ears?"

The slender young pooka sighed dramatically as he settled himself on one of the bar stools. With one hand he smoothed the pair of graceful, soft brown rabbitlike ears that draped his expressive face. "I've been stuffing myself all day," he said, "and I couldn't eat a thing." Fizzlewig nodded gravely. "It'll take a few minutes for everything to be ready," he said. He drew a cup of hot cinnamon coffee, pouring it into a mug hand painted with scenes from the Black Forest, chosen from his prize collection.

"I hope you're not going to serve me anything in one of those antique things," Rasputin said. "Your standard coffee cups are quite superior in my book to those ornate pieces of crockery you honor your special friends with." Even Fizzlewig could hear the wistfulness in his voice that belied the words. The talented pooka was a regular at the Toybox, and his inspired antics had livened up many an evening.

"The last time I served you something in one of my mugs, it ended up as part of an impromptu juggling act," Fizzlewig grumbled. "I'll think about it." On his way to Tor's booth, he stopped by the door to the kitchen to call Rasputin's order for food in to Barklie, a fellow boggan who enjoyed nothing more than puttering around the Toybox's cooking facilities.

The door burst open to admit a diminutive whirlwind, as a crowd of childlings, led by a sharp-faced boy in torn jeans and a Bart Simpson T-shirt, shoved their way unceremoniously into the coffee shop. All of them but the leader and a spindly-legged little girl with sad, wild eyes clustered around the toy chest, pulling up chairs to reach its tantalizing puzzle-top. The boy scrambled onto a barstool and was halfway across the bar itself before Rasputin put out a hand and snagged him by the back of his jeans, halting his progress.

"It's far more annoying to sit on the stool and make a polite request instead of helping yourself, Edmund," Rasputin cautioned gravely. The young redcap gave him a sneer that might have been a smile.

"I'm supposed to believe that crap?" he said. "Hey, Fizzleface, got any lady fingers?" he yelled.

Fizzlewig hurriedly placed the mug of cinnamon coffee in front of Tor, shrugging as he did so. "Guess we'll have to chat later," he said. Tor nodded his thanks and wrapped a gigantic hand around the delicate mug, inhaling its spicy aroma as the steam wafted past his nose.

"Let me know if you need help with him," he rumbled, gesturing with his head toward the bar and Edmund.

"He's just rambunctious," said Fizzlewig, his voice uncharacteristically soft and lacking its usual critical overtones. Nevertheless, he made his way quickly back to the bar. "Lady fingers are out," he said to the boy. "You'll have to settle for gingerbread men. You can let go of his trousers, Rasputin. He knows better than to come into my territory without asking."

"Just trying to cause trouble, as usual," Rasputin said casually. "You know me, always ready to risk my neck when danger threatens."

"A dozen gingerbread men and a beer, then," Edmund said.

"Root beer," Fizzlewig amended, "and don't eat the glass this time." He noticed the little girl standing patiently at the bar. Even on tiptoe, she could barely be seen from his side of the counter. "Something for you?"

"Yeth, pleathe," she mouthed, her voice barely audible over the background conversation and the excited chattering of the childlings. "We need thome paper and crayonth tho we can draw the pictureth on the chetht."

"I have some colored pencils and some paper placemats," Fizzlewig said, pulling out one of the drawers on his side of the bar. "Will those do?"

The child's head bobbed up and down. Fizzlewig handed her the desired items and watched as she skipped over to join her companions. Soon all the childlings were busily arranged around the chest, drawing or tracing the fanciful figures that decorated its exterior.

"It's a contest," Edmund said disparagingly. "It was Ilith's idea to see which one could make the best drawing from the chest. At least I think that's what she said."

"She can't help the way she talks," said a new voice. "All sluagh speak in whispers." A tall ebony-skinned man with eyes like two onyx pools slid onto the stool between Rasputin and Edmund.

"Hi, Valmont," said Edmund with a tone in his voice almost akin to respect. "How's the Shadow Court these days?" The noise level in the room dropped instantly, and several heads turned toward the bar.

"The court is as it is, and their doings are of no concern to the folk here," Valmont said sharply. "As I was saying, my young omnivorous friend, the little sluagh cannot help her manner of speech or her lack of audibility. No more than you can resist the impulse to say and do things that most others consider vile and ungainly."

"I was just going to say those very words," Rasputin mumbled to no one in particular. Fizzlewig decided that things would sort themselves out without his attention and busied himself with taking and filling orders for food and drink while the coffee shop continued to fill with its usual small crowd of changelings. Later, some of the current patrons would wander out to enjoy the evening. Some, he knew, would go in search of places redolent with Glamour — the club scene in San Francisco provided a steady source of inspiration for many of the area's wilders, who soaked up the creative energies of the local musicians. Others would find art galleries or attend one of the many dramatic offerings of the city. Fizzlewig himself rarely left the Toybox. His private rooms and his workshop were above the coffee shop, and his own skill at woodworking and carving, along with the ambient Glamour that clung to the freehold, sustained his connection to his faerie self. Like other havens for the changeling community, the coffee shop's faerie nature emanated from the Balefire that spread its magic throughout the holding, warming it against the cold winds of Banality. In addition, no small part of the Toybox's Glamour came from the toy chest.

Her parents left the house promptly at 6:45. Morgan kissed them good-bye and watched out the window until their car disappeared from view. Mrs. Goherty, who had arrived at 6:30, consulted the list of instructions given her by Morgan's father. They were no different from the do's and don't's that she had received on earlier occasions, but she always made certain that Mr. Daniels' wishes were followed to the letter. When she was familiar with the evening's routine, she placed the list in the pocket of her sweater.

"Your parents won't be home until very late, Morgan," Mrs. Goherty said. "Your father's notes say that you haven't had dinner yet. Why don't we go in the kitchen and see what we can fix together?" The elderly woman prided herself on her ability to relate to children, mostly by combining a lack of condescension with a no-nonsense attitude.

Morgan smiled up at her. "That would be nice, Mrs. Goherty," she said sweetly. She started toward the kitchen, ahead of her babysitter, then stopped abruptly and turned, a look of surprise on her face. At least she hoped it was the same look she had practiced earlier in the afternoon. "Oh! I almost forgot," she said, reaching into the back pocket of her crushed-denim split skirt. "I made this for you after school today in my mother's studio," she said. She pulled out a silver-coated walnut shell with a cluster of three tiny flowers on each half. "I painted it myself," she said. "It's a keepsake."

Mrs. Goherty's usually stern face softened. "Why, child," she began, holding out her hand to take the small object from Morgan. "It's perfectly lovely. Thank you." Morgan turned her face upwards, as if expecting a kiss, and watched through partially squinted eyes as Mrs. Goherty obligingly bent down to press her lips against the child's forehead. Morgan kissed the woman on the chin.

"I really, really hope that when I go upstairs in a few minutes you'll be convinced that I've gone to bed for the night, and you'll be so sure I'm fine that you won't even check on me, and if you do check on me, you'll think you see me in bed asleep, and if my parents call to see if everything's all right, you'll tell them everything's fine and they should stay as long as they want."

Morgan stepped back and took a breath. Her heart pounded so loudly that she was afraid Mrs. Goherty could hear it. She had practiced the wording of her speech to make sure that it covered all the possibilities she could think of. Lady Alyssa told her that sometimes it was necessary to use the vulgar forms of faerie magic — particularly on mortals — to get important things done, so she had reluctantly arranged for Morgan to learn how to muddle a person's thoughts. She looked up at Mrs. Goherty anxiously, trying to see if she had been successful.

Her sitter's face looked mildly perplexed. She was still holding onto the silver walnut token Morgan hoped would strengthen the connection between the two of them, making it easier to weave her illusionary beliefs into Mrs. Goherty's mind. She thought that maybe her enchantment had worked, but she wouldn't know until she tested it.

"Dinner was great, Mrs. Goherty," she said. "I'm a little tired, though, so I'm going to bed now." She turned again and started up the stairs toward her room.

Mrs. Goherty followed her to the foot of the stairs, where she stopped. "Good night, Morgan," she called. "Sleep well."

Leigh picked up her week's wages, hung up her server's apron and left the restaurant. If luck was with her, she would have time to go home and try out Georges' new recipe for smoked salmon salad. The chef at Mardi's, where Leigh waited tables three afternoons a week, shared her own passion for creative cuisine, and his approach to the art of cooking kept her regularly supplied with Glamour. All Georges was aware of was that the restaurant's veteran server was also his favorite taster. Leigh liked to think that her encouragement inspired the feisty Frenchman to greater culinary achievements.

Her small apartment in the Upper Market district of San Francisco occupied the uppermost floor of a spindly, wooden frame house that dated from the last century. Leigh had been drawn to it because of its large, light-filled kitchen. She had acquired an impressive collection of cookware, skimping on cheap furnishings and poster art and splurging on a variety of saucepans, skillets, and state-of-the-art utensils to indulge her passion for cooking. Once inside her three-room castle, she changed from her server's black-and-whites into her customary bodysuit and jeans and freed her long, flame red hair from the pins which confined it in a secure bun for work. Her head still buzzing with ingredients and instructions for preparation, she ensconced herself in her culinary workroom. She glanced at her wall clock and noted that she still had nearly two hours before she was due in Pacific Heights, where a little girl waited for an escort to accompany her to visit her grandfather. She marveled at the child's determination and the ingenuity she consistently had to employ to keep her parents from finding out about her secret life, a life that Leigh herself knew only too well.

Leigh had been living in the apartment for nearly a year since she moved out of her parents' house in North Beach. Her parents still worried about their oldest daughter leaving home. Her policeman father had yet to reconcile himself to the thought that Leigh no longer needed his protection or his repertoire of old Irish sayings and maxims. Her mother's approach to Leigh's "abandonment" of the security of the family was simpler. She had cried nonstop for a week. Leigh was still trying to patch together the rifts she had caused in the family. Sunday dinner with them was her attempt at compromise, and little by little her parents were beginning to accept the fact that Leigh was determined to live a life they hadn't planned for her.

Nearly two years ago, Leigh had attended a concert by Aeon, a local band noted for its passionate and innovative music as well as for the magnetism exerted by the band's leader, an enigmatic and compelling young man known simply as "Aeon." She had gone with one of her classmates from cooking school, who had insisted that she hadn't lived until she had heard Aeon perform. Her friend had been right, for during the concert, a wave of something had swept over Leigh and her world had come crashing down around her. She went into the concert hall as the seventeen-year-old daughter of an Irish cop and an Italian housewife, and she had come out with the realization that she was much more than that. She was Eleighanara of House Fiona, a noble sidhe trapped in the body of a mortal woman. Her companion had seemed nonplussed by Leigh's apparent seizure and subsequent fugue state. She was only vaguely aware at the time of being hoisted into the air by a pair of strong arms and being carried away to the backstage area of the concert hall.

Aeon himself had welcomed her into the community of changelings, and to the Duchy of San Franciso, which he held as Duke for the Queen of Pacifica, Aeron ni' Siobhan. For Leigh, her introduction to the Seelie Court of San Francisco had been both the beginning of a new life and the end of her old one. At first she had tried to juggle her growing awareness of changeling society and its demands on her time with her normal existence, but she soon began to run out of excuses to explain her sudden absences from home or her need to keep hours that conflicted with her family's strict schedule. Her father began to suspect that she was on drugs, her mother feared that she was sleeping around, and her brothers and sisters didn't understand why she was no longer available to take them to ball games and Girl Scout meetings. She eventually realized that in order to keep hold of her sanity while living a double life, she would have to separate herself — at least partially — from her family. It hadn't been easy, but she had saved enough money by working three waitress jobs to rent an apartment. She suspected that her landlord was influenced by one of her friends at court, because the rent was surprisingly reasonable.

The salmon salad took shape under her nimble fingers. Most people looked at her as if she were a little touched when she tried to explain the delight she gleaned from the simple art of preparing food. Even some of her fellow changelings looked down on her cultivation of cooking and chefs, claiming that she couldn't possibly get the same inspiration from her chosen art as they did from painting, music, poetry or one of the other lofty arts. A few, however, understood the visceral and aesthetic beauty of cooking, one of the oldest arts in the history of mortals and changelings alike. As she admired, sampled, and finally sat down to savor her latest creation, she was beginning to feel giddy with Glamour.

By the time she left her apartment for her rendezvous with young Morgan Daniels, the policeman's daughter had succumbed fully to her changeling self. Eleighanara, knight-in-training to the court of Duke Aeon, began the journey to Pacific Heights, where the Baroness Morgania awaited her arrival.

"Valmont," Rasputin said loudly, "you promised me you'd tell me the story of that chest someday. Is it someday, yet?"

Valmont's face registered an expression of gratefulness as he turned toward the pooka. "I did, didn't I?" His mellow voice carried across the room, and the conversation, which had begun to rise again as it became clear that news of the Shadow Court of the Unseelie was not forthcoming died down once more. Valmont was an eshu, and the storytelling abilities of his kind were legendary. Even some of the childlings looked up from their drawings as they anticipated a story.

The door to the Toybox opened and a strikingly beautiful red-haired woman, her delicate features and pointed ears marking her as one of the sidhe, entered in the company of a raven-haired child who looked for all the world like a fairytale princess.

Rasputin launched himself from his place at the bar and cleared the space between himself and the new arrivals in the blink of an eye. He executed a sweeping bow before Leigh and Morgan.

"On behalf of everyone here, except myself, of course," he proclaimed as he straightened up and brushed some imaginary dust from the tips of his ears, "I welcome you to our most humble freehold."

"Hello, Rasputin," Leigh said, smiling at the pooka, although her eyes strayed beyond him to focus on Valmont. The eshu gave her an almost imperceptible nod. Morgan held out her hand for Rasputin, and giggled as he kissed it and pressed it to his heart.

"Lady, I am undone by the softness of your skin and the unmistakable sweetness of...butterscotch...that hovers in your vicinity," the rakish pooka intoned.

Then Morgan spotted the massive troll sitting in the back booth. "Grandpa!" she exclaimed. "Pardon me," she said to Rasputin. "I have urgent business that calls me from your company," she said, remembering Lady Alyssa's lecture on polite conversation. She ran toward the rear of the coffee house and clambered into Tor's lap. The weary look on Tor's face disappeared as he embraced his granddaughter.

"Did you have any trouble getting here?" he asked.

Morgan shook her head. "It was easy, now that I learned a neat trick. Mrs. Goherty thinks I'm upstairs in my room sleeping. Mother and Daddy are at the symphony and won't be home until late."

Fizzlewig ambled to the booth and placed a mug of hot cocoa in front of Morgan. "It's the unicorn mug!" she exclaimed in delight. "Thank you, Sir Charles...oops...I mean, Mr. Fizzlewig."

The boggan gave her a mock frown. "My lady can call me whatever she wants," he said gruffly, "but I may not answer to a name I rarely use."

Leigh finished chatting with Rasputin and joined Morgan and Tor in the booth. "Valmont's getting ready to tell a story," she said. "At least that's what I think Rasputin meant by his references to show-offs and oratorical displays." She greeted Fizzlewig warmly.

"I suppose you want the usual," he said.

Leigh nodded. "Spiced cider, if it's not too much trouble." She rose to accompany Fizzlewig to the bar, but he motioned her back into her seat.

"I'll bring it to you," he said. He nodded toward Valmont. "Don't want to disturb the evening's entertainment."

As if on cue, Valmont rose from his place at the bar and strode toward the center of the room. Someone pulled out a chair for him. "I'll stand, thank you," he said. "That way, I can see everyone — and everyone can see me." He drew himself up to his full height and stretched out his hands, palms facing upward, in a gesture that commanded everyone's attention.

"Listen, companions of the Dreaming," he began, "to a story of a mortal who lived his life on the fringes of a world he could not entirely comprehend but which colored his perceptions and brought the world of the Dreaming and the world of harsh reality close together for a brief, glorious, and ultimately tragic time."

"He's on a roll tonight," Edmund whispered. The redcap childling grinned broadly, his over-wide mouth seeming to split the lower half of his impish face in half.

Valmont walked slowly across the room to stand in front of the toy chest. The children moved aside to make way for him. The handsome eshu placed one hand atop the chest, making it an extension of himself. "This chest is more than it appears to be," he said. "It once belonged to a man...a mortal, yes...but a mortal with the blood of the Dreaming coursing through his veins. His name was Joshua Abraham Norton, and he came to the city of Saint Francis in the middle of the last century, hoping, like many others, to make his fortune. But, like so many others, he failed, and failed miserably. He disappeared for three years. No one knows where he went or what happened to him during that time, but some say that he touched the Dreaming, and that even though he was no changeling, it changed him forever."

Morgan was the first to sense the quickening in the air of the room. She leaned back against her grandfather's chest and tilted her face upwards. "He's doing it, Grandpa," she whispered. "Can't you feel it?"

"Doin' what?" Tor said in a low rumble that passed for a whisper.

By then, Leigh had noticed it too, and Rasputin's nose was twitching with excitement. "She's right," Leigh said. "Valmont's raising the Glamour." All around the room, there were small murmurs as first one group of listeners and then another felt the tingle of faerie magic brush lightly across them. The childlings, nearest to Valmont, seemed frozen in ecstasy.

"It was 1859," the eshu continued, "and San Francisco was caught between the last of the gold rush and the beginning of the search for silver. Joshua Norton reappeared in the city dressed in a military uniform and carrying himself with the grace of a born leader ready to assume his new role as the Emperor of the United States and Protector of Mexico." Valmont punctuated this statement with a rich, throaty chuckle, which was soon taken up by a few other listeners. The childlings, missing the humor, waited to hear what came next.

"No one knows why people believed him," Valmont said, his tone becoming almost scholarly, "but believe him they did. In fact, the entire city believed — or pretended to believe — that he was their emperor. He taxed the businesses of the city, and they paid him. He enacted laws, and some of them were actually obeyed." Spontaneous laughter greeted that statement. "He abolished slavery and outlawed discrimination years before the rest of the country mimicked his actions, but most importantly, he decreed that a Christmas tree be erected each year for the children of the city. He was a good emperor. He ruled for twenty years, and during that time, the hearts of San Francisco opened to him. Everywhere, people accepted the coins he had minted for him, restaurants fed him regally at no cost, and he was gifted with opening night tickets to the theatre. People brought him presents, too, in tribute to his equitable and compassionate leadership. This toy chest was one of those gifts, so they say, given to him by a changeling craftsman in appreciation for bringing back a little Glamour to a city awash in a wave of concupiscence — that means greed," he turned toward his childling audience for a moment. "You may wonder what he kept in the chest..." his voice trailed off while a gaggle of small heads bobbed up and down. "That," Valmont said crisply, stepping away from the chest and walking abruptly into the center of the room, "is another story for another evening."

"What happened to ol' Norton?" Edmund's voice rang out from the bar, his words garbled by the half-chewed spoon in his mouth.

As Valmont turned to answer the young redcap, the door to the coffee shop opened suddenly. Something slim and dark hurtled through the air, catching Valmont in his shoulder. Valmont screamed as a sharp, cold pain wracked his body. He fell to one knee.

"Take that as a warning from those you would betray," a woman's voice, full of steel and ice, resounded from the doorway.

Before the voice had stopped speaking, Leigh was on her feet, pushing past a startled Rasputin to race for the open door. "Someone stop them!" she called. Rasputin stood up to follow, but found Tor blocking his way.

"Watch my granddaughter," he said. "Let nothing harm her or else answer to me." With a quickness that belied his bulk, he moved toward the door. Rasputin nodded, mute for once, and planted himself between Morgan and the rest of the room. Morgan's face was drained of color, her green eyes wide with concern and fear. "Grandpa?" she said, her voice trembling. Rasputin turned to her.

"It's all right, lady," he murmured. "I'm certain everything will be just fine."

Morgan peered past Rasputin into the center of the room. "What about Valmont?" she said. "Shouldn't someone help him? Let me go to him." She ducked under the booth, intending to crawl past the pooka, but found herself in a tangle of legs as Rasputin began sneezing violently. Finally she gave up trying to get past the pooka. Disgruntled at being kept out of the action, the sidhe childling made the best of her position underneath the table.

From her vantage point at floor level, Morgan could see Edmund and Fizzlewig hustling toward the fallen eshu. Edmund reached Valmont first. The scrawny redcap bent over Valmont's body, extending a hand slowly toward the object, visible now as a slender throwing dagger, imbedded in his right shoulder.

"Don't touch it!" Morgan heard Fizzlewig bark in a commanding tone. At the same time, Edmund straightened up and stepped backward, his toothy mouth agape.

"Iron!" he said, awe filling his voice. "It's made of cold iron."

Outside the Toybox, Leigh and Tor tried to catch a glimpse of the unknown assailant. A September fog had settled over the city streets, and the misty tendrils made it difficult to see clearly.

"There," Leigh said suddenly, catching a glimpse of furtive movement in the shadows near the corner of Haight and Clayton Streets. She darted through the pedestrian traffic along the sidewalk. Behind her, Tor's heavy footsteps seemed to shake the ground as he half-trotted in her wake. She reached the corner just in time to hear the roar of motorcycles. Tor caught up with her just as two figures mounted on twin Harleys pulled out of an alley halfway down the block and sped south into the fog.

"Damn," she breathed, and readied herself to give chase on foot. Tor put an arm out to stop her.

"It's too late," he said. "You won't catch them now."

"We should at least try," Leigh said bitterly. "We need to find out who they were, why they attacked Valmont—"

"So, maybe we should ask Valmont," said Tor. Leigh's disappointment showed as she wheeled around and began trudging back to the Toybox. This time, Tor had no trouble keeping pace with her.

By the time Leigh and Tor returned to the coffee shop, the chaos had begun to sort itself out. Most of the crowd had departed, seeking a more congenial end to their evening, but a few regulars still sat talking quietly among themselves. Leigh sought out Fizzlewig to report her failure, while Tor headed straight for Morgan. Rasputin surrendered his charge gratefully.

"Valmont's upstairs in my rooms, resting," Fizzlewig replied when Leigh asked to speak to the eshu. "No one disturbs him until he's fit to talk," he added. "Not even the duke himself. You might, when next you visit the court, take him this, however," Fizzlewig said, pulling a heavily wrapped object out from behind the bar and placing it gingerly in Leigh's hand.

"What is it?" she asked, although she already knew what the answer would be as a vague discomfort engulfed her from the weight of the package.

"Someone's idea of a sick joke," Fizzlewig said. "An iron throwing knife. An assassin's weapon."

"I knew he should have told us what was going on with the Shadow Court," Edmund said, appearing suddenly at Leigh's side. "No one ever takes me seriously."

chapter

three

The mansion on Nob Hill attracted few prying eyes. Most passersby saw it, if they noticed it at all, as a faded relic from the hill's heyday, an old-fashioned, slightly seedy manor house that at one time might have served as home for one of San Francisco's millionaires, but which had not stood up to the passage of time. Perhaps a few people wondered why the derelict house had not yet fallen prey to the wrecking crews or why no attempt was made to renovate it in the interests of preservation. Most mortals, however, failed to make even a passing attempt at speculation, for their eyes were distracted by other sights and sounds just across the street or around the corner, and once past the grounds, the memory of the house's existence faded quickly from their minds.

This was exactly what the duke and his court, the Seelie Court of the fief of Goldengate, wanted — to be ignored by the mortal world. The weave of Glamour and dreaming that surrounded the mansion and its grounds provided a barrier of protection from the outer world. To those with faerie kenning, the true nature of the Nob Hill residence stood revealed in all its palatial splendor. Gleaming spires and balconies graced an exterior which caught the rays of the rising and setting sun, coating it with rainbow prisms of color. Immaculately tended lawns in both front and back surrounded perpetual gardens of riotous blooms and arbors of stately trees.

Inside the ducal palace, rich tapestries and velvet hangings decorated the elongated walls of the duke's high-ceilinged audience chambers, the ballroom, and the other rooms which served the functions of the court. As she stood in the anteroom awaiting Lady Alyssa, the duke's chamberlain, Leigh nervously adjusted her courtier's silks. Although she told herself repeatedly that as one of the sidhe, her presence at Duke Aeon's palace was unquestioned, she could never quite shake the slight discomfort she felt at being surrounded by so much elegance. She had heard that the duke's personal tastes ran to simpler forms of beauty, and that his own apartments upstairs in the palace were less overwhelming.

She heard soft footsteps approach the inner door, and turned just as a childling page entered, bobbing her head in acknowledgment of Leigh's marginally superior rank. Leigh forced a smile to her face.

"The Lady Alyssa will see you now," the page chirped. "Please follow me."

Leigh allowed her young escort to lead her past the open door and into a comfortable parlorlike reception room. Seated in a wine-colored damask chair, Lady Alyssa raised her head a fraction of an inch as Leigh entered. A dark-haired woman with classic features, the duke's chamberlain radiated competence and efficiency. Leigh opted for a knight's bow instead of a lady's curtsey. Lady Alyssa acknowledged Leigh and dismissed the page in a single gesture.

"Since there are none about to look askance," she said in a low, cultured voice, "let us dispense with further formalities. Please be seated, Eleighanara." She motioned to a smaller chair slightly in front and to one side of her.

"Thank you, my lady," Leigh mumbled, wishing that her own voice held more of the court and less of the street in its timbre. She sat gingerly on the edge of her seat.

"You did well in bringing us the weapon that caused such a stir in Sir Charles' fief last night," the chamberlain said. "We have taken precautions against its baneful effects and will attempt to make some determinations as to its origin and intent."

"Its intent was obvious, Lady Alyssa," Leigh blurted. "At least, at the time, it seemed..."

"No need to smooth over an honest reply," Alyssa laughed wryly. "I fully agree that its immediate purpose was to cause harm to the eshu Valmont, but I fear that there may be some darker meaning behind the attack which we have yet to fathom." She hesitated, as if considering her next words. Leigh waited.

"This Valmont," Alyssa began, "is he not known in the circles of the Shadow Court?" Her voice conveyed a carefully studied casualness.

Leigh, in turn, considered her own reply.

"I am not aware of his standing with the Unseelie, my lady," she said, her voice slow with deliberation, "but he has never acted in open opposition to the Duke's policies." Her own words amazed her as she realized that they sounded almost polished despite the basic emptiness of their content.

"Last Samhain, it is said, the Shadow Court elected him its prince," Lady Alyssa said. "In truth, it is but an empty tradition left over from a past that is no more, but still it does suggest some affinities this court does not condone. You have questioned the eshu about the attack?" Alyssa asked.

"Who'd want to hurt you, Valmont? Cold iron's a killing weapon." Fizzlewig asked.

Leigh had returned to the Toybox after escorting Morgan back to her home over the young baroness's protests, finally appealing to her grandfather for common sense. The weathered troll had asked a favor of his granddaughter, worded in a way that was impossible for Morgan to refuse, and the childling had swallowed her disappointment with admirable grace and only a few tears. When Leigh rejoined the small group that had agreed to help Fizzlewig explore the evening's mystery, she had found Edmund and Rasputin awaiting her arrival in the darkened coffee shop, now closed for the evening. Edmund was playing half-heartedly with the puzzle atop the toy chest, while Rasputin was busy mounting the drawings the childlings had made, arranging them in gallery fashion on the wall behind the chest. When she invited them to come up with her to Fizzlewig's upstairs apartment, Rasputin had smiled and muttered something about vital duties to the aesthetic community, while Edmund was characteristically blunt.

"The old grumpball doesn't want us up there," he said. "So he stuck us on guard duty." Privately, Leigh suspected that Charles had asked Edmund to guard the shop and Rasputin to guard the shop's contents from Edmund. She had hurried upstairs, arriving in time for his first question to the still-groggy eshu.

Valmont groaned as he struggled to raise himself to a sitting position. He lay diagonally across Fizzlewig's boggan-sized bed, the only position which could accommodate his lanky body. Tor stood near the center of the room, where the building's sloped ceiling was highest. Even then he had to stoop slightly to avoid bumping his head.

"How should I know?" Valmont said, pain coloring his voice. "I didn't even see my attacker."

"Who are your enemies, Valmont?" Leigh had asked, joining Fizzlewig at Valmont's bedside.

The eshu's laugh, though cut short by a twinge of pain, still held some of its usual richness. "Better to ask, who are my friends?"

"Maybe it wasn't Valmont who was being attacked." Tor said, more to himself than to the others.

Fizzlewig turned at the unexpected comment. "What?"

toybox

"Maybe Valmont was just an accident waitin' to happen," he said. "A lucky shot."

"Are you saying that the attack was intended as a warning to the Toybox? Or to Sir Charles?" Leigh stopped herself from immediately apologizing to Fizzlewig for the inadvertent use of his title. Fizzlewig glared at her, but made no further comment.

Tor nodded, but added nothing more. Both Fizzlewig and Leigh had looked to Valmont for confirmation or denial. The eshu shook his head.

"It's always possible," he said, "though personally demeaning. I have no lack of both friends and enemies, I assure you," he said, "but I presently know of no one who would so desire to hurt me that they would employ a weapon of such devastation." A half-smile tugged at one corner of his mouth. "I might consider it an honor to have such an enemy, but if I do, I can put no name to him — or her." His eyes turned toward Leigh.

"Yes, lady," Leigh said, aware that several seconds had passed between her answer and Lady Alyssa's query. "We questioned him late last night, but I believe he has no more idea about who attacked him than we do." She related Valmont's words to the chamberlain. Lady Alyssa listened carefully.

"It is unfortunate that the eshu is either unknowing or unwilling to share his knowledge," she said. "We shall conduct our own investigations, thanks to your initiative in bringing us the weapon."

Leigh shook her head. "Fizzlewig...Sir Charles...asked me to bring it to the duke," she said. "I don't know if it would have occurred to me to do anything other than get rid of it."

"Nonsense." Lady Alyssa's voice was sharp, almost a reprimand. "You are a sidhe noble, one of those destined to wield authority over our lesser kin." She paused, and her next words were spoken more gently. "Do not doubt your judgment, Eleighanara," she said. She rose from her seat, holding out a hand to Leigh, who stood quickly and assisted Alyssa to her feet. She sensed an end to the audience and prepared to take her leave.

"Fall Court approaches," the chamberlain said before Leigh could make her farewells. "You have, of course, received the duke's invitation?"

Leigh thought about the gilded scroll carefully stored in a small jewel chest in her bedroom. "I have, my lady," she said.

"It is customary to bestow knighthood on worthy candidates at that time." Alyssa smiled. "The duke and I both feel that your comportment, including your most recent actions on behalf of the court, warrants a suitable reward. Sir Cumulus, of course, concurs."

Leigh felt her face grow warm at the note of praise that flavored the chamberlain's voice. It reminded her of the few times when something she had done had elicited approval from her father, and evoked the same awkwardly self-conscious response from her. At the same time, she felt uncomfortable with the fact that she should place such importance on outward approval.

"I...I'm honored, my lady," Leigh sputtered, feeling very uncourtly. Lady Alyssa's words replayed themselves in her head. "Sir Cumulus vouched for me?" she asked, incredulous. "Really?" The duke's herald and one of his greatest warriors, Sir Cumulus was at the end of his wilder years; many who knew him mistook him for a grump, one of the "old men and women" of the changeling community. The ornate eyepatch he wore to mask the loss of his right eye in the duke's service added to his appearance of age. His blustering propriety made him a severe critic toward younger sidhe, and Leigh often felt her own inadequacies most keenly in his presence.

Lady Alyssa nodded gravely. "He recommended you to the duke, as a matter of fact," she said. "And in the light of your courage in accepting such a dangerous charge as Sir Charles imposed upon you, it seems his faith in you is justified. You will do well to prepare yourself for knighthood. In the meantime," the chamberlain's voice changed yet again, becoming brisk and matter-of-fact, "you will keep us posted on anything that transpires with regard to last evening, and we shall notify you of such discoveries as we may make."

"Give my regards to Duke Aeon," Leigh said somewhat belatedly, as she sensed a definite dismissal in Lady Alyssa's words.

"I shall, of course, bring him greetings from his newest knight." There was a subtle undertone to the chamberlain's voice that Leigh could not identify, and caution prevented her from further speculation on the matter. The Lady Alyssa left the parlor, and a tiny cough informed Leigh that the young page was waiting to show her out of the palace.

Across the bay from San Francisco lies the city of Oakland, a community wracked by internal strife and ravaged by economic woes. Here the councils of the sidhe were often cause for derision and opposition. The changelings who felt disenfranchised by the Seelie Court and its commoner supporters clustered in the working-class neighborhoods, clinging to each other for a sense of community.

From his residence in Oakland's Old Town, Count Elias tried desperately to hold his fief together despite the general tenor of resentment for the privileged "others" in San Francisco. As an eshu, ennobled by Duke Aeon and awarded the county of Oakhold as his domain, Elias commanded the respect of the area's changeling population, a mixture of nockers, boggans, redcaps, eshu like himself, and other commoner kithain, with only a smattering of disgruntled sidhe. To command their obedience in addition to this was more than anyone could rightly expect. Still, out of friendship to Aeon, Elias tried, although privately his sympathies drew him daily farther from the auspices of Seelie society. The sidhe, with their penchant for pomp and ritual, rarely paid heed to the real problems that beset the changeling community in their backyard — the dumping ground that was Oakland. In some ways, he mused, the people he thought of as "his" were still paying for their part in the Accordance Wars, and for being on the losing side in the struggle that established the supremacy of the sidhe after their return from Arcadia.

The eshu who now stood insolently before him typified the attitude of most of his "subjects." Blade's arrogant stance and his refusal to adhere to even the minimal protocol Elias sought to impose on the area's changelings were a continual source of irritation to the count, but the power base that Blade commanded was too significant to be shunted aside. Elias had, consequently, made Blade one of his advisors. By the time-honored method of co-opting the opposition, the count hoped to avoid any open power struggle between them. Last night, however, Blade had crossed the boundaries of acceptable behavior.

"This time you've gone too far," Elias said curtly. "Do you not think that the duke's forces will be looking for whoever attacked one of his fiefs? Do you want to provoke him into sending his knights out in search of those attackers? Are you so blind as to think he will not come here first, or do you think he will suspect Countess Evaine and her tame satyr have designs on his beloved city?"

Blade shrugged, a practiced gesture that sent ripples through his long black mohawk. "Rumor has it his dukeness is in such a funk that he wouldn't notice if his whole palace got up and walked away from him." Shoved through one corner of his mouth, his words were a barely intelligible mumble.

Outside his window, Elias heard the roar of motorcycles as members of Blade's gang, the Oakland People's Front, circled the block. The count shook his head. Sooner or later it would come down to a challenge. For his part, it would be later.

"Get out of here," he said. "I'm tired of this posturing. Go play with your friends." He gestured toward the window and the now-idling engines in the street below. "I will send for you when next I have need of your advice."

The surly eshu gang-leader gave Elias a mock bow before withdrawing. Elias watched him go with a heavy heart. By all rights, he should at least send a warning to the duke. Anything more, such as an apology, would be admitting to Aeon that the County of Oakhold was in less than capable hands. Not for the first time, Elias wondered just how long he could maintain his Seelie attachments in the face of overwhelming pressure from Blade's group and other factions who saw only continued frustration in their second-class association with the sidhe-dominated realm of Pacifica.

He waited until the sound of the motorcycles faded into the distance before he summoned one of his trusted agents, a furtive sluagh known only as Runt. The scrawny wilder crept into the count's chamber, and cowered as far away from Elias as

possible. Elias strove to conceal a shudder as he
acknowledged Runt's presence.

"Find Valmont," he said. "Tell him we must talk,
and soon."

He saw Runt's lips move, and only his skill in
reading lips allowed him to interpret the sluagh's
whispered "Yes, of course, whatever your Excellency
wishes." He smiled bitterly, and turned his head in order
to spare Runt any further ceremony. When next he
looked toward the doorway, the sluagh had gone.

The old satyr woke from a dream of shameless lust.
For a moment, as he became aware of the abandoned
warehouse in which he had taken shelter, he wondered
what he was doing so far from the duke's court and the
nubile sidhe maidens who had graced the silken sheets
of his dreaming. The incessant pounding on the back
door of the building soon brought back his sense of who
and where he was. He smiled and rubbed the sleep from
his eyes, a gesture of habit now, and not necessity.

His plans were beginning to fall together nicely. He
struggled to his feet, pushing back the weariness and
the continual aches that plagued him in the autumn of
his life. The dream stirred up faint twinges of
remembered pleasure in his loins. In his wilder days,
he would have been led by his horns; now he lusted
after more than carnal pleasures.

The pounding continued. The satyr brushed
himself off, and donned the velvet topcoat that lay
draped across one of the stacks of boxes that filled the
cavernous building. It was important that he impress
his visitors with the trappings of wealth and power

despite the seediness of their meeting place. He hobbled toward the door and undid the locks, neutralizing his wards in the process.

Blade and three of his companions, a scraggly pair of nockers and a rat-faced pooka, shoved their way inside.

"Well?" the satyr demanded, staring directly at the foursome, making no attempt to hide the glittering red and green jewels that served him for eyes. With this crew, he needed all the intimidation factors he could get, and the obvious magic that he possessed served his purposes well.

"It's there, all right," Blade said, "just like you said it'd be. Whiskers delivered the fake message." The eshu gestured toward the pooka, who giggled nervously and twitched her nose in response to the attention. "Sounded just like some sidhe bitch when she did it, too," one of the nockers added. The other nodded in confirmation.

"And the dagger?" the satyr asked.

Blade's hand barely moved, but the satyr felt a whisper of air pass his left cheek and heard a deadly "ping" sound from behind him. He did not need to look to know that the eshu standing before him had neatly placed a knife in one of the boxes just behind his head.

"I don't make a habit of missing," Blade replied. "It's a professional thing."

"I hope that one was steel," the satyr said.

The eshu gang-leader smiled. "Of course." He snapped his fingers, and one of the nockers darted past him to retrieve the weapon. He handed it back to Blade in full view of the satyr, its steely glint obvious in the late afternoon sunlight that penetrated the grimy windows of the warehouse. "Only those who court Banality use cold iron." Blade's grin mocked his words.

The old satyr reached into a pocket of his coat and withdrew a small pouch of fine fawn-colored deerskin. He tossed it into the air toward the four wilders. One of the nockers snatched it with a gnarled hand. He was about to open it when he became aware of Blade, who hadn't moved except to stretch out his arm, his hand held palm up. The nocker placed the pouch in his leader's hand.

"Don't worry, Limbo," he sneered. "If it's what it had better be, there'll be enough to share." He opened the pouch and looked inside.

"There's enough Dross in those pieces of moss and shells to keep you in Glamour for some time if you don't use it up all at once," the satyr said smugly. "But of course, your real payment will come later, when everything falls together." His voice was oily, seductive with promise. "You'd better go now," the old changeling suggested. "The less time we spend in each other's company, the safer we both are from those who might expose us. That would be unfortunate, don't you think, Count Blade?"

Blade nodded gravely as his co-conspirator spoke, his attention still taken up with fingering the contents of the pouch. At the sound of his name affixed to a title, however, his lips curled softly upward in a hint of a smile. He turned to go, cocking his head in a gesture to his companions. As they began to troop out the door of the warehouse, the old satyr chuckled softly to himself.

"Well done, Malacar," a soft, silken voice sounded from deep within the shadowy recesses of the warehouse. The satyr stiffened, turning slowly to face the direction of the voice.

"Come no farther," the speaker commanded, and the force which empowered her words froze the satyr in his tracks. "It is not for you to give away titles," the voice continued. "That is the prerogative of someone far greater than you...or me for that matter. Still, you play the piper well; let us see now how well you dance when someone else calls the tune."

"How may I serve you?" Malacar's voice shook slightly, as he fought the overwhelming urge to grovel before the speaker, known to him only as the lady of the shadows.

"Listen carefully," the voice said. "I shall tell you everything you need to know for the present." Entranced by her dulcet tones, Malacar drank in her every word.

Georgia sat on the hood of her cab, a purple and yellow 1957 Dodge gleaming in the bright autumn sunlight. She removed her battered cabbie's hat long enough to comb her bony fingers through her red, black and white spiked hair. Business had been slow this afternoon; in the daytime, most mortals were understandably leery of engaging the services of a middle-aged punk. If the tricolored hair didn't put them off, then the gold chain running from a nose-ring to the matching ring in her left ear did. In the evenings, she usually fared better. The nighttime crowds were less choosy, or more adventurous, and she generally did a brisk business once the sun set. Still, she enjoyed just driving around the city — a far cry from the frenetic jam-ups of New York, from which she had migrated, years ago, and where she had spent most of her wilder days. Here in the relative tranquility of San Francisco, she hoped to recapture some of the zest for living that had once threatened to slip from her grasp.

the

The nocker cabbie's skin prickled with the odd tingle that alerted her to the presence of another changeling and she peered around her to locate the source of the feeling. From a narrow alley between two nearby buildings, she heard a faint, whispery voice.

"Over here, where it's dark."

Georgia pulled her cap down lower over her forehead to shade her eyes. She could just barely make out a pale, diminutive form huddled in the shadows of the alley. She sighed, pitying what could only be one of the sluagh. Their aversion to light, and their corresponding affinity to dark, dank places was legendary. She made her way toward the alley, peeling off her bulky bomber jacket as she approached.

She recognized Runt, one of Count Elias' messengers. "Looking for a ride somewhere?" Her question was half challenge, half genuine query. "You're on the wrong side of the bridge, you know."

The scrawny, black-clad figure made a reply which Georgia barely heard. "Say again?" she asked. "Can you yell this time?"

"The Count wants to speak with Valmont," Runt answered in a voice that, for him, was loud but barely crossed the line between inaudible and audible for Georgia.

"Valmont?" Georgia threw back her head and laughed, a deep, throaty sound that made one or two heads turn as people passed back and forth along the sidewalk. "First of all," she said, looking at the lowering sun and then at her watch, "he's probably not up yet. Secondly, I don't keep Mr. Nighttime's schedule for him."

"I can pay," Runt screamed in his loudest whisper.

"Up front? Money or Dross?"

A hand with long, pale, bony fingers extended a velvet pouch toward Georgia. "Up front, for searching for him. More, later, for finding him."

Georgia held out her hand while the sluagh dropped a pair of iridescent crystals into her palm. She could feel the faint hum of the entrapped Glamour within them.

"Here," she said, tossing her bomber jacket toward her fare. "Throw this over you till you get in the cab. It'll keep the light away from most of you."

She returned to her car and opened the back door, and watched as her jacket scuttled across the sidewalk. She snatched it from the sluagh as he propelled his skinny body into the back of the Dodge. She caught a faint whiff of residual decay from the leather. Even the childling sluagh smelled vaguely like dead mice. She shook the jacket out before draping it over her shoulders and climbing behind the wheel. I'll have to remember to go by the dry-cleaners, she thought ruefully.

Inside, the car was cool and dark. Tinted glass on all the windows kept out the worst of the sunlight's glare without impeding vision.

"Hang on," she called over her shoulder. "Let's see if we can't roust that wily eshu from his lair. I hope you don't mind shortcuts."

Georgia pulled out into the traffic. Honking her horn loudly, she felt a burst of chimeric energy surround the cab. "We're on our way," she hooted as she brought her car up to speed with the surrounding traffic. What she couldn't go around, she and the enchanted Dodge went over. She never worried about the mortal drivers or their vehicles when she executed even her wildest maneuvers. Most of them never even noticed, so intent were they on their own mundane concerns. If they did, they might look around for the movie cameras for a minute before putting the incident out of their minds.

"The duke would just shit," she chuckled to herself.

Valmont's "day" had just begun. In his Victorian townhouse on the edge of the Castro district, Valmont deWinter — aka Valmont Frost, aka Valmont Adeboro, aka Valmont Duvalier — pulled on his "working clothes," a pale gray Italian suit with a wine-colored silk shirt. He hesitated over a selection of rings before choosing a broad silver band for his index finger. A few more accessories, tooled black leather belt, diamond stud in his left earlobe, mirror shades tucked discreetly into his inner coat pocket, and he was ready to hit the streets.

He pulled out a slim black leather notebook from his back pocket and flipped through the pages, finding his schedule for the evening. A private consultation at Marco and Eddy's near Castro and Market was his first appointment for the night. The elderly gay couple's domestic problems were an ongoing concern for Valmont Adeboro, personal counselor. Mostly, Valmont just listened as each of them complained to him about the other, voicing problems that neither would have been able to mention without the presence of a third party. Valmont occasionally felt ashamed of the steep hourly fee he charged for doing nothing except facilitating meaningful conversation.

Later in the evening, Valmont deWinter would travel to Russian Hill where Mrs. Gladstone, of "the" Chicago Gladstones (as she liked to remind him), would seek his aid in trying to contact the 5,000-year-old Sumerian astrologer who sometimes graced her with his presence — and mostly sound financial advice based on the stars of his time. Valmont had actually done research for that gig, and considered himself almost an expert in Sumerian popular culture. He checked his handwoven shoulder bag to make sure it contained the skullcap, ceremonial shawl and long wooden earrings he used as "the vessel of Ur Tammuz."

Sometime between clients, he would find a convenient pay phone and return the calls collected by his answering machine during the day, while he slept. He had jotted the numbers and names down in a second notebook. The firm appointments would be written into his "datebook." Business was thriving for New Experiences, Ltd.

He was on his way to the door when the doorbell chimed softly. He hesitated momentarily, not expecting visitors, and then opened the door slowly. At first he saw nothing but the darkness outside. Then his eyes focused on Georgia's purple and yellow atrocity of a car parked just across the street. Finally, a faint whiff of something rotten drew him to look toward the shadows in the corner of his front porch.

"Ah, it's you," he said softly, recognizing the figure that lurked in the darkness. "To what do I owe the honor of your fulsome presence?"

"The count wants to speak with you. Soon." Runt's voice was a whispery croak.

"Hmmm," Valmont said. "It must be important for you to come all the way out here to find me."

"Very," Runt agreed.

"But not so important that he demanded my immediate presence," Valmont continued. "Tell Count Elias that I have some urgent business to attend to, but that I shall speed my way to him sometime this evening — at least before dawn."

The sluagh muttered something in a resigned, barely audible tone.

"Give the count my regards," Valmont said, "and my apologies for not responding more speedily to his

the

invitation. Tell him I shall do my best to come to him before he retires for the night."

Valmont watched as the slight, pale figure scrambled down the porch stairs and climbed into Georgia's cab. He quickly finished his preparations, and soon his wine-colored Cadillac was wending its way toward his first appointment.

toybox

chapter

four

He shoved his fist into his mouth and bit down hard, trying to stifle the scream that rose in his throat as the belt buckle cut into his bare back. He tasted blood. "You will stop this lying, Raphael!" His father's voice matched the fury of his blows. In the background, he could hear his mother's whimpering cries. He tried to catch his breath before the next searing pain left him gasping. His back, he knew, was a mass of multicolored bruises and ugly scabs, some of which he could feel tearing open again as the metal ripped through them.

"He's just a boy," his mother sobbed. "He doesn't know any better!"

"Then I will teach him better," his father answered. "And you're no better than he is for protecting him."

The blows stopped coming. There was the sound of a struggle, followed by the dull slap of fist hitting flesh. His mother cried out once.

Raphael seized the moment. He jerked himself up from the bed and grabbed the faded sweatshirt that lay on the floor where it had fallen. His mind was filled with pain and fear and the overwhelming urge to run. Tears stung his eyes and his back was on fire, but he bolted past his parents and fled through the cramped apartment. He was already through the front door and halfway down the stairs before he heard his father's ponderous footsteps.

"Raphael! Don't you run from me, you lying son of the devil!" He ran blindly down the four flights of stairs, stumbling and regaining his balance as he propelled himself around the corners of each landing, not stopping until he had gained the street. He paused just long enough to pull *his shirt over his head, gritting his teeth against the pain as the coarse cloth touched his open wounds. Then he was running again, not certain if the pounding he heard came from his pursuing father or from the blood pounding in his temples. This time was the last time, he told himself as he ran. This time he would never go back home. Home was pain. Home was death. Home was...*

Rasputin woke sobbing from the nightmare, clutching his sweat-soaked pillow with both fists. He sat up slowly, not certain if the pain he had felt was real or imaginary, relieved when he discovered that the only discomfort he felt was the inevitable result of sleeping on a broken mattress. Outside his ground floor apartment, a bird chirped incessantly, announcing the onset of another morning. Rasputin dragged himself out of bed and groped his way toward the bathroom, pausing for a moment to view himself in the mirror. He stood looking over his shoulder, reassuring himself that the only scars were old ones and that the bruises had long since faded to invisibility. "Poor Raphael," he mused bitterly, "he should have had a happier childhood. Maybe, then, there would be room in my life for a little sadness."

A hot shower gradually restored his equilibrium. He dressed quickly, choosing a soft, Indian-print tunic and a pair of double-washed jeans with a twisted rope belt. He retrieved his wallet from the bedside table, checked it to make sure he had money for breakfast on the street, and picked up the worn leather satchel that served as his bag of tricks. Today it held a set of juggling balls, a wooden flute, and the latest set of lyrics for Pandemonium, a band of talented musicians and lousy lyricists who were only too happy to have their songs written by a "real" poet. His efforts had landed them a weekend gig at Tricksters, and he hoped that they'd live up to the enthusiastic billing he had given them.

By the time he left his apartment, his mood had improved considerably. He walked the few blocks from his home to Haight Street and started sniffing the air, hoping to catch the aroma of cinnamon buns or hot pretzels. He pushed the memory of his dream as far behind him as possible.

In the Y's locker room, Leigh donned the black pants and white shirt she was expected to wear to wait tables at Mardi's. As she combed out her hair, still wet from the showers, she thought again about cutting it. Her parents would hate it if she did, but it only got in her way during karate class, and she had to keep it pinned up for work.

She checked her watch as she left the building and slowed her pace as she realized that she had plenty of time to make the bus which would take her to Union Square. The sun had burned off most of the early morning fog, and she was determined to enjoy the day. It was still a week before the duke's Fall Court and her knighting ceremony, and she had no business worrying about it any more than she had to.

She joined the small clutch of people standing at the bus stop, returning their casual greetings with a smile that kept turning into a shaky grimace. In her mind she was seeing herself decked out in court regalia, kneeling before the duke and swearing fealty to him and to the Queen of Pacifica. She had rehearsed the ritual in her head for the last two days, and each time, in her imaginings, she stumbled over the words. She shook her head to clear her thoughts as the bus rolled up to the curb.

the

She settled into an empty seat by the window and tried to concentrate on other matters. There was the matter of Morgan to consider. She had accepted Lady Alyssa's charge to act as escort for the young sidhe baroness, but she and the childling were running out of excuses to get Morgan out of her parents' house. In some ways, Leigh was glad that she had not woken to her changeling nature until she was old enough to leave home. Being a childling and living at home meant always having to account for your time. Many young changelings simply ran away from home, abandoning their mortal ties for the protection of a freehold and the company of others like themselves. But Morgan was adamant about staying with her family.

Privately, Leigh thought the child should let her mother in on her secret, although she knew the duke would not approve. Leigh had met Morgan's mother in an art shop on Haight Street where Alicia Daniels bought her paints and canvases. As an artist, she might be able to accept that her daughter was a changeling. Leigh knew that Morgan found a regular source of Glamour in her mother's whimsical illustrations. The real problem lay in Morgan's father, who, in Leigh's opinion, was close to being one of the Autumn People, mortals who collected Banality about them to such an extent that their presence put nearby kithain in danger of losing touch with their faerie natures. His refusal to accept the existence of anything except what he could see, touch, feel and explain rationally cloaked him so strongly in Banality that Leigh could hardly stand to be in the same room with him. She had only met him once, by accident, when the Daniels family sat at one of her tables at Mardi's. She had traded tables with another server after seating them. For the rest of the evening, she suffered in the smoking section, where she felt safe from the unconscious threat he posed to her. She wondered how Morgan could stand it.

My own father is bad enough, she thought. As a policeman with an unblemished thirty-year record — and an Irishman to boot, Duncan Shaughnessy tried to foster in his rambunctious family his own abiding respect for the law, a respect that bordered on adoration. If Leigh had been a boy, they would have long ago come to blows over any one of the issues upon which they disagreed, everything from equal opportunity laws ("damned quotas that ignore merit and experience") to a woman's right to choose whether or not to bear a child ("the choice should precede the act, not try to erase the blackboard after it's been scrawled all over"). Yet there were times when she and her father connected; Leigh looked forward to those Sunday evenings when, after dinner, her mother would seat herself at the weathered upright piano that dominated the Shaughnessy's living room and her father would page through one of his many books of Irish ballads until he found his favorite of the moment. Then Leigh would lose herself in her father's soaring tenor as he sang the mournful melodies of the "auld country," an Ireland he had never seen but whose history was engraved within his heart. In those moments, Leigh, too, would find herself longing for an "auld" place, the true home of her faerie self. At such times, she understood the fundamental ties that bound her to her mortal kin, that linked her with her father in a mutual sorrow for a lost homeland.

Perhaps Morgan had something she and her father shared, something that made him dear to her. She would have to ask the childling about it when she next had the chance. Leigh's heart pounded fiercely for a beat or two, reminding her that she would next see Morgan at the duke's Fall Court, on the occasion of her own knighting. "Dammit," she muttered to herself, then swallowed the rest of her thought as she realized that the other passengers on the bus were eyeing her suspiciously. She gave them what she hoped was a reassuring smile, then settled back into an uneasy, deliberately thoughtless silence until the bus reached her stop.

Leigh disembarked and walked the half-block to Mardi's, where the noon crowd awaited her solicitations. Hoping Georges was in good culinary form, she made her way to the servers' station. She could use all the Glamour his creative approach to cooking provided.

At first, they appeared to be just another self-styled biker clique, their leathers a little too new, their boots a little too shiny to mark them as one of the established clubs. Tor hardly noticed them lounging on the grass of the Panhandle, the promenadelike strip that extended from the eastern side of Golden Gate Park into the heart of Haight-Ashbury. He had spent the morning wandering through the park, making the usual rounds that took him past the Buffalo Paddock, a favorite place for him to ruminate on his own feelings of obsolescence as he gazed at the protected herd of once-endangered buffaloes. So long as he kept up the appearance of having a purpose, even if that purpose was only self-amusement, no one bothered him or accosted him for looking like a vagrant. He had stopped for awhile at the Children's Carousel, but the sight of parents and grandparents fondly watching their progeny swirl past on the gaily caparisoned menagerie of animals reminded him of Morgan. He had cut short his stay and was letting his feet carry him toward the Toybox, where, secure in the constant atmosphere of the changeling freehold, he could settle himself in his favorite booth and forget his mortal travails or else wander downstairs to the coffee shop's basement, where Chip kept a troll-sized cot ready for him to occupy on chilly evenings.

Lost in his thoughts, Tor saw but paid no attention to the leather-bedecked foursome that approached him until they blocked his path. "Hey, look at the ogre!" a brash young voice called out in challenge. Something in their stance, the wild abandon that seemed to surround them, made Tor look at them, seeing them for what they were.

While the pedestrians, who now veered aside to avoid the incident they sensed about to develop, saw four teenage punks about to mug a helpless old tramp, Tor saw a motley group of redcaps, clad in bloodstained leather and wielding chimeric chains, invisible to the mortal eye.

He tensed and readied himself as the challenger made his move, launching himself at Tor. The old troll ducked, and in the moment of his evasion sensed a second attack, this one from behind as another redcap tried to use his length of chain as a garotte. Both attacks failed, as Tor caught his first opponent's legs with a low sweep of his massive forearm and thrust himself out of range of his rear attacker's lunge.

A well-placed kick caught him in the ribs as his attackers' two companions joined the fight. Tor braced himself against the pain and struggled to regain his feet, knowing that against his opponents' obviously quicker reflexes, he would need every advantage his size and strength could give. The end of a chain snapped perilously close to his head as he shoved his body upwards to assume a fighting stance. Gaining control of those chimeric weapons became his first priority. Formed from the stuff of dreams or nightmares, the chains had no physical reality, but the damage they caused to his faerie self could drive him deep into the clutches of Banality. The blood roared in his head, and he bellowed a wordless battle cry from deep within his warrior's soul.

All around the warrior, the battle raged as commoners clashed in desperate struggle against their noble foes. Iron weapons sang their mortal song as the angry horde of redcaps and nockers sought to banish forever the threat of disruption caused by the return of the sidhe to the land of exile. The warrior felt the force of anger directed at him as he struggled to protect the fragile lives of those so newly come into the mortal world. Many of his own kith would brand him a traitor, one who would deliver the realm of earth once more into the hands of hide-bound nobility. He saw himself as a protector of all kithain, an enemy of those who would use the tools of Banality to sunder from the Dreaming the souls of their noble brethren....

Tor's massive hand closed upon the end of one of the outflung chains. With a yank, he jerked it from his opponent's grasp and hurled it into the air, careless of where it landed. Insubstantial to all but faerie sight, it would lie unnoticed until Banality eroded its chimeric magic. A second chain caught him a glancing blow near his cheek, sending a sickeningly cold wave of pain coursing through him. For a dangerous moment, Tor forgot both who and where he was....

Private Tor Larssen was fighting for his life. The sounds of gunfire filled his ears as black-clad troops poured out of the jungle on all sides of his platoon. His M-16 jammed. He cursed and turned the weapon in his hands, swinging it

about him like a club. Screaming his outrage, he charged
into the thick of enemy fire....

Georgia stood over him, shaking his shoulder and staring into his befuddled eyes. "Tor," she called to him. "They're all gone now. Tor! Remember who you are." A small crowd of people gathered around the fallen man and watched the private drama unfold.

Tor blinked, uncertain of his surroundings. He recognized the spike-haired, middle-aged woman as his cabbie friend Georgia. He remembered a group of gangers and a one-sided battle he almost won.

"Let's get you into the cab, old-timer," Georgia said, helping him to his feet. She turned to the waiting crowd. "Show's over, folks. Move it so's I can get this gentleman where he needs to go."

She bustled Tor into the back of her cab and raced for the Toybox.

Nearly a week had passed since his meeting with Count Elias, and Valmont still wasn't certain he had discovered anything that would be useful to the ruler of Oakhold. That there were strange undercurrents among the Unseelie changelings of the Bay area was easy enough to sense. Just what those undercurrents were, however, had so far eluded Valmont's efforts.

The handsome eshu sat in a dark corner of Trickster's, an all-night coffee house not far from the Panhandle that catered to a rougher crowd than many of the other cafes in the Haight. Although the establishment was not a freehold, many of the area's Unseelie kithain made it their unofficial hangout within the world of mortals. It was an odd sort of meeting place, Valmont thought as he scanned the collection of bikers, leatherboys, hookers and blood dolls that circulated through the smoke-filled room. Ironically, the attraction Trickster's held for mortals living on the fringes of reality served as a buffer that sheltered the changeling spirit from the cold tide of Banality. Like the world of changeling Glamour, the world inhabited by many of the bar's regulars did not quite match the mundane reality in which most humans lived. Dark fantasies and delusions permeated the atmosphere, creating a demimonde of shadowy illusion that wrapped its denizens in their own protective shroud.

From behind his dark glasses, Valmont stared intensely at the people around him, spotting more than a few changelings in the crowd. Some of them he knew by sight, but there were others he had never seen, and their presence disturbed him. He nodded to a pair of trolls who made their way through the crowded room toward the rear of the coffee shop, disappearing through an unmarked door that led into a private room. Valmont suspected that the Shadow Court was holding another of its unscheduled meetings; briefly, he wondered why, if they were, he hadn't been informed. Not for the first time, Valmont considered the possibility that he might just have his fingers in one too many pies.

As one of Count Elias's advisers, Valmont was aware of his liege's wavering loyalties to Duke Aeon. Few of the changelings in the Freehold of Oakhold — Oakland — felt any allegiance to the sidhe-dominated court of Goldengate or to the Kingdom of Pacifica. Valmont's own sympathies, at least as far as politics went, lay with the commoner changelings. It was only by decree and the imposition of long-dead customs that the artificial division of changelings into nobles and commoners existed. The sidhe insisted on maintaining their dominion, and their victory in the Accordance War had solidified their control in North America, at any rate. The commoners who had opposed them had wrested some conciliations in the bloody war's aftermath, though, and Count Elias' ennoblement had been one of those small victories.

Like Elias, Valmont was being wooed by the elusive Unseelie organization known as the Shadow Court. Since Samhain last, he had occupied the honorary position of Prince of the Court of Shadows. Everyone knew that the court and its trappings were a sop to the Unseelie, a pale reminder of a time long past when the Seelie and Unseelie Courts alternated their rule over faerie society. His title held no real power, and would pass to another during the next Samhain celebration, just over a month away. For now, though, it conferred upon him some small status among the Unseelie, just as his friendship with Elias gave him some minor standing in Aeon's court.

So far, Valmont had been able to divorce his political feelings from his personal ones. Most of his friends were solid supporters of the Seelie Court, or at least of Duke Aeon's liberal attitudes. Because of the duke, places like the Toybox were able to enjoy the protection of official patronage while remaining "free"-holds in the truest sense of the word. But because he was eshu, Valmont would always be considered an outsider in the eyes of the rulers of changeling society — just like Rasputin, despite his brief stint as Aeon's court jester, would be forever barred from real power or influence. It was a topic Valmont tried to give as little consideration as possible. In Africa, where his faerie race originated, he would be recognized as nobility. In Greece, he supposed, the race of satyrs would have similar honors. But here, only the sidhe — and those few commoners they deigned to elevate as nobles — were deemed worthy of status.

Valmont's bitter train of thought was broken as he spotted the individual he had hoped to find here. She sat at the bar nursing a Bloody Mary and trying her best to look like one of the "children of the night." Valmont's kenning saw beneath her matte-black dyed hair and stark white skin to the essential redcap nature that lent a dangerous veracity to her mortal guise. It took him a few moments to summon a waiter to carry a message to the bar, and another minute for her to consider his invitation. He watched as she slithered from her stool and meandered over to his table, where she sat down, placing her half-filled drink in front of her.

Valmont caught the attention of the bartender and signaled for drinks. His own espresso had gone cold while he sat lost in thought, and his companion would undoubtedly expect a refill.

"So what brings you out slumming, Valmont?" Slique's voice was low and sultry. "Tired of your Seelie friends?"

Valmont ignored the sentiment. "I'm here on a dare," he said. "My Seelie friends, as you call them, were not able to prevent a recent attack against my person." He tested his shoulder as he spoke. Fizzlewig had used some of his own Glamour to speed the healing of the eshu's knife wound, but sudden movements still pained him. "I came here hoping to discover who it was I had offended so badly that they would seek me out with cold iron."

"Gutsy, aren't you?" Slique said, and this time her voice was tinged with admiration. A waiter brought their drinks to the table. Valmont sipped the hot, strong coffee carefully while Slique crunched away at her fresh celery stalk.

"Not gutsy," Valmont said, "just curious. If I have an enemy who wants me so badly, I wish to meet him personally and give him my regards."

"Do you think I know anything?" Slique asked. "Is that why you called me over here?"

"Not entirely," Valmont said, realizing too late that he was treading on dangerous ground. Slique was a useful source of information, but she had a habit of causing trouble for anyone she suspected of taking advantage of her. Although she rarely discovered that she was being used until after the fact, Valmont had no desire to be on the receiving end of one of her vendettas.

"Well, that's okay," she said abruptly. "I don't really care why you called me over here. I was actually looking for you." A smirk played at the corners of her mouth.

"You were?" Valmont was genuinely surprised.

"Yeah," she said. "I have an offer for you — information you want in return for a favor."

"What favor is that?" Valmont asked, suddenly wary. All week long he had been putting out feelers in the Unseelie community, trying to make a connection between the attack on him in the Toybox and Count Elias' suspicions that Blade and his supporters were part of some larger conspiracy. So far, he had turned up nothing...but perhaps he had been wrong in his estimations.

Slique smiled wickedly. "Not until you agree," she said. "After all, I think what you need to know is more important than a small service that will harm no one."

Valmont shrugged. He was doing the count's bidding, after all, he reasoned. It was in his nature as an eshu to take calculated risks, and, although he had seen better odds, this one might just pay off.

"So long as this service does no harm to the standing of my liege, I will agree to your bargain."

"Good," Slique said. "You're planning on attending

 the

the duke's Fall Court, aren't you?" Her expression belied the feigned innocence in her voice.

"I've agreed to accompany Count Elias as part of his escort," Valmont answered.

"I want you to take a guest with you," Slique said. "All he wants is an opportunity to speak to the duke, but he needs to be with someone who received an official invitation."

"I don't like the way this sounds," Valmont began.

"You promised," Slique reminded him. "Besides, it's not as if he were planning on attacking the duke or anything like that. He just wants to be heard."

"Who is this individual you so carefully refrain from naming?" Valmont asked.

"He'll be waiting for you and Elias outside the duke's palace," Slique said. The look on her face prevented Valmont from pushing the issue. "That's all you need to know. Besides," she added glibly, "you can't be held responsible for what you don't know, can you?"

Valmont nodded slightly. "It might hold up in court," he said. "Now for your part of the bargain."

It was Slique's turn to nod. "The count needs to be more wary of who advises him," Slique said. "And I don't mean you, Valmont."

"So it is Blade who was behind the attack," he said. "Where did he get the knife?"

"He had it brought in from outside the area," Slique said. "His gang's got a warehouse somewhere in Oakland where there's probably a small cache of cold iron. I don't know where, but I'm sure Elias' spies — his real spies — can find it if they try hard enough."

"Can you prove any of this?" Valmont asked.

Slique shook her head. "I have a very reliable source," she said, "but nothing hard. If I did, the favor would be considerably bigger. This way, you have something to go on, which is more than you had before."

Valmont decided to press the matter. "Count Elias already suspected that Blade was up to something," he said. "Your confirmation is just that. It tells us nothing new."

"Look," Slique snapped. "You're part of the damned Shadow Court. You should know what your own people are up to." She stopped abruptly, the look on her face telling Valmont that she had said more than she intended. He also knew that he would get nothing further from her.

"Thank you for your help," he said in his most formal tones.

Slique flashed him what could have been a grateful look and rose from the table. "I'll be on my way," she said, "unless there's something else you want...."

Valmont shook his head, trying to project a regret he didn't feel. "Not tonight," he said.

"I didn't really think so," Slique said wryly. "You're not my type, anyway."

Valmont watched her make her way back to the bar, where she began chatting up a pooka whose tight curls clung to his head like lamb's wool. He drained his cup and sat for awhile, pondering what he had just been told. Elias would not be happy with the information about Blade, although he would be relieved to have some answers, even unsubstantiated ones. Valmont wondered just how much he could reveal to the count about what Slique didn't say. That was the problem with the Shadow Court, he thought as he got up from the table and left the coffee shop. It was as deceptive and insubstantial as the shadows from which it took its name.

the

toybox

chapter

FIVE

"What do you mean, the duke refuses to see anybody?" Lady Alyssa tried to conceal her exasperation from the childling page who stood before her.

"Stefan...I mean, Sir Stefan, and Sir Lucas said they had orders from the duke himself that no one was to disturb him," the page stammered.

"Until what time?" Alyssa asked, reminding herself that the childling bore no culpability for the content of her message. Her voice remained pleasant and casual, although she seethed inwardly.

"They didn't say...m'lady," the childling mumbled.

Alyssa allowed herself a small sigh. The two trolls sworn to protect Duke Aeon were notorious for their paucity with words and their fierce devotion to their liege. "You may go now," she told the page and watched the childling scamper off. Then she went in search of Lord Cumulus, finding the duke's herald practicing feints and thrusts on the back lawn with one of his knights-in-training. She waited impatiently for a pause in the mock battle before announcing her presence with an uncharacteristically unsubtle clearing of her throat.

Lord Cumulus, the duke's First Lord of War in addition to serving as his herald, doffed his chimeric plumed helmet, tucking it neatly under his arm while simultaneously delivering a sweeping bow to Lady Alyssa.

"My services await you, fair lady," he intoned, catching her hand in his as he rose from his obeisance and kissing her knuckles with a flourish. Alyssa smiled in spite of her concern. The brawny sidhe warrior had possessed a flair for the bombastic even as a childling.

Now, near the end of his wilder years, he was positively florid in his exaggeratedly courtly behavior.

"I'm certain they do, Lord Cumulus," she replied, "but it is the duke's service with which I am presently concerned."

Lord Cumulus's posture stiffened, and his angular features took on an icy sternness. His good eye shone with a cold light. "His Grace has not bestowed his confidences upon me for some time now, my lady." He made no effort to conceal the bitterness in his voice.

Since Beltaine last, the duke's often erratic mood swings had settled into a single mood, one of ever-deepening depression. He had begun to distance himself from the affairs of the court, rarely left the freehold, and had even neglected his music, at least the songs he composed with the help of the other musicians in his band. It had been a long time since Aeon's last concert, and the changelings who regularly profited from the Glamour provided by the band's exquisite music were beginning to complain.

"I had hoped that our plans for Fall Court would arouse his interest," Alyssa said. "But he refuses to respond to any of my requests for his participation in the planning of it."

"Fall Court," Lord Cumulus said, looking suddenly perturbed. "That celebration takes place this evening, does it not?"

Alyssa nodded vigorously. "The preparations have been made for the feasting and the entertainment, invitations have been sent out, and the arrangements for the knighting ceremony are nearly complete...save for one thing." She arched an eyebrow, inviting Lord Cumulus to finish her thought.

He pondered her words for a minute. "The duke's presence is mandatory for the investiture," he said slowly. "Without him..."

"There will be no ceremony." Alyssa finished.

"But...but...that's unthinkable!" Cumulus blustered, his face clouding with consternation. "You say he refuses to speak with you?"

Alyssa inclined her head in a nod. "His personal guards have orders that he is not to be disturbed."

Lord Cumulus swore, growing bright red with anger as he did so. Alyssa stared across the lawn at the stand of birch trees, still in full summer foliage, and waited for his soldier's tongue to exhaust itself. After a time, his imprecations ceased.

"I hope that is not the full extent of your response to our predicament," Alyssa said dryly.

The duke's herald had the good grace to look abashed. "Your forgiveness, please, my lady, for my gross misconduct in your presence."

Alyssa knew that Cumulus would wait until he had her verbal pardon before he continued, so she gave it quickly.

"I shall speak to the duke personally," he said, and turned toward the palace. "I do not consider exercising my duties as 'disturbing' his Grace." He took two steps, then paused abruptly to bow once more to Lady Alyssa. "By your leave, my lady," he muttered.

Feeling somewhat relieved of her burden, Alyssa watched Cumulus's progress until he had disappeared inside the palace. She still had a list of things to do before the evening's festivities.

Morgan could hardly contain her excitement. Ever since her Chrysalis, a little over a year ago, she had looked forward to each visit to the Seelie Court of Duke

Aeon with the same anticipation she used to give to birthday parties, Easter egg hunts and Christmas. That she had chosen not to live full-time at court only made her appearances there more special. Now she was going to get a chance to see a real knighting ceremony at the Fall Court, and the fact that her friend and escort, Leigh — or Eleighanara, as she was known at court — was to be the recipient of the honor made the occasion even more important.

She only wished that Tor would be there, but as a commoner, related to her by mortal ties only, he had not received an invitation. She knew he would not be turned away if he chose to go anyway; the duke's court was open to all changelings. But she also knew that he would never willingly attend any court function. She had tried to ask him why he shunned the court, but it was something he refused to talk about.

During the last week, she had been in touch with Leigh several times, making plans to ensure that she could attend Fall Court without arousing her parents' suspicions. She had gotten very good at creeping downstairs to use the kitchen phone after her parents had gone to bed. The only time she had been caught, she was able to tell her mother that she had come downstairs for a glass of milk and noticed that the phone was off the hook. Her mother had accepted her explanation.

Lady Valeria, who had been present at Morgan's Chrysalis, which had taken place in the Toybox Coffee Shop under her grandfather's watchful eyes, and who had later presented Morgan to the court for her Saining, had used her connections with the art community to arrange a charity ball for the local Council of the Arts. Her parents had received invitations to the affair. Since her mother was to be one of the honored guests, they had been unable to refuse, even though her mother usually disliked what she called "snob parties." Her father, on the other hand, was enthusiastic about attending, insisting that it was good to be seen supporting cultural events. It was unlikely that they would be home until well past midnight. She had practiced her befuddlement trick with Mrs. Goherty over the weekend, when her parents went out for the evening. Her elderly babysitter had proven to be what her eshu friend Valmont had described as an "easy touch," falling readily under Morgan's enchantments.

Morgan looked at the wall clock in the dining room, where she was attempting to pass the time by working on a thousand-piece jigsaw puzzle depicting the Eiffel Tower, a present from her father for her A in French class. She still had three hours to wait. It seemed like forever.

It was a creature born of a nightmare, a monstrous snakelike beast with leathery skin and metallic fangs. It slithered around the small apartment, testing its strength. It possessed only minimal intelligence, but what little it had focused on one thing only, the being whose night terrors had given it form. In its brain, a word circled endlessly, the name of its creator. "RaphaelRasputin… RaphaelRasputin… RaphaelRasputin…" Patiently, with the patience of something that has no concept of time, it waited, settling finally in the darkness beneath the bed, coiled and ready to spring.

In his darkened chambers, Duke Aeon sat at his writing desk scribbling furiously, trying to capture on paper the seductive strains of music that compelled his attention. The floor of his room was littered with crumpled balls of sheet music, evidence of his failure to transcribe the complex harmonies that filled him with inconsolable sadness. Every few minutes, he would pause in his writing to caress the slender ebon harp that rested, upright, next to his desk. The music emanating from that delicate instrument spoke to him of Caliendra, his dark-eyed lady, whose lilting voice he had never thought to hear again this side of the Dreaming. It was as if her soul poured forth from the midnight-colored strings of the harp, bearing some message meant only for his ears, some indecipherable promise from beyond the realms of sadness this world had become without her presence. Day and night, the music haunted him. Day and night, almost without ceasing, he tried to unlock the secret code contained within the music, to turn the notes into words he could understand.

His mind wandered momentarily as he heard the approach of footsteps outside his door, and he lost the tune. In a rage, he snatched the sheet from atop his desk and crushed it in his hand, tossing it to the floor to join the growing clutter of failed attempts. He slumped over his desk, his head buried in both hands, his long blond hair, now matted from lack of attention, cascading over his face like a waterfall.

He heard a low rumble of voices just beyond the door and recognized the curt replies of his personal guard and the blustering tones of Sir Cumulus. Without warning, the door burst open, and his herald strode brusquely into the room.

Aeon rose from his seat, anguish and annoyance distorting the lines of his finely chiseled face.

"What is the meaning of this?" His voice, lately unused to speech, sounded strangled in his ears, lessening the intimidating effect he wished to project by several magnitudes of intensity. "I gave orders that I was not to be disturbed."

Lord Cumulus bowed, speaking with head downturned.

"My most humble pardon, your Grace, for this unannounced visit to your chambers," Cumulus began. "I did not think that a brief audience with your herald would constitute a disturbance, and I convinced your guards likewise. I accept the full responsibility for my actions. They have not faltered one iota from their sworn task."

Aeon sighed heavily and slumped back into his chair.

"Since you are here," he said wearily, "speak your mind."

"It is but a small matter of your appearance at Fall Court tonight, and the knighting of one of your loyal subjects...."

The old satyr spoke a few cryptic words and invoked the power of the gem that lodged in his right eye socket. The ruby stone began to glow, emitting a rosy light that engulfed the changeling, altering his form in small but significant ways. His crooked spine straightened, adding two inches to his height. The wrinkles in his face softened and disappeared, giving him the appearance once again of a wilder in his prime. His muscles thickened and filled up the skin that had previously hung in slack folds about his arms. Finally, the gem transformed itself and its companion, a glittering green stone that served as the satyr's left

t h e

eye, into the semblance of normal eyes — one blue and one green.

Straightening his velvet robes, their tattered finery reinfused with Glamour so that they seemed once more rich and new, the satyr allowed a small, grim smile of satisfaction to cross his face. He needed no mirror to know that none would recognize him until he chose to reveal himself. And that would come later, at the proper moment.

A new strength invigorated his limbs as he left the drafty warehouse where he had sheltered since his quarrel with Duke Aeon and his banishment from the fief of Goldengate. His new colleagues, members of the true Unseelie Court of Shadows, had made it plain that his enforced poverty and substandard accommodations were only a temporary discomfort, necessary to the unfolding of their mutual plans.

The cab was waiting for him on the street outside the warehouse, and had been waiting since he had beguiled the driver a few hours ago. The satyr climbed into the battered taxi, barking out an address as he settled himself in the back of the cab. The driver sped off without a word. Later, when the effects of the faèrie magic wore off, the cabbie would have trouble remembering how he spent the better part of the day and evening. The satyr shrugged. It wasn't his problem.

"The sun has set, my lady," Lord Cumulus observed from the broad front porch of the Nob Hill mansion.

Lady Alyssa took one last look around her. Everything was in readiness. In the dining hall, a feast had been laid out, filling the air with a tantalizing blend of spices. In the duke's throne room, a hundred candles blazed from standing candelabra and hanging chandeliers, their scintillating light reflecting in the mirrors that lined the walls of the room, making it seem as though the chamber opened onto an infinite series of brilliant rooms. Finally, she stared for one long, thoughtful moment at the figure of the duke himself, his slender — no, his gaunt — form clothed in the colors of his noble House, the crimson and silver of House Fiona. Above the palace, the banner of House Fiona wafted gently in the soft breeze that continually surrounded it, its silver lion proud against a field of red. The duke stood between his herald and his chamberlain, grasping the porch railing in his hands, his knuckles white with the power of his grip. His long blond hair had been brought into order by Alyssa's own lady-in-waiting, and now hung in soft, shimmering waves, held back from his brow by a silver circlet. If it were not for the firm set of his mouth and the sadness in his eyes, Alyssa could almost believe that Aeon's mood had come full swing and that he was once again the vital presence that brought life and vigor to the Duchy of Goldengate.

"Your Grace," Alyssa murmured softly to the duke. "It is time."

Aeon turned his head toward her, a haunted look in his eye.

"Time?" he asked, his voice indicating that his thoughts had been far away.

"The call must go out," Alyssa prompted. "You must give the orders to your herald."

Lord Cumulus, standing to the duke's left, cleared his throat and raised a slim golden horn to his lips, poised to sound. Attracted by the noise and the motion, Aeon transferred his gaze from Alyssa to his herald.

"Oh please hurry, your Grace!" A small voice from

the palace doorway startled all three nobles. A childling sidhe, all blond curls and twinkling blue eyes, stepped onto the porch. In a frilly rose-colored dress of gauze and silk layers, a tiny tiara nestled amid her curls, the Princess Aliera, the duke's protégé and his most likely successor, hovered like a bubble about to burst with excitement. Aeon's face softened when he saw her, and the childling ran to him and wrapped her arms around his waist. He loosened his grip on the porch railing to stroke her hair, shaking his head as if clearing out some inner fog.

He stood erect and threw back his head.

Alyssa let out her breath in a long sigh of relief just as Cumulus inhaled deeply, cheeks distended on either side of his face.

The duke's voice was clear and concise. "Lord Herald," he said, "the Autumnal Equinox is upon us, and throughout the realm this is a time for celebration and feasting. Sound the clarion call and summon all my subjects to Fall Court!"

Throughout the city, a sweet clear sound rang out, carried on the breeze that swept in from the bay. Though most mortals did not hear it for what it was, almost everyone within its compass — and its compass extended to the furthest realms of Goldengate and even across the bay to the borders of Oakhold and beyond — felt a lightening of the air, a freshness to the salty ocean tang, and a lifting of the heart, as though a murky veil had been drawn aside suddenly to reveal a world awash in color and light and sound. To changelings, the effect was immediate and profound.

A tidal wave of Glamour swept through the city, and even those changelings whose lives had become twisted and crusted over by the iron grip of Banality now felt their faerie selves awaken.

Leigh and Morgan were expecting it. Leigh had waited outside the Daniels' home until her charge appeared. When the clarion call sounded in their ears, they were just emerging from a cab a block from the duke's palace. Morgan giggled uncontrollably, and Leigh found she was barely able to concentrate on paying the driver. When the cab had gone, they turned to look at each other with senses bathed in Glamour. Morgan's long black hair, through which the tips of her pointed ears could just be seen, was raven-bright with a dusting of tiny jewels. She was clothed in a deep violet gown conjured from her own dreaming, real to changeling eyes though mortals saw only a pretty dark-haired girl in a lavender party dress. Leigh wore a silvery gown of watered silk, its simple lines suggesting formality without excess frills, the court garb of a knight-to-be. Her long red hair was woven into an elegant braid, held in place by silver filaments. Some part of her knew that in another world, a mundane realm where words like faerie had no meaning, she stood on a street corner in Nob Hill wearing a simple gray sheath dress, looking like a young woman on her way to meet her date. Unmindful of the cars that passed them, and of the gaze of passersby, Leigh smiled and gave Morgan a deep, formal curtsey.

"My lady Baroness," she said, her green eyes sparkling with tears as the beauty of the Glamour-touched world rose up within her, "shall we hasten our steps to the palace of the duke?"

Morgan laughed aloud, returning Leigh's curtsey with one of her own. She linked arms with her escort and tried her hardest to remember that she was a baroness and that skipping up the pathway to the duke's palace was probably an unseemly thing to do.

Outside the duke's palace, Valmont and Count Elias waited. They, too, had heard the call as Valmont pulled his wine-colored convertible into a side street not far from their destination. Both eshu were dressed in garb traditional to their tribal heritage. Elias wore his hair in many beaded braids, and a multicolored robe draped gracefully over his ebony skin. Valmont was resplendent in a gold and brown patterned dashiki that set off his rich mahogany flesh. It was not uncommon on the streets of the city to see a pair of dark-skinned men in African dress, but only those with faerie sight could see the elongated limbs and dark pupil-less eyes that marked them as eshu. The princely aura that surrounded them was invisible to mortals, but no changeling could mistake the nobility inherent in their faerie kith.

"I thought you said he'd be here," Elias said, his voice showing a hint of impatience. "It would not do for us to be late. We have not the luxury of fashionable tardiness, like many of the sidhe in the city."

"He'll be here." Valmont's reply implied a confidence he did not feel. Although Elias had been pleased by Slique's information, his spies had yet to track down the cache of iron weapons she had mentioned, and no one in Oakhold had seen Blade or any of his gang. That, in itself, was worrisome, since the Oakland People's Front's primary weakness lay in its visibility. Hidden, they could be a source of serious trouble.

The pair stood by the side of the street and watched as a small parade of changelings passed them by, all dressed in court regalia, all filled with the Glamour of the clarion's call. Valmont nodded to Leigh and Morgan as they approached arm in arm. Morgan waved. Leigh matched his gesture with her own nod. Valmont shook his head. She was a cool one, he thought ruefully.

"Come with us!" Morgan called out to him.

Valmont shook his head. "Later, little one," he said. "We shall see you in plenty of time for the feast."

A satyr clad in velvet robes approached Valmont and Elias, stopping as he came even with them. He bowed, first to Elias, then, less deeply, to Valmont. "Your Excellency," he addressed Elias. "I believe I have the honor of accompanying you to the duke's celebration."

Valmont looked at the satyr warily. His robes were fitting enough for any noble's court, and his civility left nothing to be desired, yet there was something odd about him, something the eshu, for all his familiarity with subtlety, could not quite put a name to. He finally decided it was the odd-colored eyes, one blue and one green, that made the satyr's face seem strangely disturbing.

Elias nodded curtly to the new arrival, motioning him to his left side. Valmont fell in at the count's right and the three changelings joined the throng of Seelie kithain who streamed toward the duke's palace.

Inside the Toybox Coffee Shop, Chip Fizzlewig heard the dulcet tones of the clarion and bustled over to fling wide the door to the street. A gust of air from the outside filled the coffee shop, bringing with it the invigorating energy of faerie Glamour. In the fireplace at the rear of the cafe, near the kitchen, the chimerical Balefire that — along with the toy chest — provided Glamour for the freehold burned with renewed energy.

Tor, drowsing in his customary booth, snapped awake suddenly, a memory pulling at the back of his mind, the ghost of another clarion call, a call to... The old troll shook his head, as even his greatest efforts at concentration failed to wrest a clear image from the mists that clouded his past. He, too, however, felt the influx of Glamour and basked for a moment in its soul-cleansing purity. He had been reluctant to leave the safety of the Toybox since his encounter with the redcap bikers. He had come too close to losing himself completely to the grip of Banality. Now, however, he felt almost young again.

Inspired by the wave of Glamour, Rasputin propelled himself atop the bar and grabbed a handful of drinking glasses from their hanging racks. His hands barely seemed to move as he juggled first three, then four, then five of the fragile glasses in the air in front of him.

"Do it on one foot, rabbit-ears!" Edmund, his spiky hair crackling with the infusion of faerie magic, began pulling objects from his pocket — a bright-colored stone, a man's leather wallet, a pocket-knife, and a dog-whistle — and tossing them in Raputin's direction. The pooka caught each one in turn, and added it to his ever growing circle.

Fizzlewig ambled over to Tor's booth and squeezed into the space left by the troll. "It's Fall Court," he said quietly.

Tor nodded.

"I could go, if I wanted," Fizzlewig added.

Tor nodded again.

"I could even bring an old friend with me, without any trouble at all." The boggan wiped at a spill on the table in front of them as he waited for a response from his friend.

"You could go, all right," Tor said finally, not looking at the proprietor but concentrating on his broad hands which rested flat on the table top. "We'd be fine here if you did," he said.

"I don't suppose you'd care to go along," Fizzlewig muttered.

"Hey Tor!" Edmund called out, his eyes still on Rasputin. "Whynt'cha go get fancy and visit the duke? Morgan'll be there." His raucous voice made Morgan's name into a leer.

"That's enough, Edmund," Rasputin said suddenly, his voice quiet and deadly. The objects he had been juggling hovered, motionless, in front of him. Absently, Rasputin picked them from the air, one by one, and placed them carefully on the bar. Then he sat, cross-legged, ears wilting, on the counter.

Edmund stalked over to the bar to retrieve his possessions, pocketing everything but the wallet, which he unfolded and crammed into his mouth. "Mfmrfrrp," he said, and wandered over to stand near the toy chest, which had begun to glow softly as the Glamour surrounded it. The carvings on its side seemed to cavort in place as Edmund watched, fascinated.

Tor turned his head away from his friend, resting his forehead against the cool dark wood of the wall beside him.

"I'd rather stay here," he said. Fizzlewig stood up, giving the table one last swipe with his apron.

"So would I," he agreed. "There'll be a crowd tonight. Lots of folk don't want to be bothered with the shenanigans at the court. We'll be in better company here." He went back to the bar and spent the next few minutes wiping down the glasses that had so recently starred in Rasputin's performance. He avoided looking in Tor's direction, unable to bear the pain that emanated from his friend.

toybox

chapter

six

Lady Alyssa watched as the guests filed into the duke's palace, smiling to herself as she noticed the change that came over them inside the ducal freehold. In anticipation of the evening, the chamberlain had spoken the words of protocol, a ritual formula which endowed the public rooms of the palace with a special sort of faerie magic. While the duke presided over the court, all who entered would abide by the formal rules which governed courtly behavior. Seelie or Unseelie — the thought of the presence of the latter made her shudder involuntarily — all would be compelled to conduct themselves according to the familiar rituals so long ago laid down by the sidhe in their domains throughout the world.

She greeted each arrival in turn and deftly steered them toward the dining room, where a table full of rich confections and heartier fare awaited the guests. Later in the evening, the court would officially convene. She glanced over her shoulder, where she could see Sir Cumulus assiduously squiring the duke through the crowd. She had asked Princess Aliera to stay near Aeon as well, knowing that her guileless good cheer would be the best preventive measure against a recurrence of the Duke's profound melancholy.

She marked the arrival of Count Elias, accompanied by his advisor Valmont...de Winter?...de Something, at any rate. A rangy satyr in fine robes seemed to be part of the count's entourage. His bearing momentarily reminded Alyssa of another satyr she seemed to remember seeing at court, but her attempts to put a name to him were interrupted by a pair of wilder sidhe and a long-nosed pooka who accosted her with bows and curtseys.

"Excuse us, my lady," one of the sidhe, a haughty-faced, chestnut-haired female wearing a court gown cut far lower than Alyssa thought seemly, spoke for her companions. "But is the duke's band going to perform tonight?" Her friends looked on expectantly.

Lady Alyssa blinked, caught by surprise at the request. It had been months since Aeon's band had even called a rehearsal, yet she had seen the other members of the group arrive. It had been a custom of Aeon's court for the band to present a short concert of their newest songs for the entertainment of the attendees.

"I shall find out from the duke himself," she said. "In the meanwhile, there is a fine young troubadour performing on the verandah for those who wish to take their meals outside." She gently prodded the trio toward the dining room and then went in search of Aeon.

Dr. Adrienne Walters' hands trembled as she put down the journal she had finally managed to locate. For the last ten days, she had conducted an exhaustive search for any references to Morgan Daniels' particular delusion. The professional journals had turned up nothing until, two days ago, she had come across a reference to a book by a psychologist named Anton Stark. Its title, *Chimera: Living Within Our Dreams*, had reminded her of some of the words Morgan had used in describing her fantasy life. She had spent yesterday searching for the book or for other references to it, and only this morning had her research paid off — and in a most unlikely place.

She had been browsing on her lunch hour in a bookstore across the street from her office, and had noticed a slim periodical in the "New Magazines" section of the store. Normally she would have ignored its garish cover, but its title, *Perils of the New Age*, and its lead story, entitled "Glamor-Mongers of the Soul," attracted her attention. She flipped through the pages, passing by articles on demonic worship and psychic frauds, until she located the cover story. Skimming the first few paragraphs, she found enough in it to convince her to purchase it.

The article, which focused on religion as a cure for sufferers from delusions, contained mostly rubbish, but the author quoted Anton Stark in one paragraph and later on made reference to some work by an avid investigator who had uncovered "a race of demons who spread their foul gospel of seductive fantasies, believing themselves part of an insidious world of dreams and glamor." She took out her notebook and copied down the publication's address and phone number. First thing in the morning, she decided, she would call their office and attempt to locate either Stark or the unnamed — and quite possibly delusional — investigator.

Her last visit with Morgan had been frustrating. It was almost as if the child had been briefed on how to appear perfectly normal. She smiled to herself. No one was "perfectly" normal, or else she would not be spending so many hours courting the fringes of her profession. Somehow or other, she would not give up until she had the answers she sought. She would not release the child from her care only to have her suffer a relapse into a neverland of fantasy.

Aeon readily agreed when Alyssa suggested that he and his band perform. The duke's chamberlain rejoiced to see Aeon showing some of his former animation as he and his bandmates retired to the music room for a quick run-through of their songs. A ripple of anticipation swept through the court as some of the palace retainers, commoners sworn to the service of the duke, brought out the band's equipment and set up a small stage in the ballroom. This was the last event on the agenda before the formal convening of the duke's court and the promised knighting ceremony.

Alyssa located Sir Cumulus, relieved for a while of his burden of squiring the duke, and suggested to the warrior that he might want to find Eleighanara and brief her once more on the ceremony. The Princess Aliera had found Baroness Morgania and the two childling sidhe were busily sampling the desserts in the dining room. Her duties forced her to miss the beginning of the band's performance, but from the enthusiasm Alyssa felt as the soaring music rocketed through the palace, she knew that the crowd was enjoying the show.

It was only when the music changed that she began to grow worried. The familiar sound of the band's ensemble work began to lose form as she heard the wailing tones of Aeon's guitar, a vintage Rickenbacker twelve-string, cut loose from the group. The melody he played was at odds with the framework of his band's music, throwing their rhythm out of kilter. One by one, she heard the bass, keyboards, and, finally, the drums drop out of the blend, leaving only Aeon and his guitar. Alyssa paused at the threshold of the ballroom, standing on tiptoe to get a glimpse of the stage and its solo performer. A restive murmur spread through the audience, as the listeners tried desperately to follow the strange directions the duke was taking with his music.

Alyssa saw the duke's head bent low over his instrument, his slender fingers wrestling with the strings of the guitar. It was not that the music was inferior, just that it was utterly alien to anything she had ever heard before. Beyond its strangeness, it was more painful than anything Aeon had ever played. A sudden ache filled her heart, and a great sadness washed over her.

The music stopped abruptly, and the duke raised an anguish-ridden face to the crowd. Even from her place in the rear of the room, Alyssa realized that Aeon was seeing something visible to him alone. She saw the band's bass player, a dark-haired female sidhe who had been with the band since its inception, nudge Aeon and whisper something into his ear. Aeon nodded absently, and the band started another tune, a lively Celtic-based number they had once referred to as "Rock and Reel." It was their last song of the night, and though the applause that greeted the concert's end was enthusiastic, Alyssa thought she could sense a general relief that the evening's strange music was over.

Caught between two worlds, he who had once been a prince of the sidhe in Arcadia waited for what seemed like centuries for the opportunity to escape his cage. It had taken almost all his patience to wait for the proper moment. The walls of his prison were not as solid as his enemies had hoped, and little by little he had found a way to send his dreams beyond the magical barrier that trapped him. The world beyond the Dreaming contained a few kindred souls who were receptive to the messages he sent. He had seen the weakness of the Seelie rulers in Arcadia. Like him, the ones who heard his call recognized the impotency of the Seelie Court beyond the Dreaming. These allies would form his Shadow Court. They would

*be his arms of vengeance against those who branded him
an outlaw and a fugitive. Through them, he would find
a way to free himself. In the Banal world, he would
collect the treasures which would give him the key to
impose his will upon Arcadia.*

*His milk-blooded Seelie cousins professed their
dedication to a time when Earth and Dreaming would
become one again, but they were blind to the way — the
only way — such union could be achieved. They had
condemned him for trying to open their eyes. Soon,
however, they would find themselves shoved into a rude
awakening....*

Leigh tried to ignore the rapt attention of the
changeling courtiers as she approached the duke's
throne. Out of the corner of her eye, she glimpsed
Valmont, standing quietly to one side of Count Elias.
She felt the force of his gaze and struggled to keep her
face impassive, although she could not control the
heat that rose to her cheeks. She breathed deeply,
drawing on the lessons she had learned from her
martial arts teacher, and brought herself to a center
of enforced calmness. *Nothing will go wrong,* she
thought furiously. She could recite her knight's oath
in her sleep. Sir Cumulus and Lady Alyssa had drilled
her in the ceremonial particulars so that her part in
the ritual seemed almost second nature.

After what seemed like an eternity of slow,
measured steps, she paused at the foot of Aeon's
throne. She raised her head to look upon the face of
the individual to whom she was about to swear fealty,
and knew an instant of panic. Aeon's pale blue eyes

were unfocused, his attention seemingly directed toward something at the rear of the throneroom. She stifled the urge to turn her head as well. She saw Lady Alyssa inch closer to the duke, murmuring something indistinct as she did so. Aeon's face changed and he shifted his gaze to Leigh, greeting her with a gentle, almost sorrowful, smile.

Leigh knelt. She hoped the gesture looked more practiced than it felt and that the onlookers remained unaware that her knees seemed to collapse beneath her. She bowed her head and awaited the duke's pleasure. Aeon rose from his carved ebony throne and towered before her.

"The burden of knighthood is not lightly undertaken," Aeon began, intoning the prescribed words in a voice that seemed strained with the effort of speaking. The duke paused unexpectedly. Leigh could just hear a breathless whisper from Lady Alyssa's direction. She suddenly realized the duke's chamberlain was coaching him, and her heart missed a beat. She dared an upward glance and saw Aeon glare fiercely at Lady Alyssa. "I know the words," she heard him mutter under his breath. She lowered her eyes quickly as he turned back to her.

"The words you are about to speak will bind you to me, whether you like it or not," he said, departing from formula. A restless murmur began in the back of the throneroom, then quieted as Aeon once again raised his voice.

"Is this something you want?" he asked, his voice a harsh question. A shocked gasp escaped from Lady Alyssa. Just behind the duke, Sir Cumulus made a quiet choking noise in his throat.

Taken aback, Leigh lifted her face and met the duke's eyes with her own. She knew with a certainty that came from deep within her that Aeon was floundering in some inner chaos and that he was reinventing the words of the ceremony in a desperate attempt to keep himself grounded in his immediate surroundings. Leigh swallowed hard and felt her jaw tighten. So be it, she thought. If I'm to be his knight, my duty is to assist him in any way I can.

"This is my heart's desire," she answered, and despite her earlier misgivings, she knew at last that it was just as she had spoken. There was another round of quiet whispers as the audience responded to her own abandonment of the ritual.

"Then make your oath before all who would bear witness to your desire," Aeon said, his voice poised on the edge of pain. He held out his hands to her and Leigh placed her own clasped hands within their grasp.

"I swear fealty to you, my lord," she said, thankful to be on familiar ground. "Your command is my desire, and your request my desire as well. May my service always please, and may my sight grow dark if it does not. As the tides to the moon, my will to yours, my liege."

Aeon sighed heavily, his hands dropped away from hers. "If you but knew the full import of your words," he said in a voice meant for Leigh alone but overheard by the first few ranks of changelings.

He turned his head abruptly and nodded to Sir Cumulus, who stepped forward bearing a sheathed sword, resplendent with chimeric newness. Sir Cumulus made to draw the virgin weapon and proffer it to the duke, so that Aeon might continue with the ceremony by investing his newly sworn knight with a sword from his own hands. Aeon shook his head. "Not yet," he said aloud. "I choose to accept her by the laying on of hands rather than at the point of a blade."

This time the stillness in the room behind the tableau sounded like thunder. Aeon stepped closer to the still kneeling Leigh and placed both hands upon her head.

"I take you as my vassal and my knight." His voice was ethereal, as if spoken from some distant place far from the palace on Nob Hill. "You are of my house, even as the very stones. I pledge to hold you, to guard you, and to keep you. I pledge to honor your service as it deserves, and to reward loyalty in kind. As the moon to the seas below, my will to yours. I—"

"This knighting is a farce, as your rule has been for nigh on many passings of the moon!"

A strident voice rang out, followed immediately by a chorus of indrawn breaths. From between Valmont and Elias, a wizened old satyr emerged. In his face, two glittering gems — one red, the other green — shone balefully.

"Malacar!" Leigh heard Alyssa exclaim in a low, rage-filled voice.

"I demand a turning of the wheel, a change in the tide of rulership that, if left unchecked, will bear us all to our doom! I declare you unfit to hold the throne and call for a lottery, as is my right before the laws of all the faerie kithain. Let the withering of the symbol of your rule witness the truth of my words!" As he spoke, the satyr pointed a gnarled finger toward the sprig of flowering mistletoe that hung above the ducal throne.

The throneroom erupted in a confusion of voices and movement as some members of the court jostled one another in an attempt to distance themselves from the intruder while others tried to lay hold of the twisted figure.

"Seize him!" Sir Cumulus spouted. He dropped the unsheathed sword onto the floor in front of Leigh as he charged forward, drawing his own weapon, the legendary Arcbiter.

Before Cumulus had taken a half-dozen steps, Malacar gestured, hiding himself within a bright explosion of light and smoke. The courtiers nearest him screamed and threw themselves aside. By the time the duke's warlord closed the gap, the smoke had dissipated, revealing only emptiness where Malacar had stood.

"He's gone!" Cumulus stood bewildered.

"Count Elias and the eshu Valmont brought him here," Lady Alyssa's voice cut through the commotion. She turned to the duke, her eyes blazing in anger and mortification. "Your Grace," she hissed, "act now or prove the truth of the traitor's words."

Aeon jerked his hands away from Leigh, who found herself at once both ready to leap to her feet and uncertain that her legs would support her. She had not yet been given leave to rise, yet it seemed ridiculous to remain on her knees when everything was collapsing around her. The duke fastened on his chamberlain's words.

"Detain the Count and his advisor," he commanded. "Bring them to me at once. Sir Cumulus, see if you can find out where that piece of foulness went."

Someone grasped Leigh's elbow, and a pair of small hands held the forgotten sword out to her. Leigh looked up and saw Morgan, her face pale and determined, on one side of her, holding the sheathed weapon gingerly. On the other side, equally as pale, her blue eyes brimming over with tears, Princess Aliera held Leigh's arm and tried to pull her to her feet.

"Rise, Dame Eleighanara," Aliera said in a high-pitched voice. Her face was solemn as she added, "I have the right to say that, you know."

Leigh stood, grasping the sword sheath in both hands, not sure whether she should draw the blade. She turned to face the crowd, searching for Aeon, waiting for some guidance.

Across the bay, in a shadowy room redolent with the scent of jasmine and patchouli, Lady Glynnis sat upon a heart-backed teakwood chair. Before her, on the carpet at her feet, rested a delicate ebony harp. Her eyes were closed, her features bore the stillness of death — or of one intent upon an inner vision. Her hands reached out to caress the ebony strings of the harp, which vibrated with an agonizing sweetness. "Remind the duke of what he has lost," the dark-haired lady of shadows murmured. "Let his pain become a blazon for him to bear before all who stand before him...."

Aeon's body convulsed as he heard the music in his head, soft strains of heartbreak and anguish which sliced through the noise of the throne room and beckoned him to join his soul to their forlorn melody. He doubled over, clasping his head in both his hands to drive away the utter desolation that swept over him.

"It is too much to bear!" he groaned, his voice a howl that hovered on the edge of madness. The inner pain drove him to his knees. "Why can I have no surcease from this torment?"

Near him, the startled members of the court began to back away from the duke's twisted form, whispering among themselves. Lady Alyssa hastened to his side and took him by the arm. Aeon shoved her brusquely aside. "Leave me," he commanded, his voice stretched to breaking, pain a blanket across his lusterless eyes.

"Do something," Morgan whispered fiercely to Leigh, then turned to comfort Aliera, who stood sobbing helplessly at the spectacle before her. On impulse, Leigh stepped forward until she was at the duke's side. She knelt in front of Aeon and placed her hands under his elbows.

"My liege," she said, urgency filling her voice. "Tell me what causes you so much pain."

Aeon lifted his head and stared into her eyes, a puzzled expression on his face. His features softened, taking on a look of quiet joy and unabashed relief.

"Caliendra..." he murmured and reached to clasp Leigh's forearms with trembling hands. Leigh braced herself and helped the duke regain his feet. For a moment they stood face to face, arms locked, nearly embracing. As he looked at her, Leigh sensed that he was seeing someone else standing in her place. She released Aeon's elbows and with that simple movement shattered the vision that stood between them. Aeon lowered his head and dropped his hands.

"No," he whispered to himself, "not Caliendra. Eleighanara."

He drew himself up, as if suddenly remembering where he was, and looked about him at the anxious crowd still enthralled by what they had witnessed. Aware that Aeon's attention was once more upon them, the courtiers began to quiet their furious whispers and frantic mutterings.

"Your Grace!" Leigh heard Valmont's voice above the gradually dying tumult. The eshu stood, along with Count Elias, in the midst of a group of Aeon's knights, supervised by Sir Cumulus' brooding presence. "By your leave, there is something I must say in the defense of my lord." Valmont extended his arms in front of him, palms out and pointing downward, in a gesture of supplication. His words were directed toward Aeon, but his eyes found Leigh. He stared at her.

"His missing companion has already said quite enough," Lady Alyssa cautioned quietly, coming forward to stand just behind the duke. If her rude dismissal had affected her, she gave no outward evidence of the fact.

Leigh returned Valmont's stare. She saw the pleading look in the eshu's gaze, knew what it cost him to make even this silent request of her. The duke had stepped away from her and now stood on the edge of the low dais before the throne. Leigh turned from

Valmont and approached Aeon, bowing before him as her knighthood demanded.

"Please, your Grace," she said. "May I speak on behalf of Valmont?" Slumped in his throne, Aeon turned his head toward her, acknowledging her words. His face seemed carved from granite.

"Why should I not allow my newest, and fairest, knight to voice her thoughts?" he said. Leigh felt her face grow red with the reference to her appearance.

"I know Valmont," she said. "I do not believe that he will say anything that does not need to be said." She started to say more but then realized that in truth she had no idea what Valmont might say. At least he's not Rasputin, she thought to herself and remembered that Rasputin himself had served for a time as Aeon's jester. He had been asked — politely — to retire when the court complained that his comments were too bitter for their liking. Although she knew that Valmont, like many other commoners in the city, had his differences with the Seelie Court, she had never heard him voice any criticisms of the duke. She hoped that he would not choose this moment to start.

"Already it seems I have another advisor," Aeon murmured. His expression remained stern, but his voice sounded detached and gentle. "For the love that I bear for Count Elias, until I hear something to convince me that my feelings are mislaid, I will hear the words of his advisor," Aeon said to the listening courtiers. "You may speak," he commanded, his words aimed at Valmont.

The eshu gave Leigh a look of gratitude before fixing his eyes upon the Duke.

"The count is blameless in this whole affair," Valmont said. "Malacar came into this court as a result of an agreement that I made, although I did not know at the time that it concerned him. If there is any fault to be laid upon any present in this assemblage, it rests solely upon my shoulders. Count Elias chose merely to honor my agreement."

"Are you in concord with your vassal's words?" Aeon asked Elias. The eshu count ignored the wary glances of his guards and placed a hand on Valmont's shoulder.

"It is as Valmont has spoken," he replied. "Yet I will stand by him as his lord. His censure will be mine as well."

Aeon nodded gravely. "There has been no talk of censure, my friend," he said. "But I would question those with any knowledge of this mishap. I see no reason for you to remain in custody, though I would request the company of your vassal for the information he can provide." The duke motioned his guards to step away from the count and Valmont.

"Sir Cumulus, your weapon is not needed for our defense at this time, although I cherish the timeliness of its display." The knight returned Arbiter to the scabbard at his belt, his face glowing with pride at earning his liege's warm approval. His single good eye sparkled with a fierce satisfaction.

"There are still some hours left in the celebration," the duke said, directing his statement at the courtiers milling uncertainly about the throne room. "I declare the formal proceedings of Fall Court to be concluded, that you may all avail yourselves of the offerings of the palace and grounds." He watched in silence as people began to drift from the throneroom, talking in small groups as they wandered toward the dining room or sought the pleasures of the moonlit gardens outside the palace. Count Elias spoke briefly with Valmont.

"I will find my own way home," he said, "unless you wish me to stay. My instinct is to return to Oakhold as soon as possible...."

Valmont nodded. "Whatever happens here should not add to your difficulties, your Excellency," he replied.

"I will return to you as soon as I am able, or send word if I cannot."

Elias clasped Valmont's shoulders in farewell. "We stand together in this place," he said. A wry smile tugged at one corner of his mouth. "But I, too, would have more words with you about tonight's occurrence."

Valmont nodded as meekly as he could. He watched the count leave the room before he approached the duke in answer to his summons. Cumulus stalked behind the eshu. Aeon inclined his head as Valmont neared the throne. He gestured toward a door at the rear of the throneroom, its presence all but concealed by the massive bulk of the ducal throne.

"We will speak privately in here," he said, motioning Cumulus forward to open the door. A small sitting room lay beyond. The duke gestured for Valmont to precede him through the doorway. Before he followed, Aeon looked over his shoulder, catching Leigh's eye as she and Alyssa waited before the throne. "Dame Eleighanara, Lady Alyssa," he said, "I would have the wisdom of your counsel as well."

"May we come, too?" Princess Aliera asked, hope written boldly on her face. Aeon paused for a moment, on the verge of denying her request. Then he shrugged. "You and Morgania were witnesses as much as any of us here," he said. Morgan squeezed Aliera's hand tightly, her own face flushed with excitement and anticipation. Alyssa opened her mouth to admonish the duke, but a look from Aeon silenced her before she could utter a word.

Within her scented chamber, the lady of the shadows smiled a secret smile. Her hands rested idly in her lap; the harp stood silently at her feet. The inner window of her mind revealed a scene of confusion and dismay, as noble courtiers and commoners clustered together, gossiping nervously among themselves about the duke's erratic behavior. Later,

the

when the beglamoured Aeon was once more ensconced within his chambers, she would take up the harp again, and send him dreams that would serve to drive him deeper into the madness she desired, the madness that was necessary for the fulfillment of her plans. For now, she had other work to do. The duke's fall from power was but the first step in a greater scheme, one which would result in the entry into the world of a great prince from Arcadia, an Unseelie lord who would bring true power to the Shadow Court. The Lady Glynnis warmed herself with the thoughts of the destiny which would soon be hers.

Halfway between Nob Hill and Haight-Ashbury, Malacar lounged in comfort in the back seat of the sleek black car that wound its way through the city's hilly streets. His escape from the duke's court had gone without a hitch. Although he had been denied his rightful position as Aeon's court wizard, it had been due to his political differences with the duke, not the competency of his art. It had required only a few gestures and the strewing of some flash powder to draw upon his reserves of Glamour to cloak himself with an aura of misdirection, so that all eyes were drawn to every place where he was not. For all practical purposes, he had disappeared, walking brazenly through the throne room and leaving via the rear door in the kitchen. The palace and its routines were familiar to him, so he knew which exits were most likely to be unguarded. Once he had gained the street, the first of a series of vehicles, a paneled van, was waiting to take him from the area. Now, in the third leg of his journey to his next destination, he felt he had the leisure to spend a few minutes reveling in the consternation he had caused.

He had little hope that his words before the court, true though they were, would effect an immediate change or result in Aeon's overthrowing. Although his real task lay elsewhere, the satyr knew that the seeds he had sown this evening would provide sufficient distraction to give him room to maneuver.

Once again, he congratulated himself on the wisdom of his decision to cast his lot with those who would overturn the old regime. Despite the fact that he was not privy to the Shadow Court's innermost councils, already he had only the greatest respect for the subtlety and forethought that had gone into preparing for this night. Thanks to their hidden orchestrations, his words to the duke and the Seelie Court had been given the force of truth. The timeliness of the duke's public display of unseemly emotion could not be denied. Aeon's hold over his reason and his realm were unraveling; the voice that spoke to Malacar from the shadows had seen to that. Through a simple gift to the Duke, an ebony harp inserted into the heap of presents from his vassals at the last Beltaine festival, the seeds of discord had been sown. The inevitable erosion of Aeon's sanity would deprive the Duchy of Goldengate of the wisdom of its ruler.

Malacar instructed the redcap driver to pull over just before they neared the intersection of Haight and Ashbury Streets. Concealed behind the car's darkened windows, he once again invoked the Glamour contained within the ruby gem. He wished the power of the stone were such that it could change his essence to one of the other kith — a boggan, perhaps — but he would have to work with what he had. Before he left the vehicle, he steeled himself for the final step in his preparations. Reaching up with one hand, he clamped his jaws together against the anticipated pain and plucked the emerald gem from his left eye. From within the pocket of his robes, now a patchwork duster that seemed hand-made from an assortment of rags, he withdrew an eyepatch. Pulling it into place over his empty socket, Malacar stepped out of the car and slowly limped toward the Toybox Coffee Shop.

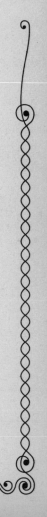

chapter

seven

"It's not that pookas never tell the truth," Rasputin proclaimed from his makeshift throne in front of the Emperor Norton's toy chest. "It's just that our version of the truth does not always correspond with majority opinion."

"You lie," said Edmund, chewing thoughtfully on the remnants of a plastic Frisbee he had found near the Children's Carousel earlier in the evening.

"You shouldn't speak that way to your duke," Rasputin murmured languidly, tossing back an imaginary mane of long hair as he spoke. "And stop chewing on your shield, Lord Cumbersome, it's unseemly."

The crowd of childlings that habitually followed Edmund in his wanderings about the city giggled appreciatively at the pooka's words.

Behind the bar, Fizzlewig wiped down the counter. "I wonder how long he's going to keep this nonsense up," he remarked to Georgia, who sat at the bar alternately sipping from a tall, frosted glass and munching on an oversized sandwich.

"Until he gets tired of giving the little brats a lesson in proper court etiquette, I suppose," she replied.

Many of the regular patrons of the Toybox Coffee Shop had responded to the duke's call to Fall Court, since only the most marginal noble connection was necessary for admission. Theoretically, the meetings of the Seelie Court were open to everyone. Those who refrained from attending did so either because they opposed the Seelie nature of Aeon's rule or because they felt uncomfortable surrounded by the pomp and ritual of noble gatherings. Most of the changelings who clustered in Fizzlewig's freehold this evening fell into the latter category; those whose sympathies lay with the Unseelie found other places to be. Aside from Georgia, Rasputin, Edmund, Tor — dozing as usual in the back booth — and the Brat Patrol, as Edmund's admirers called themselves, there were only a half dozen other changelings in the room.

The boggan bartender glanced nervously at one pair that had come in a few minutes earlier. Slique rarely visited the Toybox, and to Fizzlewig's mind, never was once too often. Her insistence on playing the vampire queen got on his nerves; it was too close to the bloodthirstiness of her redcap nature. She generally circulated among the Unseelie changelings who gathered at Trickster's or one of the freeholds in the Tenderloin or across the bay in Oakhold. So far, she and the sheepish pooka who fawned on her had occupied themselves with talking quietly and sampling the coffee shop's specialty drinks. Every now and then, the pooka would glance toward the door as if anticipating someone's arrival.

A raucous round of laughter from the direction of the toy chest drew Fizzlewig's attention. One of the childlings, a kittenish pooka named Mai-Ling, was kneeling before Rasputin, who had styled himself "Duke Millennium" for the evening's farce. Rasputin tapped her on the shoulders with a ladle, purloined, Fizzlewig realized, from his own kitchen.

"Now that you have spoken your oath of faultiness," he proclaimed, "I feel the sudden urge to entertain you with some of my overwhelmingly ornate music." Rasputin reached inside the pocket of his trousers and pulled out a toy harmonica. A tortuous version of "Red River Valley" soon had the children in stitches.

The outside door swung open and a decrepit-looking satyr clad in a faded patchwork overcoat and wearing a patch over his left eye hobbled unsteadily into the coffee shop. His steps took him toward the side of the room where the children were clustered around Rasputin and the toy chest, where he stopped for a moment as if to watch the proceedings. Then he seated himself at the end of the bar nearest the mock-Seelie court.

"Coffee," he muttered in a phlegmy voice.

Fizzlewig set a mug of steaming coffee in front of the old changeling. "Don't recall seeing you here before," he said in what was intended to be a conversational tone but sounded more like a challenge.

The satyr cackled. "Don't get out much," he replied. "At my age, it's not safe to be away from the fold for too long, if you know what I mean."

Fizzlewig nodded. He himself rarely left the confines of the coffee shop lest his fading grasp on the Dreaming be swept away by the insidious pull of mundane reality. It was the inevitable withering away of his changeling nature. It was this death of the spirit that he, like other grumps — as mature changelings were called — feared more than anything, even the death of his mortal body. The boggan felt a twinge of sympathy for the satyr, but contented himself with grunting his agreement.

Leigh listened carefully as Valmont told the duke of his meeting with Slique and the bargain he had made. She stood, somewhat self-consciously, a little behind the duke's chair. Opposite her, on the other side of the Duke, Sir Cumulus hovered like a storm cloud, filling the room with his lowering presence. Lady Alyssa sat on a low divan, with Morgan and Aliera on either side of her. Valmont remained standing as he spoke in defense of Count Elias and in explanation of his own actions. Leigh found herself admiring the eshu's coolness. She doubted that she could have shown the same composure as Valmont; but then, she also doubted that she would ever have placed herself in his situation.

Aeon concentrated on the eshu's words. To Leigh, he seemed completely in control of himself once more, as if nothing had gone wrong.

Valmont finished speaking. For several long minutes, silence filled the room. On the couch, Aliera fidgeted, her interest in the proceedings rapidly waning. Morgan sat hunched over, her elbows resting on her knees, her chin propped up with her fists. Her brows wrinkled in concentration. The duke reclined in his seat, his head tilted backward, his eyes closed.

For a panicky instant, Leigh feared that he had fallen asleep, and wondered what protocol accounted for such an occurrence. Just as she sensed that Lady Alyssa was about to make an effort to rouse the duke, Aeon opened his eyes and sat upright.

"I thought Malacar was banned from the fief," he said, looking upward at Sir Cumulus.

"You banned him from the court, your Grace," Cumulus said, "and from Goldengate. I would suspect that he took shelter in Oakhold...." The knight's inadvertent glance at Valmont implied more than his words.

"Your Grace," Valmont interjected quickly, "I hope you will not assume that if Malacar has been living in Oakhold that it has been with the knowledge or sanction of the County's lord."

"Do not tell me what I assume," Aeon snapped. "I have had enough of being told what to do and how to conduct myself. Malacar's appearance in the court this evening was more than a spontaneous attempt to challenge my power. Tonight's display had to have been carefully orchestrated, and not by that disgruntled wizard alone. I have no doubt that through you," he said, indicating the eshu, "Malacar sought to implicate Count Elias and drive a wedge between me and my vassal. He is up to something, and I will know what treacherous game he plays."

Morgan watched the exchange, only partly hearing the words that were spoken. The evening's excitement had brought something to mind, but she could not make herself remember precisely what it was. She chewed on her lip, trying to bring the memory to light.

Lady Alyssa stirred for the first time since the group had retired to the duke's private audience chamber. "Your Grace," she said, "perhaps you should appoint Sir Cumulus to lead an inquiry into what is going on in your holding."

Aeon glared at her, his face gone icy. "Perhaps I should appoint someone of my own choosing," he said.

Alyssa lowered her head, rebuffed. "Forgive my importunity," she said mildly.

Aeon turned toward Leigh, his face set with determination.

"Dame Eleighanara," he said, "Through no fault of your own, your knighting was deprived of the solemnity it deserved. As token of my trust in your worthiness," he continued, "I charge you to undertake a search for the traitor Malacar. Find him and discover what his full intentions are." The duke's voice resonated with authority.

Leigh started, unprepared for the suddenness of the duke's proposal. She reacted instinctively — and rebelliously — to the paternal authority in his tone, an authority she had spent most of her growing years fighting.

"No daughter of mine is going to spend her life waiting tables," her father shouted across the dinner table. "Waitresses marry truck drivers and mechanics," he said,

his face growing red. "I want something better for you!"

"And what about me?" Leigh countered. She was sixteen years old, and had just announced to her parents that she had gotten her first part-time job, waiting tables at McCready's Restaurant. "What about what I want to do? I need to know about restaurants if I'm ever going to become a chef. I don't want to go to college, and I don't want to marry anybody!"

Without thinking, Leigh stepped backward from the duke.

"Me?" she said incredulously. "I'm not ready to take charge of something this important! You have other knights who are much more suited...."

Alyssa drew in her breath sharply; Cumulus began to sputter.

Aeon's expression grew cold. "Do you refuse my express command, Dame Eleighanara, vassal of my fief and of the House to which we both belong?"

"I wish you and your father wouldn't go at it like that." Leigh's mother sat on the edge of the bed, her hand stroking her daughter's hair. Leigh lay on her stomach, her face buried in her pillow, trying to hold back the sobs that wracked her body.

"He doesn't understand, Mama," she said. "He thinks he can just order me to do something and I'll snap to it like one of his rookie cops." She could taste the saltiness of her tears. "I can't be what he wants me to be."

"You're his pride and joy, Leigh," her mother said softly. "He can't stand it when you act like you think you're not good enough for college. He's worked hard all his life to save up enough to send you to school so you can make a future for yourself, a real future with a good husband and a good home. Why can't you just be happy that he cares so much about what happens to you?"

"I can't," Leigh said over and over, losing control to the tears and the heavy ache inside her. No matter how hard she tried to explain to both her parents that it was impossible for her to go along with their plans for her life, she couldn't seem to get it across to them. She didn't want to be forever defiant, but there was something inside her that continually raged against being told what she had to do.

Leigh knew that she should beg the duke's mercy for her unthinking outburst. She tried to make herself kneel and speak the words of acceptance of the ducal charge. Instead, her knees locked, and an unexplained fury built up within her. She felt an eerie sense that she had experienced this very confrontation before, in another place and time. She felt trapped within a loop, compelled to speak the words of denial. She lost all sense of where she was as voices filled her mind, as if from far away....

"She will not bend her will to yours." The speaker's voice, her mother's, was silver, like the brilliant moonlight that shone through the crystal trees of the Arcadian forests.

"Then she must pay the price for her excessive pride and her rebellious heart." The second voice, belonging to her father, rippled like the wind through the golden grasses along the mirrored lake. "There is but one way that her passion can be tempered so that her destiny may come to pass."

"Have I no part in my own future?" This time, the voice was her own, and in it was the desperation of fear and defiance.

"The path that you are fated to follow, the story that is the seed of your existence, has many choices which are yours to make. The one choice you may not make is to refuse that path." Her father's golden eyes gazed upon her with a mixture of fondness and sorrow. "Your foolish alliance with the enemy of our House has cost you the

the

freedom to choose. Your mother and I must make that choice for you, though it will be many years before you understand — or even remember your purpose in the world to which we must send you."

"I will not forget who I am and what you do to me," she replied, passion filling her voice with a fiery intensity.

"Those who pass beyond the Dreaming into the mortal world always forget," her mother said softly. "In time, when the eyes of the warring brothers look upon each other once again, you will remember all...."

Her father's voice came as a harsh interruption. "Tell her no more, lest you soften the road which she must travel. The path to memory is sometimes more important than the memory itself, and hers will be a journey which will test her strength and forge the sword of her will upon the inner fires of her passion."

"Can you not give her something to carry with her in the long night to which we must condemn her soul?" Her mother's plea was softer than a whisper.

"She will have her honor," her father said. "That alone must be her guide."

The voices faded, and Leigh became aware once more of where she was. Her hands shook with anger, but she could not put a name to its source. She knew the duke was waiting for her answer, sensed that he was losing patience.

She forced herself to speak, although her throat was tight. "I am uncertain of my fitness, your Grace," she began.

"Your hesitation shames your calling, Dame Eleighanara!" The harshness of the duke's words struck Leigh like a blow. Aeon rose to his feet. "By the crown of my office, I will put an end to this equivocation." His figure began to shimmer in the dim light of the small room as he surrounded himself with the Glamour of his faerie nature. He towered, proud and terrible, filled with the naked beauty of the sidhe. His eyes burned from within. Lady Alyssa's face grew pale, while on either side of her, Aliera suddenly became very still and Morgan sat up straight, her concentration broken. Sir Cumulus uttered a reverent curse.

Leigh felt the weight of his grandeur forcing her to her knees in spite of herself. Her face burned, hot with humiliation. Valmont, who had watched the exchange between Aeon and Leigh with growing concern, forced himself to avert his eyes, lest he fall prey to the noble sidhe's commanding presence.

"Since you will not willingly accept my charge, I find that I must change my request to a compulsion. By your oath as a vassal of my House and holding, by the honor of your knightly calling, by the moon whose eternal radiance has borne witness to your promise, I geas thee to serve me in the fulfillment of my desire. Lest you be known henceforth as a traitor and a coward, I compel you to go forth and find the satyr Malacar, and having found him, to repeat to him my ban upon his presence in my fief. I further charge you to discern the purpose of his machinations and bring back to me the knowledge you have gained. By the power of the dream, the word, and the deed, so must your will be bound to mine."

Leigh trembled as Aeon's words swept over her like a storm of fire and fury. She felt her will begin to dissolve, as the force of his geas tried to take root in her soul. The oath which earlier she had sworn seemed as shallow as an idle promise compared to the overwhelming magnitude of the formal binding ritual. Most powerful of all the faerie oaths, a geas, once imposed, could not be broken without suffering the penalty spoken at the time of its pronouncement. Its power extended beyond that of a simple command to try; it was an order to succeed. Leigh bowed her head, helpless to do anything except surrender to the consequences brought upon her by the stubbornness of her denial. All thoughts fled from her awareness as something within her stretched to breaking. Her vision blurred. And then, something snapped back into place, forcing the binding to unravel, returning her will to her control. Still kneeling, she raised her head, confused at the sudden calm that filled her — and the sudden void.

Aeon stood looking down at her, surprise and puzzlement on his face. The grandeur which surrounded him had faded, and Leigh found that she could meet his gaze without fear.

"I don't understand it," Aeon said. "The binding does not hold. It is as if some other, stronger compulsion stood in its way. Why did you not tell me you labored under another geas?" he asked Leigh.

"I don't," she said. "I have sworn no previous oath to anyone but you." The blush that had receded with the overcoming of the geas returned as Leigh remembered how she had incurred the duke's displeasure.

"There's no point in your kneeling before me," Aeon said. "Please stand or sit, whichever suits you." He looked around him at the others in the room. His gaze settled on Valmont, as if suddenly remembering the eshu. He gestured toward an empty chair next to the sofa where Alyssa and the two childlings sat. "I have been remiss in my duty," he said. "I lay no blame on either you or your lord. Sit and take your ease." Valmont moved to the chair designated by the duke and sat gracefully, murmuring his thanks in a distracted voice.

"Your Grace," Morgan's voice was small but clear, bidding for the duke's attention.

"Baroness?" Aeon responded, inclining his head toward her as he returned to his chair.

Morgan stood up and curtseyed deeply. "On behalf of Dame Eleighanara, who I know would never truly deny you anything, I accept your charge to find out why Malacar came here tonight."

Aeon shook his head, a bemused smile on his face. "That is not necessary, Morgania," he said. "You will have plenty of time in the future to undertake your own quests, when you are older...."

"I am a noble of House Eiluned, your Grace," Morgan said. "I have studied the uses of Glamour with Lady Alyssa and others who have mastered its many forms. I was a witness to Malacar's words, and I was at the Toybox when Valmont was attacked. It's my right to ask that you grant me the chance to serve you. Besides," she added, looking over her shoulder at Aliera, wide-eyed on the couch behind her and flashing a small, conspiratorial smile at her fellow childling before she turned back to the duke, "Princess Aliera and I finished the knighting ceremony for you. We gave Leigh...I mean Dame Eleighanara...her sword, so that means she's our vassal, too." She walked over to Leigh and took her hand. "Dame Eleighanara, if Duke Aeon grants me this quest, will you promise to help me complete it? Please?"

Leigh stared down at the childling, her eyes suddenly misty with pride, not for herself, but at Morgan's sweet determination. "My lady, and my lord," she said, finding her voice. "I have been blind to my duty as your vassal. If you will have me, I will do as you command."

Aeon looked from Morgan to Leigh, studying each of them carefully. He saw Lady Alyssa start to rise from her seat, a frown of disapproval on her face.

"I accept," he said quickly. "Baroness Morgania, I grant you and Dame Eleighanara the favor you seek."

Leigh bowed, relief flooding through her. Morgan curtseyed once more to the Duke. Then she turned to

Valmont. "Will you help us?" she asked. "After all, you're a part of this already."

Valmont nodded to Morgan. "The honor of my lord is at stake," he said. "It is my quest as well."

Morgan held out a hand toward Valmont, and started to voice her thanks. Suddenly, the dream that she had been trying to remember came to her.

She stood in her mother's studio, staring at a painting of a young woman in a long white tunic kneeling in front of an elaborately decorated chest which stood open before her. From inside the chest a throng of shadowy creatures rose into the air, some of them with wings like bats, other with horns protruding from their heads. The woman's hands were held in front of her as if to shield her from their onslaught. It was a painting of Pandora, who opened the magical box that loosed all manner of ills upon the world. As she looked more closely at the painting, it changed, and the woman became Morgan herself, standing in horror in front of an open chest....

"The Toybox!" Morgan cried out. "We have to go there before it's too late!"

"What do you mean?" Leigh asked, her question echoed by Valmont. Cumulus reacted to the childling's sudden cry by jerking to attention, casting about for the cause of her alarm.

"I had a dream last night," Morgan said. "The Toybox is in danger."

"Morgania," Lady Alyssa began, her face pale with worry, "this evening has been too much for you."

"No, it's real, I swear it," Morgan sounded near tears.

"I believe the child," Valmont said. "I will not be the one to mock a dreaming. My car is nearby," he added. "We can be there in a few minutes if we make haste."

Morgan had already made her way to the door and

was preparing to open it when she heard Leigh mutter an apology to the duke and his advisers, followed by a similar word of farewell from Valmont. The three changelings hurried through the palace, ignoring the festivities that continued around them. In moments they reached Valmont's convertible, clambered inside, and began their frantic journey to the Toybox Coffee Shop.

Left alone with his advisers and the Princess Aliera, Aeon sat lost in thought, trying to make sense of what had just occurred. Alyssa was admonishing him about something, and Sir Cumulus had begun to pace furiously about the small room. Aliera watched the antics of her elders with open astonishment.

Then he heard the sad, sweet call of the harp, piercing the jumble of thoughts in his mind, filling his awareness with an irresistible pull. Aeon rose with the stiffness of a sleepwalker and left the room without another word. Lady Alyssa stopped in mid-sentence and stared helplessly after the duke.

"Shall I go after him, lady?" Cumulus asked.

Alyssa shook her head. "It's pointless, Sir Cumulus," she said dully. "We were lucky to have his company for this long...." She sighed once, then lifted her skirts and looked over her shoulder at the princess. "Aliera, sweetling," she said, "it's nearly time for you to go to bed. Come with me to say good night to the guests." She stalked out of the room, the childling trailing in her wake.

Sir Cumulus followed them from the room, but turned from the party to wander toward the grand stairway in the center of the palace. He reached it just in time to see Aeon's forlorn figure disappearing into his chambers at the head of the stairs. With a heavy heart, the duke's herald wandered back toward the ballroom, the night's celebrations quickly becoming only a bitter memory.

Malacar was growing more and more impatient as the evening progressed. Rasputin showed no signs of bringing his parody of the Seelie Court to an end. The satyr muttered an idle curse under his breath. He remembered Rasputin's brief stint as court jester. More than once, the pooka's bitter insights had driven some of the more sensitive of the sidhe nobles to tears rather than the laughter they so ardently desired. Although privately, Malacar thought Rasputin's exaggerated portrayals of the members of the court showed an uncanny accuracy, he had joined with the others in pressing Duke Aeon to replace him with a more suitable — and less perceptive — court fool. Rasputin saw only too clearly, and although he could not, by his nature, speak truly without some form of embellishment, Malacar had been afraid that someone would eventually decipher the pooka's secret language and uncover a number of dangerous truths concealed in his wayward speech.

His own dismissal from court and his banishment from the fief of Goldengate had come about prematurely, a matter that still rankled whenever the satyr dwelled on what had been denied him. After all, it had been his own meticulous research that had led to the discovery of the twin gems he wore, and had it not been for the malicious interference of Lady Alyssa, he would have gained a clearer understanding of their original purpose and the uses to which they could be put.

The little he had discovered, however, had been enough to make him valuable to the rulers of the Shadow Court — not the mock court which made a feeble pretense of rulership once a year, at Samhain, but the real Court of Shadows, which convened in secret to plan how to restore its rightful place in the changeling community. His mysterious contact, whom he thought of as the "lady of shadows," had welcomed his arrival and had commiserated with his enforced defection from the Seelie Court. Although she had cautioned him that, like others who had turned their back upon the outdated, stagnant traditions of the Seelie fae, he would have to prove his commitment to the Shadow Court before he could be brought into its innermost circles of power, she implied that the faithful execution of his current task would result in his elevation to a position of leadership. She had made no effort to conceal her delight with Malacar's possession of the magical eyestones, as she called them. Through her instructions, he had learned to use the power of the ruby gem, which she called the Changestone, to allow him to travel unrecognized throughout the fief of Goldengate. She had also orchestrated the events that were about to lead up to the use of the emerald stone, the Eye of Opening.

Malacar cast a wary glance about him at the few changelings remaining in the Toybox. Slique and her companion were still awaiting his signal to act. Everything was in readiness for him to make his move. All he needed was for the damned pooka and his court of brats to end their foolishness and clear the pathway to his goal.

Edmund was beginning to get bored with playing knight of the Seelie Court. He'd eaten his way through two Frisbees and was considering whether or not he could surreptitiously consume the tablecloth he wore draped across his shoulders like a cloak.

Rasputin had the rest of the childling "court" in stitches as he demonstrated yet another of "Duke Millennium's" many talents, assuring his audience that secretly the real duke was a consummate juggler and acrobat.

"Hey, your Dukeness!" Edmund called out, catching the pooka in mid-handstand.

Rasputin lost his balance momentarily, teetering back and forth precariously until he managed to steady himself on his palms, feet waving in the air.

"Are those the dulcet tones of my First Lord of Warts that so gently beg for my attention?" he responded.

"Yeah, it's me," said Edmund. "I'm tired of being Sir Cumbustible."

"So, I'm certain, is said Sir Cumbustible," said Rasputin. At the bar, Fizzlewig caught himself smiling wryly at the pooka's comment. He knew of nothing that could be further from the truth.

The street door of the coffee shop opened suddenly. Morgan, her long black curls in disarray, burst through the doorway, followed closely by Valmont and Leigh, both in their court finery.

Edmund seized the opportunity to make his break. "It's an invasion, your Dukeness!" he exclaimed, charging forward to intercept the three changelings. The rest of the "court" scrambled to their feet and swarmed after Edmund. Rasputin, finding himself abandoned, let his legs fall forward, rolled into a standing position, and trailed after the childling horde.

"Evicted from civilized company so soon?" he drawled as he approached his friends.

Malacar jumped at the opening provided him by the sudden entrance of Valmont and his companions. Their arrival, although it drew Rasputin and the childlings away from the toy chest, meant that he would have to work even more quickly than he had intended, but he prided himself on his ability to improvise. According to the lady of shadows, any one of the items contained in the toy chest should serve his purpose. He had privately hoped to acquire as much of its contents for himself — and his new associates, of course — as he could stuff inside the inner pockets of his cloak. Now he would have to content himself with a simple hit-and-run maneuver. He wheeled about on his barstool, upsetting his drink with one arm in what he hoped appeared to be an unintentional display of clumsiness.

As the mug clattered to the floor, Slique went into action.

"You filthy, wool-faced, slime-soaked muttonbag!" she shrieked, jumping to her feet and taking a swing at her companion. The pooka ducked under the table and ran, bleating frantically, straight for the center of the room, upsetting tables and chairs as he passed them.

Malacar noted his position relative to the toy chest, then muttered a pair of nonsense syllables. Darkness filled the room. Trusting his memory for detail, the satyr, his limp abandoned, raced toward the toy chest, pulling the emerald gem from his pocket as he ran.

The childlings' screams filled the air as an impenetrable blackness engulfed the interior of the coffee shop.

Blinded by the sudden darkness and trapped by the miniature army of childlings clustered around her, Morgan found herself unable to move.

"He's going for the chest!" she screamed, trying to make herself heard above the panicked shrieks of the other childlings.

"Let me through," she heard Leigh's voice, strident with authority.

"It's too bright in here!" Rasputin exclaimed. "Somebody turn off the lights!"

The panicky sound of his granddaughter's voice jolted Tor from his sleep. He opened his eyes and saw only an inky darkness. A confusion of screams, scuffling and scraping noises, and a few childish sobs assaulted his ears.

"Morgan," he bellowed, rising from the booth and shoving his way into the room. "Where are you?"

"Grandpa!" Morgan called back to him, her voice rising in urgency. "The chest! Do something!" Tor groped his way toward the center of the room, heedless of the overturned furniture in his path.

"Everyone sit!" Valmont cried out, projecting his voice in a range calculated to cut through the high-pitched cries of the childlings and resonate through the room. A barrage of nearly simultaneous thuds answered his command, as the young changelings near him — and, by the sound of it — some of the other patrons in the coffee shop reacted instinctively to the forcefulness of his tone. "Rasputin!" he called. "Can you counter the darkness?"

"With my eyes closed," the pooka responded from somewhere in front of Valmont. "Although it's rather soothing to the nerves..."

"Just do it," the eshu snapped. He felt an elbow poke him in the ribs as someone shoved past him. He made a wild grab, hoping to connect with the fleeing individual. His fingers closed on some silky fabric, and he heard a ripping sound as a swatch of cloth came away in his hand. Beside him, he sensed Leigh slowly picking her way through the gaggle of seated, sobbing childlings. At least she would not have to contend with trying to predict where they might be had they not followed his earlier orders to sit, he thought grimly to himself.

"When day is night, and wrong is right, when horses fly, and fish walk by, when two makes three, the light we'll see!" Rasputin drew on his reserves of Glamour, channeling it through his sing-song rhyme into the air around him. A brilliant light exploded through the room, soaking up the chimerical darkness, though its unexpected brightness blinded everyone in the room for an instant.

"Don't forget to keep your eyes open," Rasputin warned belatedly, his own eyes tightly shut against the sudden light.

Once Morgan's eyes had recovered from the dual assault of darkness and light, she started for the toy chest, only to find herself swept up in the arms of her grandfather.

"Are you hurt?" he asked. "What happened?"

"I'm fine, honest," Morgan said, trying to wriggle out of his grasp. "Stop trying to protect me," she said, her voice betraying her frustration. "I need to get to the toy chest!" Abashed, Tor placed Morgan gently on the floor. Taking her hand, he turned and began walking toward the chest. Morgan gave a soft moan as her eyes took in what she had both expected and feared to see.

Leigh and Valmont looked around the room. At the front of the coffee shop, the still-seated childlings were beginning to stir, making their way to the back of the room and taking shelter in one of the side booths. The center of the room was in shambles, as overturned tables and chairs formed random piles from one side of the coffee shop to the other. At the rear, near the booth lately occupied by Tor, Georgia poked

the

a chair, legs pointed outward, toward something underneath the table. Behind the bar, the door to the kitchen opened and Fizzlewig, looking flustered, hurried out, pulling his pale-faced apprentice, Barklie, behind him.

"Barklie says he got out the back door," Fizzlewig announced, then stopped abruptly in the center of the room, mouth agape. "By the lady of the moon and all her starry children!" he whispered. "It's been opened."

The room grew still as all eyes turned toward the toy chest. The ornate steamer trunk still rested on its low table, but now its top was thrown back on its hinges. A soft, iridescent glow emanated from within it, making ripples in the air above its exposed interior.

Morgan and Tor continued their steady progress until they stood directly in front of the open chest. Leigh and Valmont, seeing where Morgan had gone, joined them. With a sigh and a mumbled, "I have absolutely no interest in seeing what's inside," Rasputin sidled up to stand next to Leigh. Someone jostled the pooka at knee-level, and he looked down to see Edmund squirming past him to grab the edge of the chest with one hand, peering inside. His other hand disappeared into the chest.

"Don't!" Morgan gasped as she saw the redcap childling dive for the toy chest. She started after him, but Tor's hand, still firmly closed around hers, held her back.

"What do you see?" Valmont asked, his voice quiet, his body tensed to move quickly. Leigh found her hand straying involuntarily to the sword she wore belted around her waist.

"Toys!" Edmund said, awe muting his voice to a whisper. No sooner was the word out of his mouth than he jumped backward, slamming into Rasputin and bringing the two of them crashing to the floor. "They're alive!" he said, eyes wide with amazement.

"Look!" Morgan called out, pointing to the chest. A pair of gloved hands emerged from within the toy chest, gripping its sides. Tor dropped Morgan's hand. Closing the gap between himself and the chest with one long stride, he grasped the trunk lid and attempted to wrest it into place. Given his massive size and proportionate strength, it should have been an easy task. The lid refused to budge. Tor strained, and managed to pull the lid a few inches forward. He set himself for another mighty tug, but the lid slipped from his grasp and sprang open again. At the same time, a head popped up behind the pair of hands, eyes scanning the room. Both head and hands disappeared back into the box.

"Oh, leave it open!" Rasputin called from his position on the floor, partly underneath Edmund's sprawled form. "Just be quick about it!" Leigh moved forward to lend her assistance to Tor. The lid remained unmovable.

"It's stuck," Leigh cried.

At that instant, a soldier, dressed in the regalia of a bygone century, stood up inside the box. Morgan recognized the gloves and face from its appearance seconds earlier. The life-sized figure's dark curly hair, muttonchop sideburns, and carefully groomed mustache looked as if they had been applied with paint. Placing one hand on the side of the chest, the soldier vaulted over the top and stood looking perplexed at the people standing frozen before him, fascinated by the spectacle. His gaze finally focused on the door of the Toybox Coffee Shop, still standing slightly ajar. He nodded once to himself, then turned back to the toy chest. With lightning swiftness he drew his sabre from its sheath at his side and pointed it toward the open door. Still looking over his shoulder, he opened his mouth.

the

"Charge!" he called. "To the front, lads! Follow me!" Hurling his body forward, he ran toward the front of the coffee shop. Leigh released her grip on the trunk lid and moved to interpose herself between the charging soldier and the open door. Valmont joined her. Tor backed away from the chest and placed his bulk squarely in front of Morgan, his body a formidable shield against whatever might follow. Rasputin and Edmund untangled them-selves from each other and struggled to their feet just in time to see a pair of mounted cavalrymen leap over the edge of the box, followed by a second pair.

Leigh's face grew pale as the four horsemen bore down upon her. Valmont grabbed her arm with one hand, touched his forehead with his other hand, and leaped out of the way, pulling Leigh with him.

Pandemonium descended upon the coffee shop as more and more creatures began swarming from the toy chest, assuming life-sized proportions as they did so. A group of footsoldiers crawled over the side of the trunk and ran outside onto the street. A bear clutching a pair of brass cymbals shuffled its way out of the box, the first in a chaotic parade of phantasmagoria.

"There's an ostrich!" shrieked a childling voice from the rear of the coffee shop. "I see an elephant!" another voice exclaimed as the figures continued to spew forth in an endless stream, each one stranger than the one before. Something resembling a large golden lizard with batlike wings flew out of the chest, filling the doorway of the coffee shop with its bulk before disappearing into the night. Nothing more emerged from the box.

"That was most definitely not a dragon," Rasputin said, his nose twitching furiously. Edmund glanced surreptitiously at the small object he clutched in his hand, then shoved it quickly into his pocket, smiling to himself.

Both Leigh and Valmont rushed from the coffee shop, intending to give chase. At the doorway, Valmont pointed Leigh in one direction, his steps already taking him in the other.

Inside the coffee shop, Morgan stepped out from behind the wall that was her grandfather and started toward the open toy chest. Tor extended a protective hand to stop her, but the childling reached upward to clasp hands with him instead, trying to pull him with her.

"I don't think anything in there can hurt us," she said. "I just want to look inside....Please?" Together the eager childling and the reluctant troll walked carefully to the chest. Morgan peered inside.

The inside of the toy chest was lined with a rich, silvery satin interwoven with iridescent threads, and marked by faint depressions made by the once closely packed "toys." It was empty, or almost so.

"What's that?" Morgan asked, staring at something tucked into one of the corners of the chest. She tried to reach into the chest to retrieve the object, but it remained just outside her grasp. Instead, Tor leaned over and plucked it out of its corner.

"It's a cat!" Morgan said, staring at the painted metal figure — a small gray sleeping cat curled into a circle — that now rested on Tor's flattened palm. Rasputin and Edmund, followed by Fizzlewig, came nearer to look. The cat's body began to glow softly.

"It's getting bigger," Tor said, as he brought his other hand into line with the hand that held the cat, which now extended across the entire width of his palm.

"I think it's probably a good idea to let it grow to its full size," Rasputin commented. "I'm sure the toy chest will be unaffected if everything is emptied out of it."

Morgan looked back at the empty chest. The light that once radiated from within it was beginning to dim.

"Rasputin's right!" she cried. "The toy chest needs something in it to feed its magic. Put it back, quick!"

The cat was almost to full size, and had begun to sprout a pair of tiny golden wings. Hesitantly, Tor closed his hands over the figure and bent to lower it into the chest, tucking it into the spot where it had originally rested. The glow from the figure quickly faded, and it receded in size, wings disappearing back into the painted fur. Within the chest, some of the brightness returned.

"It's the guardian of the chest," Morgan breathed. "I know it is! Like Pandora's Box!"

The door to the coffee shop opened as Leigh and Valmont returned, failure evident on their faces. Fizzlewig looked at them expectantly. Valmont shook his head.

"Nothing," the eshu said. "I went as far as the Park and saw no sign of any of them."

Leigh's face echoed Valmont's dismay. "I thought I saw something near Buena Vista Park," she said, "but I ended up chasing shadows. They've disappeared."

"Now what do we do?" Edmund asked.

"They have to be retrieved somehow," Fizzlewig said. "I was afraid this would happen someday."

"Did you know what was inside it all this time?" Edmund asked. "And you never told anybody?" The childling's voice sounded accusing.

Fizzlewig shook his head. "I knew there had to be something in it that was giving off all that Glamour, but I never could get the dang thing to open!"

"You mean you actually tried?" Rasputin asked. "And here all this time I thought you weren't any good with tinkering."

"I could use some help over here," Georgia's voice called out from the back of the room. Fizzlewig looked around him. The coffee shop was nearly empty. Aside from the group that stood with him near the opened toy chest and the gang of childlings who still chattered nervously in the booth they had claimed as a refuge from the confusion, only Georgia remained, hunkered over near the rear booth. In the relative silence, Fizzlewig thought he could hear bleating noises coming from somewhere near the nocker cabbie.

Fizzlewig looked at Tor, a question in his eyes. The troll nodded gravely and strode toward Georgia.

"He's under the table," she said. "He changed his form and tried to four-leg it out of here by the back door along with the old coot, but I grabbed him by the tail and threw him under the table. I've had my eye on him ever since, so he can't change back."

Tor bent down and peered under the table. A grim chuckle escaped him as he knelt down and shoved an arm into the dark corner formed by the booth and the wall. He groped around for a few minutes as Georgia looked on.

"Got him," Tor said, finally. He stood up, his large hand gripping a struggling, bedraggled sheep by the scruff of its neck. Tucking the bleating creature under one arm, he returned to Fizzlewig and the others.

The boggan's face brightened. "That's the scoundrel who was with Slique," he cackled.

"Slique was here?" Valmont asked. "Who else?"

"Some old satyr," Fizzlewig answered. "He was sitting by the bar when you three came in," he said, including Leigh and Morgan as he spoke.

"Malacar," Morgan said. "It was Malacar, I know it!" Behind her, Leigh nodded agreement.

"But why?" she asked.

"Who's Malacar?" Edmund demanded.

"He was once the court wizard for Duke Aeon," Valmont said. "He had some differences with the duke's other advisers, and stirred up a fair amount of unrest in

the

the Seelie Court. The duke ordered him to leave his court and the fief of Goldengate." The eshu hesitated, as if trying to decide whether to say any more.

"He was one of the nicest people I ever met," said Rasputin. "It's a pity such a loyal servant of the duke had to leave."

"So did he join the Shadow Court, or what?" Edmund asked.

Valmont shrugged. "How should I know?"

"I thought you knew everything that went on with the Unseelie Court," the redcap said. "At least that's what I've heard."

"That's neither here nor there, Edmund," Valmont said sharply. "What is pertinent is that thanks to Georgia," he glanced toward the back of the room where Georgia was brushing off her leather jacket and straightening her cap, preparing to leave the coffee shop, "we have a potential source of information about what happened tonight."

"I was just leaving," Georgia said as she crossed the room and headed for the childling group. "I thought I'd see these tykes to their homes, if they have any." She stopped in front of the children. "Anyone interested in a ride?" she asked diffidently.

"In your cab?" a childling nocker asked, his face incredulous. "Can I sit up front?"

"Can you make it fly?" "How about wheelies?" Still asking questions, the childling group followed Georgia out the door into the street.

"You're gonna question a sheep?" Edmund's tone was derisive.

"There's something else we need to talk about," said Leigh, looking at Morgan as she spoke, "but I don't think it's wise to do it in front of strangers...." Her eyes strayed toward the creature that sagged listlessly in Tor's grip.

Fizzlewig nodded sagely. He turned to Tor.

"Why don't you take him into the kitchen and tie him to the carving table." The sheep's eyes grew wide and he began bleating furiously, trying to kick his way free from the troll. Tor squeezed his prisoner sharply around his stomach, driving the wind from the sheep's lungs. He stopped struggling.

"To the table leg," Fizzlewig added impatiently. "I hate mutton," he said. Then the boggan looked at Barklie. "I want you to go back into the kitchen and keep an eye on our guest. He can't change form if anybody's watching him. We'll talk to him later." Barklie nodded his head up and down. Fizzlewig accompanied Tor and Barklie toward the rear of the room, ducking behind the bar while they continued onward into the kitchen.

A few minutes later, Tor returned alone to join his friends, who had spent the intervening moments putting the coffee shop's dining area in some kind of order. Fizzlewig emerged from the bar carrying a tray of mugs, steam rising from the hot drinks they contained. He made his way over to the largest table in the room and waited while the others joined him.

"The cocoa's for you," he said, placing a large mug shaped like a dragon in front of Edmund. "Butterscotch for the baroness," he continued, giving Morgan a mug formed like a fairytale castle. Morgan frowned. "Where's the unicorn mug?" she asked, a tone of petulance creeping into her voice.

"I wasn't exactly expecting you tonight," the boggan said. "I thought you'd stay at the court festivities." Fizzlewig regarded the childling dubiously. "Do you want me to change mugs?" he asked.

Morgan shook her head. "It's all right," she answered.

"I have some spiced tea for the rest of us," Fizzlewig said, setting the tray with its remaining drinks down in the center of the table.

"You were saying," he said to Leigh.

Leigh took a sip of the spicy tea to moisten her throat and to allow her to put her thoughts in order.

"Valmont and I came here tonight because Morgan had a dream that this was going to happen," she began. "Obviously, we got here too late to prevent Malacar from opening the toy chest. But something else happened earlier this evening at court, and I think the two events may be related."

As briefly as she could, Leigh recounted the details of her knighting, and of Malacar's sudden interruption of the ceremony, avoiding the mention of how the satyr had gained entry into the court and playing down Aeon's peculiar behavior as much as she could.

"So he quested you to find Malacar and give him the boot?" Edmund said, his voice excited and not a little envious.

"If you'd gotten here sooner, that might have been the longest quest in Seelie history," Rasputin observed.

"It wasn't just Leigh he quested," Valmont said quietly. "Baroness Morgania accepted the quest along with her...as did I."

"Morgan..." Tor began, his expression stern.

"Grandpa, not you, too!" Morgan's voice betrayed her exasperation. "I had to do it. It wasn't fair for Leigh to get stuck with it all by herself. She's going to need help."

"Well, obviously, she won't get any help from us," Rasputin said.

"Will you help us?" Morgan asked, her face bright with expectation.

"Didn't I just say that I wanted no part of this?" Rasputin rolled his eyes.

"I knew you'd help," Morgan said. Leigh smiled at the pooka. "Thanks, Rasputin," she said softly. "I don't know just what we're getting ourselves into. We might be up against some very dangerous people," she added, looking inadvertently in Valmont's direction. The eshu flexed his tender shoulder thoughtfully before nodding, his face concealing whatever thoughts passed through his mind.

"Then I'm in," said Tor. "Morgan will need me."

"We'll all need you," answered Leigh.

"Yeah," Edmund interjected. "An old fart like you must know a few tricks we can use."

"Are you offering to join us, Edmund?" Valmont asked mildly. "I didn't think this sort of thing would appeal to you."

"Why not?" the redcap childling countered. "It's not as if this were a Seelie-only gig after all," he said, his voice tinged with maliciousness. "If it were, you wouldn't be here."

"Edmund!" Morgan snapped. "No one asked you to be a part of this." Her dark eyes glowered at the boy.

"I don't see how you could possibly be useful, Edmund," Rasputin said mildly. "After all, you know nothing of what's going on among the hoi-polloi and riffraff that clutter the fair streets of this ancient metropolis of harmonious concord. Morgan and Leigh are quite capable of rubbing elbows with the worst sort of people. Valmont and Tor and I are obviously included as a sop to the masses and can't be anything other than a burden...."

"I think we get your point, Rasputin," Leigh said, smiling in spite of herself. "Do you want to join us, Edmund?" she asked.

Edmund stood up, arms folded across his scrawny chest, a sneer on his face. "I don't know," he said. "Maybe I'll just leave you in the lurch." He looked pointedly at Morgan. She returned his glare.

"I suppose an apology would be impossible at this juncture," Rasputin remarked. He turned to Valmont. "I think staring contests do wonders for one's eyesight," he said.

Morgan sighed and looked down at her cup, tracing its intricate designs with her fingers. "I'm sorry, Edmund," she said finally. "I had no right to say what I did. Please, will you help us?"

His pride mollified, Edmund uncrossed his arms and sat down. He drained the last of his cocoa and looked thoughtfully at the cup. Fizzlewig held his breath until Edmund set the cup down again in front of him. "I'm not hungry," he said.

"Well?" Valmont prodded.

Edmund shrugged. "I guess," he said, looking at Valmont.

"Sir Cumbersome has spoken," Rasputin intoned. "How can we help but fail?"

Tor turned to Fizzlewig, who had sat quietly listening to the conversation around him. "What about you, old friend?" the troll asked. "Are you up for joining us?"

Fizzlewig pursed his lips and frowned. Watching his face, Leigh could almost see the boggan weighing the pros and cons of Tor's invitation. Finally he shook his head.

"Someone has to hold the fort while the troops are out gallivanting around," he said. "But I'd certainly appreciate your trying to find all those damned...s'cuse me, ladies...danged critters before they hurt themselves out in the world."

"That's right!" Leigh exclaimed. "They are chimerae, aren't they?"

Valmont nodded. "They would have to be. How else could they exist?"

"But they were just a bunch of toys when I saw them," Edmund protested. "They were really cool toys," he added, "but they weren't anywhere near as big inside the box as they were when they came out of it."

"It's just that, well, I swore I'd keep the toy chest safe...and that included its contents," Fizzlewig mumbled.

"You're the head of this freehold," Tor said. "We're all beholden to you for all the times we've come here. If you ask us to round them up for you, we won't refuse."

"Then consider yourself duly charged with returning them to where they belong." Fizzlewig looked about him. "Does this place seem a little gloomier than usual?" He asked, worry evident in his voice.

"I shouldn't think that all that Glamour running out the front door would have any effect on the freehold," Rasputin said.

"I know," Fizzlewig muttered. "It worries me, too. But there's not much that can be done about it this late at night," he said.

"Morgan!" Leigh said suddenly, springing quickly to her feet. "We have to get you home!"

Morgan's face grew pale. "My parents have probably been home for hours!" she wailed. "How am I going to explain this to them?" She rose hastily.

"I seem to be playing chauffeur tonight," Valmont said, rising to his feet. "Let me drive you home. Maybe it's not too late."

"Some quest," Edmund grumbled. "Let's take a break 'cause it's the princess' bedtime."

"Why don't you come back to the kitchen with the rest of us," Fizzlewig said to Edmund. "Let's get some answers from our leg of mutton. We can do that, at least." The boggan got up and steered Edmund toward the rear of the coffee shop as Valmont and Leigh took Morgan's hands and hurried out the front door.

Alicia Daniels leaned sleepily against her husband's arm as Gordon turned onto their street.

The party had been better than she had expected. Although the requisite socialites had been in attendance, fawning over the guest artists and uttering facile words of praise for their work, Alicia had managed to extract herself from most of them. She had found a small group of artists and genuine art patrons whose company she enjoyed for most of the evening. Gordon had courted all the important people in the room, using his good looks and articulate speech to advantage as he circulated systematically through the crowd. Alicia had no doubt that his efforts this evening would pay off in a wealth of new contacts.

A light mist had moved into the neighborhood in the wee hours of the morning, giving an impressionistic blurriness to familiar objects. Suddenly, her drowsiness left her and she clutched Gordon's arm.

"Look!" she said, sitting up and leaning forward in the seat to peer intently ahead of her. "Is that Morgan?"

Halfway down the block, just in front of their house, a long, dark red convertible had pulled up to the sidewalk, discharging what looked like a slender young woman in gray and a child about Morgan's size, wearing a lavender party dress.

Startled, Gordon slowed the car down, trying to see what had attracted his wife's attention.

"Here we are," said Leigh, stepping out of Valmont's car and helping Morgan out onto the sidewalk. "Can you get into the house by yourself?"

Morgan nodded, smoothing the wrinkles out of her skirt. "There's a key to the house hidden near the back steps. Mother's always locking herself out of the house."

Inside the car, Valmont saw headlights in his rearview mirror. He watched as the vehicle slowed to a crawl. "Is the car behind us anything you should be concerned about?" He spoke conversationally, but made sure his voice was loud enough for both Leigh and Morgan to hear him.

Morgan turned around to look.

"It's my parents!" she whispered frantically. "I'll bet they've seen us!"

Leigh thought quickly. There were certain ways to use the natural magic of the fae to alter the perceptions of others. It was too late to change the fact that Morgan's parents had seen them, but there was a chance that she could make them uncertain of what they saw. An idea occurred to her.

"Get ready to start pacing me," she said to Valmont. "Morgan, get set to run around the back of the house."

Leigh took a moment to tap the Glamour of her faerie nature, mumbling a word over and over to herself to direct the illusion she wanted to create. When she was satisfied, she signaled to Morgan.

"Run!" she whispered. "Get in the house as quickly as you can!"

Taking a deep breath, Leigh bent over on the sidewalk and mimed the act of checking the laces on a pair of nonexistent running shoes.

Trusting her friend, Morgan sprinted for the back of the house. She found the key by the back steps, let herself in and, taking off her shoes, tiptoed quietly up the back stairs. Panting with excitement, she ran to her bedroom and undressed hurriedly. By the time she heard her parents' key in the front door, she was in bed, the covers tugged around her and her party clothes stuffed underneath the mattress.

Gordon Daniels thanked Mrs. Goherty for her services and escorted the elderly woman to her car. When he returned, Alicia was coming from the kitchen, carrying two glasses of water. She handed one to Gordon to carry upstairs with him.

"You gave me a scare," he said as he followed her

up the stairs to their bedroom. "You must have been dreaming about Morgan."

Alicia nodded, her mind still puzzled at her misperception. "Who would have thought anybody would be out jogging at this time of night?" she murmured.

"At least she had sense enough to bring someone along to pace her," Gordon said, putting the incident out of his mind. Nevertheless, he paused and stood behind Alicia as she eased open the door to Morgan's bedroom and looked in. Together, they listened to the soft breathing of their sleeping daughter.

toybox

chapter

eight

Malacar stood in judgment, surrounded by a circle of tall, grim figures cloaked in velvet darkness and terrible in the sinister radiance of their power.

"Tell us again how you failed to perform the ritual," one of the figures spoke, his voice colder than iron.

The satyr trembled and clutched his cloak tightly around his worn body to conceal his tremors.

"I have told you truthfully all I remember," he began, but his words were cut off as one of the figures moved with lightning swiftness. Malacar cringed in terror as one slender hand grasped his chin while the other held a dagger to his neck. The satyr felt a wave of sickness as the sharp iron point pressed into his skin.

"Again," the figure whispered. "And this time you will show us the respect that we deserve. On your knees, commoner!" the voice ordered.

Malacar knelt as quickly as he could, taking care to keep his head — still trapped between the hand and dagger of his tormentor — motionless.

"Stand away," a third voice commanded. Malacar thought he recognized the sultry female voice as that of his contact, the lady of shadows. "I think our point has been made."

Malacar nearly wept with relief as the figure standing at his side withdrew the tip of the dagger from his neck and released his grip on the satyr's chin.

"You were saying..." the familiar voice prompted.

Trying to keep himself from babbling, Malacar began to speak.

the

"Unless you want to spend the rest of your miserable life tied in sheep-form to my cutting table, you'll take advantage of the next ten seconds to change back to something that can talk without bleating." Fizzlewig's voice was sharp. Rasputin, Edmund and Tor stood around the table in the kitchen of the Toybox. Seated cross-legged on the floor, head propped up in his hands, Fizzlewig's cook, Barklie, stared unblinking at the forlorn animal secured to a stout table leg by a sturdy rope around its neck.

"Everybody look away while I count to ten," Fizzlewig said. Tor looked at the ceiling. Rasputin wandered over to inspect the rack of pots and pans hanging on one wall. Edmund went to the large oven, pulled it open and stuck his head inside. Barklie shut his eyes. "One, two, three..."

On seven, they heard a sharp thud followed by a startled cry. Looking back, they saw a young, woolly haired pooka crouched awkwardly in front of the table, his body bent forward by the rope still encircling his neck. He rubbed the top of his head with one hand where it had cracked against the corner of the tabletop.

Tor reacted to the cry, reaching out to snag a handful of the prisoner's hair. "I wouldn't go anywhere, if I were you," he rumbled in a menacing voice. The other changelings gathered around the flustered pooka, who sat on the floor, weighed down by the burden of Tor's fingers wound tightly in his curls.

Fizzlewig, hands on his hips, placed himself in front of the pooka and frowned.

"You and that redcap Slique were ready when the satyr made his move," Fizzlewig said. "I want you to tell us why he did it and what you all hoped to accomplish. And don't lie to me either!"

"He's doomed!" Edmund called out cheerfully, his childish voice echoing from the depths of Fizzlewig's oven.

"Get out of there!" Fizzlewig called over his shoulder.

"Just cleaning your oven for you," Edmund returned, backing out of the oven and slamming the door after him. He chewed furiously on something and swallowed before speaking again. "Spic and span, now..." he said.

"It would be a bad idea for me to question him," Rasputin said, coming forward to sit on the floor opposite his kithmate. Fizzlewig looked up at Tor. The old troll grimaced as he considered the implications of Rasputin's offer. Finally he nodded.

"Let 'im give it a shot," the boggan said.

"Why didn't you do anything to create a diversion?" Rasputin began, his face intent, his large rabbit eyes glittering.

"I swear nobody paid us anything. We thought of it all on our own!"

"Just as I surmised." Rasputin said sagely. "So who didn't pay you? And why did this person tell you not to come to the Toybox tonight?"

"He'll be just thrilled if I tell you his name," the pooka said.

"We'll be even happier if you don't, and we're too far away from you to do anything about it," Rasputin countered.

"It wasn't Malacar," mumbled the pooka.

"I didn't think it was," Rasputin said. "Please don't tell me what he had in mind..."

The pooka tried to lower his head and look away from his captors. Tor pulled his head back up.

"Ow!" the pooka complained. "That didn't hurt a bit. All I know is that Slique and I were supposed to sit quietly and do nothing when Malacar knocked his cup off the bar. He wanted us to make it as easy as possible for people to get to him by arranging the furniture in a neat path. Then we were supposed to stick around until everything was over."

Edmund scrambled under the table and wedged himself as close to the pooka as he could. He smiled broadly, displaying his teeth.

"I've never had leg of lamb before," he said. "Can I just have a taste?" he asked Fizzlewig. The pooka jerked away from him, pulling the rope taut around his neck and slamming his elbow hard into the table leg.

"Wow!" said Edmund, his voice full of admiration. "Let him torture himself! What a great idea."

"Edmund, you're being very helpful," Rasputin said, "but I'm sure our conversation will go nowhere if you keep trying to calm our friend down."

Edmund sat back, looking confused.

"Now," Rasputin continued calmly, "I believe I forgot to ask you just what purpose was furthest from Malacar's thoughts...."

The woolly-haired pooka looked nervously at Edmund and swallowed audibly. "He had some sort of ordinary gizmo, not magical at all, that he was going to use to keep the toy chest from opening up. He didn't want anything that was in it and he didn't want to let all those things inside it loose. He told me exactly why he wanted to do that, too."

"I don't suppose you have a name or anything like that," Rasputin said.

"Don't call me Larry," the pooka mumbled.

"Fine, Larry," said Rasputin, "let's suppose you're lying to me for the moment. I don't want to know where Malacar met you two or what he offered to pay you."

"We were nowhere near Trickster's when Malacar found us," Larry said. "He didn't split a pouchful of Dross between us, either. He was really polite about it, too. He told us to ask all the questions we wanted and he'd be happy to reply to them and that the more we knew the safer we'd be." He sounded worried as he spoke.

Rasputin nodded. He stood up and brushed off his hands, then turned to his companions, who were staring at him, their faces full of questions.

"I think we need to keep him here," Rasputin said. "It's obvious that he's got a lot more to tell us and we can spend our time most profitably by questioning him."

"What exactly did you learn from all that?" Fizzlewig asked, immediately regretting his question.

Rasputin sighed.

"He never said the following: Malacar met him and Slique at Trickster's and offered them a sizable amount of Dross up front to come here tonight and, on his signal, create a disturbance and make certain that no one could get to the toy chest before Malacar succeeded in opening it with a fairly potent magical treasure, retrieving something of value from it and allowing the rest of the chest's contents to break free of their confinement. He also didn't say that Malacar refused to tell them why he wanted what was in the box, and he most emphatically avoided telling me that Malacar implied that knowing what he was up to would be dangerous."

"Is that all?" Edmund asked, incredulous.

"Oh no," Rasputin said, nodding. "There was a lot more."

"I think Rasputin's right," Tor said, releasing his hold on Larry's head. He leaned down and untied the rope, freeing the pooka. "Get out of here," he said.

The pooka scrambled to his feet and bolted for the kitchen door, which led to an alleyway behind the coffee shop.

"That's the way the other one went," Barklie said, pointing to the pooka's departing form. "He was gone before I could stop him...."

"Don't worry about it, son," Fizzlewig said. "You couldn't have known."

"Well, at least we found out something," Tor remarked.

"We did?" Edmund asked. "I'm gonna go look at the chest again," he announced, stomping back into the coffee shop's dining room.

"I'd better go with him," Tor said and followed the young redcap out of the kitchen. Fizzlewig regarded Rasputin with a new respect in his eyes.

"Thanks," he muttered. "I couldn't have done better myself."

Rasputin bowed low, his elongated ears nearly touching the floor.

"You're most unkind," he said. "We'd probably better leave the other two alone out there," he continued, moving to follow Tor into the front room.

"I'd better lock the place up for the night," Fizzlewig said. "I'll want some help moving a mattress downstairs so I can keep an eye on the toy chest overnight."

"Don't ask me," Rasputin offered. "Barklie, don't give me any help carrying some bedding downstairs, all right?"

"Um, sure," Barklie said, looking toward Fizzlewig for help in translating the pooka's remark. Fizzlewig nodded at him.

"After you've helped Rasputin, you can shut the kitchen down and go home until tomorrow...unless you'd rather make a bed for yourself in one of the booths. I could use an extra pair of eyes in case anyone tries to come back here." Fizzlewig pulled out a ring of keys from his pocket and left the kitchen.

For time beyond reckoning, they had dreamed their restless dreams, steeped in the Glamour of their confinement. The suddenness of their awakening had shocked them. Lumbering, clawing, running, slithering, marching, leaping, soaring, scrambling — each according to its nature, they poured from the place that had been their home and their prison, their sanctuary and their cage. The world outside called to them, despite its coldness and its strangeness.

Some of them remembered. The soldiers, the ballerina, the marionettes — to them the streets bore some resemblance to streets contained within their memories. A battle had raged throughout the city, and many of them had taken part in that great upheaval. Commanded to fight, they fought, and some of them remembered dying. Dying, and awakening again, crowded together within a haven replete with Glamour. Now they were free once more, and that meant there was something for them to do, some enemy to fight.

Others remembered nothing, for they had no capacity for memory. They knew how to run and leap and kick and claw and bite. They tumbled headlong into the streets, some feral instinct warning them to dodge the cold bodies of the ones-they-could-not-touch. The whizzing giants that sped back and forth along the hard, black ground were also things to be avoided. Caught in their eternal present, they hurried onward, without direction. From time to time, one of them would pause and sniff the air, catching the scent of something irresistible. Some turned toward the scent of grasses

the

and trees while others sensed the presence of a source of Glamour just around the corner. One by one, the creatures from the chest dispersed, vanishing into the night.

Valmont parked his car outside the ducal palace and waited while Leigh went back inside to make her report to the duke. Later, he knew, he would be making his own assessment of the evening's events in the presence of Count Elias. How much he should tell the count of his own involvement with the Shadow Court still remained uncertain. He had spent most of his life treading on dangerous ground, trying to steer a middle course between conflicting cultures. He was the changeling in the mortal briarpatch, the Unseelie bird in a Seelie nest. And most of the time, he made it work. Like Rasputin, he was good at juggling.

Now he could not escape the feeling that his control was beginning to slip. He prided himself on being able to maintain relationships and connections that crossed boundaries. That, along with their shared eshu heritage, was why he had embroiled himself in changeling politics enough to act as an adviser for Count Elias, who had the unenviable task of ruling, in the name of the Seelie regime, a fief populated almost entirely by Unseelie changelings.

He rankled at the thought that he had been used as a means of insinuating Malacar into the duke's celebration. Regardless of Aeon's protestations of friendship with Elias, in the minds of many of the Seelie Court, Malacar's challenge would be inextricably linked with his appearance at the count's side. Valmont shook his head wearily. On top of everything else, he had foolishly accepted the duke's charge to involve himself even further in things his reason told him he would rather avoid. He had responded almost instinctively to Morgan's request. The childling had an uncanny ability to bend those around her to her own particular vision, and when she asked for his help, he had found it not only impossible but unthinkable to refuse her.

In retrospect, however, he realized that his agreement was also due to Leigh. He wondered what it was about the flaming-haired, Seelie sidhe that both annoyed and attracted him. He wondered if others sensed the anger coiled inside her like a snake about to strike or if he were the only one who saw beneath the veneer of self-assurance she tried to project. That image had failed her in the privacy of the duke's chambers, he realized, when she had faltered in her acceptance of the charge that was originally directed to her. Valmont pondered the idea that he had volunteered his assistance partly to prove a point to Leigh. Idly, he wondered what point it was. He could think of several, not all of them admirable.

The sound of footsteps caught his attention. He looked toward the duke's palace and saw Leigh returning, her report apparently delivered. Valmont studied her for the few seconds it took her to make her way down the walk to the car. The way she carried herself gave him cause to worry. She did not appear pleased. He leaned over and opened the door for her.

Valmont felt Leigh's distress as she got into the car and slammed the door. He pulled away from the curb in silence, not looking at her, waiting for her to explain the sudden iciness that collected in the air around them.

"The duke was indisposed," Leigh said bitterly.

Valmont said nothing, waiting for her to continue. When she gave no indication of elaborating, he drew in his breath and braced himself for a possible explosion.

"Did you see any of his advisers?" he asked.

"Oh yes," she breathed, nearly hissing her words. "Lady Alyssa informed me that she and Sir Cumulus were far too busy with ducal affairs right now to offer me any advice on how to pursue the duke's commission. When I asked her whether she had learned anything more about the dagger I turned over to her, she told me to be patient. Personally, I suspect she had forgotten about it. I tried to tell her about what happened at the Toybox, and she cut me off."

"You told her that Malacar had loosed a trunkful of chimerae onto the streets of the city, and she cut you off?"

Leigh nodded, and Valmont sensed that she was on the verge of tears. "I don't know if she really heard me," Leigh said, her voice a little more controlled. "She seemed preoccupied. When I mentioned the Toybox, I think she stopped listening. When I finished telling her about trying to chase down the chimerae, she interrupted me. She reminded me that it was Malacar and not a bunch of magical creatures that we had been told to pursue."

"So she wasn't interested in the fact that a chest that has been mysteriously locked for who knows how many years has suddenly been opened and its contents released to roam around the city?"

Leigh muttered something under her breath.

"What did you say?" Valmont asked.

"She said we couldn't be bothered with the affairs of commoners," Leigh said.

Valmont's hands tightened inadvertently on the wheel.

"I see," he said quietly, hearing his own voice grow

cold. "Now do you understand?" he asked, a dangerous softness coloring his speech.

"Understand what?" Leigh asked.

"That not everyone loves your duke," he said. "That the care which he so lavishly bestows on his loyal subjects is seen as directed only toward those of royal kith. That we *commoners*," Valmont spat, uttering the word as if it were a curse, "enjoy only the leavings of his largesse."

"That's not fair!" Leigh said, her voice hot with anger.

"No, it's not," Valmont agreed, deliberately misinterpreting her comment. He felt something inside her explode and wondered for a moment if she would exorcise her frustrations by attacking him in his car. He swerved sharply, as if to avoid something in the road. The car's sudden lurch threw Leigh against the door. She swore. When she had finished, Valmont relaxed. She had needed the release.

"I'm his sworn knight," she said finally.

"And that is part of the problem," Valmont said. "This medieval pretentiousness adopted by the nobles has no real place in a world that has outgrown such trappings. For the sidhe, it is as if nothing changed in the centuries they were gone from this realm. But everything has changed. The old ways are...old ways."

"They're meaningful traditions," Leigh countered. "They help us keep away the dreariness of the everyday world. Without them as a barrier between us and Banality, we'd lose ourselves."

Valmont chuckled. "The delicate natures of the sidhe might wither and blow away at the first mortal breeze that touched them, but we common changelings have existed here much longer than the nobility. We have learned to find our inspiration from the things around us. We don't have to create an artificial society to sustain our creative impulses."

"You ravage," Leigh said sharply. "You strip others of their inspiration without bothering to give anything back. That's how you keep yourselves in Glamour."

"When we must," Valmont said. "But I didn't mean to start an argument between us...."

"Didn't you?" Leigh asked. Valmont shrugged in response. He had actually hoped that she would expend some of her pent-up rage in her defense of what he considered to be an indefensible position. The lessening of tension in her body as she leaned back into the car's plush interior made him think that she had.

"I thought I'd pass by the Toybox and see if anyone is still there...besides Fizzlewig," he said, changing the subject as he turned the car onto Haight Street. "We should at least let Tor know that Morgan got home safely. I'll drop you off there or take you home, as you desire."

Leigh nodded absently. Abruptly she sat forward in the car. "I just remembered," she said, concern once more lacing her voice. "I passed by the duke's throne room before I left the palace. I don't know if it was a trick of the lighting or not, but the mistletoe that hangs above his throne..." she hesitated, looking at Valmont.

"The symbol of his eternal rule," Valmont said. "A quaint convention."

Leigh ignored the disparagement in his voice.

"It's dying," she said.

Rasputin stumbled into his apartment and threw himself on the bed, fully clothed. The evening had been considerably more exciting than he had anticipated, and he was exhausted. On his way home from the Toybox, he had tried to keep an eye out for any stray chimerae, but nothing out of the ordinary had caught his eye. He mulled over the events of the last few hours, particularly the part about joining Morgan and Leigh in some quest on behalf of the duke. The idea of charging around the city trying to round up the creatures from the toy chest while simultaneously searching for an apparent traitor to the Seelie Court appealed to his sense of theatre. Already he was imagining the elaborate choreography the dual mission would involve.

He stroked his ears thoughtfully as he let his mind wander in search of sleep. It was an odd assembly of questers, he mused. Morgan and Leigh, both of them seekers at heart, were natural choices, and where Morgan went, her grandfather-guardian would follow without question. He only hoped that Tor could put up with his own presence in the small company. His mannerisms grated on the troll's nerves after more than a few minutes, although tonight he had demonstrated an uncharacteristic tolerance. Rasputin suspected that it had something to do with the fact that he had spent a good part of the evening entertaining the local childling population. Tor had a soft spot for the little ones. Even Edmund. Rasputin felt a sudden pang of sympathy for the scrawny childling. More than once he had been tempted to offer Edmund a place in his apartment. He suspected that the young redcap had no real place to call home. The one time he did ask, however, Edmund had just sneered and threatened to eat Rasputin out of house and home. He knew Edmund despised Morgan, and Rasputin felt that he was, perhaps, one of the few people who could understand why. He hoped Valmont would be able to keep Edmund in line, since the eshu obviously ranked high in Edmund's estimation. He was beginning to ponder the prickly relationship between Valmont and Leigh when sleep finally overtook him, muddling his thoughts into a hopeless tangle.

Coiled beneath his bed, the creature waited. Soon the nightmares would begin again, and it could feed on the pain and terror that surrounded his creator's sleeping form. Its time had not yet come, its small brain told it. When it was bigger, when it was stronger, it would emerge from the darkness and do what it had been born to do....

It was nearly dawn before Edmund finally gave up his search. Since leaving the Toybox, the redcap childling had scrounged through every dumpster in every alley between the coffee shop and his current "home," hoping to catch sight of one of the creatures from the toy chest. Preferably the dragon. He imagined himself swaggering into the Toybox sometime tomorrow, giant lizard in tow. His search had turned up nothing except a few cardboard boxes and a bent coat hanger. At least his stomach was full.

A stray cat ran past him, almost close enough to kick. Edmund briefly considered trying to run the animal down. It looked less scrawny than most alley cats he had seen and would probably be tasty, but then he realized that he was beginning to feel the urge to sleep.

The old Ford was still there. For the last two days it had sat, abandoned, on a side street just outside the Haight. The surrounding neighborhood was a little seedy, and Edmund suspected that no one had bothered to report the vehicle's presence. All the houses around him were dark, the roads deserted. Edmund walked up to the car, kicked its front tires once each for luck, then popped the lock on the front door and scrambled inside. Whoever had left the car had also left an old army blanket in the back seat. It was scratchy and smelled faintly of dried blood, but it served to keep out the evening chill.

Edmund climbed into the back seat of the car and pulled the blanket over him. Before he went to sleep, he retrieved from his pocket the object he had snatched from the toy chest, examining it closely for the first time. It was a garishly painted clown, about three inches tall, and it tingled with suppressed Glamour in Edmund's hand. Edmund thought for a moment about trying to invoke its power here, in the privacy of his present sanctuary. From everything he had heard, listening to other changelings gossip about chimerae, he suspected that he would have to trigger it with his own stored-up Glamour.

It occurred to him then that he had no idea what he would do with the clown if it suddenly became a life-sized replica of its inert form. His brows wrinkled as he remembered that chimerae weren't supposed to have physical substance. They were dreams come to life, not real objects. He stared at the toy in his hand. Its grotesque face seemed to stare back at him. It didn't look like a particularly friendly clown. Maybe he needed to find out more about the knack of handling chimerae before he tried anything with this one. Clutching it firmly in his fist, Edmund tucked the blanket tightly around himself. He shoved the hand that grasped the clown firmly in his pocket and turned on his side, trapping the toy with the weight of his body. He fell asleep, his head cradled on his bent forearm.

In the basement of the Toybox, Tor settled down for what was left of the night. He lay on the army cot Fizzlewig kept for him, his hands locked behind his head, staring up at the ceiling. Above him, near the kitchen, the Balefire burned, spreading its Glamour throughout the freehold to protect it from the chill of the world of mortals. Protecting me as well, Tor thought.

Since last week's attack, Tor had spent most of his time within the confines of the Toybox, reluctant to confront the outside world's constant threat to his changeling nature. Tomorrow, he would have to do just that and hold as tightly as he could to the Glamour inside him, Glamour gleaned from the time spent in the freehold.

He had offered to spend the evening upstairs, helping Fizzlewig and his apprentice keep watch over the opened toy chest, but Chip had brushed him off, saying that he'd need his sleep for the next day's work. Tor held little hope that they would succeed in rounding up all the chimerae that had escaped from the chest. Morgan was right when she said it was like the story of Pandora, where all the ills and evils of the world had escaped from that other box to torment the world. Still, he thought, we will have to try. For Chip's sake.

And then there was Morgan's quest, a far more dangerous one than running down a bunch of overgrown toys. He should have gone with her to the Fall Court. If he had been there, he never would have allowed her to accept something that would endanger her. He cut off his thoughts abruptly, aware that they were leading nowhere. He was a commoner, a troll. Morgan was a noble changeling, one of the sidhe, and despite her youth, her words carried more weight in the duke's court than his ever would. If Morgan wanted this quest, his protests would not deter her.

Tor closed his eyes and tried to will sleep to come. Unlike most people, he never drifted off to sleep, passing through a series of semiconscious states of hazy thoughts and waking dreams before finally sliding into the restful darkness. Somewhere in his past, those years whose memories remained just outside his recall, he had lost the ability to dream.

Malacar writhed in agony as the chimerical fire engulfed his body, consuming his thoughts in sheets of white hot pain, preventing him from any action more complex than drawing breath enough to scream. He felt his skin crisp and bubble, felt the bones inside him char and blacken. Had he natural eyes within his head, they would have long since burst in the searing heat that robbed him of all reason.

From within her place in the circle that stood around the helpless satyr, Lady Glynnis watched impassively. The thrashing creature was amusing to watch, she noted, as a despairing scream resounded through the subterranean chamber. Were he able to think clearly, she thought, he would know that no real harm was being done to him, that the agony he suffered was only in his mind, placed there by the will of those more powerful than he. But that was the irony of pain, that it blocked all capacity to reason clearly. He had within him the key to his release, but the agony that dominated his thoughts made it impossible for him to free himself.

She shrugged. There was still much that had to be done. With a lazy gesture, she gave an unspoken command to the figure standing to her right. The figure stepped toward the prone satyr, clapped his hands together twice and uttered a word.

The pain disappeared. For a moment Malacar felt only numbness and utter cold. He staggered to rise, gasping with relief as cool air filled his lungs. As his sight returned, he noticed that he was unharmed, his skin intact. He doubled over, head in his hands, as harsh, tearless sobs wracked his body.

"You have earned a second chance." The lady's voice washed over him like a soothing balm. Malacar dared to raise his face in the direction of the speaker. Although a heavy cowl concealed her face in shadows, he could just make out a hint of the beauty that cloaked itself in darkness.

"You will repeat the ritual, this time with a more powerful chimera, not just the first object you happen to close your hands upon." The male voice came from behind him. "It shouldn't be too difficult for you to find one of the creatures you loosed from the chest," the voice continued, heavy with sarcasm.

"Indeed, the task may be more simple than you think," a third voice, that of another female, interjected. "From my own calculations, the chimerae should not have strayed too far from the source of their Glamour. Just make certain that this time you sacrifice something more potent than a wind-up monkey."

One of the figures snorted derisively.

Malacar opened his mouth to speak.

"You have already given us your excuses," the lady's voice snapped before he could utter a word. "The ritual's instructions were explicit on the nature of the sacrifice. It requires a chimera born of a powerful dream...."

"Do you think this simple task is beyond your puny abilities?" This voice came from the snorter.

Malacar shook his head quickly. "I have a question, noble ones," he stammered, flinching as he spoke.

The lady's laughter sounded like ice cracking on a frozen pond. "Only one?" she said, cruel amusement in her voice. "How modest! Ask your question," she continued. "Perhaps you will even get an answer."

"You have given me directions as to how to perform the ritual, but I have no knowledge of the ritual's purpose. Since it involves the Eye of Opening..." he hesitated, uncertain as to whether he dared voice the question after all.

"You wish to know what it is that you are opening," the lady said, her voice soft with danger. "I would have thought you'd guessed by now."

"No, most gracious lady," Malacar mumbled, surprised that she had not taken his query amiss.

"*Within the place of eternal flowers lies the gateway to undying powers,*" she quoted, her voice elegant with silken tones. "Your actions will open a gateway that has long been closed to us, one through which the Dreaming will be reborn. For you to be chosen for the task despite your common nature is an honor," she said. "Do not throw it away so carelessly this time. You will be taken from this place to discharge your duty."

With that, she turned and disappeared into the darkness.

chapter

nine

178

Morgan's father dropped her off at school on his way to his downtown office. As she leaned over to kiss his cheek, Morgan hoped he wouldn't notice her nervousness or the extra bulk inside her schoolbag.

"Have a good day, darling," Gordon Daniels said. "Study hard."

"I will, Daddy," Morgan said. She got out of the car and walked toward the Stratton School, trying to look nonchalant. Stopping on the steps of the school, she turned and waved at him, their signal that she was safely to her destination. She stood on the bottom step and watched until his car was out of sight. Then she ran quickly up the stairs and into the school. At the door to the principal's office, she paused and waited while some of her classmates passed her on their way to homeroom. She nodded at the ones she knew and tried to look as if her stomach hurt. The traffic in the lobby cleared, and Morgan took advantage of what her father would have called her "window of opportunity." She took several rapid breaths, saturating her lungs with air. Then she stuck her thumb in her mouth and blew out as hard as she could, letting her cheeks puff up as she trapped the air. She felt herself grow dizzy and stopped blowing before she fainted.

Catching sight of herself in the mirror that hung on one wall of the lobby, she noticed with satisfaction that her face was flushed. Still reeling from her near-swoon, she careened into the principal's office.

"I feel really sick," she moaned. "Can I call my mom to pick me up?"

The principal's secretary took one look at the red-

the

faced child and pushed the telephone toward her, coming out from behind her desk to steer Morgan into a chair. Crouching low over the phone, Morgan dialed Leigh's number.

"Her car's in the shop," Morgan informed the secretary as she replaced the phone in its cradle. "She'll have to pick me up in a cab." She got up suddenly, clutching her stomach. "I think I'm going to throw up," she croaked, and fled for the girls' bathroom. As she huddled in the stall, making retching noises and flushing the toilet repeatedly just in case anyone was listening, she hoped that no one would insist on accompanying her to the taxi, or if they did, that they wouldn't object to her "Aunt Olivia" picking her up.

By mid-morning, the group had assembled at the Toybox, where Fizzlewig, red-eyed and bleary from lack of sleep, insisted that they help themselves to the plate of oven-fresh sweet buns and either coffee or tea before embarking on their search for the errant chimerae.

"Reports have been coming in all morning," he muttered. "I guess your friends," he looked at Edmund, who was happily downing his fifth cinnamon roll, "spread the word about a bunch of critters on the loose."

"Great!" said Leigh. The Fiona knight had clothed herself in chimerical armor, light enough to allow her to move freely. "At least we have some idea of where to start looking."

"Have they managed to catch any of them?" Morgan asked. She had changed in the back of the cab from her school clothes into jeans and sneakers and was busily braiding her long hair to keep it from getting in her way. Unlike Leigh, the garments she wore in her faerie seeming — a loose-fitting tunic worn over a pair of soft linen leggings —afforded her no protection, but they were the best her imagination could come up with for the moment. She concentrated briefly and a split tabard emblazoned with the twin crescents of House Eiluned draped itself over the tunic.

Fizzlewig shook his head. "Not many people are willing to tackle a full-grown lion or a trumpeting elephant, even if they do have enormous keys sticking up from their backs...."

Morgan giggled. Across the table from her, Tor gave her a stern look. The troll wore a mail shirt and metal guards on his forearms and thighs.

"Don't underestimate them," he said. "They may be overgrown toys, but they can hurt you."

"Yeah, but the damage they do can't kill you," Edmund snorted. "They're chimerae!" Edmund sported a patchwork assemblage of protective gear: A jaunty leather cuirass topped a metal-plated skirt, below which his knobby knees poked through the holes in the dirty jeans that formed the basis for both his mortal and changeling attire.

"They can destroy the Glamour inside you," Leigh said. "That's worse than dying for some of us."

"A lot of good folk were lost to Banality during the Accordance Wars," Fizzlewig added. "Some of 'em were done in by chimerical creatures who got the better of them. They just collapsed where they stood, and when they woke up, they had forgotten they were changelings. They just got up and wandered off, with a battle going on all around them...." Fizzlewig stopped abruptly, noticing a pained look on Tor's face. He clamped his mouth shut.

"Cool!" Edmund said. "Welcome to Banality Central...for the rest of your life!"

"That's not funny," Morgan said. "It's horrible. I

never want to forget what I am!"

"Of course you do," Rasputin mumbled sleepily, resplendent in soft forest green leathers and a feathered archer's cap. He had been troubled by strange dreams again last night, ones he couldn't quite remember, but which had left him feeling unrested when he had woken, too early, this morning. "Forgetting is what it's all about."

"Where's Valmont?" Edmund asked suddenly.

"Late, obviously," Leigh said. "I don't know if we can wait for him. I'm getting edgy just sitting here as if there's nothing to do."

"I suppose we shouldn't tell you that we examined the lid of the toybox last night," Rasputin said.

"I was the one who thought of it," Edmund interrupted. "You know what? The top of the box isn't a puzzle anymore. I mean, it's still a puzzle, but it's been all put together. It shows this great battle scene with lots of men on horses and people dying and flags waving and stuff, but there's this round hole right in the middle of the picture."

"Like a missing piece?" Morgan asked, her interest piqued in spite of the fact that the information was coming from Edmund.

Edmund rolled his eyes. "What else?" he said smugly.

"It obviously can't be something else, such as a marble or a signet ring or a ball of wax or the tip of a really fat fountain pen or the ball hilt of a dagger," Rasputin added.

"Okay, so maybe it's not a missing puzzle piece...but something round must have been used to trigger the opening of the chest," Edmund insisted.

"That's very useful information, Edmund," Valmont said, coming from the street door to stand behind the young redcap. The eshu's appearance drew an admiring gasp from Morgan and an appreciative smile from Leigh. Valmont's changeling form was clothed in a flowing caftan, belted at the waist with a broad sash. On his head he wore a turban, from which hung a veil, loosened at one side to reveal his face.

"It's the sheik," said Edmund.

"When did you get here?" Tor asked, mentally rebuking himself for not noticing the eshu's arrival. He was slipping.

"In time to hear Edmund's report," Valmont said, eyeing the coffee and sweet rolls. Fizzlewig pushed the platter toward him as the eshu pulled up a chair beside Edmund and joined his companions at the table. "And it's Moorish," he confided to the young redcap.

"You look a mite pale," the boggan cracked.

"I had a long night," Valmont said, pouring a cup of coffee for himself. He listened carefully as Fizzlewig went over the information brought to him by the local childling population.

"Most of the chimerae seem to be hanging around the Haight, or else they've wandered as far as Golden Gate Park," Fizzlewig said. "At least most of the animals have fled the streets for greener pastures." The plump boggan rose from the table and retrieved a long, flat, cloth-wrapped package from a nearby booth. He presented the object to Tor.

"You'd better take this," he said gruffly. Tor looked at his friend blankly as he accepted the bulky item, turning it over in his hands.

"It's yours," Fizzlewig said. "I've been keeping it for you in case you ever needed it again. This might be the time." Without opening it, Tor shoved the package lengthwise through his belt, nodding absently at the boggan.

"Are we making the assumption that we'll have to fight all these creatures?" Leigh asked, looking at Fizzlewig in expectation. The boggan nodded.

"It's my suspicion that these are some of the same chimerae used as support troops during the Accordance

Wars," the boggan said. "I wondered what had become of them." He chuckled slightly. "If that's the case, they'll be geared up for attacking whatever comes their way. Unless you can figure out some other way of rounding them up, you'll just have to slug it out with them until you kill them...figuratively speaking, of course."

Morgan's brows creased. "You mean we have to destroy them?" she asked plaintively.

"I don't think these chimerae can be destroyed," Valmont said. "Am I right?" he asked Fizzlewig.

"Unlike most chimerae, these seem to have physical counterparts," Fizzlewig answered. "These will probably revert to their toy-forms once they've been subdued."

"Then what?" Edmund asked, curiosity overcoming his growing impatience.

"If they're replaced in the toy chest, they should eventually absorb enough Glamour so that they can reform some other time," Fizzlewig said.

"You're just guessing," Edmund sneered.

"It's an educated guess," Fizzlewig retorted.

"So can we go now?" Edmund asked, pushing his chair backward as he spoke.

"Not yet," Morgan said.

Edmund groaned. "Now what?"

Morgan rose from the table, her face grim. "I was thinking about this all last night, and I talked to Leigh about it on the way over here. If we're going to work together, we need to do it the right way." She looked at Leigh, who nodded her approval.

Edmund looked around the table, seeing the others, even Rasputin, nodding their heads in agreement.

"What are you talking about?" the redcap demanded, feeling suddenly left out of the group.

"She's talking about swearing oaths to one another," said Valmont. "It's an ancient faerie custom...and one not without merit, unlike other traditions I could mention."

"Please don't," said Leigh quickly, flashing a hard look at the eshu. Valmont gave her a small smile and inclined his head toward her.

"An oath bond," said Rasputin, "what a terrible thought."

"So, how do we do this?" Morgan asked. "It needs to be a group oath...."

Hands clasped across the polished table, the shining companions spoke the ancient words in unison. She looked into the face of the knight who stood opposite her in the circle, felt the heart within her pound as she fell into the cerulean pools that were his eyes. When the words were spoken, and the binding of the Glamour fixed within their souls, his hands lingered in hers a few seconds after the others' hands had dropped away. He smiled at her, but unlike the enfolding tenderness of his gaze, the smile he gave was hard and cold.

"We are oathbound." The prince of House Ailil spoke to all his companions, but his eyes focused on hers, and his words embedded themselves in her heart. "My cause is yours. Our fates are bound forever by these words. We go now to do battle with the forces who would hold Arcadia back from her destiny."

Leigh rose quickly, stopping the memory before it could go any further. Whatever it was that had flashed into her mind, she had no desire at the moment to pursue it. Still, there was something of use in its sudden appearance in her thoughts.

"This is what we need to do," she said, extending her arms toward the center of the table. "We all clasp hands and speak the words together."

Fizzlewig stepped backwards out of the circle as the others rose and followed Leigh's instructions. Valmont, seeing Edmund hanging back, grasped the redcap's hands and guided them inward to join with the other hands.

"I'll feed you the lines," Leigh said. "All you have to do is repeat them after me." Just before she began, she looked questioningly at Rasputin. "I've never sworn an oath with a pooka before," she began, her voice betraying its uncertainty.

Rasputin smiled cockily. "Don't be so sure," he replied. "But if I were you, I'd be terribly concerned. After all, we pookas have no way of insuring that what we say can be believed." He paused and winked at Morgan. "Let it be known that the words I shall pronounce in tandem with this assembled group are as meaningless as the wind, and that they don't come from the bottom of my heart," he nodded to Leigh.

"Blood for blood," she began, feeling within herself the familiarity of having spoken these words at least once before. "Bone for bone, life for life..."

When the others had repeated the opening words of the Oath of Clasped Hands, she continued, pausing after each phrase, until the pledge was finished. "...Until only we stride the Earth. My life is in your hands, my blood is in your veins. Hold me well and I will lend you my strength; break your bond and may we all perish. Friendship I swear to you, an oath of clasped hands and shared hearts."

During the speaking, she had closed her eyes, listening to the rich combination of voices that surrounded her. When she finished, she opened her eyes and looked around at her sworn companions. Morgan's face was streaming with tears. Valmont was looking at Leigh curiously, as if taking her measure. Edmund looked bored. Rasputin's eyes were wide and guileless. Tor's face was hard to read, but she saw the tightness in his jaw. Gently she disengaged her hands from the group as a signal to the others that the ceremony was at an end. Only Tor and Morgan still held hands, her little ones engulfed between his two enormous palms.

Before Leigh could say anything, the troll, looking like nothing so much as a Viking warrior or one of the ancient Norse giants, began to speak, his eyes fixed upon his granddaughter's tear-streaked face.

"As the sun guards the earth by day, as the stars by night, so shall I serve thee. This my duty as protector of my granddaughter Morgania I shall not abandon till one or the other of us returns to the Dreaming from whence we came, else may the stars close their eyes and sleep."

"What was that?" Edmund whispered loudly to Valmont. "Do we all have to do that?"

The eshu shook his head. "That, my young friend," he said, "was the Oath of Guardianship. It is something all trolls who might one day be called upon to act as guardians or protectors must learn."

"Well," Rasputin said, "Let's take all day to be about our business."

"It's about time," said Edmund. "Where do we go first?"

"You'll probably stumble across something up near the Panhandle," Fizzlewig began, just as the door burst open and a nocker childling poked his head into the coffee shop.

"There's a bear in front of the tattoo shop!" he yelled excitedly.

The others had to run to keep up with Edmund as the redcap whooped with glee and barreled out the door into the street.

Across the street, near the corner of Haight Street and Masonic Avenue, an enormous, shaggy brown bear loomed before the garishly painted doorway of Tattoos and Twilight. A large brass cymbal was strapped to each of its forepaws, and the bear alternated between performing a series of shuffling, dancelike steps on its hind feet and clashing the cymbals together. Its head bobbed from side to side as it sniffed the air, occasionally emitting a mournful groaning growl.

As Edmund, heedless of the cars suddenly braking as he darted in their path, raced into the traffic toward the creature, the bear lurched sideways to avoid a leather-clad couple emerging from the tattoo shop. Caught up in the examination of their latest acquisitions, the pair strolled by, oblivious to the chimerical creature towering only a few feet from them. One of the couple cocked his head, as if in response to some sudden sound, then shrugged and followed his partner down the street.

Taking advantage of the path Edmund had carved for them through the traffic, Leigh and her companions dashed across the street, converging upon the bear.

Edmund skidded to a stop inches away from the chimera.

"Do we attack it, or what?" he yelled, looking back at the others.

"Oh, definitely what!" Rasputin answered him, springing nimbly past his companions, then belatedly called out, "Ducking is bad!"

Morgan's high-pitched shriek was more direct. "Look out!"

A resounding clash of cymbals shattered the air above Edmund's head, narrowly missing the scrawny childling, who managed to throw himself to the pavement just in time. Scrambling to his feet, this time armed with a dagger, he confronted the bear.

"Edmund, get back!" Leigh called out, charging toward the bear. She drew her sword from the sheath at her waist, angling it to slash upward at the creature's raised foreleg. At her side, Valmont slipped a gracefully carved scimitar from the sash wound around his waist and began to circle around behind the chimera.

Morgan started forward, only to feel a pair of strong arms catch her up and deposit her in front of Rasputin, who had stopped just before the tattoo shop to consider the battle evolving in front of him.

"Keep her out of the way," Tor snarled, then reached for the still-wrapped package at his side. The wrappings fell away as he pulled it free of his belt. In his hand gleamed a mighty battle-axe, its double edges glinting in the sunlight beginning to pierce the morning's mist.

Swinging the axe's shining blade before him, the warrior plowed through the field of battle. Where weapon met flesh, his opponents fell to the ground, driven from the realm of the Dreaming by the warrior's potent strength and the accuracy of his strike. Up ahead, the blazon of the silver lion fluttered in the breeze, its defenders struggling to protect it from the angry horde that surrounded them....

"Watch where yer' goin', ya seedy bastid!" a nasal voice jolted Tor into the present, as a bespectacled, balding man in a plaid shirt and ill-fitting trousers lurched into the troll's side. Tor clutched the axe in both hands and shoved his way past the man, who caught sight of the immense weapon and, eyes agog, hurried down the street muttering to himself.

The bear reared backwards, and Leigh's stroke clashed harmlessly against the cymbal nearest her. Valmont took advantage of the creature's movement and brought his scimitar downward, feeling the blade slice through matted fur and sensing some of the chimera's power diminish with the blow. He smiled to himself as he felt a seldom used rhythm return to him. The dance of blade and battle, the eshu thought. Like riding a bike.

Edmund stabbed viciously at the bear's foot, swearing loudly as he missed his target and jammed the dagger's point into the concrete. The creature's knee caught Edmund in the face, and the redcap sprawled on the ground, rolling out of the way of the bear's other foot, now lifted in the air.

On the sidelines, Morgan caught a flurry of motion as a figure in motley, strings trailing from his wrists and ankles, cartwheeled down the sidewalk toward the battle.

"Behind you, Grandpa!" Morgan screamed. The puppet came to a stop just behind Tor, a pair of blue and yellow juggler's clubs materializing in its hands, poised to throw.

Tor wheeled around, his axe perpendicular to his bulk. A solid blow sliced the puppet in half through the middle, the clubs clattering on the ground around his feet. Tor looked down where the two halves of the juggler shimmered for a moment and disappeared. He snatched something from the pavement and shoved it in his pocket, then continued to jog heavily toward the bear.

"You shouldn't scream things out like that," Rasputin said to Morgan. "It's only a distraction."

"Thanks," Morgan said. "I was feeling useless just standing here watching everything. I don't have a weapon."

Rasputin nodded. "I have weapons aplenty," he said. "Although I'd never think of using my faerie magic at a time like this..."

"Oh," Morgan said. "I never thought about that."

"Excuse me, young man," a matronly woman with a small boy attached to one arm accosted Rasputin. "What are those people doing over there?" She pointed in the direction of the mêlée.

Rasputin considered the woman carefully. To her eyes, the bear was invisible. Like most mortals, all she could see was a dark-skinned man and a red-haired woman apparently miming some mock battle while a scrawny, dusky-hued boy with spiked dreadlocks pounded a butter knife into the sidewalk at their feet and a tall, broad-shouldered man in a worn trenchcoat swung a large double-bladed axe and turned in slow circles a few feet away from them. The lightweight chimerical battle armor worn by Leigh and Tor, Valmont's North African martial costume and Edmund's comic Roman attire eluded her perceptions, as did the chimerical weapons wielded by the battlers. Only Tor's axe, visible to Rasputin with both mortal and faerie sight, could be seen for what it was.

"They're wearing funny clothes, Nana," the boy said, his eyes popping. "And there's a bear!"

Morgan looked up at Rasputin expectantly. The pooka arched an eyebrow and gave the woman his brightest smile.

"Street theatre," he said. "A political commentary on the decaying of family values and the fracturing of the nuclear family performed in four carefully choreographed scenes for the enjoyment and edification of the strolling public." He extended a hand, palm up, toward the woman. "If you would care to contribute to the Bootstrap Performing Arts Band...?"

The woman looked confused. She regarded the fracas for a moment, frowning. Then she shook her head. "I don't see it," she said. She pursed her lips and looked sternly at Rasputin. "They need more practice before I'll support shenanigans like that. Come along Jonathan David," she commanded, dragging her grandson behind her, as she stalked away from the pooka and a giggling Morgan. The boy waved good-bye to the bear.

Tor reached the bear just as Leigh thrust her sword into the chimera's midsection. She let out a war cry as the creature roared in obvious pain and brought its paws together, attempting to trap Leigh's head between its cymbals. Remembering Rasputin's advice, Morgan imagined that the luck she seemed to attract was a round, palm-sized ball in her hand. She made a tossing motion with her arm and mentally saw the "ball" arc in the air toward Leigh, sending her own good fortune to her battling companion. The red-haired knight pulled her head backward just before the cymbals collided. Seeing his opening, Tor swung his axe in a high circle, catching the bear between the eyes.

Suddenly the space where the creature had towered was empty. Still on the ground, Edmund found himself staring at a small stuffed bear, a pair of shiny cymbals strapped to its fuzzy paws.

"Yugh!" he exclaimed. "It's cute!" He seized the toy and drew it toward his mouth.

"Not on your life," Leigh said, snatching it from the redcap's grasp. She held the bear at arm's length. "What now?" she asked.

Rasputin and Morgan joined them. "That was terrible," Rasputin said approvingly.

"Oh yeah?" challenged Edmund. "What did you do, pink nose? I didn't notice you or Morgan doing anything while we risked our lives." Morgan started to reply to Edmund, but realized that she couldn't prove that she had been of any assistance. Her face burned with suppressed anger.

"I believe we were discussing what to do with the body of our recent foe," Valmont said, returning his scimitar to the loop in his sash.

"Bodies," Tor said, pulling the marionette out of his coat pocket and displaying it by the strings. Both Valmont and Leigh nodded a silent thanks to the troll.

"We put them back in the toy chest," said Morgan with conviction. "I know we do. They'll...they'll get better there."

"She's got it all wrong," Rasputin said, his belief evident in his tone.

The persistent honking of a car horn drew their attention. Georgia's purple and yellow cab pulled up alongside the group. The nocker leaned across and called to them through the open window.

"You're not gonna believe what's assembling on the Panhandle," she said. "Get in! There's plenty of room in the back seat."

Tor held the back door open, while everyone piled inside a back seat that seemed to stretch to accommodate them. Tor saw there was still space for his bulk, and climbed inside, pulling the door shut behind him.

"Don't tell us, please," said Rasputin to the back of Georgia's head.

All of them could see her grin through the rearview mirror as she replied, "Soldiers! It looks like the Battle of Waterloo is getting ready to start."

Malacar watched impassively as the young maiden clad in antique finery struggled in the clutch of the swarthy eshu. A horrified young man in a turn-of-the-century tuxedo flailed helplessly at his partner's abductor.

"Don't harm the bride," Malacar called from the doorway of a chapel-like building, now converted into a trendy cafe. He congratulated himself on being able to locate and enlist Blade's help on such short notice. The eshu's obvious martial arts training made him more than a match for the chimera he was attempting to overcome.

Blade's foot lashed out, catching the dapper man on the jaw. The figure collapsed to the ground and disappeared. Malacar hurried over and retrieved the chimera, a bridegroom doll made from hand painted china and cloth.

"Hold her while I immobilize her," Malacar said to Blade as the eshu concentrated on subduing the whimpering old-fashioned bride doll. Pulling several lengths of silken rope from the pockets of his cloak, the satyr quickly bound the wide-eyed, life-sized chimera. As an afterthought, he gagged her with a stained linen handkerchief. "She might scream," he said to Blade. "You never know...."

"What are you gonna do with her?" Blade asked, his eyes implying that he already knew the answer.

"That's my business," Malacar replied evasively, "but I'm sure you can figure it out for yourself." He took the trussed bride from Blade and heaved her over one shoulder like a rolled carpet. He began trudging away from the chapel-cafe, Blade moving as if to follow. Malacar stopped and rounded on the eshu. "Our business is concluded," he snapped. "You were paid before we began this operation, so there's no more reason for you to hang around."

The eshu shrugged and ambled away. "Have fun!" he called over his shoulder. Malacar ignored him and concentrated on bearing his burden westward from the Haight, paying no attention to the odd glances from people who, in passing, saw an old man struggling under an invisible weight.

"I just hope she's a virgin," he muttered to himself.

Along the length of the Panhandle, the block-wide strip of green that extended east from Golden Gate Park for more than half a mile through the Haight, a line of bicyclists pedaled in single-file toward the Park. Once intended as a carriage entrance to the splendors of the

Park itself, the grassy promenade now played host to an assortment of regulars from the surrounding streets, taking advantage of the late September sunshine to enjoy a few moments away from the bustle of the city around them.

No one seemed to notice the assembly of cavalry and foot soldiers that had secured a broad space screened by oak trees for use as a drilling ground. Under the watchful eye of their commander, resplendent in gold braid and cocked hat, the horsemen executed a series of precise mounted maneuvers while a small unit of regulars marched in formation nearby. A five-man cannon team worked at readying its mounted cannon. Oblivious to the rattle of sabres and the jingle of spurs, a stooped woman, burdened by a pair of shopping bags bulging with collected junk, trudged wearily across the clearing, heading north toward Fulton Street with her booty.

"There they are!" Edmund scrambled across Valmont and onto Tor's knees to point through the cab's open rear window at the figures he saw moving beyond the trees that lined the Panhandle.

Leigh opened her mouth to ask Georgia to pull over to the curb just as the nocker slid her vehicle to a smooth stop.

Tor opened the door, grabbing Edmund by the shoulder to keep the redcap from tumbling headfirst onto the ground. Still holding onto Edmund, he stepped from the cab and waited for the others to join him on the grass.

"This time we stay together," he warned. "These are soldiers, not some stuffed bear."

Edmund snickered. "They're just big toys!" he said. "They're cool, but they're only..."

"They are only capable of thrusting their swords through your metaphysical heart," said Valmont, reaching across his face to attach the loose end of his veil to the rings dangling from his turban. He slid his scimitar softly from its sash.

"I suggest we approach with caution, and be prepared to fight," he said. He looked toward Leigh in mock deference to her position as titular leader of the group. Leigh nodded in agreement, her lips pressed tightly together. She, too, drew her sword, wondering if the motion would ever seem natural.

As quietly as they could, the six companions made their way through the trees to the clearing.

"Intruders in the trees, sah!" a voice called out from over their heads. Edmund looked up to see a soldier perched in the branches above them, a spyglass in one hand.

"Charge!" screamed Edmund in response and broke free from Tor's grasp, dashing into the clearing.

"Caution is suddenly the watchword of the day," said Rasputin, pulling Morgan behind him.

"Oh, hell!" Leigh swore. "Back him up." She sprinted after Edmund with Valmont and Tor just behind her. Rasputin took Morgan by the hand and, raising the index finger of his free hand to his lips in a request for silence, he led the childling through the trees around the area that was quickly becoming a battlefield.

"Pygmies!" The soldier's cry marked Edmund's approach.

"Sound the charge, bugler!"

"Bugler's down, sah!"

"Blast him, then! Forward the charge!"

Edmund screamed as a horse bore down on him, the rider leaning forward with outstretched sabre. The redcap held his breath and dove under the animal's legs, emerging on the other side just as a second cavalryman thrust at him with his sword.

Coming hard behind Edmund, Leigh dodged the first cavalryman's sword, then rolled to the ground as she felt the soldier's mount gather his haunches for a backward kick. Nearby, she saw Tor drop to his knees just in front of another horse and rider, his battle axe held horizontally in the horse's path. He braced his weapon with both hands and waited.

Valmont danced dervishlike between two cavalrymen, who circled him warily, each unwilling to attack for fear of missing their target and landing a blow on the other soldier.

The oncoming horse stumbled against Tor's axe handle and pitched forward, screaming. Its rider leaped from the fallen animal, landing inches in front of Leigh, who now stood, ready to meet the grounded attacker. The cavalryman halted, and raising his sword to his face, saluted Leigh, his meticulously hand-painted face expressionless. Leigh returned the salute before drawing her weapon back for a thrust at her opponent. Beyond her she saw Tor rise up to meet still another horse and rider, his axe angled toward the cavalryman's outstretched sword arm.

Past the cavalry charge, Edmund bore down upon the footsoldiers, who now advanced upon him in precise formation. His first thought was that there were only five of them; his second thought was that there was only one of him. Frantically he looked over his shoulder. Leigh, Valmont and Tor were busy with the cavalry. Rasputin and Morgan were nowhere to be seen.

Suddenly the line of soldiers buckled as the grass beneath their feet rose upward in entangling ropes of greenery. First one, then another of the smartly dressed warriors toppled over. Edmund's sharp eyes caught sight of a pair of familiar figures hidden among the trees opposite him. He saw something else, too. "Look out!" he yelled.

Morgan screamed as she caught sight of the soldier coming up behind Rasputin, who still faced the tangle of footsoldiers, beaming at his handiwork. She recognized the spyglass tucked into the sentry's belt.

"Don't hurt him!" she called out. A word came to mind. "Parley!" she shouted.

The sentry stepped back and extended his sword in Rasputin's direction, holding it steady. Rasputin turned slowly to face the soldier, hands held out to either side.

"I suppose you're not going to accept our parole," Rasputin said.

The soldier nodded curtly. "You made a request for parley," he said, "which I am enjoined to honor. Both of you precede me onto the field."

Seeing a clear shot between him and the cannon, Edmund ran past the still struggling muddle of footsoldiers. Four soldiers busied themselves with loading the weapon's barrel, while a fifth soldier stood some distance behind the cannon holding a harnessed mule by the bridle.

"Fire cannon!" one soldier called. A second soldier touched something to the cannon's fuse. All of the cannoneers ducked. Edmund threw himself flat onto the ground, arms folded around his head.

"Incoming!" he screamed into the dirt.

A loud boom followed by a whistling sound filled the air above the battle. Matching blows with her opponent, Leigh was beginning to tire, her arms aching from the prolonged strain of strike and parry. Her opponent showed no signs of fatigue, and Leigh realized, for the first time, the disadvantage inherent in facing a chimerical foe. The sudden boom brought both combatants to a halt.

"Down!" the soldier barked, obeying his own order. Leigh dropped to the ground, grateful for the respite. Gasping for breath, she looked around.

Surprised by the unexpected blast of cannon fire, the cavalrymen fighting Tor and Valmont reined their horses back and stared upward, trying to gauge the arc of the oncoming missile.

"We're out of its range," observed Valmont to no one in particular. Drawing the same conclusion, Tor ignored his opponent long enough to trace the cannonball's arc to its apparent point of impact. Sudden terror clutched him as he spied Rasputin and Morgan, followed by a soldier with his sword leveled at their backs, standing in the middle of the field, heads turned upward toward the piercing sound that grew increasingly louder around them.

"Morgan!" Tor roared and started running toward his imperiled granddaughter, aware that he would not reach her in time.

Rasputin felt like a bull's eye. "It's nowhere near us," he called over his shoulder. He reached for Morgan, who stood rigidly in front of him, her eyes wide in her upturned face. Grabbing her by the waist, the pooka swung her behind him. "Break a leg," he muttered softly, as he reversed his swing and pitched the childling as far away from him as he could. Then the world exploded around him as the cannonball landed between Rasputin and the entrapped huddle of footsoldiers, raising a cloud of chimeric dust and smoke with the force of its impact.

Rasputin barely had time to see the sentry behind him fall to the ground, his chimerical body shimmering and dissipating as the Glamour that had powered it shattered under the shock wave of the cannonball. "Medic?" he called faintly before he fell into a dark whirlpool that seemed to open at his feet.

Morgan landed on the ground at Tor's feet, just outside the perimeter of the cannon's fury. The troll threw himself forward on his hands and knees, trapping Morgan underneath him. His massive bulk rocked slightly as the explosion's outer edge buffeted him, but he leaned into the invisible force that pushed at him and held his ground.

"Cease fire!" a commanding voice carried over the field, followed by repeated blasts from a whistle.

A mounted officer, the one who had earlier overseen his troops' maneuvers and who had sounded the charge to battle, rode into the center of the field. Leigh stood up and glared at her opponent, who was also clambering to his feet. She jerked her head in the direction of the officer and, lowering her sword, strode purposefully toward him. Valmont took advantage of the hiatus to extricate himself from both his opponents and raced toward the fallen pooka.

Leigh presented herself before the officer, her eyes blazing in anger.

"This stops now!" she said, pointing to where Valmont knelt cradling the pooka's head in his arms.

The officer turned his head, following Leigh's outstretched arm. Then he looked around at his own fallen footsoldiers, reduced to small painted figures by the errant cannon blast. He turned back to Leigh and nodded his head once.

"Agreed," he said. He dismounted and bowed to the Fiona knight, sheathing his sword with a flourish. "Nasty business, wot?" Swallowing her anger, Leigh ignored the officer and trotted toward Valmont and Rasputin. The cavalry leader followed her, mumbling to himself. "Tend to the wounded first, splendid idea!"

Morgan crawled out from beneath Tor and ran to Rasputin, tears streaming down her cheeks. Tor pulled himself to his feet and plodded wearily after the childling, a sinking feeling in the pit of his stomach. Edmund passed them in a blur and reached Valmont's side seconds before the others. Peering over the eshu's shoulder at Rasputin, he gave a low whistle.

toybox

"He's fading," he called out as the others approached. "Look," he pointed, "you can hardly see his ears anymore."

Valmont stroked the pooka's head, murmuring an atonal chant in time to the movement of his hand. He looked up at the group standing around him. "I'm trying to keep him from slipping away," he said, pain threatening to crack his usually sonorous voice. Morgan sensed the healing Glamour as it passed from the eshu to Rasputin. She dropped to her knees beside the pooka and placed her hands on his chest. "Let me help," she said and began to mimic Valmont's eerie tune. Leigh held her breath as she watched Morgan and Valmont struggle to transfer some of their own Glamour to the wounded pooka. Slowly, Rasputin's elongated ears regained their former solidity. His nose twitched, and his eyes, full of rabbity softness, opened.

"That was fun," he whispered, and made a game effort to sit up.

"Stay," Valmont told him, relief accomplishing what pain could not as his voice broke. The crisis over, Edmund busied himself with picking up fallen soldiers and stuffing them into his pockets. Leigh watched him carefully, counting each figure as the redcap picked them up. His pockets bulging, Edmund sauntered over to stand beside her. Leigh nodded her approval.

"Take charge of them until we can get them to safety," she said. "And..."

"I know," Edmund said. "Don't eat them." He made his voice into a bad imitation of Leigh's and gave her the redcap version of a rakish grin. Leigh shuddered.

"Sorry about the mishap," the officer on the edge of the group said. "As commander of this multipurpose attack unit, I accept full responsibility for all casualties. We're missing our bugler, you see..." he said.

Rasputin made another attempt to stand up. Tor extended a hand to help the pooka to his feet.

"What's a bugler got to do with anything?" Edmund asked. The commander looked down at Edmund.

"Why, without him to organize our attacks and sound the call to arms, the charge, the retreat, the volley, the forward thrust, the..."

"I get it already," Edmund said. "You're like a film crew without a director..."

"I say, what?" the officer sounded perplexed.

"Never mind," said Leigh. "Where is this bugler?"

"Well, in hospital, of course," the officer replied. "He was wounded in our last skirmish. His bugle hand snapped right off in the middle of an 'about face' and he was carried off the field. He should have been back by now. Dr. Kurtzweiler usually works very quickly."

"Hospital?" Morgan asked, looking up at her grandfather. "Does he mean the toy chest?" she whispered. Tor shook his head.

"I dunno," the troll muttered.

Leaning against Tor to keep his balance, Rasputin closed his eyes as a memory pushed its way to the forefront of his mind.

"The children's drawings," he murmured softly. "I distinctly forget that one of the drawings — not the drawing of a bugler — featured a large "K" in the background. It couldn't stand for Kurtzweiler, though," he said.

"Not a toy chest," Valmont said, realization dawning. "A toy shop!"

"Try as we might," the officer continued, oblivious to the discussion around him, "without our bugler we are only an isolated detachment of soldiers. Only the bugler can summon our other allies and deploy them to their best advantage...."

"Other allies?" Leigh asked, her attention caught by the commander's insistent monologue. "Other soldiers?"

"The puppeteer squad, the aerial attack unit — the

dragon, that is — the ursine assault squad...all the others!"

"He's talking about the other chimerae!" Edmund said excitedly. "The bugler can get the chimerae to come to us! We don't have to spend all friggin' day hunting them down!"

"The language in your ranks is scandalous, ma'am," the officer observed. Leigh bristled at the rebuke, then decided to ignore it.

"I don't suppose you can locate Dr. Kurtzweiler for us—" she began.

The officer shook his head sadly.

Rasputin stepped back from Tor and took a few exploratory steps. Sure of his footing, he turned away from the group and headed back toward the street.

"Hey, hare-brain!" Edmund called out. "Where are you going?"

"To find the most useless thing I can think of," Rasputin called cheerily over his shoulder. "A phone book!"

Leigh turned to the commander. "Sir," she began.

"General, actually," the officer corrected her.

"General," Leigh said. "Please direct the remainder of your troops to stand down and take no further actions until we return or until you hear from your bugler."

The general nodded his head. "Hostilities temporarily suspended," he said, turning away and barking commands to the remaining cavalrymen and the cannon team. Leigh followed her companions trailing after Rasputin.

Kurtzweiler's Toy Shop stood sandwiched between a pawn shop and an adult book store on the lower end of Masonic Avenue, not far from Buena Vista Park. A

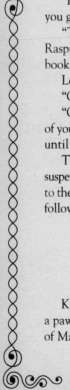

t h e

small metal plaque next to the door read: *Kurtzweiler's Toy Emporium. Est. 1892. F. Kurtzweiler, prop.*

A more prominent hanging sign, lime green with purple lettering, proclaimed KURTZWEILER'S TOYS 'N' GAMES. The shop's window displayed a variety of computer and video games crammed in amid battery-operated action figures and radio-controlled race cars.

Edmund pressed his face up against the glass, pulling back only when he had left a good-sized oily smear on its surface.

"There's a bunch of video game cartridges inside..." he said. "I don't see many toys."

Leigh pulled the door open and stepped inside. She reeled from the cold wave that hit her as she crossed the threshold into the shop. The toy store was utterly lacking in magic. She stepped backward quickly, her face pale.

"Brace yourselves," she said. "This place feels like it's made of iron."

Edmund grinned wickedly. "Banality Outpost number 147!" he said. "Let me at 'em!" Valmont slipped between Leigh and Edmund and strode into the shop. Edmund ducked inside after the eshu.

Rasputin looked at Tor thoughtfully. "It would probably be a bad idea for the three of us," he said, including Morgan in his statement, "to wait out here while the others retrieve the bugler. The place is obviously saturated with Glamour that we desperately need."

Morgan nodded her head. "Rasputin's right," she said to Tor. "They might need reinforcements to come in if they run into trouble."

"What's the problem?" Tor asked, still uncertain whether to follow his companions into the store.

Leigh paused in the open door, waiting for her stomach to stop lurching. "I've never felt such a gathering of Banality in one place," she said, pausing as she remembered her single encounter with Morgan's father. She shook her head. Compared to this shop, Gordon Daniels was a cornucopia of Glamour. "I think our "Dr." Kurtzweiler is one of the Autumn People."

"Here!" Morgan said suddenly, reaching inside her tunic and pulling out a silver chain with a heart-shaped locket hanging from it. She looked up at Tor. "Can I let her borrow it?" she asked. Tor nodded, his grizzled features softening.

Morgan handed the locket to Leigh. "Put this on," she said. "It's full of Glamour. I keep it with me to help me remember."

Leigh took the necklace and slipped it over her head, pushing it under her armor. She felt it glow warmly just above her breasts. "I'll treasure it, Lady Morgania," she said. Taking a deep breath, she entered the shop.

Valmont walked deliberately toward the counter at the rear of the shop, where a thin-faced young man with a brush cut and wire-rimmed spectacles stood nervously watching the eshu's approach. The sickeningly cold waves of Banality that permeated the shop's interior seemed to focus on the shopkeeper.

Edmund shuddered as he ran inside the shop and headed for the display rack of video games just inside the front door. "Awesome!" he muttered, running his hands over the shrink-wrapped surfaces of the cardboard packages. He began to poke each one in turn, relishing the topsy-turvy feeling that came with touching their shiny surfaces. "Bet I can make it all the way through them without losing it," he said to himself. He knocked one of them over and it fell to the floor with a hollow thunk.

"Hey, gyp!" he called toward the back of the store. "These things are empty!"

"Don't touch those," the young man proclaimed in a nasal tenor. "Those are for display only! You'll smudge the covers." Valmont cleared his throat and smiled as he saw the man twitch with surprise.

"May I help you?" the man sneered.

Valmont reached up and unhooked his veil, aware that his action would make no sense to the mortal standing across the counter from him. The man blinked and waited, his gaze darting nervously past Valmont to fasten on Edmund. Leigh looked around her as she stepped inside the shop for the second time. Sizing up the situation, she located a dusty doorstop near the inside of the door and used it to jam the door open. Behind her, Rasputin, Tor and Morgan hovered just outside the store. Leigh tapped Edmund on the shoulder as she passed him.

"Help me look for the bugler," she whispered. "Let's hope Valmont can keep the old man's attention."

"He's not old," Edmund whispered back to her. "He's kind of a thirty-something fart...."

"Trust me," Leigh said. "He's old. He's one of the Autumn People, can't you tell?"

Edmund's mouth dropped open. Leigh looked away quickly, then forced herself to turn back and stare at the redcap childling with desperate intensity, studying his grotesque mouthful of teeth, a physical impossibility among mortals. Banality collected around certain mortals, so infusing them with skepticism and disbelief in anything that smacked of imagination or creativity that they functioned as walking wet blankets, squelching Glamour wherever they went. The Autumn People are like iron bulls in a changeling china shop, Leigh thought to herself. She concentrated on feeling the Glamour that nestled next to her skin and felt a wave of affection for Morgan.

"Way cool!" Edmund said.

"We need to work fast," Leigh said, "or we could all walk out of here without remembering why we came in." She shoved Edmund toward the left side of the shop, while she began wandering down the right-hand aisles, grimacing at the garish objects that lay on the shelves, passing themselves off as toys.

Valmont smiled at the man across the counter.

"I'm looking for Mr. Kurtzweiler," he said.

"I'm Mr. Kurtzweiler," the young man replied. "Is there something you want?"

"I'm interested in tracking down a toy soldier that was brought here for repair some time ago."

"I don't do repairs," the man snapped. "If something's defective, you need to mail it back to the factory. I hope you mailed in your warranty card. I don't do trade-ins either. Or refunds."

Valmont cringed inwardly but managed to remain outwardly impassive.

"The toy was brought here for repair some years ago," he said. "It must still be here unless it's been thrown away." Once spoken, the thought became a sickening possibility.

"That was probably when my great-uncle owned this dump," the young man said. "Felix Kurtzweiler. My name is Ernst."

"Then it's your great-uncle with whom I have business. Does he still repair toys?"

Ernst Kurtzweiler giggled, a harsh, snorting sound that grated on Valmont's ears. The eshu looked down quickly and saw that his scimitar was beginning to take on a hint of insubstantiality.

"Hardly," Kurtzweiler said. "Old Uncle Felix died years ago and left this place to me. "He was a real loser," the man said. "Made and repaired everything in the shop. He never understood the concept of mass marketing, you know?"

"I'm afraid I must share his ignorance," Valmont said. "I myself prefer personal services whenever possible." He was beginning to panic as he felt his own Glamour disappearing into the creative vacuum that surrounded the shop owner. Reaching into the folds of his fading robes, he located his wallet in the back pocket of his trousers. Without removing the wallet, he extricated a pair of bills and laid them on the countertop.

"I really need to find the toy bugler," he said. "A hundred dollars should buy some of your time, if nothing else." Ernst looked at the money. Snatching it up, he ducked down below the counter. "My great-uncle kept a register somewhere in here," he said, his voice muffled but no less unpleasant. "I have everything on computer, myself. They've got a great package for inventories..."

Leigh had reached the back of the shop, near the counter where Valmont struggled to hold onto his changeling identity. She brushed up against a bulky wooden display case jutting out from behind a shelf full of NFL trading cards and bingo paraphernalia. A cloud of dust filled the air. She turned to see the object of such neglect, and found herself staring at a glass-fronted oak cabinet, grimy with caked-on dust. From inside it, she felt a faint glimmer of faerie magic.

"Over here! I've found it," called Leigh excitedly. "Valmont, get out!" she hissed at the eshu. Valmont looked at Leigh, then made a hasty retreat from the shop. Edmund, his head buried in a bin of marked down toys, swallowed quickly and ran across the shop to join Leigh.

Outside, Valmont staggered. Morgan ran to him and took his hand. "Look!" she said, and closed her eyes while she blew an imaginary soap bubble into the air in front of her. She transformed her utile tunic into a

toybox

frothy pale blue ball gown patterned after the dress Princess Aliera had worn to Fall Court. A faerie glow surrounded her, showering the eshu in Glamour. Valmont drank in the childling's offering with gratitude.

"That is the second time you have come to my aid, young one," he said. "Once more and I am bound to your service."

Morgan giggled, her pure laughter falling like sparkling water on the eshu's ears.

"I've never heard of that custom," she said.

"It's an eshu thing," Valmont said.

"Where did he go?" Ernst Kurtzweiler stood up behind the counter, a dusty leather-bound register in his hand. He plunked the massive book on the counter in front of him and looked around.

"Quick, do something!" Leigh said to Edmund, pointing to the cabinet. Edmund pulled something that looked like an unfolded paper clip from his pocket and shoved it in the rusted lock on the glass door, jiggling it while jumping up and down on one foot. The glass door swung open.

"Hey! What are you doing?" Kurtzweiler called out, rushing from behind the counter toward Leigh and Edmund, a look of horror on his pinched face. "Stop that!"

"I stumbled on this!" Leigh said, picking up a pack of trading cards and shoving them into the shop owner's face. "My elbow hit the glass. The lock must have snapped." Lame as it sounded, she hoped the man would believe her.

Behind her, Edmund shoved his head into the dark interior of the cabinet. Lying on its side, behind an antique replica of a Model T, the bugler rested under a layer of dust. Edmund stuck his finger down his throat as far as he could. Forcing his stomach to spasm, he threw up.

"Get out of my shop!" Kurtzweiler yelled, his voice rising to a shriek. "I don't care what you want or why you're here, just get...out...of...my...shop."

"I feel sick, Mom," Edmund groaned, grabbing Leigh's hand and pulling her out of the shop. "This place sucks eggs!"

Leigh kicked the doorstop aside and slammed the door shut behind her as she burst into the street. "We came so close," she said, and looked around for somewhere to vent her frustration.

Tor started to make his way toward the shop. "If it's in there, I'll get it out," he said grimly.

"Wait," Edmund said, and spat something out into his hand. Slimy but cleansed from the layer of dust that had covered it, the toy soldier, bugle pressed against its lips, began to glow in the center of Edmund's palm.

"Better not drop it," Rasputin drawled. "It shouldn't need any room to expand."

A few seconds later, a life-sized bugler stood blinking in the mid-afternoon sun. Taking the measure of the group that stood before him, expectant looks on their faces, the soldier slowly lowered his instrument and bowed from the waist. Straightening up, he saluted first Leigh, then the others.

"A lady knight and her noble retinue," the soldier said. "My thanks for rescuing me from that abominable internment camp." He cocked his head to one side, as if listening to something.

"Alas!" he cried. "The royal bride is in great danger! We must move quickly! Have you horses?"

"We have a chariot," Rasputin said, steering the bugler in the direction of Georgia's waiting cab.

chapter

ten

Malacar entered the place of flowers, carefully retracing his steps to the spot where last he had attempted the ritual, whose purpose even now he only dimly understood. From his earlier research, while he still served the Seelie Court, he had deduced that the green gem, the Eye of Opening, would unlock a portal of some sort. Before the sidhe had abandoned the earth at the time of the Shattering, centuries ago, leaving behind the "lesser" kithain to fend for themselves, the lands of North and South America had contained numerous faerie freeholds. In the western lands of the Summer Country, as the fertile continents came to be called, mortals dreamed, and Glamour remained long after disbelief had closed off most of Europe, labeling the things of faerie superstition at best, heresy at worst.

His own kith, the satyri or satyrs, existed as living proof of how far the children of the Dreaming had fallen into disrepute and infamy. Once the embodiment of passion itself, the satyri had led the mortals of the balmy Mediterranean lands in revels of sensual enjoyment, celebrating the splendor of physical sensation. Theirs had been a noble calling; their lust, the pure expression of the dance of love and death. Now the world perceived them as mere creatures of myth, rutting goat-footed lechers or minor devils.

When the triumph of rationality destroyed the belief in magic and the fires of the Inquisition burned the spirit of the Dreaming from mortal hearts, many faeries sought refuge in the relatively unspoiled lands west of the Atlantic Ocean. Before explorers from Europe discovered the New World, the American continents afforded the children of the Dreaming a sanctuary far from the Banality that had infected their homelands. But the reprieve was only temporary.

When the Shattering came, the delicate sidhe deserted their hearths, forts and glens, sealing many of them with wards that prevented the commoners they left behind from claiming them. The years between the Shattering and the return of the sidhe had seen the formation of new freeholds and, in some cases, the rediscovery of lost sites of faerie Glamour. But far too many places which had known the touch of faerie remained concealed. When the moon landing had infused the world with a wave of Glamour so strong that it blasted open the locked portals to Arcadia, home of the Dreaming, many sidhe returned to earth, thinking that the tide of Banality had been reversed. Instead, they found themselves stranded on an earth still too tainted by the denial of dreams to sustain their pure Arcadian selves. Ironically, their reentry into the mortal world made them unfit to return to Arcadia. The sidhe remained, and proclaimed their sovereignty over the other kithain, those who had suffered through the years of Darkness after the Shattering.

The sidhe quickly staked their claims to some of the ancient freeholds held by their houses, but there were other places, belonging to houses whose members had not chosen to return to the world of mortals, which still remained fast against any attempts to open them. The faerie treasures and Glamour that reputedly lay dormant within those concealed holdings were the stuff of changeling myth.

One of Malacar's fondest hopes, while he was wizard to the Duchy of Goldengate, was to discover the whereabouts of some of these hidden treasures. With them, he had hoped to improve his standing in the Seelie Court, perhaps even extending his influence as far as the Court of High King David at Tara-Nar. Now that his fortunes had changed, he still held out the hope that his service to the Unseelie would put him in a position to better himself. At least the lady of shadows made no secret of her contempt for commoners, unlike

Duke Aeon and his toadies, who covered their disdain for other kithain with honeyed words and plied them with bribes of Glamour to ensure their loyalty. With the lady and the others of the Court of True Shadows, he knew where he stood. Despite the evidence of his senses, he still could not shake the feeling of charred bone beneath the surface of his skin.

He would find their precious gate and retrieve whatever treasures rested beyond it. Then he would make his own way in the world, armed with the fruits of his own efforts and the reward for the humiliation and pain he had suffered. The lady and her companions, too preoccupied with their own secretive plottings to waste precious time and energy dealing with the world of mortals, relied on agents such as him to do their dirty work. Well, he would do it, but on his own terms. He had begun to dream of carving out a place for his own power base, one untroubled by the haughty ways of the sidhe. A satyr's paradise, with him as its lord.

The chimerical woman on his shoulders had long since ceased to struggle as Malacar made his ponderously circuitous trip to the designated spot. The lady had been certain that the garden in which he stood met the criteria for the "Place of Eternal Flowers" mentioned in the ancient rhyme which Malacar had brought to her as the price of his admittance to the Unseelie Court after his expulsion by Duke Aeon. Certainly, the satyr thought as he deposited his sacrificial burden on the ground and began making his ritual preparations, there was evidence that the site held traces of Glamour. But then, Glamour collected in a number of other places throughout San Francisco, and flowers were not unique to this location. Still, the ambiance seemed right. Malacar put aside his worries and concentrated on the task ahead of him. He had to assume that the lady was right. His future depended on it.

All around him, flowers bloomed in the late afternoon sunlight. Malacar paused in his activities while a human family strolled through the pathways between the profusion of flowering shrubs and late summer blossoms. The children looked at him with undisguised curiosity, while their parents' expressions contained a mixture of pity and disgust for the wretched vagabond his mortal guise revealed to them. He waited until they had disappeared from his view, then returned to his preparations. He would have to move quickly, before the advent of yet another group of mortals. While much of the ritual would not be visible to those without faerie sight, he had no doubt that anyone stumbling upon a homeless tramp stabbing an imaginary target with a dark-bladed knife would raise the alarm. The last thing he needed was some good samaritan's interference.

When everything was ready, Malacar turned once more to his bound victim. For the first time, he examined her in detail, noting the crown that formed part of her bridal veil and the ermine trim along the edge of her flowing train. Those were indications of royalty in the mortal world. This was not only a bride, with everything that word symbolized, but a royal bride. Malacar hoped the combination would result in a chimera powerful enough to serve his purpose.

He lifted the chimera and carried her into the center of the circle he had prepared where the traces of Glamour seemed to intersect at a nexus which should correspond to the portal he sought to open. Four stakes with scarlet ropes attached to them marked a square within the circle. He placed the chimera gently in the center, bending over her to undo the ropes which bound her. He freed the bride's wrists, and attached them securely to the pair of stakes nearest her head. Her eyes stared at him in silent protest. He stopped to pat her on the cheek with a gnarled hand.

"Don't worry," he whispered, "it's not the 'fate worse than death' that I have in mind for you."

Just then the sky above him darkened. Looking upward to see if a storm was in the making, Malacar saw a monstrous dragon begin its dive. Panic overtook him and, abandoning the place of flowers, the satyr fled for his life.

Edmund swore they were flying as Georgia's cab careened through the streets of the city, guided by the shouted directions of the bugler who rode up front with her. The chimeric soldier periodically thrust his horn out the window, sounding an variety of cadences and calls.

Leigh was the first to notice that they were heading toward Golden Gate Park.

"Stop by the Panhandle," she called from her place sandwiched in the back between Valmont and Morgan, who sat on Tor's lap. On Valmont's other side, Rasputin tried to keep Edmund from leaning too far out the cab's rear window. "The rest of the soldiers should be there. I told them to wait until they heard the horn."

"I have already sounded the call to arms, lady knight," the bugler replied. Leigh thought she heard a hint of smugness in his clipped, precise tones.

"Will they know where to go?" Morgan asked.

"Everything they need to know is in the sequence of notes," the bugler said.

Georgia sped down Oak Street, paralleling the Panhandle. "Up ahead is Stanyan Street," she advised the bugler, "and beyond that is Golden Gate Park."

"I know the Golden Gate," the bugler said. "The

bride lies within a grove of flowers. Take us there quickly." The bugler pointed out the window.

"As the crow flies," Georgia said, turning the steering wheel in the direction indicated by the bugler's outstretched arm.

From every corner of the Haight, they answered the call of the bugler. Striding from his newfound lair in the basement of Calling Card Stationers, the tawny lion shook his magnificent mane in the afternoon sun, the horn's music ringing in his ears. Following each other in order of descending height, a troupe of nesting dolls paraded past the lion, while overhead a plump, rosy-colored pig fluttered a pair of tiny wings and propelled itself in fits and starts. A Viking longship passed them by, its rowers straining to push their vessel along its perilous course through unseen gray waters filled with crashing metal floes.

From within the Park, atop a promontory over-looking the Buffalo Paddock, a tiger turned from his contemplations and ambled in the direction of the bugler's blast. Below, a painted bison broke free from the herd and lumbered past the restraining fences, following the irresistible command. Acrobats, archers, ballerinas, calico cats, dancing dervishes, mustachioed nutcrackers, zebras on wheels — all converged upon their destination.

There were a few, however, who managed to resist the bugle's command. Ensconced between a rearing charger and a two-humped camel, the chimerical ostrich ignored the blare of the horn call in favor of the sprightly music of the Children's Carousel. It had found its place, surrounded by the natural Glamour embedded in the small mortals who perched atop their fantastical mounts and spun dreams of dangerous quests and fearsome battles. In a tiny apartment above the Passionate Heart Bookstore, where a pinch-faced sluagh named Ellen made her home, a wind-up mouse nestled deeper into the dog-eared paperback romances spilling from the corners and nibbled on the lonely changeling's impossible dreams.

"Stop here!" the bugler called out suddenly as Georgia's cab approached the Japanese Tea Garden. The cabbie obliged him, pulling her car to the side of JFK Drive. The bugler fumbled with the handle of the door, finally releasing himself from the confines of the cab. "My duties call me in that direction," he said, and, putting the bugle to his lips once more, marched toward the exotic garden.

Leigh and her companions followed the bugler.

"Look!" Morgan called, pointing east toward Stanyan Street, where a parade of chimerae were making their way across the Park, the general and his cavalrymen in the lead.

"There's more over there," Edmund yelled, as the redcap spotted a second chimerical army coming from further within the Park. "There's a buffalo, a tiger and an elephant!"

The back of Rasputin's neck prickled. "We're perfectly safe here," he said suddenly, bolting for the shelter of some nearby trees. "Stay!" he called, pointing skyward as he ran.

Without bothering to look, Tor grabbed Morgan and

Edmund and bore them into the trees behind Rasputin. Leigh and Valmont raised their faces upward and for the second time that afternoon caught a glimpse of falling doom.

"The dragon," Leigh said, her voice filled with equal parts of fear and wonder. "It's passing by," she added. The monster dipped one wing and banked in a graceful arc away from the changelings. Valmont nodded wordlessly. Then his sharp eyes caught sight of a figure running west, hugging the trees along the road through the Park.

"That's Malacar!" he proclaimed. "The beast is after him!"

Leigh felt a surge of determination rise within her. Her vow to Duke Aeon rang inside her, needing no geas to tell her where her knightly duty lay.

"Dragon or no," she heard herself say, "Malacar belongs to me!" She drew her sword and raced after the fleeing figure. Valmont motioned to the others in the trees and followed the Fiona knight.

Edmund struggled in Tor's vise-like grip. "Let me go, you rock-faced lumberjack!" he cried angrily, trying to twist his head around to get his teeth on the offending hand that held him back. "We gotta go after them!"

Morgan tugged on her grandfather's other hand. "We swore an oath, grandpa," she said. "We have to help them. They can't fight Malacar and the dragon by themselves."

"Oh, they'll surely get help from somewhere," Rasputin said, calmly, readying himself to follow his companions. "I'm sure it won't matter if we're there to see them die or not."

Swearing, Tor let go of Edmund abruptly. Still holding onto Morgan's hand, the troll looked down at her. "You stay with me, or else where I put you," he ordered. Morgan pressed her lips together tightly and flashed Tor a look of frustrated resignation. "I'll be careful," she promised. "But we need to hurry."

In the vanguard, Leigh tried to keep her eyes on both Malacar and the dragon. It seemed that the beast was herding the satyr, for as she watched, it flew past him and described a lazy circle in the air ahead of him. Seeing his approach cut off, Malacar reversed his course, cutting back toward the Tea Garden.

"He's heading back inside," Leigh said, and changed her course to one that would take her within the garden's confines. Ahead of her a booth advertising admission fees blocked her path.

"Valmont!" she called over her shoulder as she sprinted by the startled woman operating the booth. "Do something." Looking behind her, she saw Valmont pause for a second and whisper something to the woman, miming the act of blowing something in her face as he spoke to her. Leigh crossed a wooden bridge over a stream filled with black and gold carp. Behind her, she heard the others hurrying to catch up with her. She felt a wave of grim satisfaction that they had all chosen to follow her as she plunged into the lush foliage of the ornamental gardens.

Tor's footsteps clattered heavily over the wooden bridge as he entered the garden with Morgan, a few steps behind the others. Rasputin and Edmund had caught up and passed Valmont and were gathered near Leigh, preparing for battle.

"Do dragons breathe fire?" Edmund asked excitedly.

"Let's hope this one doesn't," Valmont said in a dubious voice. Tor looked around him, trying to find a place where Morgan could be safe. His eyes met the placid gaze of a huge bronze statue, a nine-foot tall Buddha, whose serene presence dominated the area around it. A man in a flowery Hawaiian shirt stood a few feet from the statue, aiming a shiny camera at a woman in pink knee-length pants who held the hand of a stocky child. A bright flash went off, and the trio moved away from the statue, wandering in the direction of the pagoda-like Tea House that doubled as a gift store.

Tor carried Morgan over to the statue and placed her in the Buddha's lap. "Stay there," he said. He closed his eyes and stomped his foot heavily on the ground. His craggy face broke out in a sweat as he seemed to be reaching for something buried deep within him. To her horror, Morgan realized what Tor was doing.

"Grandpa, don't!" she cried. "Don't waste your Glamour on me. I can protect myself." Tor opened his eyes, a grim smile on his face. He patted the hilt of his axe. "I got it covered," he said. "This will keep me going for awhile." He turned to join the others.

"Over there, near the waterfall," Valmont pointed. "That's where we'll meet up with them if we move quickly." The eshu turned to Leigh. "Follow me," he said, his dark eyes adding force to his command. "Arriving at the right place in a timely fashion is the prerogative of my kith." Leigh hesitated, then nodded brusquely.

"Do it," she said.

"I love constructive struggles for power," Rasputin mumbled to himself. The pooka looked around for Edmund and finally found him scrambling through the sculpted greenery, making his own path toward the waterfall.

Malacar's only thought was to get to water. There, he hoped, he could invoke some of his affinities with the element to bolster his waning Glamour. Without it, he had no hope of surviving an attack by anything as large as the dragon. His heart raced wildly in his chest as he considered the horror of losing himself to Banality so close to real power.

Up ahead, he spied the waterfall, a spot he had noticed and dismissed in his earlier reconnoitering of the garden in search of the spot where the portal had to be. As he neared the sound of splashing water, the satyr noticed a group of people waiting for him, then cursed loudly as he recognized them.

The armored Fiona knight, whose ceremony he had chosen to interrupt for the sake of dramatic timing, took a step toward him, her sword at the ready. Just then, the dragon began to dive.

During her race through the garden, Leigh had rehearsed the words she would say when she and Malacar came face to face. She was opening her mouth to deliver the duke's message of banishment when a sudden rush of wind prompted her to look above her. It occurred to her that just because both she and the dragon had targeted Malacar, the chimerical monster would not necessarily recognize her as an ally. The creature seemed to have Malacar cornered.

"Retreat would be a bad idea!" Rasputin's voice, accompanied by the rustle of leaves, came from some distance behind her, seeming to echo her own thoughts. If she ran now, she would have time to find shelter of some sort from the dragon's assault, whatever form it took. But then, she realized, so would Malacar. Within her a red fury kindled and burst into flames.

"Our cause is lost, Eleighanara! Save yourself and the others!" Her oathmate's voice rang in her ears as they stood upon the craggy tor, watching as death approached them from the sky, driven by the rush of wings. His gauntleted hand brushed her cheek as gently as it could. "This is your

fight no longer." Nearby, the rest of the rebels, all sons and daughters of the noble Houses of Arcadia, steeled themselves for what would likely be their final battle in a doomed uprising.

"I will not leave you." Tears and desperation softened her voice to a near whisper.

"Neither will our oathmates, save you lead them to safety while there is still time." Something unspoken hovered on the edges of his voice. "Your families will grant you clemency," he said, "for you act out of love and loyalty."

"Together we may yet prevail," she insisted.

"This time, perhaps," he countered, "but they will never accept what we have chosen to do. They will remain locked forever in the dreams of their noble pasts rather than accept the inevitability of the changing of the cycle. Your part in this is over. Go. Take the others with you."

"You will die in this place," she said, "without our help."

"With your help, we will all die," he said. A grim smile hardened his face. "There are risks I am willing to take that you and the others would never countenance. Leave, now," he ordered harshly, "and leave me free to take those risks."

Blinded by her tears, she turned and led the others from the battle, knowing as she did so that she was abandoning the prince she loved.

Leigh swallowed hard and turned to Valmont, who had stopped just behind her. "Get the others to safety," she said.

"You can't fight this dragon by yourself," Valmont said, looking about him nervously as the dragon approached, giving every indication of leading off its attack with an elemental blast.

"I don't intend to," said Leigh. "I intend to keep Malacar from running away."

"This is foolishness!" Valmont said, his temper flaring.

"This is my right, and I command you to take the

others aside!" Leigh called upon the Glamour within her, feeling Morgan's locket radiate warmth next to her skin. Her form began to shimmer as an aura of power surrounded her. The sidhe had maintained their rule through their ability to inflict awe upon other kithain who challenged them. She was playing dirty pool, but she saw no other recourse open to her.

Valmont's face grew taut with silent fury. His nostrils flaring and his dark eyes hard with anger, he turned and ran quickly toward Rasputin and Edmund. Reaching out to snag a hold on each of them, the eshu muttered the refrain of a popular traveling song. A soft pop of displaced air marked the place where the three disappeared.

Malacar cursed as he saw his path to the waterfall blocked by the Fiona. Glancing upward, he saw the dragon's head rear back, heard the sudden intake of air and saw its chest expand.

"Out of the way!" he shrieked as panic overtook him. Hands outstretched, he barreled forward, ready to push his way through the knight toward the refuge of the water. "I'll give you anything you want," he babbled, out of control as he succumbed to terror. "My greatest treasure...my service..."

Leigh waited until the satyr was nearly upon her, then sheathed her sword and reached for the arm nearest her. Pulling him in the direction of his momentum, she fell backward, flipping the satyr headfirst into the water at the base of the ornamental cataract. Adjusting her grip on his wrist, she let him pull her into the pool as well, landing solidly atop him.

Where they had stood, a gout of chimeric flame struck the ground. For an eerie moment, Leigh saw, through the rain of water that poured down on her from the crest of the waterfall, the sight of carefully tended paths and flowering shrubs limned in an insubstantial flame. The dragon's fiery breath, deadly to a changeling's faerie nature, could not affect the scenery of the mortal world.

"Yield to me," Leigh said, "and I will accept your service in the besting of this beast. It's said you are a wizard besides being a traitor. Use your powers now, or I will use you as my shield in single combat with the dragon. Unless we join our forces in this fight, we will both be severed from our natures, but unlike you, old man," she spat, "my Glamour will return. You risk much more."

The dragon came to ground upon the spot where it had last seen its opponents. Its serpentine eyes spotted the pair of changelings and it trumpeted a challenge in their direction.

Malacar nodded glumly, gasping for breath as the knight's shin guard weighed heavily upon his chest.

"I yield," he said in a strangled voice. "Let me up. I need room to work."

Leigh released her hold upon the satyr, and watched him struggle to his feet. "If you betray me or try to run away," she began, drawing her sword and stepping from the pool toward the dragon, "I swear..."

"He will go nowhere." Valmont, arm in arm with Edmund and Rasputin, appeared within the pool. "You forced my obedience a moment ago," he said. "But that danger is past, and you will not so easily order me away again."

"Or me!" said Edmund hotly, flashing his dagger first at Malacar and then in the general direction of the dragon. "I'm not some wimp that needs to run from everything...."

A scream of pain erupted from the dragon as an axe blade buried itself in the beast's scaly haunch.

"It's Tor!" Edmund screamed. "Look at the old fart go!" The redcap yanked his arm from Valmont's grasp and ran toward the dragon.

"Go," the eshu said to Leigh. "Seek your claim to

glory. Rasputin and I will help keep Malacar honest."

"I'm very good with honesty," Rasputin mumbled, brushing water from his ears.

From within the protective barrier Tor had constructed around the statue of the Buddha, Morgan watched the progress of the battle with farseeing eyes. Lady Alyssa had told her that she possessed a rare ability to alter the fortunes of those around her for good or ill, so the childling proceeded to pour her Glamour into doing just that. She would never be able to prove that she had anything to do with delaying the dragon's fiery breath long enough for Leigh to get out of its path, or that she kept its attention focused on the figures in the water so that her grandfather's attack from behind went unnoticed until too late, but she felt a private satisfaction in being able to do her part, even from a distance.

Tor felt the blood sing in his ears. His temples throbbed with the frenzy of battle. Now that he had discharged his duty to protect his granddaughter, he was free to do what his trained responses told him he did best: fight. Still some distance from Leigh when the dragon's breath billowed upward in a fiery pillar, at first he feared that he would arrive too late. His worry abated when he came to the waterfall and saw his companions unharmed within the water. Even

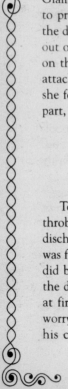

better, he faced the dragon's back; its attention was focused on the others. He rushed the creature from behind, his glowing axe slicing deeply through scale and hide to bite into flesh and sinew.

Leigh charged forward, aiming her sword's thrust for the dragon's vitals. She caught Tor's eye across the dragon's bulk and nodded grimly to him. She hoped that Malacar would do something to aid them. She saw Edmund dance around to one side of the dragon, looking for a place to stab his knife.

Malacar reached into the pool at his feet and picked up a stone, worn to a point at one end. "To hurt, you must sometimes be hurt," the satyr growled, gritting his teeth and jabbing the sharp stone into his forearm, scraping the edge down the length of his arm. "It works better with a holly branch," he said through clenched jaws.

Beyond him, the dragon's head jerked violently backward, as if struck by a blow from an unseen assailant. Its tail lashed out, catching Tor around the midsection and tossing the troll to the ground. On the dragon's other side, Edmund ducked to avoid the backlash from the tail swipe.

Morgan screamed as her inner sight saw her grandfather fall. She focused on his prone form, and imagined herself kneeling over him, planting a kiss of healing on his forehead. She held her breath and crossed her fingers.

Leigh reeled as the dragon swept its wings forward, catching her on the shoulder with its spiny ribbing. Blindly she lunged into the beast, jamming her sword at the dragon's bulk.

Rasputin saw Leigh's brave reaction to the blow. Letting out a yodeling screech, the pooka reached into the air in front of him, hands locked together as if behind someone's neck. He jerked down hard, bringing one knee upward into his clasped hands.

The dragon lurched forward, impaling itself on Leigh's blade. From behind the dragon, Edmund thrust his dagger into the tendon at the dragon's heel. Using the blade to pull himself forward along the ground, he opened his mouth and bit into the creature's spiny foot. The dragon howled in agony and toppled forward, shimmering and shrinking as it fell.

From her seat in the Buddha's arms, Morgan let out a yell of triumph, followed quickly by one of relief as she saw her grandfather shake his head and raise himself from the ground, the mark of the guardian warrior still stamped upon his faerie form. She felt the barrier around her crumble. She scrambled to the ground and ran for her companions.

Tor brushed himself off and retrieved his axe from where it lay on the ground beside the foot-long painted wooden dragon with jointed wings and tail. He scooped up the figure with his other hand and offered it to Leigh. She started to refuse it, but the look in Tor's eyes cautioned her that the wisest course would be to accept the offering.

"Are you hurt, Grandpa?" Morgan cried, launching herself at her grandfather. Tor caught her up with one hand.

"Just a little dusty," he said.

Valmont and Rasputin, with Malacar between them, emerged from the water and joined the others. Edmund ran up to the satyr and made a show of patting him down, rifling his pockets until Valmont pulled him away. Leigh stared at the satyr for a moment before speaking.

"By order of Duke Aeon, you are henceforth banished from the Duchy of Goldengate and the counties, baronies and all freeholds contained within the duchy. May no one give you shelter or succor who honors the Dreaming; save for the Right of Life, your

the

life blood would be forfeit. So long as Glamour remains in the world, may you bear the stigma of betrayer, pariah, and outcast."

Edmund gave a low whistle. "That's harsh," he whispered. Rasputin stepped on Edmund's foot.

Malacar felt the words fall upon him with the force of a binding. The sidhe were experts at using words to bind their subjects, and the satyr heard his doom within Leigh's careful speech. More than that, he sensed Duke Aeon's will in her pronouncement.

"If you are finished, may I take my leave to begin the exile to which you have condemned me?" Malacar could not suppress a sneer. He had already made plans to quit the fief, although he had hoped that his pockets would be heavy with purloined treasures.

Leigh seemed to hesitate. "You made certain promises," she said.

"And I discharged those promises during the battle," Malacar replied angrily. "I offered you treasure or service, and you chose service."

"Give her the Eye."

The voice resonated through the satyr's mind, filling him with a sick chill like the touch of cold iron upon his heart. Malacar did not recognize the speaker, but he could not fail to acknowledge the sheer power and majesty which resonated through his being. He fought to resist the force of the command.

The imprisoned prince had sensed the ritual's beginning, felt the wrongness of its setting. His ability to reach beyond the barrier of his prison-realm was still too feeble to allow unimpeded communication. His ally in the world beyond, the silken Lady Glynnis, had sworn herself in a dream to his service. She received his sendings only faintly, and though he could guide her to the general area of his imprisonment, he could lead her no nearer than the verses she had so neatly misinterpreted.

Just as he knew when the satyr, the lady's tool, began the ritual, so, too, he felt its interruption. Only by his most powerful kenning, focused on the eyegems borne by the wizard Malacar, could he follow the pathetic creature's panicked flight from some unknown foe. Then he sensed another presence within the bounds of his perceptions. Emotions long since atrophied by time and bitterness stirred faintly in his ancient breast. Eleighanara had returned, her glory undiminished despite the cloak of mortality she bore about her faerie form, her passion still seething just below the surface of her will. For the first time since he had been thrust into his wretched cage of broken dreams, he felt true passion fill his empty spirit. She would be the one, he decided. Once, in Arcadia, he had won her love and loyalty. He would win her again. Together they would change the mortal and immortal worlds....

Malacar felt the emerald gem within his left eye socket begin to burn. He blinked to soothe its growing heat with forced tears. A molten fury raged within his head. He screamed.

Leigh and the others watched speechlessly as the satyr doubled, grasping his head between his hands and screaming.

"He's glowing!" Morgan finally said, as a luminous green light radiated from the satyr's face.

"He's not," corrected Edmund, staring in fascination at the spectacle. "It's his eye! He looks like he's gonna pop!"

"The Eye. Give it to her." The captive prince gathered all his power within him and directed it toward the puny form of the gem's possessor. This working would leave him drained, he knew, and only the passing of time would allow his slow recuperation. But he was not used to failure...

the

Malacar fell to his knees. The torments of the lady of shadows were nothing compared to the pain that seared his nerves and turned the blood in his veins to liquid fire.

"Remove the Eye and give it to her, now!" Overcome by weariness, depleted of most of his faerie magic, he loosed his failing hold upon the mortal world and collapsed within his prison. Having uttered the three-fold compulsion, he could only hope that the satyr's will was not strong enough to resist him. He cursed the limitations that bound his power, making it impossible for him to know the outcome of his working.

Malacar grasped the gem in desperation and ripped it from his eye socket, heedless of the wounds opened by the violence of his pain-wracked fingers.

Morgan screamed and hid her face in Tor's neck. Valmont set his jaw and watched impassively. Leigh's face registered the horror that coursed through her.

"Too gross!" Edmund said admiringly. Next to him, Rasputin's face grew thoughtful. "I hope this isn't one of those eye for an eye things," he murmured.

Malacar extended a trembling hand to Leigh, palm upward. A round, translucent green stone rested on his open palm. "Here," he screamed, still wracked by a pain that was only beginning to recede. "Take it! It will serve me no longer!" When Leigh failed to take the gem from his outstretched hand, Malacar dropped it on the ground. Before anyone could react, he staggered to his feet and fled the serenity of the Tea Garden.

Valmont started after him.

"Let him go," said Leigh. "We have discharged our duty." Numbly she knelt to pick up the gem, still glowing with an inner light. She held it gingerly between her fingers, before finally letting it rest flat on her palm.

"It's cool," she said, watching as its glow diminished to a single pinpoint of light hidden deep within its core.

"Too cool," breathed Edmund. "But what's it do?" he asked.

Leigh shook her head as the others gathered around her to examine the gem. Rasputin wrinkled his nose. "It's nowhere near the size of whatever opened the toy chest," he commented.

"Company's coming," Tor said, as a horde of chimerae appeared from deep within the gardens, led by the bugler and his military companions. Among them, escorted by one of the footsoldiers, walked a slightly rumpled bride.

"Her royal Highness is safe and unharmed," the bugler announced to the gathered company. "The foul ritual was interrupted before she could be sacrificed."

"I suppose the dragon's arrival had nothing to do with the interruption..." Rasputin said.

"Oh, wow," said Edmund, running up to the bugler and handing him something from his pocket. "I'll bet she'll need the groom!" He looked at Valmont. "Malacar had it stuffed in his pocket."

"Why does he always have to sound so proud of himself?" Morgan whispered to her grandfather. Tor shrugged.

"No one else will do it for him," the troll surmised. Morgan thought about that for a while.

"Request permission to return to the barracks," the bugler said.

Morgan's face lit up. "He wants to take them all to the toy chest!" she said. "Permission granted," she replied gravely. Following the soldiers, the chimerae from the toy chest left the Tea Garden and paraded eastward on their journey homeward.

"I hope Georgia didn't decide to leave us," Valmont said as the companions made their own way back to where they had last seen the cabbie. The eshu looked around as the fading daylight bathed the gardens in pools of shadows. "We should all return to the Toybox," he said. "It's been a long day...."

Morgan suddenly gasped, covering her mouth with both her hands. "It's nearly dark!" she said, her voice muffled. "I should have been home from school hours ago."

"Don't worry," Leigh said, not wanting to spoil the moment of victory for any of them. "We'll think of something to explain your absence."

"Yes, don't worry," said Rasputin. "Everything will turn out fine."

chapter

eleven

Morgan sat in the child-sized wicker chair and stared across the table at Dr. Walters. It had not been a good session for either of them and Morgan was glad that it was almost over. Since the battle with Malacar and the chimerae, she had been in disgrace. After seeing the chimerae safely inside the toy chest and watching in amazement as the bugler — the last one in — pulled the otherwise immovable lid shut with a flourish, Morgan had accepted Georgia's offer to take her home.

Her parents had been waiting for her, her mother red-eyed from crying and her father white-faced with anger.

"The school called this morning," her mother had said. "They wanted to know if you'd gotten home all right and if I wanted them to give me your assignments for the weekend or if you were too sick to study. I called your father."

Her father had been more direct.

"Where were you?" he demanded. Morgan could see that in spite of his anger, he, too, was close to tears.

Morgan tried to tell them that she had been with friends, that she had been safe and that they shouldn't have worried about her, but they kept pressing her for details. Finally, in desperation, she said the only thing that she knew they might believe, even though she felt rotten inside for dragging him into her problems.

"I went to see my grandfather!" she had said, bursting into fortuitous though unintentional tears. "You won't let me see him any other way so I had to find some way to do it myself." Unable to stop sobbing once she had started, she shoved past both her parents, knocking aside her mother's outstretched arms, and ran up the stairs to her room. No one came after her. She thought she heard her mother start up the stairs, but then her father's voice, sounding harsher than usual, stopped the footsteps.

Then the phone calls began. By kneeling on the floor and pressing her ear against the polished wood around the edges of the carpet, Morgan could hear muffled voices, mostly her father's, and could make out a few words: "Walters... emergency... whatever you advise" worried her.

Later in the evening, her father came upstairs and took her door off its hinges, while her mother brought in a tray of food, supper she had apparently missed, and set it down on the end of Morgan's bed. She looked as though she wanted to say something to her daughter, but then her eyes clouded with tears, and she hurried out of Morgan's room and fled to her studio, slamming the door behind her.

"I've canceled all our weekend plans," Gordon said, his throat muscles working furiously to keep his voice expressionless. "We're keeping you out of school on Monday, and I'm taking the day off as well. Tuesday, you have a nine o'clock appointment with Dr. Walters. It's the earliest she could fit you in."

For the last three days, Morgan had been under the watchful eyes of either her mother or her father every minute. The hour she had just spent sitting in Dr. Walters' fake playroom of an office had been the first time she had been out of the sight of either of them. The worst thing had been the silence. Neither of her parents had spoken to her except to inform her when it was time for bed or meals. Morgan suspected that the "silent treatment" had been Dr. Walters' idea, and had decided that she would give the psychologist a taste of her own medicine.

For the last hour, Dr. Walters' questions had gone unanswered. The psychologist had begun cheerfully, asking Morgan if she felt like discussing her recent truancy. Morgan had only shaken her head. The doctor's questions had grown more personal, wanting to know if Morgan had been in contact with her grandfather, if she had ever thought of running away from home before and if she was so unhappy that she wanted to punish her parents. Morgan had ignored those questions entirely, hoping that Dr. Walters could read the look of disgust on her face. When the doctor started asking Morgan about her fantasies, Morgan seriously considered breaking her vow of silence to insist that she had given up all her notions of real faeries in the modern world. She realized, just in time, that a sudden burst of denials would probably be worse than continuing her refusal to speak. She substituted a look of boredom instead. Deep inside, Morgan was filled with terror.

When Dr. Walters looked at her watch and announced in a crisp voice full of fake cheeriness that the weekly session was over, Morgan felt as if she had been released from a cage. She leaped from her chair and ran from the doctor's office into the cheerful waiting room, where Gordon Daniels stood waiting for her. Wordlessly, Morgan threw her arms around her father, grateful for his familiar presence, even if he was still angry with her.

Gordon Daniels absently stroked his daughter's head, as Dr. Walters appeared in the doorway of her office.

"I'll be in touch with you later in the week with my recommendations," she said, the same false brightness in her voice.

"Thank you for your help," Gordon Daniels replied, his usually strong voice sounding almost pathetically grateful.

Gordon drove Morgan to her school. "I spoke with your teachers," he said, as he escorted her up the walkway and inside the building. "They've been made aware of our concern for your safety, and have promised us that one of their staff will be with you every day until either your mother or I arrive to take you home. Do you understand?"

Morgan nodded sullenly. Her father knelt in front of her and hugged her tightly. "Morgan, sweetheart," he said softly, "your mother and I just want what's best for you. Please try to understand that."

Morgan relented, and returned his hug. "I know, Daddy," she said. She knew her voice sounded small and sad, but she hoped her father did not realize the profound depth of her sorrow. "I love you," Morgan said suddenly, "and Mother, too." She kissed her father on the cheek and detached herself from his embrace and headed for her classroom.

Despite their promise to keep an eye on Morgan, no one noticed when she slipped inside the office of the principal's secretary during lunchtime to use the phone.

After she had spoken to Gordon Daniels, Dr. Adrienne Walters informed her secretary that she wanted no interruptions until further notice. She walked across the playroom to a door that led into yet another office, this one more traditional. Here she saw some of her older patients, teenagers who disdained the "playroom atmosphere" she used for her pre-teen cases.

The man who had been waiting in the office during Morgan's session now rose from his chair as Dr. Walters entered the room.

"So that was the famous Morgan Daniels," he said, gesturing toward the two-way mirror on the wall between the two offices. Dr. Walters had seldom had the occasion to use it since its installation last year, but she now hoped that in the last hour the device had justified its expense.

Dr. Walters nodded. "I'm afraid she was extraordinarily uncommunicative today," she said. "I hope I haven't wasted your time."

The man shrugged as he removed his wire-rimmed glasses and tucked them neatly into the vest pocket of his suit-coat.

"On the contrary," he said smiling. "What I have just seen, in combination with the files and the transcripts of the young lady's previous sessions, seems to suggest that your suspicions are justified."

Dr. Walters walked to her desk and sat down. Her colleague resumed his seat in the chair he had occupied near the mirror to view Morgan's session.

"I don't know whether to be relieved or worried that Morgan Daniels seems to fit the paradigm outlined in your book," Dr. Walters said. "The measures you recommend are—"

"I realize that they are extreme," the man replied. "But the important thing is that they work. The delusions which overwhelm these people are extremely potent. Gentler methods simply cannot penetrate them."

"I have broached the subject of institutionalization with the child's parents before," Dr. Walters began, "but they were reluctant to send her away for any length of time."

Her colleague nodded. "Many parents feel that no institution can provide adequately for their children's welfare," he said. "I read the report of your conversation with Mr. and Mrs. Daniels. The hospital in Colorado was an excellent choice, by the way," he added. Dr.

Walters felt a momentary anger at the blatant condescension in his voice, but suppressed the emotion as puerile and waited for him to continue. "Still, there is the matter of distance. It is possible that the Daniels might be inclined to accept sending Morgan to a hospital here in San Francisco."

"Do you have some place in mind?" Dr. Walters asked.

The man nodded. "As a matter of fact, I know of a small, privately funded operation in Presidio Heights that could handle the Daniels' child with minimal trouble. I serve as an adviser to their board of trustees," he said complacently, "so gaining admission for her will be no problem."

Dr. Walters closed her eyes, collecting her thoughts. She had gone over and over in her mind other alternatives for treating Morgan, whom she now believed to be manifesting signs of serious disturbance, and she had come to the conclusion that the man sitting in the office with her held out the best hope for a cure for the child's deteriorating condition. Nevertheless, she could not shake the feeling that she had failed in her duty to Morgan Daniels. She opened her eyes. Her colleague sat calmly awaiting her decision.

"Very well," she said. "After Morgan's disappearing trick last week, I think that I can persuade the Daniels to sign the necessary commitment papers."

"And I shall start the wheels turning for Morgan's admission to Ironwood Hospital." The man rose to leave, extending his hand toward Dr. Walters.

"Thank you for your help, Dr. Stark," she said, shaking his hand and getting up to see him to the door. She watched as he left the room, and continued watching, through the two-way mirror, as Dr. Anton Stark, author of *Chimera: Living Within Our Dreams*, made his way through her outer office. Only when he had gone through the door into her waiting room and, presumably, from there out of the building, did Dr. Walters return to her desk and allow herself to ponder the enormity of what she had just done.

Upon his arrival in San Francisco, Cyprian Ryder wasted no time checking into the hotel where he had confirmed reservations. He traveled with minimal baggage, and once his few necessary items were carefully stored away in the single bureau or hung on the rack provided by the hotel, he made his way from his room to the gift shop which fronted the hotel lobby and purchased a map of the city. Taking a moment to get his bearings, he placed the map in the inside pocket of his jacket where he could reach it easily, and hit the streets.

The publishing company which had solicited his expertise for an article on demonic influences in the modern world had forwarded to him a request from a Dr. Adrienne Walters for his assistance in a matter regarding one of her clients. Though the doctor's request had been vague, presumably in keeping with ethical constraints, Ryder's interest had been roused. More importantly, his left palm had begun to ache since he picked up the brief letter from Dr. Walters at his post office box.

The ache was still with him, in fact it had grown measurably stronger since entering the city. Cyprian Ryder could gauge the relative intensity of the familiar pain as it waxed and waned, sometimes so faint it was nothing more than an inconvenient itch, sometimes so overwhelming he could hardly concentrate on anything else. It was a feeling he both savored and dreaded.

Ryder walked quickly through the city, taking note of the variations in pain. Ignoring occasional twinges,

the

usually when he passed an art gallery or specialty shop, he concentrated instead on the erratic spasm that made him clench his hand to relieve the pain. On those occasions, he would take careful note of his surroundings, pull out his map, and draw a circle with a red pencil to mark his location. He made no attempts to investigate those areas further. He had set aside today and possibly tomorrow as well for reconnaissance, for discovering the areas where an abundance of Glamour indicated the presence of his quarry. Later tonight, in his hotel room, he would study the map he had marked and begin to work on his game plan. If necessary, and he suspected it would be, he would call in some allies.

Cyprian Ryder drew his comforting cloak of Banality close about him as he continued his exploration of the city, looking for signs of the infernal ones. He no longer thought of them as changelings, though he knew that was the name they gave themselves. To him they were, if not demons, then something very like — creatures from an alien dimension whose presence threatened the security of the rational world. He knew this with a conviction no one could uproot, for like those he hunted, he was — had been — a changeling.

Even now, Ryder knew that he could summon enough residual Glamour from within him to assume his other form — the aspect which changelings referred to as their faerie natures or their fae forms. To normal humans, he would appear unchanged. Only other changelings could see that hidden inner self. Once he had gloried in that alien body; as a changeling, he was one of the sidhe, the rightful rulers of the hidden race of faerie. Like his mortal self, his fae form was tall and trim, with rich, chestnut colored hair and dark hazel eyes. One of his changeling lovers had compared his looks to a hawk: cruel, predatory and proud. In his early years, before he realized the true horror of his condition and swore to atone for his existence, he had reveled in his appearance. As a knight of the Seelie Court in the midwestern Kingdom of Grass, he had been known for his courage and had been elevated to the status of paladin, a champion of the court.

The event that had brought him to his senses, so to speak, had been simple and utterly devastating, and had resulted in the death of a child. Nearly a decade ago, he and a group of wilder friends, all of them court nobles, had attended a Shadowstorm concert in Chicago. The band members were all changelings, and all Unseelie, but the Glamour raised by their music drew Seelie and Unseelie changelings from all over the midwest. The Ravaging started somewhere during the band's third song, their showcase number. A group of redcaps from Detroit started a fight with some local commoner changelings as everyone tried to extract as much Glamour from the band's music as they could, even stealing it from other changelings in the crowd.

The violence spread, engulfing most of the audience on the floor of the concert hall, even the mortals. Ryder, whose faerie name was Chevalier, and his friends were caught up in the riot, losing themselves to the frenzy of Glamour-for-the-taking. Someone called in the police, who stopped the show and arrested several of the more prominent rioters as well as all the band members. Chevalier had escaped the round-up, but had stayed behind until he was forced to leave. The devastation wrought by his fellow changelings was epitomized in the last thing he saw as he finally fled the concert hall — the lifeless form of a young girl, no more than thirteen or fourteen, trampled under the feet of the heedless crowd. He recognized her as someone who had brushed up against him in the thick of the disturbance. Casually, he had knocked her aside with his elbow and had seen her go down. He had given the incident no further thought until the sight of her dead body brought home to him the brutal evidence of what he had become.

Since that night, he had forsworn his faerie nature. Adopting the name Cyprian Ryder, he cut his ties with the court and dropped out of changeling society, immersing himself in the real world with an intensity born of desperation. For years, he avoided any evidence of Glamour, wanting nothing more than to live out his mortal life span untainted by faerie madness. But for the clear blue stone embedded in his left palm, visible only to those with faerie kenning, he would have succeeded in his desire.

What splendidly vicious stroke of irony singled him out as its target, he had yet to discover. Even now, he had trouble remembering the occasion which forever condemned him to a state of perpetual inner conflict. All he could recall was a seemingly chance encounter with a street musician, a wandering minstrel who accosted him one evening in a bar, plied him with liquor and began asking him questions that at first struck him as bizarre. Too late, he realized that his drinking partner was a changeling and that his questions were intended to confirm his own changeling nature. Ryder had gotten up to leave, but before he could get away, the minstrel had grabbed his hand — his left hand — and pressed something into his palm. "Take this," he had said in an urgent whisper. "It will remind you who you are and lead you to your destiny." He felt a searing pain in his palm, as if someone had driven a hot nail into its fleshy center. He rushed from the bar and into the street, running blindly from the agony that sealed itself within his hand.

Now, despite his efforts to deny it, he was never far from his faerie nature. At first he considered having the hand amputated. While he was still debating the pros and cons of radical surgery, he began to notice that the pain in his palm seemed to ebb and flow in direct proportion to his proximity to a source of Glamour, particularly the kind of Glamour that indicated the presence of changelings. With that discovery had come the revelation of his true mission, to hunt down changelings and end the danger they posed to the unknowing world. Not long after that, he ran into others like himself. From his court days, he remembered hearing rumors of individuals who spent their time tracking down and destroying changelings. Dauntain, they were called, anathema to both Seelie and Unseelie, for they made no distinction between the two divisions of changelings. Some Dauntain were mortals, survivors of Ravagings or jilted lovers abandoned by the fickle winds that governed the affections of changelings. Others were changelings themselves; like him, they had come to despise their inner natures.

Darkness had settled on the city before Ryder finally decided to call an end to his day's wanderings. He returned to his hotel, ordered a meal from room service, and sat down at the desk in his room to eat and study the marks he had made on his map. He smiled grimly as he interpreted his private system for noting relative concentrations of Glamour. He had been able to cover nearly a quarter of the city since he began his travels this morning, and already the map was pockmarked with red dots and circles. According to the information relayed to him by the fluctuations of his pain, the greatest concentration of Glamour he had discovered so far centered around the section of the city known as the Haight. Somehow, that didn't surprise him in the least.

Before he went to bed, Ryder reread the brief letter from Dr. Walters. He replaced it carefully in his wallet when he had finished. He hoped she would not be too disappointed at his failure to reply to her appeal for help. Although there was every likelihood that she would be able to lead him to one changeling, he doubted that the doctor would approve of his suggestions for dealing with her client — apparently a child. Instead, he preferred to take the doctor's letter for what it was, a sign that he had been called to San Francisco to purge

the area of its changeling taint. He would just as soon
not have too many mortal witnesses to what he would
have to do to accomplish that task.

"We must begin to consider the possibility that the
duke is succumbing to Bedlam, Sir Cumulus." Lady
Alyssa walked with the Duke's Herald in the formal
gardens at the rear of the estate's grounds.

"His Grace is noted for his moodiness, my lady." Sir
Cumulus's reply came after a long moment's thought
and did not sound convincing.

"His current mood has lasted for quite some time
now," Lady Alyssa observed.

Sir Cumulus mumbled a gruff concession to her
statement.

"Since last Beltaine, as a matter of fact," the duke's
chamberlain added. "More than four months."

Sir Cumulus sighed heavily. "I fear there is nought
we can do, my Lady, save maintain as best we can."

"We can appeal to Queen Aeron," Alyssa said.

"Absolutely not!" Sir Cumulus exploded, his furor
causing a shower of chimeric sparks to erupt about him
in the twilight. Alyssa waited patiently for the sparks
to dissipate.

"This morning, he made a brief appearance only to
order all the furnishings of his room removed and to
commandeer bolts of black velvet. I worry about his new
taste for morbidity," she said.

"I understand black is quite the rage among the
mortal youth these days," Sir Cumulus observed.

"It is also quite the rage among the Unseelie," Lady
Alyssa said sharply.

"Surely you are not suggesting that the duke has forsaken his allegiance to the Seelie Court!" Sir Cumulus exclaimed, horror evident in his voice.

"I suggest nothing, Sir Cumulus," Lady Alyssa said. "I only desire to express my concern for the welfare of the duchy — not to mention the duke."

"The duke is the duchy," Cumulus pontificated, expressing a variation on the faerie belief, once part of mortal cosmology as well, that the destiny of a realm was bound to that of its ruler and that the land itself prospered or suffered according to its ruler's fortunes.

"Precisely," Lady Alyssa said. "Or have you been so out of touch with the world outside this sheltered freehold that you have failed to notice that there seem to be far fewer hours of sunlight and a greater density in the fog that clings so tenaciously to this city?"

"It is autumn, my lady," Sir Cumulus observed. "The weather is usually less clement in the fall season. And there have been some sunny days." The knight's voice sounded almost petulant.

"It is early autumn," Alyssa replied tartly, "and for the last week there has been a persistent and increasing grayness to the weather. It is my opinion that the brief spates of sunlight are largely due to the influence of Princess Aliera. As Aeon's heir-apparent, she does exercise some small control over the realm as well."

Alyssa smiled one of her rare smiles as she thought briefly of Aliera's sweet disposition and pristine sense of wonder. It had been a wise decision to remove the child early from the influence of her mortal parents and raise her entirely within the freehold. Her childling nature could be preserved intact for many decades so long as her exposure to the erosive character of the mortal world was severely curtailed. At least, she thought to herself, Aliera gave her no trouble. Ensconced in her own suite of rooms amid her chimerical toys and devoted fosterling companions, the princess could indulge her playful nature shamelessly, protected from the duke's brooding presence.

"I have not seen the princess lately," Sir Cumulus said. "I do hope she is well."

Alyssa nodded emphatically. "I decided that it is best for the childling to remain in her rooms for the nonce. She shouldn't have to suffer the pall of gloom that troubles the rest of us. I have, myself, elected to avoid the pleasure her company affords me rather than infect her with my cares."

Sir Cumulus patted Lady Alyssa's hand. "I admire your forbearance and your fortitude in bearing so nobly the burdens that have been thrust upon you by the duke's latest... temporary... infatuation with melancholy." He emphasized the word "temporary" with an arched eyebrow.

Together, the couple turned and paced slowly back along the garden path toward the rear of the duke's palace. As they passed the heated pool behind the house, they paused to look upward at the rear balcony just outside Aeon's second floor suite. In the growing darkness, they could just make out the black curtains that covered both windows and the door onto the balcony. Silently, chamberlain and herald resumed their progress toward the house.

Until last night, Glynnis feared that she had been deserted by that regal presence whose wisdom had directed her recent activities. Since the apparent failure — a second time — and subsequent disappearance of the vile satyr who had claimed to be a wizard of great potency, she had heard nothing from her imprisoned lord. Then, last night, the captive prince had sent her another dream. It had been a faint sending, as if performed at great cost to its sender, but from it she had been able to extract two important pieces of information.

First, that the Eye of Opening had been passed to a more fitting subject and that the prince himself would oversee its eventual use in his behalf. Second, that she was to concentrate specifically and exclusively on achieving the downfall of Duke Aeon. Her primary duty now lay in reducing to chaos the Seelie Court of the fief of Goldengate.

The dream had renewed her devotion to its sender. She had failed, yes, but she had also been forgiven. Reaching for the familiar ebon harp, she clutched it firmly between her knees and began to play with all the dark passion of her Unseelie nature.

A single candle ensconced in an open globe of ruby-colored crystal shone on Aeon's desk. The sidhe lord sat hunched over his piles of ruined sheet-music, frantically trying to capture the notes that rang from the ebony harp at his side. Caliendra's harp, he now called it, for he was certain that her spirit was entrapped within its wooden form. Once they had been lovers, oathbound for eternity. She had been his constant companion in both the changeling and the mortal worlds. When he and his band toured nearby cities, playing for changelings and mortals to inspire them with the Glamour of their music, she had traveled with him, the source of his private inspiration and the sharer of his deepest passions.

Seven years ago in Sacramento, at the final performance of a fortnight's tour, she had somehow been discovered by a group of Dauntain, who had managed to separate her from Aeon and his band, snatching her off the street and dragging her into the back of a van. Aeon had chased them through the night, unable to catch up with them and frantic at the thought that she was in malevolent hands. Finally, they had flung her body out of the rear of the van into the path of Aeon's own vehicle before fleeing into the darkness. She was already dead when he skidded to a stop and rushed outside to cradle her lifeless body, full of gashes that appeared more like scorch marks than stabs from a knife. His faerie sight told him that her murderers had used cold iron to destroy her faerie nature, signifying the utter annihilation of the bright, joyous spirit that was Caliendra.

He had mourned her, but despite his overwhelming sorrow, he knew his duty as Duke of Goldengate. He had tried to put aside his grief and lose himself in music and affairs of state. He thought he had succeeded in living without hope until last Beltaine, when among the gifts he had received from his subjects, he discovered a graceful ebony harp that sang with Caliendra's voice, but in an unknown tongue.

Since then, he had determined to unlock its secrets, certain that the spirit of his love was trying to show him a way to return her to him in the flesh. Every moment he could spare, he now devoted to transcribing its elusive notes. All else was mere distraction.

Sighing as he regarded yet another page of indecipherable markings, Aeon crumpled up his latest effort, the work of an entire evening, and reached for a clean sheet of paper. His hand trembling from exhaustion and his eyes bleary from lack of sleep, he strained once more to hear the elusive words of Caliendra's song.

chapter

twelve

Leigh paced back and forth along the Rose Walk, a private garden surrounded by tall hedges that lined one wall of the duke's palace. Since their battle with Malacar five days ago, she had been coming to the Nob Hill mansion daily, hoping to gain an audience with the duke. So far, she had met with no success. She looked at the immaculately trimmed path beneath her feet for signs that she was wearing a rut in the raked earth.

"I thought I was a knight, not a lady-in-waiting," she muttered to herself, kicking a rock from the path just to disturb the symmetry.

She told herself repeatedly that Duke Aeon had many responsibilities, and that he and his advisers could not be expected to drop everything to hear a knight's report of her partially successful mission. She wondered if Aeon would be angry that she and her oathmates had not gotten more information from Malacar before the satyr fled. She had already berated herself for failing to question him after the defeat of the dragon, but somehow the sight of Malacar ripping what had seemed to be his left eye out of his head, followed almost immediately by the arrival of the chimeric horde, had driven from her mind the second part of the duke's charge. She hoped Valmont was right in insisting that they would find out more about what the wily satyr had intended by keeping an eye out for some of his known allies than they would have gleaned from Malacar himself. Valmont implied, although he did not say, that he had an idea as to who those allies were. Privately, Leigh wondered about Valmont's reputed connections with the Shadow Court and how the eshu reconciled his position as an adviser to Count Elias with his plethora of Unseelie contacts.

She reached for the small velvet pouch that now hung from her waist. Feeling through the cloth for the gemstone resting within it, she contemplated whether she should turn the item over to the duke. After they had safely returned the chimerae to the Toybox and received Fizzlewig's formal thanks, she and the others had argued about what to do with the emerald. Both she and Morgan wanted to take it to the duke. Edmund and Valmont had argued against that. Tor refused to commit himself, while Rasputin wholeheartedly supported the idea of placing the gem in the safekeeping of the Seelie Court. The pooka's opinion tipped the scales in favor of keeping the gem, at least long enough to discover something about it.

Leigh felt as though she had been waiting for hours. Usually she had been turned away, politely but firmly, after only a few minutes of pacing the garden walk. She wondered what would happen if she insisted on seeing someone in the duke's confidence. She would gratefully accept an audience with Lady Alyssa or even Sir Cumulus if such a meeting could be arranged with more alacrity than an appointment with Duke Aeon.

There was also the matter of her phone conversation with Morgan yesterday morning. The childling had been on the verge of tears as she confided to Leigh, whispering so that her words were almost incomprehensible, that she didn't think she could continue to live at home anymore. She begged Leigh to tell the duke that she wanted to come live at the court. Morgan had sounded so upset that Leigh had promised to pass along her request. Once again, Leigh felt lucky that she had not become aware of her changeling nature until her childling years had passed.

Leigh heard the sound of footsteps on the gravel behind her. She turned, expecting to find a page arriving with the information that she would have to wait until a more suitable time — the message that had concluded all her previous trips to the palace.

Instead of a page, however, a slender eshu childling whom Leigh had seen in the company of Princess Aliera stood self-consciously in the middle of the path.

"The princess will see you now," the childling informed her. "Please come with me."

Mystified, Leigh followed her escort into the palace.

The Princess Aliera was royally bored. Since Fall Court, no one except her personal retainers and playmates had paid any attention to her. It wasn't that she was neglected, she realized. She had hundreds of toys and thousands of things to do to occupy her time in her own suite of rooms in the west wing, but Lady Alyssa and Duke Aeon hadn't visited her in days.

From the whispered conversations she overheard when people thought she wasn't listening, she knew that something was wrong with Duke Aeon and that the palace was in an uproar — a quiet one — but an uproar just the same. When she tried to ask her governess about that, she was told not to bother herself about things that didn't concern her.

She was supposed to be taking a nap, something Lady Alyssa insisted was still necessary for one of her "tender years." She had retired to her bedroom and tried to sleep, but no matter how hard she worked at feeling drowsy, she was wide awake. And bored.

Aliera rose from her ruffled canopy bed and

wandered aimlessly about her room, picking up and discarding toy after toy. Nothing held her interest. She peered out the window that overlooked the Rose Walk and saw Dame Eleighanara pacing back and forth along the path. She thought about pecking on the window and catching the knight's attention so she could wave hello. At least that would be more contact with the world outside her rooms than she had had for some time. Her trips outside to play now involved using the servants' stairs and avoided all the main rooms of the palace. She felt as if no one wanted her around. As she watched the knight below her kick a small rock from the path, seeming to echo her own frustration, Aliera decided to take matters into her own hands.

Opening her bedroom door, she beckoned for Layla, one of her playmates, to come into her room. The eshu childling had been brought to the court as a favor to Count Elias. Within a few days of her arrival, Layla had discovered two secret passages in the palace and had quickly shown them to Aliera. One led from the library to the duke's private receiving chamber on the ground floor, and the other led from the palace wine cellar to the cabana near the swimming pool outside. In time, Layla had assured Aliera, she was certain she could find many more.

"Can you find out why Dame Eleighanara is here?" she asked her companion, who stood beside her looking out the window down at the pacing knight.

Layla cocked her head smugly and smiled. "I already know," she said, her childish voice ringing with importance. "She's here to see the duke, but she'll be turned away again."

"Why?" Aliera asked innocently.

Layla's expression grew serious. "I'm not supposed to tell you," she said.

"Nobody tells me anything," Aliera complained. "Will you tell me anyway?"

"You are my princess," Layla said coyly. "If you command me to tell you, I can't refuse."

"Tell me, then," Aliera said. "I command it."

Layla went over to the throne-shaped rocking chair in the corner of Aliera's room and seated herself on its rose-colored velvet cushion. Resting her elbows on the arms of the rocker and steepling her fingers, she gave Aliera a look of practiced wisdom. The princess perched on the edge of her bed and waited for the eshu's answer.

"Duke Aeon is writing a great song," the eshu child said, "and he has commanded that no one disturb him until it is done. Lady Alyssa and Sir Cumulus have orders to keep away anyone who might prove to be a distraction."

"Oh," said Aliera, glad to finally have a believable explanation for the strange behavior around her. "But that's not fair to Eleighanara!"

"She has come here more than once requesting an audience," Layla informed her. "I heard she has returned from a great quest."

Aliera clapped her hands delightedly. "I know about her quest!" she said, excitement in her voice. "Baroness Morgania was part of it, too. I was there when the Duke quested her."

Layla shook her head sadly. "It is a pity that there is no one to hear the story of her deeds," she said mournfully.

Aliera's eyes sparkled. "That's not true," she said. "I'm here, and it's about time I started accepting some responsibility at court." She slid off the bed and walked over to Layla. Taking the eshu's hand, she raised her out of the rocker and pulled her to the door.

"Go downstairs and tell Dame Eleighanara that I want to see her. Can you bring her up here without anyone knowing?"

Layla gave the princess a broad grin. "I have been waiting for the opportunity to show you my latest discoveries," she said, walking away from the bedroom door toward the door to Aliera's closet. Opening the door, she stepped inside and disappeared behind a rack of dresses and gowns. Aliera heard something being slid to one side within the closet.

"Wait here." Layla's voice seemed to come from deep within the closet. "I'll bring her to you in a few minutes."

Leigh emerged cautiously from the dark passage, stooping to keep from hitting her head against the low door frame. She was so elated at finally being admitted into the palace that she had not dared question the route taken by the eshu childling. Once she realized that her destination was the Princess Aliera's bedroom, the strangeness of her journey became very clear.

Aliera sat in a small rocking chair, shaped like a throne. In her hand she held a miniature scepter. Leigh bit her lip to keep from smiling at the grave look on the princess's face. Reminding herself that royalty — even childling royalty — deserved a proper show of respect, Leigh bowed to Aliera. The princess gave her a stately nod of acknowledgment.

"We understand you have been seeking an audience," Aliera said. "Will I do?"

Edmund was on his way to the Toybox with his news when the dark-haired man accosted him, seemingly coming out of nowhere to stand in his path. Edmund looked around him, and realized that he was in a part of the Haight noted for its plethora of bizarre — no, downright weird — shops. He'd heard rumors that sometimes vampires prowled this area late at night, but he'd never seen one. If it weren't for the fact that it was still daylight, the predatory look on the face of the man who blocked his way might lead him to believe he had just met his first real live member of the undead. Edmund looked up at the man suspiciously, reaching into his pocket for the comforting feel of his knife as he spoke.

"You want something?" he asked, wishing his voice would go ahead and break so that he didn't sound so much like a kid.

The man stared at him, dark eyes flaring in his hawk-like face. Edmund noticed that he flexed his left hand repeatedly, as if limbering his fingers up in case he had to make a quick grab for something. Like a fleeing child.

"I have need of information," the man said, his voice stilted.

"Go get a newspaper," said Edmund, pointing past the man to a rack of papers that stood outside a corner drug store. He grimaced when the man failed to turn his head in the direction Edmund had indicated.

"A newspaper will not tell me what I need to know," the stranger said.

Edmund backed up a step. When the man allowed him that much distance, the redcap relaxed. Maybe this wasn't a snatch and grab after all.

"What do ya' want?" he asked. The man smiled at Edmund, giving the redcap a brief glimpse of his teeth. The childling felt a little disappointed at the lack of points on the man's eyeteeth.

"I am newly come to this fief," the stranger said, placing a heavy accent on "fief" and raising an eyebrow to further emphasize the word. "I seek congress with others of my kind."

Edmund felt an odd, prickly sensation travel up the back of his neck. He hadn't been aware that he'd been projecting his faerie nature so strongly. Usually, when he traveled around town, he tried to keep his true self under wraps. Unlike the Seelie wimps he'd been hanging around with lately, Edmund wasn't as afraid of slipping into the Banal world as they were. Some of his friends in Oakland did it all the time, and had shown Edmund how to use Banality to protect himself from other changelings. He hadn't really had a chance to experiment on anyone, although his recent encounter with the overwhelmingly Banal atmosphere of Kurtz-whats-it's toy store had proven to him that he could absorb more disbelief than most of his fellow kithain.

Edmund decided to risk a peek with faerie sight. What he saw was not comforting, but it was cool. Too cool. The "man" looked like some gothic knight of no court he had ever seen. His dark brown hair, pulled back at the neck in a long ponytail, hung nearly to his waist. He wore a killer suit of black chain mail. At his belt, where a sword would normally be, was an empty scabbard. On his other side, a slim sheath held a dagger, its black tipped pommel just visible above the top of its casing. The dagger was real, Edmund saw, and the man wore it in such a way that it was concealed beneath the jacket of his mortal clothing. It was also iron.

"I don't know what you're talking about, mister," Edmund said, deciding it was time to try the old Banality trick for real. Swallowing hard, he thought about nuclear bombs and oil spills and public schools and electric chairs and politicians and Muzak. Edmund saw the man frown, and tried to imagine what the man must be seeing. He thought of

Rasputin's ears slowly fading after he got smoked by the chimeric cannonball.

This time, the man stepped backward, an awkward expression on his face.

"I must have been mistaken," he said.

Edmund turned and fled. He ducked into an alley, panting, and panicked as he tried to remember what he had been doing a few minutes before. His hand, still in his pocket, clutched a rusty butter knife. Edmund wondered what it was doing there. He started methodically searching his pockets for some clue. None of the junk he carried on him made any sense until his hand closed on what felt like a metal figure. He pulled out a miniature painted clown, and stared at it. It began to glow softly, and suddenly, Edmund remembered everything.

He breathed a low whistle of relief. This Banality trick was more dangerous than he'd figured. Maybe he'd need a few more lessons before he attempted it again. Still, it had worked. He peered in both directions before leaving the alley to resume his trek to the Toybox.

"Thanks, pal," he muttered to the clown, its glow now dampened to a faint glimmer. "I hope you didn't get wasted," he said, stuffing the figure quickly in his pocket and edging his way carefully down the street, keeping his eye out for anyone who might be following him.

Now he had two pieces of information to tell Valmont and the others if they showed up tonight. The trouble was, he wasn't sure what the meeting with the strange knight meant. Just before he reached the Toybox, he remembered one thing more about the stranger. With his faerie sight, he had noticed a strange blue glow coming from the knight's left hand.

If nothing else, Leigh thought, Princess Aliera was a good listener. The childling sat quietly with a thoughtful expression on her face as Leigh described the chimerae's escape from the toy chest, the harried pursuit through the Haight, and the encounter with Malacar and the dragon in the Japanese Tea Garden.

When Leigh confessed that although she had delivered the duke's formal order of banishment to Malacar, she and her companions had neglected to learn the reasons behind the satyr's actions, Aliera's face had twisted into a frown. Then the princess shrugged, looking like a miniature Lady Alyssa, and the frown faded away.

"At least you put the ban upon him," she said. "And you saved all those wonderful creatures from a horrible fate and got them back where they belonged."

"I still feel that we should have accomplished more," Leigh said. "Valmont thinks that he might be able to locate Malacar's associates and get some information from them about Malacar's intentions."

Princess Aliera nodded. "I like Valmont," she said. "He's polite enough to be nobility."

"Among the other eshu," Leigh replied, "he is nobility."

"I'm glad," the princess said, sounding relieved. "He deserves to be more than just a commoner."

Leigh heard the innocence behind the princess' pronouncement and decided against turning her royal audience into a lecture on the arrogance of the sidhe. Instead, she told Aliera about Morgan's troubles.

"We shall have to do something to help her," Aliera announced when Leigh finished. "She shouldn't have to be so miserable!"

Leigh nodded glumly. "I told Morgan I would ask the duke for help."

"That's all right," Aliera said, her voice firm. "I promise you I shall pass her request on to someone who can assist her with her problem."

Leigh gave the childling a grateful smile. "Thank you, your Highness," she said. "It is my hope that you will have more influence in this matter than I do."

Aliera asked Leigh a few more questions about Morgan's home life and asked to hear again about the chimerae from the toy chest. Then she stood, signaling that the audience was over. Leigh left the princess's bedroom by the secret passage through the closet, which led, via a winding set of stairs, to a small room just off the pantry. From there, Leigh slipped quietly through the kitchen and outside the palace.

It was only when she reached the Toybox Coffee Shop that she realized that she had not told the princess about the emerald stone.

After Leigh had gone, Aliera turned to Layla, who had been sitting quietly in the corner of the princess' room amid a pile of velvet and satin pillows.

"We must to do something to help Baroness Morgania," Aliera told her companion.

The eshu nodded solemnly, her dark eyes growing wide with concern.

"Here's what I want you to do," she said.

the

"But what's it do?" Edmund said, as Leigh brought out the stone once more for the others to examine. With the exception of Morgan, the five oathmates had gathered at the Toybox to decide what they needed to do next to fulfill the remainder of the duke's command. They had commandeered a table near the rear of the coffee shop, near Tor's usual booth. Valmont, Leigh, Edmund and Rasputin sat at the table, while Tor looked on from his accustomed place.

"We know that Malacar used it to open the toy chest," Valmont said, reaching for the gem and rolling it around on top of the table. "It feels almost hot to me," the eshu observed.

"Let me see it!" Edmund said, grabbing the gem up and dropping it again just as quickly. "Yowch!" he cried.

Rasputin caught the stone before it could skitter off the edge of the table. "Oh, yes," he said. "I can feel the heat coursing through my bones." The pooka held the gem up to the light before passing it on to Tor.

Tor held the stone gingerly in the palm of his massive hand. He frowned as he studied it.

"What is it?" Leigh asked, catching the troll's expression.

Tor shook his head. "Nothing. I thought it reminded me of something but—"

"Well, I just remembered something," said Edmund, sounding full of self-importance. "I went to Oakland this morning to see some friends of mine — yours, too, Valmont," he added conspiratorially. Valmont raised an eyebrow.

"Who were these people?" asked Leigh.

"I promised I wouldn't betray my sources of information," Edmund replied smugly. "They claim that the Oakland People's Front — that's Blade's gang — have been spreading around a lot of Dross, like they'd just been paid for something big."

toybox

"This 'they' you keep mentioning couldn't possibly be Ragger's Band?" Rasputin asked, his soft eyes full of apparent innocence.

Leigh looked questioningly at first Edmund, who shrugged, and then at Valmont. The eshu folded his hands on the table and leaned forward.

"An assortment of scoundrels, thieves and rogues who follow a boggan by the name of Ragger," he informed the others. "Among other things, they're noted for their anti-sidhe sentiment, though the reason for their dislike of the fae nobility escapes me." He smiled to soften the sarcasm in his voice.

"I never said it was Ragger's Band," Edmund said, giving Rasputin a sneer. "Anyway, they — my contacts — said that Blade and his group have gotten hold of a bunch of iron weapons, swords and knives and arrows and stuff."

"Like the knife that wounded Valmont?" Leigh asked.

"By the way," Fizzlewig said, coming up to the group with a tray of drinks, "not to be nosy, but didn't you take that blasted thing to the duke to have it examined?"

Leigh nodded. "I delivered it to Lady Alyssa," she said. "So far I haven't heard anything more about it."

"Bad move," said Edmund. "Those jerks probably threw it away on trash night."

"There are problems going on at court," Leigh began, stopping herself as a look from Edmund told her that explanations would be useless.

Fizzlewig snorted.

"The court's always having problems," he said. "That's why nothing ever gets done around here. All they do is stand around and gab and look at each other to see who has the best duds. That's why I stay away from all that." He picked up his empty tray and ambled back to the bar.

the

"Are you saying that Malacar paid Blade for something in Dross and iron?" Valmont asked.

Edmund nodded. "My sources say that Blade was bragging about how close he came to taking out his 'competition' and that if he hadn't been instructed to wound instead of kill, he'd have nailed his target."

Valmont suppressed a shudder. "Blade has a certain reputation for his expertise with throwing knives," he said quietly.

"So why would Malacar pay him to hurt you?" Tor asked.

"Maybe he wants to be head of the Shadow Court instead of you," Edmund said to Valmont.

"Edmund!" Valmont's voice sounded like the crack of a whip. Rasputin flinched. The eshu took a deep breath and stared at the redcap childling. "For the last time," he said, "the Shadow Court convenes once a year — at Samhain — to elect a mock ruler for one night of misadventure. It is a reminder of a time when Seelie and Unseelie alternated their rule of faerie society, dividing the year at Samhain and Beltaine in homage to the balance of dark and light that exists within our natures. The title means nothing!" His last words sounded like the hiss of a snake poised to strike.

"Okay!" Edmund said, throwing his hands up in mock surrender. "Fine! It's no big deal. I just thought it sounded like a cool motive for someone to want to off you."

"Edmund!" This time the cry came from Leigh. "We're trying to put together a puzzle from a few mismatched pieces, not discuss the politics of the Shadow Court or the political sympathies some of us might entertain."

Edmund picked up his mug and sipped the dark cocoa sullenly. "Hey, Fizzlewig!" he called in the direction of the bar. "When can I have a beer?"

"When I think you're civilized enough to appreciate one," the boggan snapped.

"Just suppose," Rasputin said, "that the following statement is patently false." For the last few minutes, the pooka had been lost in contemplation, leaning back in his chair, his eyes closed. "Someone opens the door of this establishment, slings a dagger and a warning at Valmont. Shortly thereafter, Malacar challenges the duke at his own party and throws a wrench into the Seelie Court. That same evening, he and his two confederates execute a well-choreographed plan to open the toy chest and loose an army of chimerae into the streets of the city. Then Malacar kidnaps a bride doll and brings her to the Japanese Tea Gardens for some as yet unknown foul purpose." Rasputin paused, opening his eyes and staring at each of his companions in turn, looking for signs of comprehension in any of their faces.

No one responded to him. The pooka sighed in frustration, and began again. "Malacar, Slique and Larry are regulars at the Toybox, right, Fizzlewig?" he called over his shoulder.

From the bar, Fizzlewig shook his head. "I don't remember any of 'em coming here," he said.

"Exactly!" said Rasputin, directing his comment once more to his companions. "They're regulars."

"Get to the point," groaned Tor.

"I'm being as circuitous as possible," Rasputin replied. "Anyway, it didn't seem at all strange to me that these regular customers should know the precise layout of everything in the coffee shop — including the position of the toy chest and how to cause as much chaos as possible in the dark...."

Edmund jumped up from his chair, upsetting his half-finished mug of cocoa in his excitement. "I get it!" he chortled. "The point of the attack on Valmont

the

wasn't really to hurt Valmont. It was to distract people from what was really going on." He looked around at the others expectantly. Only Rasputin shook his head approvingly. "They used the time it took to open the door, throw the knife and yell out a threat to case the joint!" He sat back in his chair to Rasputin's applause.

The others looked in astonishment at the pooka and the redcap. Finally Valmont nodded his head slowly.

"I'm afraid it makes sense," he said.

"But why the Japanese Tea Garden?" asked Leigh. "Do you think we should go back there and look around to see if we can find out any reason for Malacar to have gone there?"

Tor rumbled his agreement.

"Tomorrow, then," said Valmont, "we meet here and go to the Park."

"If Malacar's gone," said Leigh, "won't the trouble stop?"

Valmont laughed. "Malacar is a powerful and dangerous individual in his own cretinous way," the eshu said, "but I don't think he is the source of the trouble. He seems to have amassed enough resources to engage the services of some of the duchy's most acquisitive elements. We're looking for whoever was plucking his strings, and that person is not going to be easy to find."

"I just remembered something else," Edmund said in an unusually subdued tone. "I met someone today." The redcap proceeded to recount his meeting with the strange changeling, dwelling in great detail on the suit of black armor and the iron dagger at his belt and carefully omitting his own precise method for dealing with the suspicious sidhe knight.

Leigh shook her head. "There's no one like that at court," she said.

"I told you he said he was a stranger," Edmund responded sneeringly.

"Whoever he was, you did well to get away from him," Valmont remarked. "It would probably be a good idea for us all to be on the alert for this person, and to avoid contact with him until we are certain of who he is and what he represents." The eshu rose from the table and looked toward the street door. "I have a few appointments — consultations...to tend to." Leigh looked at him curiously.

"Bread and butter, so to speak," the eshu replied, rubbing thumb and fingers together in an unmistakable gesture. The rest of the group began making motions to depart. Tor rose from his booth to return the emerald stone to Leigh, who replaced it carefully in her pouch. Leigh started to mention her phone conversation with Morgan's decision to leave her family, then decided she would wait for some response from the court before troubling the troll with his granddaughter's unhappiness. She watched the troll wander toward the back of the coffee shop and through the door in the rear that led to the building's basement. Then she, too, left the Toybox.

Rasputin and Edmund sat alone at the table after the others had gone.

"I'm glad Morgan wasn't here," Rasputin said, more to himself than to his redcap companion. "It's always so much harder being understood when she's around." Edmund nodded his agreement.

"Ain't that the truth," he mumbled.

Since her frantic phone call to Leigh, Morgan had been waiting anxiously for something to happen. She had been scrupulously good for the last two days, and her behavior was finally rewarded when her father replaced her bedroom door on its hinges. Although she appreciated the small gesture of trust, she was also disturbed by her parents' reactions to a phone call they had received earlier in the evening. She had tried to listen, but her father had spoken so quietly that she couldn't make out any of the words. Afterward, her parents had closeted themselves in her father's study for over an hour. When they finally emerged, Morgan could see that her mother had been crying.

Well after midnight a furtive scritching on her window roused Morgan from a fitful sleep. She rose from her bed and tiptoed to the window. An eshu childling, one of Princess Aliera's companions, waved to her from a tree just outside Morgan's room. As quietly as she could, Morgan eased her window open. The childling on the limb nodded, then waved her hands in the air in a complicated pattern. A moment later, she launched herself into the air, landing softly just inside Morgan's room.

In a few brief words, Layla explained to Morgan the plan she and Princess Aliera had devised.

Morgan's first reaction was one of delight. Then she had second thoughts.

"Isn't the princess taking a terrible risk?" she whispered.

Layla bobbed her head up and down vigorously. "Of course she is," the eshu said proudly. "But then, her honor as a princess requires that such risks be taken. Besides," the childling added, "spending some time in the world outside the freehold is something she has always wanted to do. She has remembered everything you have ever told her of your life with your parents, and she wants this experience for herself."

"But we don't resemble each other at all!" Morgan said. "My hair is dark and curly—"

"And the princess' hair is blond and curly," Layla said. "There are simple ways to change one's appearance, both with and without faerie magic."

"Are you sure this will work?" Morgan asked, her hopes beginning to rise.

The eshu nodded emphatically. "Absolutely. It will only be for a few days, anyway, until the duke finishes his masterwork and can turn his attention to solving your problem in a more permanent fashion."

"Even if Aliera can fool my parents," Morgan said, still doubtful, "won't Lady Alyssa and the princess' tutors know the difference?"

"No one has paid any attention to the princess in days," Layla said. "The only ones who might suspect are Aliera's playmates, and we have all sworn to assist her in this."

The two childlings made a few more plans, and then Morgan watched, fascinated, as Layla climbed out the window and slipped out of sight. A moment later, the rustle of branches told Morgan that the childling was on her way back to the duke's freehold.

Morgan returned to her bed and tried to fall asleep, but anticipation had replaced anxiety and sleep evaded her. She counted sheep, then dolls, then chimerae, before her eyes finally began to close of their own accord. She drifted into sleep wondering if her parents would realize that the child her father took to school tomorrow morning would not be the same child her mother would bring back home.

Rasputin ran from a hail of iron-tipped arrows. He ducked swiftly down the alley that beckoned him with its promise of safety from the barrage of archers that pursued him from one

the

end of the city to the other. Then he heard the cruel laughter at the far end of the narrow passage. Ahead of him, blocking his way, loomed a tall knight in black armor, a gleaming sword in one hand and an iron dagger in the other.

"You're not a Dauntain!" he screamed at the figure. "You're not a hunter!"

Rasputin awoke in a cold sweat, gasping as if his flight had been more than just a dream. He sat up in bed and reached in the dark for the cloth juggling balls that he kept next to his mattress. Their familiar rhythm helped him slow his breathing. He tossed the balls back and forth until his hands grew numb and his eyelids grew heavy. Letting the balls fall softly to the floor, he sank once more into sleep.

The sound of the familiar voice woke the creature from what passed for sleep. "Hunter," the voice of his creator said, and the creature's brain fastened on that single word. "Hunter... Hunter... Hunter...." The sound echoed through its chimeric being like a caress. Now it had what all real things must have. It had a name.

chapter

thirteen

Leigh sighed with relief when her lunchtime shift at Mardi's ended. Either the late hours and her near-constant immersion in the world of the Dreaming were beginning to extract a toll on her reflexes, or else she was in the early stages of some neuromuscular disorder. Even in her earliest days as a waitress, when she was still learning the ropes, she had never demonstrated such a lack of coordination as she had today.

Twice in her first hour at work she had managed to prematurely spring open the cash drawer, invalidating the bills she was ringing up. Georges had removed her from her usual kitchen prep duties — normally her opportunity to glean a few cooking tips from the master chef — after she had somehow managed to upset a sealed barrel of fresh coffee beans, spilling them all over the kitchen floor. She usually had no trouble threading her way between tables, snaking past the clutter of purses hung from chairs and briefcases perched near their owners' feet; this morning, however, three purses and a locked briefcase had sprung open at her passing, emptying their contents in her wake. She hadn't remembered brushing up against any of the items.

She considered herself lucky that she hadn't actually dropped anything. Briefly, she entertained the idea of stopping by a bookstore and browsing through the popular medicine collection to see if she could find evidence of a degenerative disease that started at the hips. Instinctively, her hand strayed to the pouch containing the stone. At least her rampant clumsiness hadn't shaken it loose from her waist. She poked tentatively at her left hip, just below the spot where the pouch dangled, for signs of soreness.

Halfway across the street to her bus stop, Leigh stopped, bringing traffic around her to a screeching halt.

"It's not me, it's the damn stone!" she said, as the explanation for her morning mishaps suddenly became clear.

"Get out of the road, lady!" On either side of her, annoyed drivers honked their horns and gestured through their windows.

Hastily, Leigh finished crossing the street. All the way to the Toybox, she kept her hand firmly wrapped around her pouch and tried to stay as far away as possible from anything that had a lock, catch, clasp, or latch.

Morgan and Aliera switched places at noon, during the lunchtime confusion at the Stratton School. Layla and the princess were waiting in the girls' bathroom, where amid muffled giggles, Morgan and Aliera switched clothing, and Layla braided Aliera's newly dyed "black" hair to imitate Morgan's single, waist-length plait. Morgan wondered briefly how the two childlings had gotten onto the school grounds without being detected. She decided it was Layla's eshu skill at being in the right place at the right time.

Hurriedly, Morgan explained her afternoon schedule to Aliera and told her how to open the combination lock on her locker. Aliera nodded excitedly as Morgan tried to brief her on everything she might need to know.

Finally, the princess held up her hand to silence Morgan.

"Enough!" she said. "It isn't as though I don't know anything about you, Morgan Daniels. Concern yourself no further with me, except to tell me whether I look enough like you to be convincing."

Morgan studied the princess, now dressed in her own pleated skirt and fashionably baggy pullover.

"It's really a very good likeness," she said after a minute. "I understand about the hair, but how did you do the rest?"

Aliera and Layla exchanged knowing looks, then Aliera beamed at Morgan.

"The duke has many faerie treasures in the palace," she said primly. "It is my duty as his appointed heir to learn of their natures." She held her right hand out, palm downward, so that Morgan could see the thin silver ring that circled her middle finger. "This ring was fashioned beneath the shade of an elder tree by a great faerie smith ages and ages ago. At least so I was told. With it, I can make others see me as you."

"Doesn't the duke keep things like that locked away somewhere?" Morgan asked.

"Oh, yes," Layla said gravely. "There are many lovely things in the royal treasury that no one ever uses. It is so sad."

Morgan decided not to ask any more questions about the ring. She looked down at herself, clad in Aliera's clothing, and wished that the princess did not have such a strong fondness for pink and ruffles. Her hair, hanging in loose curls over her shoulders, caught her attention.

"What about me?" she asked, in a sudden panic. "They'll never believe I'm you just because I'm wearing your clothes—"

"It will not matter," Layla spoke up, as if anticipating Morgan's concern. "If anybody sees you, we shall make

the

it known that you are visiting the princess. Everything at the palace is so topsy-turvy that it is not very likely that anyone will even notice that you are there — or that the princess is not."

"I think it is time to begin our adventure," the princess said, looking at Morgan's watch on her own wrist. "It is nearly one of the clock," she announced triumphantly.

"O'clock," Morgan corrected. "Maybe you'd better not go around telling people what time it is," she added.

"Why should I?" Aliera asked. "Do not they have their own arm clocks?"

"We must go quickly, while there is no one in the hall outside," Layla said, pulling Morgan toward the rest room door. Morgan eased the door open and peeked outside before leaving the bathroom. The hallway was deserted.

"Good luck," she whispered to Aliera, and hurried out the door. No one stopped the pair of childlings as they left the school building and headed across town to the palace.

Aliera straightened her braid before the mirror in the bathroom, took a deep breath, and pushed the door open into the hallway. As she made her way past the other students returning from lunch, she heard a loud bell resound throughout the building. She looked about her wildly for a moment before remembering that bells announced the beginnings and endings of classes. She stared down the long hallway at the rows of doors that lined both walls and tried to remember if Morgan's next class was in Room 4A or 6C. Finally, she walked up to one of the older children and dropped a small curtsey in front of the startled boy.

"Prithee, sir," she said, remembering that as Morgan, she needed to act as if these mortals were

t o y b o x

her equals, "can you direct me to the classroom of science?"

She listened carefully to the boy's directions, expressed her profuse thanks, and made her way down the hall, pleased with her first success in dealing with the mortal world.

Layla took Morgan from school to the palace, where she helped Morgan install herself in Aliera's rooms. The princess' playmates were all there to greet her and to assure her that they would do their best to make certain Aliera's absence remained unnoticed. The eshu helped Morgan find some clothes that suited her own tastes, and then took her on a tour of the palace via a maze of servants' corridors and secret passages.

At one point, as they neared the top of a narrow set of back stairs, Layla stopped Morgan on a landing and pointed to a small indentation set into the wall. Next to it was a tiny hole.

"The duke's chambers are on the other side of this wall," the eshu informed Morgan. "And this," she tapped the indentation lightly with a forefinger, "I believe will open a door into his rooms. I have not tried it, because I think it would be unwise to disturb his Grace."

"Does everyone know about these places?" Morgan asked.

"I do not think this one has been used in some time," Layla replied in a whisper, shaking her head. "I suspect such passages had their uses when rich mortals desired for servants to appear to be invisible."

When she was confident that she could slip into and out of the palace without being noticed, Morgan thanked her newfound friend and made her first unaccompanied foray across town to the Haight.

Rasputin was already at the Toybox when Leigh arrived. The pooka waved a hand languidly in her direction.

"Everybody's here, as you can see," he called out.

Leigh joined him at what she had begun to think of as their table and waited while Fizzlewig brought her a glass of iced tea laced with heavy cream. "It's a variation on what they drink in Thailand," the boggan informed her. "I spiced it up a little."

"How did you know I was in the mood for something cold and creamy?" Leigh asked, bemused.

Fizzlewig shrugged. "I've been doing this for a long time," he said. Before Leigh could compliment him on the drink, the boggan had slipped back to the bar.

Leigh turned to greet Rasputin, but the sight posed by the bedraggled pooka stopped the words in her throat.

"What's the matter?" she asked instead, her brows wrinkled in concern.

Rasputin made a feeble attempt at a smile. "Nothing," he said. "I had a perfectly restful night and woke up completely refreshed."

"I'm sorry," Leigh said. She looked past Rasputin at the empty back booth. "Where's Tor?" she asked.

"I didn't notice he was missing," Rasputin mumbled so half-heartedly that Leigh almost believed him.

The door to the coffee shop opened and Morgan bounded in, wearing a dark, rose-colored belted tunic

toybox

over a pair of black tights and soft leather boots laced to her knees. At her waist, she carried a small, silvery dagger. She ran up to Leigh and threw her arms around her neck.

"Thank you for helping me!" she whispered into Leigh's ear. "Have you told the others?" she asked, her voice still hushed. Leigh shook her head.

"No, why?" she asked, instinctively matching her voice to Morgan's.

"Must you yell so loudly?" Rasputin complained.

"I'd rather handle it myself," Morgan said, disengaging herself from Leigh and taking a chair at the table just in time to accept a frothy strawberry drink from Fizzlewig. She started to thank the proprietor when she noticed two figures entering the coffee shop.

"Grandpa!" she cried, getting up from her seat and running forward to meet Tor. Just behind Tor, Valmont held the door open as a redcap whirlwind dashed past him, skidding to a stop just before he collided with the table.

"Hello, Edmund," said Leigh.

Edmund looked back over his shoulder at Morgan and Tor.

"What's she doing here?" he asked. "I thought she had to go to school." He plopped himself into a chair next to Rasputin. "Hey Morgan!" he called across the room to her. "Playing hooky again?"

"That's none of your business," Leigh answered for the childling.

"Are we all here, then?" asked Valmont, joining the group at the table. Tor and Morgan, hand-in-hand, followed him.

"You look worse than I do," Rasputin said to Tor, brightening a little as the company of his friends drove away the vague anxieties that had been plaguing him all morning.

the

"Hey, yeah!" said Edmund. "You look nearly decent today, Tor. Where ya' been? I thought you never left this place."

Tor seated his bulk at the table and allowed Morgan to scramble onto his lap. "I get out sometimes," he said.

"Tor and I have been visiting some of the curio shops in the neighborhood," Valmont said.

"He means pawn shops, I'll bet," Edmund whispered to Rasputin.

"Did you find anything interesting, Grandpa?" Morgan asked, looking up at him as she spoke. Unseen by her, Edmund mouthed Morgan's words, feigning a look of stupefied adoration. Valmont frowned at him.

"I saw a few antique swords in one of 'em," the troll said.

"Tor and I share an interest in old weaponry," Valmont said quietly. "I thought the contact with some pieces of military history might help inspire him."

"Hmph," Rasputin mumbled. "I always knew that was where he collected Glamour."

"Can we go now?" asked Edmund. "Or do we have to sit around and talk some more?"

"Go where?" Morgan asked.

"The Japanese Tea Garden," Leigh said. "I forgot to tell you that we decided to go back there to see if we could learn what Malacar was doing when we found him." As Leigh started to get up from her chair, her hand brushed against her waist pouch. She sat down quickly. Edmund groaned.

"This is important," Leigh said, trying to forestall any more comments by the redcap. "I think I know what this does." She patted the pouch. "It opens things."

"We already knew that," said Edmund. "It opened the chest."

"Not just the chest," Leigh said. "It opens anything."

As quickly as she could, she related the events of her morning. "I think it has to touch something to open it, though," she said. "Otherwise, there wouldn't have been a closed purse in the restaurant, and I'd hate to think of what might have happened in the kitchen before Georges made me leave."

Valmont nodded. "I'm certain we can discover several ways to prove the truth of your theory," he said.

"Like maybe on the way to the Japanese Tea Garden?" Edmund asked hopefully.

As they started out the door, Leigh caught Morgan's attention and pulled the childling aside as the others walked out onto Haight Street.

"Here," she said, unfastening the silver chain around her neck and handing Morgan's locket back to her. "I'm sorry I kept it so long."

"That's all right," said Morgan, replacing the locket about her own neck and tucking it inside her tunic.

"Shouldn't we go ahead and tell the others that you're living at the palace now?" Leigh asked. "They might need to know that your parents will probably report you missing and start searching for you."

Morgan shook her head. "That's all been taken care of," she said. "Let's catch up with the others!"

Leigh followed Morgan out the door, wondering why the childling's apparent lack of concern should leave her feeling uneasy. By the time they reached Golden Gate Park, the sensation had passed.

Even at a brisk walk, the journey from the Toybox to the Japanese Tea Garden took a little over a quarter of an hour. As they neared the entrance to the Tea Garden, Leigh stopped Valmont.

"Do you think they'll recognize us from the last time we were here?" she asked, remembering their mad dash into the area a few days earlier.

Valmont chuckled. "I made certain that our

entrance was perceived as unexceptional," he said. "But this time, we'd probably better pay to get in."

Aliera stood outside the school, waiting for Morgan's mother to come pick her up. She knew that Mrs. Daniels drove a gray Mercedes, but she had seen a lot of gray cars pass and she didn't know how to tell one type of car from another. Finally, a car fitting the general description Morgan had given her slowed to a stop in front of the school. She clutched her books in front of her and walked toward it, wondering if she should kiss her mother on the cheek or on the hand after she had greeted her.

She was a little surprised to see both Mr. and Mrs. Daniels sitting in the front seat of the car. Morgan's father got out and held the back door open for Aliera to climb inside.

"Good afternoon, Father and Mother," Aliera said as she settled herself in the back seat. Morgan's father shut the door after her, then resumed his place in the driver's seat of the vehicle. Morgan's mother turned around to look at Aliera, then burst into tears.

Aliera looked puzzled. "Have I done something wrong?" she asked. Morgan's father started the car and pulled out into the traffic before answering.

"Your mother and I have decided that you need to go to a special hospital for a few days," he said in a tight voice. "They called us this afternoon to say that they had a room ready for you."

"But I'm not sick," Aliera protested.

"I'm afraid you are," Morgan's father said. "But this place has promised to make you well."

Aliera looked helplessly out the window of the car as she rode through the city. Despite her growing apprehension that something had gone terribly wrong with her carefully constructed plan, she was fascinated at the buildings that rose on either side of her and the infinite variety of people she glimpsed as Mr. Daniels guided the car through the afternoon traffic. Neither of Morgan's parents spoke, but slowly, Mrs. Daniels' sobs grew quieter. After climbing a steep hill, Morgan's father slowed the car to a stop in front of a massive iron gate. A tall brick wall on either side of the gate surrounded what looked like a large estate. A man in a uniform opened the gate and motioned for them to drive through. Aliera felt her stomach lurch as the car passed through the iron gateway and started up a long, paved drive.

Mr. Daniels stopped the car again in front of a three story brick mansion. Stepping from the car, he opened the back door and took Aliera firmly by the hand. Aliera had no choice but to walk with him up the steps leading to the mansion's front door. Morgan's mother followed them, wiping her eyes with a handkerchief.

As soon as she stepped inside the house, Aliera felt a sick coldness invade her body. A young man wearing a long white coat over a dark suit approached her. He looked at Aliera and smiled, then turned to Morgan's parents.

"So this is Morgan Daniels," he said, his voice oozing with shallow cheer. He leaned over to pat Aliera on the head with one hand, while his other hand secured a grip on her arm. At his touch, Aliera began to scream.

The bound prince sensed her presence once more, though she was still no nearer to him than the last time. He had recovered most of the power he had expended in his efforts to ensure that she achieved possession of the Eyestone. Soon he would use those powers again, this time to draw her closer to him so that he could begin to achieve his destiny. He would have to send another dream to his servant on the other side, Glynnis of the ebony harp, informing her of another task she must accomplish for him.

Even through the barriers that prevented him from seeing clearly beyond his prison, he was able to concentrate on the Glamour that radiated from the Eyestone, drawing enough power from it to gain a hazy image of his beloved Eleighanara and her companions. For the time being, he would simply watch and wait.

Edmund found the spot where Malacar had staked out the chimeric bride — inside a circle of flowering shrubs, just past their peak.

"Over here!" he called.

When the others joined him, Edmund pointed proudly to the four small indentations in the ground.

"He was gonna stake her out and cut her throat," the redcap said, a vicarious pleasure lacing his voice. To illustrate his statement, Edmund stretched out on his back in the middle of the circle, his arms and legs splayed in imitation of a spread-eagled victim.

"Look!" he cried. "I'm a sacrifice!"

"Be careful what you wish for," Valmont said. Edmund scrambled to his feet.

Leigh and Rasputin began searching the circle's perimeter, while Tor and Morgan stood to one side, watching their companions' efforts and keeping an eye out for unwanted visitors.

"It looks like someone came along and filled in the holes," Leigh said, "but I don't see any sign of the stakes—"

"Maybe Malacar returned here later and removed them," Valmont suggested.

"Or one of the groundskeepers," said Tor.

"Somebody's coming!" Morgan's voice was an urgent whisper. A few seconds later an elderly couple strolled toward them, stopping suddenly at the sight of the group. Leigh stood up quickly, brushing herself off. Edmund shoved his hands in his pocket and tried to look innocent, while Valmont affected a sudden interest in a clump of flowers. Rasputin continued to crawl around on his hands and knees, patting the ground in front of him. He looked up at the visitors' arrival.

"Contact lens," he said. "Be careful where you step."

"Good luck, young man," the woman called, tugging on her husband's elbow to pull him away from the area. The couple meandered off in the direction they had come. Morgan giggled. The search resumed.

Leigh found a few dried rose petals scattered near the edge of the clearing. "These don't match any of the flowers I see," she said.

"Some of the grass looks silvery from here," Morgan said. Following Morgan's directions, Valmont combed his fingers through the ground cover. He examined his fingertips.

"Powdered silver," he announced. "It describes a circle around the four holes Edmund discovered."

"A ritual circle," Edmund added. "Maybe he was gonna summon a demon or something!"

Valmont wiped the silvery powder from his fingers with a black silk handkerchief. He offered it to Leigh. She deposited the dried petals into the handkerchief's center. Valmont folded the silk cloth carefully and placed it in his pocket. The eshu turned to Morgan.

"Baroness Morgania," he said, bowing to the childling in mock formality. "It is said that the members of House Eiluned are conversant with the arcane arts. Do the circle, the silver and roses, and the sacrifice call anything to mind?"

"It's not like anything I've learned so far," Morgan said, shaking her head.

"Is there no one at the duke's court who might enlighten us?" Valmont asked.

"No!" Morgan said emphatically. "Don't ask them at court!"

"Why not?" countered Edmund. "This is their stupid quest, after all."

"Morgan's right," said Leigh. "I don't think anyone at court will have the time to spare for us." Involuntarily, she looked at Valmont, saw the faint smirk on the eshu's face and quickly turned away from him.

"We should stay here for the rest of the day," Rasputin said, turning to leave.

"Yeah," said Edmund. He glanced at Leigh, a hopeful look on his face. "Can we play with the stone?" he asked, holding his hand out to her. Leigh placed a hand over her pouch, covering it possessively. The redcap scowled.

"Who said you could hog the stone, anyway?" His question was a challenge. Leigh felt her face grow red.

"Malacar gave it to me!" she retorted. Hearing the sharpness in her voice, she wondered why the thought of giving the gem up to anyone else, even temporarily, bothered her so.

"Actually, Malacar threw it on the ground after you refused it," Valmont corrected. "You chose to pick it up."

"Yeah!" said Edmund. "You just grabbed it first."

"Let's spend the rest of the afternoon arguing about

who should have the stone," Rasputin said. "I think that's a splendid way to conclude our investigations."

"Why don't we take turns?" Morgan suggested. "If Leigh doesn't mind, we can each try to use the stone to open something."

Edmund rolled his eyes upward. "I feel like I'm back in kindergarten," he said.

Valmont stared at Leigh. Finally, she shrugged and removed the gem from the pouch. "Here!" she said, thrusting the green stone toward Edmund. He grabbed it greedily, then winced as the gem burned in his hand. He juggled it from hand to hand, determined not to give it back so easily.

Rasputin offered the childling a brightly-colored scarf from his bag of tricks. "Take this," he said. "It probably won't do any good." Edmund placed the gem between his teeth while he wrapped the scarf around his hand.

"Don't you dare swallow that!" Leigh said, horrified.

"I 'on't 'wallow it," Edmund said. Using his wrapped hand, he retrieved the gem. "It's not even scratched." He held it up for Leigh's examination before darting off down the nearest path. Rasputin sped after him.

"I'll try to lose him," the pooka called as he ran after Edmund. Leigh and Valmont turned to follow them.

"Are you coming?" Leigh asked Tor and Morgan.

"You go on," Tor said. "We'll catch up. I'm too old to run."

Alicia and Gordon Daniels returned home in silence. Once inside their house, Alicia ran upstairs to her studio and shut the door behind her. Gordon lingered downstairs, wandering from room to room in a house that suddenly seemed too large yet strangely claustrophobic. Finally, he climbed the stairs and made his way to Morgan's room. He leaned inside the doorway, looking at the array of dolls in one corner, the doll house castle that Morgan and her mother had assembled last Christmas and which now stood on a card table near the bed, the collection of stuffed rabbits accumulated at the rate of one per year, the small bookshelf filled with fairy tales, and the careful selection of clothing laid out upon the bed — clothes Morgan had apparently intended to wear that afternoon when she came home from school. His chest grew tight.

Gradually, Gordon became aware of the noises coming from his wife's studio, a methodical rip and clatter punctuated by an occasional harsh sob. He crossed the upstairs hall and tried the knob on the studio door, afraid for a moment that Alicia had locked herself in. The knob turned. Gordon opened the door and stepped inside.

Alicia sat in the middle of the floor, surrounded by a growing pile of ripped canvases and snapped wooden frames. She looked up as Gordon entered, her face streaked with free-flowing tears.

"It's all my fault," she whispered hoarsely. "I encouraged her with these drawings. I let her think that it was all right to believe in...faeries...and...magic...and—"

Gordon knelt by Alicia's side and took her in his arms.

"Don't," he whispered, his lips brushing her hair. "It's not your fault."

"She's only eleven," Alicia said, her voice breaking. "She's too young to have to stay in that horrible place with no one who understands her or loves her." Her voice trailed away. Gordon removed the partially-torn painting from his wife's lap. It depicted a dark-haired faerie princess with gossamer wings standing in a circle of flowers, which were, themselves, faeries in disguise. The princess in the picture looked like Morgan. He laid the ruined canvas on the floor and stood up, pulling Alicia to her feet and guiding her toward the door. She leaned on him like a sleepwalker.

"I'm so tired," she said.

Unresisting, she let him steer her to their bedroom, where he helped her undress and then, as if she were a child, tucked her into bed.

"Can you sleep?" he asked her. "You look exhausted." He sat beside her on the bed and held her hand, watching as she closed her eyes, still wet with tears, and plummeted into sleep. He drew the curtains to darken the room and stood near the window, listening in the semi-darkness to the sound of her slow, rhythmic breathing. Still restless, Gordon left his wife in the safety of her slumber and trudged downstairs again.

In his study, Gordon sat at his desk, looking over his copy of the commitment papers. As he stared at his signature, he seemed to hear his daughter's anguished cries echoing in his head. He reached for the phone on his desk and dialed Dr. Walters' office, where he left a brief message on her machine, wondering as he did so if entrusting Morgan to the care of strangers had been a terrible mistake.

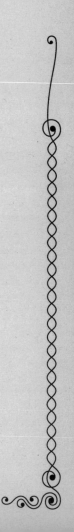

chapter

fourteen

"It's not like I don't come from a good home or anything like that. I come from a lot of good homes, all of 'em foster homes. You probably don't know what a foster home is, do you?"

Edmund and the clown sat in the basement of an abandoned house on the southern end of the Haight. The city had towed away the Ford yesterday, so the redcap childling had spent most of the night wandering the streets looking for shelter. Just before dawn, he found a partially demolished residence on the edge of a housing development. From the weeds which had grown over the remaining outer walls, he reasoned that the wrecking crews would be unlikely to finish the job anytime soon.

His hand still tingled faintly from its brief contact with the stone. Even so, it was worth a little discomfort to handle something really magical. He and the others had spent the afternoon experimenting with the stone. It really could open just about anything — car trunks, locked doors, fire hydrant valves (his idea), vending machines, even the cages in the back of Department of Animal Control trucks (Rasputin's idea). When he settled down for what was left of the night it had seemed natural for him to spend a little of his own Glamour to activate the clown.

At first, Edmund was disappointed. The clown was short, not much taller than he was. He had been hoping for something a little taller and a lot more sinister. What he got was Mr. Dumpy. Dumb Mr. Dumpy, because the clown didn't talk either. It smiled a lot, and frowned (it could look really sad). But it made a good listener, and it occurred to Edmund that someone who couldn't talk to him couldn't yell at him, either.

He had fallen asleep with his head in the clown's lap, and when the sound of a distant lawnmower woke him, sometime near noon, the chimera was still there, grinning down at him. Almost an hour later, he was still working on the story of his short, eventful life, and Mr. Dumpy showed no signs of tiring.

"When your real parents don't want you, and mine didn't, they start shoving you into foster homes where other people get paid to act like your parents. Only 'cause they get paid, they're more concerned with making a profit from you than with spending any more money on you than they have to. And they'll put up with a lot just to keep getting their monthly check."

Edmund grinned, remembering some of his former homes. "One family finally gave up on me when they caught me feeding their parakeet to their cat. It was a stupid bird, and the cat deserved something for putting up with being called Snoozums all the time. I spent some time in a sicko ward but they had to let me go because my social worker threatened a civil liberties suit or something. They tried putting me with an upscale family, and that was a little better, but I was always getting dragged around to places where they could show me off to their hip friends 'cause I was an ethnic minority. I figure I'm at least six minorities, only I don't know what most of them are."

The clown smiled sympathetically. Edmund decided it looked like it wanted to hear more. "I changed into a redcap when I was eight. I was so freaked I ran away from home. Ragger and his gang found me and helped me hide out for a while, but the cops eventually picked me up and turned me in. I did time in juvenile hall after that, and it was hell being a changeling locked up in Banality Central.

It took me awhile to figure out how to eat my way out of that hellhole. Since then, I've been careful to avoid getting caught. I figure next time it's the slammer."

Edmund had a sudden thought. "You don't mind living in my pocket, do you? I mean, it's not the most exclusive residential area in the world, but it must be better than being crammed in that old toy chest with everyone else. Can you understand what I'm saying to you?"

The clown nodded, smiling.

"Cool!" Edmund said. "If you turn into a toy again, will you be able to come back to life?"

The clown pointed to Edmund.

"I don't understand," the redcap said.

Mr. Dumpy shrugged, then pointed to Edmund and back to himself. He kept repeating the gesture until Edmund finally realized the clown was describing a connection between the two.

"I can give you some of my Glamour and you'll get big again! Is that it?"

The clown wiped its forehead in relief and nodded.

"All right!" Edmund exclaimed. "I'm glad, cause I'm gonna have to make you get small again so we can go back up to the Toybox and see if anybody's missed me...yeah, right," he added. "As if anyone would miss me with little Miss Morgan around to spoil. I hope they spoil her so much she rots."

Mr. Dumpy frowned sadly. He waved at Edmund and, placing one white-gloved hand on top of his head, shrank down into the miniature clown the childling had scavenged from the toy chest. Edmund scooped up the now inanimate figure, tucked it back into his pocket, and set out for Haight Street.

 t h e

On his way to work, Gordon Daniels stopped by Dr. Walters' office unannounced and demanded a conference with the psychologist. In between her nine and ten o'clock sessions, Adrienne Walters listened while Gordon expressed his belated concerns about the wisdom of putting Morgan in an institution.

"I'm wondering whether or not we have acted precipitously," he said. "My wife is still very upset." He paused, trying to overcome his natural reluctance to discuss his own feelings. The image of Morgan panicking as she was led away from him and her mother loomed in the front of his mind. "I'm still...uncomfortable...with the idea that we've surrendered our responsibility for our daughter to someone else."

Dr. Walters nodded, then offered Gordon an encouraging smile.

"Of course you're concerned," she said. She swung her chair around and plucked a book from the bookshelf behind her desk.

"Here," she said, handing the volume to Gordon. "This book gets a little scholarly in parts, but it covers Morgan's syndrome very thoroughly. Take it home with you and read it. I think you'll decide that you and your wife have made the right decision about Morgan."

"I certainly hope so," Gordon said. "If we decide we've made a mistake—"

"We'll talk about it at that time," Dr. Walters said, standing up to signal to Gordon that his interview was over. "I really must see my next patient."

Gordon left her office feeling only a little better. He ate lunch — yogurt and black coffee — at his desk and began delving into the book Dr. Walters had loaned him. Halfway through the introduction to *Chimera: Living Within Our Dreams* he buzzed his secretary and sent her to a bookstore in search of a dictionary of psychology.

When he returned home from work, he found Alicia upstairs in her studio, reworking the painting of her faerie princess on freshly bought canvas. He noticed that the colors on her palette were all dark ones. Alicia smiled brightly at him before turning back to her work.

"I don't have to think when I paint," she said. Leaving his wife to her own form of therapy, Gordon went downstairs to his study and spent the evening immersed in Anton Stark's book.

Valmont crossed off the last of the evening's appointments; this one involving a speculative real estate deal with a client who only kept evening hours — late evening hours. Under the name of Valmont Duvalier, he had managed to sell proprietary rights on a tract of land in Transylvania to a wealthy, aging dilettante who clung desperately to the belief he was of "Count Dracula's immortal blood," and, hence, unlikely to die anytime soon. Valmont reasoned that the absence of mirrors in the old man's house served a dual purpose, since what those mirrors would reveal might destroy his client's faith in his ability to resist the ravages of time. The eshu had long since failed to wonder at the casualness with which some of the rich bestowed their funds. He was only glad that, this time, he had been fortunate enough to be one of the recipients.

It was just before closing time when Valmont slipped into Trickster's, where, in a splendidly ironic reversal, he would assume the role of buyer, rather than seller, of intangibles. His back pocket bulged with a clip of crisp bills, enough to purchase the information he sought. Most changelings who lived in the mortal world recognized the necessity of feeding and clothing their mortal bodies. Despite their preference for Dross, the portable sources of Glamour that served as currency in changeling society, few kithain would turn down the opportunity to acquire the wherewithal for next month's rent or a new set of threads.

The eshu purchased a drink, which he intended to ignore, and worked his way through the crowded bar toward an empty booth in the rear. He hoped that putting the word out on the streets that he was seeking knowledge of certain specific matters would bear fruit.

As the hour grew later and the mortal customers in the bar wandered out into the street, a small but steady stream of kithain informants made their way to Valmont's booth to sit and talk for a few minutes before leaving, enriched by their brief conversation.

A disheveled satyr lugging a battered guitar case informed Valmont that Malacar had last been seen rapidly heading south, presumably toward Mexico where he could lose himself somewhere in the Kingdom of the Feathered Snake, which reputedly harbored no love for its sister Kingdom of Pacifica.

"He burned a lot of kithain," the satyr said bitterly. "He talked a good line about toppling outworn structures and the sunset of the Seelie tyranny. He threw titles around like candy at a Christmas parade...." The wilder musician shook his tangled mane and snorted. "He promised me a barony. Claimed he had powerful friends — some queen of shadows and her knights or some such — who were backing his activities."

A pair of sluagh, both shrouded in the layered black clothing most favored by their secretive faerie race, whispered their information to Valmont, somehow making themselves heard through the din of the bar's clientele.

"For awhile, Malacar was hiring people to run his mysterious errands, paying them in Dross that looked like it had come from somewhere exotic—"

"—brilliant pieces of coral and volcanic glass like nothing that could be found near San Francisco—"

"—he was asking a lot of questions about a storehouse of lost chimerae somewhere in the Haight—"

"—supposedly used in the final battle that won the Accordance War for the sidhe—"

"—and he hinted at something else, a horde of faerie treasures hidden in a secret glen when the sidhe abandoned the commoners and shut down the gates to Arcadia—"

"—he had something that he claimed would help him open up the doorway—"

Valmont had trouble deciding whether the pair's information warranted full payment for each of them. In the interests of maintaining his reputation for generosity for services rendered, the eshu paid them both for their time and trouble.

Georgia surprised Valmont by showing up and flopping into the seat opposite him, a half-chewed cigar clamped between her teeth. Valmont coughed as the pungent smoke hit his lungs. The nocker cabbie flashed him a smile.

"I won't take up too much of your breathing room," she said jauntily. "But I figured since you were paying for information, I'd take advantage of the windfall."

"I would have expected the ties of friendship to have a stronger pull than the lure of filthy lucre," Valmont said mildly.

Georgia let out a raucous laugh. "Friendship don't pay the rent," she replied. "Cough it up — what I've got is something you need to hear." Valmont laid a pair of crisp bills on the table. Georgia eyed them dubiously. Shrugging, the eshu added a third. Georgia leaned across the table, carefully blowing her smoke away from Valmont before speaking.

"Someone is funneling a shitload of iron into the fief. Most of it's going to Oakland, which suggests that it's coming through the port there. You might ask the count to check out the warehouses along the docks."

"Is this something else we can lay on Malacar's doorstep?" Valmont asked.

Georgia shrugged. "Maybe, maybe not," she said. "But I have seen some strange kithain wandering around late at night in long, dark cloaks. From the way they moved, I'd say they were sidhe, but if so, I don't think they'd be welcome at the duke's court—" she left her words dangling significantly in the smoky air.

"Unseelie," Valmont said, feeling that he was stating the obvious.

"In a big way," said Georgia. "You and I are one type of Unseelie, and we have a lot of friends in the other camp. The ones I saw were different, somehow, like an assassin is different from a hired thug—"

Valmont smiled. "I hope you're not implying that we're the hired thugs," he mused.

"Would you rather be compared to an assassin, then?" the cabbie countered.

"It's a tough call," Valmont said after a few seconds' hesitation. "I see the distinction, though."

Before Georgia left, Valmont warned her — as he had warned all the others who spoke to him — about the sinister knight in black armor that Edmund had encountered.

His final visitor was Blade. Resplendent in what looked like a cross between pirate's garb and voodoo chic, the muscular eshu greeted Valmont with a salute that startled him with its implied deference. Valmont raised an eyebrow.

"Have you come here to finish your work?" Valmont asked, flexing the shoulder that had borne the brunt of the iron dagger's impact.

Blade held his empty hands outward.

"That's past," he said. "I came here to congratulate you on your latest coup as Prince of the Shadow Court."

Valmont stared blankly at his fellow eshu, trying to mask his ignorance.

"Oh?" he said, his voice carefully noncommittal. "What was so special about it?"

"Most Shadow Courts hold their Samhain Revels in some secret meeting place," Blade said. "Word has it that, thanks to you, the duke has agreed to hold this year's bash at the palace. Everyone's invited."

Valmont's composure slipped. Blade leaned over, placing his hands on the table and bringing his face to within inches of Valmont's.

"You mean you didn't know?" Blade asked. Then he stepped back, slowly shaking his head and chuckling softly. "I must be mistaken, then," he said. "Maybe it was arranged by the other Shadow Court." Before Valmont could say anything, Blade turned and stalked across the bar and into the street.

Pondering everything he had learned, Valmont left Trickster's and made his way to his car, watching his back every step of the way.

october 1, 1995

After three days in which she might have been a wall hanging for all the attention anyone paid her, Morgan came to the conclusion that Princess Aliera had been right. Everyone at the duke's freehold was far too busy to notice the comings and goings of the palace's childling contingent, who were largely left to fend for themselves. Morgan also concluded that something was very, very wrong with Duke Aeon.

Although her suite of rooms — Aliera's suite, actually — was separated from the duke's chambers by several hallways and a number of guest rooms, Morgan could hear the sound of eerie music wafting through the corridors of the palace late at night. An almost physical gloom had settled over the palace itself. Only in the princess' rooms was there any levity unmarred by the presence of the older members of the court.

Morgan and Layla had taken it upon themselves late one night, when everyone else in the palace was asleep, to wander quietly through the darkened downstairs rooms. Carefully dodging the few palace guards who patrolled the house and grounds, the childlings tiptoed through the vast dining room, the ballroom with its velvet draperies and finely polished floors, the kitchens (where they helped themselves to a few choice tidbits) and, finally, the throne room, where only a little over a week ago Morgan and Aliera had stood witness to Leigh's knighting.

Egging each other on, Morgan and Layla approached the duke's enormous throne, which loomed in the dark like some great ebony beast, waiting to ensnare anyone so foolish as to venture too near its outspread paws and gaping mouth. As her eyes adjusted to the darkness, something white on the seat of the throne caught Morgan's attention. In spite of her apprehension at approaching the ducal throne, she crept closer to see. Leaning over the seat to peer at the object, she gasped and quickly covered her mouth with both hands. Layla joined her, staring in amazement. A withered cluster of mistletoe, its leaves cracked and dry, rested forlornly where it had fallen from its branch atop the throne.

"The duke's mistletoe," Layla breathed. Morgan could only nod her agreement.

t o y b o x

An agonized moan, followed by a weird, atonal wail that sent cold chills through Morgan's body, sent both childlings scurrying frantically for the safety of their rooms, where they whispered long into the night about the possible doom portended by the fallen symbol of the duke's power.

Gordon Daniels spent the weekend submerged in the psychological theories of Anton Stark. What he read, instead of reassuring him, only left him feeling uneasy. The book accurately described Morgan's fantasy world and echoed his own sentiments about the serious problems those who suffered from "chimeric delusions" faced in dealing with the everyday world. What Gordon couldn't accept was the method of treatment outlined by Stark.

The thought of his daughter undergoing a series of controlled convulsions — seizures — as currents of electricity were poured through her brain left Gordon feeling queasy. He had an even dimmer view of aversion therapy, wondering what kinds of associations could be dredged up to make his daughter afraid to think of unicorns or faeries.

By the time he reached the conclusion of the weighty tome and had read Stark's recommendations for a two-year treatment program to ensure a comprehensive reorienting of the delusional personality, Gordon was certain that he had made a terrible mistake in delivering Morgan into the hands of psychic butchers.

Adding to his disturbance was Alicia's behavior. By Sunday, his wife had seemed to accept Morgan's absence. Although she still spent most of the day in her studio, she had joined him for brunch and chatted about inconsequential matters, and later, as he was struggling through the final pages of Stark's book, Gordon heard her humming to herself as she put away the evening's leftovers. It was only when he heard her voice raised in animated conversation that he stopped reading long enough to listen to what she was saying. Quietly, he made his way through the house until he stood in the kitchen doorway where he watched in quiet horror as Alicia Gordon cautioned an imaginary Morgan to "behave yourself around your father or he'll send you away again."

Monday morning, Gordon called Dr. Walters' office, only to be told by her secretary that the doctor had flown to New York for a five-day conference and would not be back until Friday. His next call was to the Ironwood Hospital, where he asked to speak with Morgan. Informed that new patients could not receive phone calls, he asked to speak with the doctor in charge of her treatment.

"I want to bring my daughter home," he said brusquely.

"I'm sorry," the doctor told him. "That will be impossible. The commitment papers you signed specify a mandatory thirty-day residency in the hospital." Gordon heard the sound of rattling paper as the doctor apparently consulted his files.

"We've already begun a preliminary program of intensive treatment for her," the doctor said. Gordon's hands were shaking as he hung up the phone. Opening his briefcase, he retrieved his copy of the commitment papers and reread the densely worded text. Cursing himself that he, an attorney, had paid so little attention to the fine print, Gordon crumpled the document in his hands. For the first time since he was twelve, Gordon Daniels wept.

"I realize that Morgan isn't here yet," Valmont said, "but this information is too important to wait any longer. We'll just have to tell her about it later if she can get away from home long enough to join us." Leigh folded her arms across her breast and looked down at the table, unwilling to look directly at her friends. She wondered when Morgan would tell the others that she had left her parents. Without raising her head, she glanced at Tor. Morgan had indicated that she wanted to tell her grandfather about her decision first. Leigh supposed the childling hadn't yet had the opportunity. For a moment, she debated whether to go ahead and let the others know that Morgan had sought asylum at the palace. She had not sworn an oath to Morgan, but she knew that in the childling's mind, a promise was a promise. She would not be the first one to go back on her word once she had given it.

The table where they sat now displayed a "Reserved" sign at its center, hand lettered by Edmund in something that looked suspiciously like dried blood — although the redcap insisted it was only chocolate paste and red food coloring. The sign wasn't necessary, since the regulars at the freehold had tacitly ceded the back table to the "saviors of the toy chest," as they were beginning to be known, but no one had the heart — or the nerve — to mention to Edmund that his sign was superfluous.

With no immediate crisis and only a vague idea of what they needed to do next to follow through with their quest, the oathmates found the demands of their mortal lives once again impinging on their participation in kithain society. Leigh had taken on an extra shift at Mardi's to scrape up the rent on her apartment, and Rasputin was busily planning his next "happening," a pre-

Halloween event the pooka was advertising as "The Lying Truth." It had taken Valmont three days to contact everyone except Morgan and agree on a meeting time.

In as few words as possible, Valmont related most of the information he had purchased at Trickster's. Blade's comment about the "other Shadow Court" he kept to himself, although he did casually mention that the duke had decided to host the Unseelie Samhain celebration.

"Maybe the old duke's not such a jerkoff after all," said Edmund.

"I think it's the wisest thing his Grace has done in a long time," Rasputin concurred. Leigh stared at Valmont in astonishment.

The door to the coffee shop swung open and the group looked up, expecting to see Morgan come bouncing into the room. Instead, Georgia stood in the doorway for a moment and scanned the room before hurrying over to Tor.

"Hey, Tor," she said. "There's some guy hanging around outside asking if anybody's seen you. He stopped me and showed me a picture that looked a whole lot like you in an army uniform."

"What did you tell him?" Tor asked.

"I offered to track you down for a price, of course," the cabbie said. "You know me. Only I said I'd give you the option of going to him rather than bringing him to you." She leaned forward and whispered conspiratorially, "He's mortal."

"Where is he now?"

Georgia pointed in the direction of the coffee shop door. "I left him standing across the street, about two buildings down."

Tor rose from the table and walked to the door. He opened it just enough to see into the street. A few seconds later, he shut the door hard enough to rattle its frosted glass pane.

"What is it?" Leigh asked, seeing the look of consternation on Tor's face visible all the way across the room.

"That's Morgan's father," the troll said. "What's he doing here?"

"Whatever you do," Leigh said quickly, "don't let him come inside! He might kill this place just by walking through the door." Edmund scrambled across the room and, standing on tiptoe, plastered his face against the milky glass, trying to see through it. All he could see were hazy shadows, one of which seemed to be moving across the street.

"He's coming this way!" Edmund called.

"Not if I can help it," Tor said, jerking the door open and stepping outside onto the sidewalk.

Gordon Daniels saw his father-in-law emerge from what looked like an abandoned building near the corner of Haight and Ashbury. He finished crossing the street and stopped, face to face for the first time in years with Morgan's grandfather. Staring up at the tall, worn-looking derelict, Gordon found himself amazed that a man who was at least fifty years old and who had been living on the streets since his return from Vietnam could still look so imposing. His throat, already dry, tightened.

"Mr. Larssen," he began, "I'm sorry to bother you—"

"Then get the hell away from here and you won't be bothering me." The threatening tone in his voice was unmistakable. Gordon decided to make his case as quickly as he could, before he lost his nerve.

"Morgan's been institutionalized and I need to get her back," he said, feeling like his voice was on a downhill slide. He braced himself for the old man's angry reaction.

For a moment, Tor stood, looking down at his daughter's husband, trying to make sense of the words that had come rushing from his mouth. Gordon started to relax, hoping that he would get a chance to explain further what he wanted done. Too late, he saw his father-in-law's face grow livid and noticed the sudden tensing of his massive neck muscles. He was considering stepping backward when he felt a pair of vise-like hands grip his shoulders and slam him against the wall of the nearest building.

"What have you done to my granddaughter?" Tor's voice was a bellow of rage. Gordon gasped for breath, feeling the shock of the impact in every bone in his body.

"Help me," was all he could manage to force himself to say, wheezing as he tried to fill his lungs with air. "Help Morgan." Gordon's vision began to swim as tiny red dots began multiplying in front of his eyes. He thought he said "please" before his head crashed against the wall a second time and the world dropped out from under him.

Valmont rushed outside just in time to catch Gordon's falling body. Following the eshu, Leigh ran to Tor and wrapped both hands around the troll's arm, trying to forestall another blow.

"Tor!" she screamed at him. "Stop! You'll kill him." Her scream was echoed by a woman standing nearby, and a crowd quickly began to gather around the Toybox. Rasputin, looking on from the coffee shop's open door, pushed past Edmund, who stood gaping in the doorway.

The pooka approached the crowd, holding his hands in front of him as if to push them away.

"Move back!" he called indignantly. "You're blocking the cameras! Move back or we'll have to reshoot the entire scene!" From where he stood, Edmund felt the stirring of Glamour as Rasputin worked his own brand of faerie magic on the hapless bystanders, reducing them to a gaggle of confused individuals who gradually drifted away from the area.

Tor became aware of the extra weight on his arm. Turning his head, he saw Leigh gamely trying to pull him away from his son-in-law's unconscious form. Valmont looked up at the pair.

"What now?" he asked. "We can't leave him lying on the sidewalk."

Leigh stared at Morgan's father. Somehow, he seemed different from the walking advertisement for Banality she had encountered once before.

"We'll have to risk taking him inside," she said. "I'll see if Fizzlewig will let us bring him in."

Morgan and Layla stared at the profusion of flowers that surrounded them.

"Where do we start?" Morgan asked her eshu companion. "This place is enormous!"

Layla looked up from the brochure she had acquired at the front door of the Conservatory of Flowers, inside Golden Gate Park.

"It says here that this is the oldest building in the park and that it was brought all the way from Ireland in 1878. It 'houses a splendid collection of tropical and exotic flowers—'"

"Mistletoe isn't a tropical flower," Morgan protested. "It grows on oak trees."

"'—as well as regular displays of seasonal flowers and plants.'" She grinned at Morgan. "I would call mistletoe a seasonal flower or plant," she said.

"Well, it can't hurt to look," Morgan said. "There are

gardens outside, too. Maybe if we can't find any mistletoe in here, we'll have better luck out there."

Layla closed her eyes and breathed in the heady, moist atmosphere of the large, domed greenhouse. Morgan imitated her, and let the smells of earth and flowers fill her lungs.

313

"This way," Layla said suddenly, opening her eyes and taking Morgan by the hand. Morgan blinked at the riotous colors that surrounded her as she, too, opened her eyes.

"My mother was working on a painting just like this," she said, "for a book all about a princess who lived in a garden of enchanted flowers." Morgan suddenly felt a sharp pang of homesickness as she realized that she would no longer be able to watch her mother produce miracles full of Glamour from ordinary canvas and tubes of paint.

Layla tugged on her hand. "Come on, we need to do this as quickly as we can," she said.

"How do you know we're going in the right direction?" Morgan asked, and then she remembered that her companion, like most eshu, seemed to have a knack for knowing where to go. "Never mind," she said. "Lead the way."

Layla's circuitous path took the two childlings through the length of the conservatory, past clumps of azaleas and begonias, cyclamens and ferns, floating waterlilies and rows of rare orchids. Finally, she led the way through a door in the building's rear.

"We're outside again!" Morgan said.

Layla nodded happily. "And there," she pointed, "are some oak trees. And there," she said triumphantly, "is our mistletoe!"

Gordon awoke, his head aching. He touched the back of his head gingerly, where a small knot was beginning to form. Someone gave him a cool, wet cloth and he placed it gratefully over the swelling.

"Are you all right, Mr. Daniels?" a woman's voice spoke to him. As his vision slowly came back into focus, he saw that he was sitting on a makeshift bed of chairs, lined together to support his outstretched legs. He seemed to be inside an abandoned cafe of some sort, full of run-down furniture, including a magnificent relic of a bar. A dusty old steamer trunk — certifiably antique — resting on a small table, caught his eye. There were several people with him in the room. He looked up at the red-haired young woman who had spoken to him and thought she seemed vaguely familiar. With her were a dark-skinned man dressed in clothes that even Gordon, with a successful attorney's income, could not afford and a raffish-looking youth, probably in his late teens, wearing a confusion of outlandishly stylish clothing; somehow, his face reminded Gordon of a rabbit. A dusky boy of about eight or nine years, with dark, spiky dreadlocks sticking out from beneath a tattered baseball cap, crouched near the building's doorway, taking bites out of a super-sized plastic cup. He felt, rather than saw, Morgan's grandfather standing behind him.

"Mr. Daniels?" the woman asked again. Gordon realized he was expected to reply.

"I don't think anything's broken," he said. "Who are you? I need to talk to Torvald Larssen." He tried to turn his head so that he could see his father-in-law, but the sudden stab of pain caused by moving his neck prevented him from doing so.

"We're Morgan's friends," the woman said to him. "My name is Leigh." She introduced the others briefly as Valmont, Rasputin, and Edmund. "Why don't you tell us what's happened to her?"

Gordon hesitated, uncertain about unburdening himself before strangers.

"If you want to say something to me, you'll say it in front of them." Gordon jumped as the voice of Morgan's grandfather boomed like a dull thunderclap behind his head. He winced. Then he began to talk hurriedly.

"For the last year," he began, "Morgan's been seeing a psychologist because she keeps having these delusions that faeries and trolls and things like that are real."

Leigh looked at Tor. "Did you know this was going on?" she asked the troll.

Tor shook his head. "She never said a word about it to me," he muttered, his face hard and stony.

"I could've told you that she was a loony," Edmund said with a sneer.

"Thank you for sharing your observations with us Edmund," Rasputin said sharply. "And please keep talking, this is trivial."

"The problem grew worse," Gordon continued, oblivious to the side conversations going on around him. "A week ago she laid out of school, and we called her psychologist in for an emergency consultation. Morgan refused to talk to her at all. That was when the doctor recommended that we put her in a hospital."

"For playing hooky?" Valmont asked.

Edmund nodded. "Yup," he said. "I got put in a place like that once for feeding a cat."

"It was so unlike anything she had done before that her mother and I were afraid it was a sign that she was becoming truly ill," Gordon said.

"Never mind all that," Tor said gruffly. "You put her in a hospital. Take it from there."

Gordon nodded. The pain seemed to be receding and he carefully swiveled his legs around so that he could sit sideways on one of the chairs, resting his feet on the floor.

"She's been there all weekend," he said. "I...started

to have second thoughts about what we...what I...had done after I read the book written by the expert Morgan's doctor consulted before recommending institutionalization. They use electroshock and aversion therapies and psychopharmaceutic treatments—"

"What?" Leigh was mystified.

"Drugs," Edmund informed her. "They put me on a bunch of stuff: Valium, Librium, Thorazine—"

"They've already started intensive treatments," Gordon said. "I called them this morning and told them I wanted her back. They said I had to wait for thirty days."

"In thirty days," Valmont said softly, "she'll be lost."

"I'm a lawyer, dammit!" Gordon's voice was full of vehemence. "I should have known what I was signing—"

"But you signed the papers anyway," said Leigh. "There's no point in explaining why you did it."

Gordon nodded. "I looked into going through legal channels to get Morgan back sooner," he said, "but the process will take at least ten days, maybe longer." He shook his head, disconsolate.

"So now you've come looking for me," Tor said. "Why?" His whisper was the low, menacing growl of a dog ready to attack.

"Are you guys just stupid or what?" Edmund said. "He wants us to spring her from the joint!"

"You were in Vietnam," Gordon said to Tor. "Alicia has some of your medals and your citation for bravery. I saw them when I went looking for your picture. You were part of a LURP patrol...."

The jungle had become their only home, their comrades their only resources. Deep in enemy territory, they moved like snakes through the heavy overgrowth, searching for human prey. Silent killers, they struck without warning, then disappeared into the dense forest.

the

"That's right," said Tor, understanding now what his son-in-law was requesting. "We need to do this quickly." Almost before Gordon's eyes, the old man seemed to undergo an eerie transformation. His vagabond's slouch straightened into a military stance and the lines of age on his face hardened into marks of experience. For the first time, Gordon began to feel a glimmer of hope.

"Will you be coming with us?" Valmont asked.

"Are all of you planning on going?" Gordon sounded incredulous.

"I said we were Morgan's friends," said Leigh simply. "Are you coming along or not?" She repeated Valmont's question.

"I want to," Gordon said, "but I don't know if I'll be any help. I've never done anything even remotely illegal—"

"And we, of course, do this sort of thing on a daily basis," Rasputin remarked casually. Edmund snickered.

Gordon looked embarrassed. "I didn't mean—"

"Never mind," said Leigh quickly. "Tell us what this place looks like and where it is."

Gordon began describing the drive to Ironwood Hospital. A chorus of voices interrupted him when he mentioned the iron gate. He paused, perplexed.

"You're coming with us," Valmont said. One by one, the others considered the eshu's pronouncement before finally nodding agreement.

"We'll make a plan on the drive there," Tor said. "It'll fall apart as soon as we make our first mistake, but at least we'll have a starting point." He headed toward the rear of the room. "I'll be back," he said. "I have to get something."

Gordon stood up, testing his body for residual aches and pains. Aside from the dull throb in the back of his skull, he seemed unharmed. After a few minutes, Tor returned. Gordon thought he could see an odd-shaped object concealed beneath his father-in-law's trenchcoat.

"Thank you for doing this, Mr. Larssen," he said.

"It's Tor," the old man said. "No one calls me anything else anymore."

318

"Thanks...Tor," Gordon repeated.

"I swore an oath to protect my granddaughter," Tor said softly.

Standing behind Gordon, Leigh gasped softly. "That's right," she whispered to Valmont. "If he fails, he'll lose his strength and sicken...." Leigh paused. She had learned enough about the other kithain to know that trolls were physically bound by any oaths of guardianship they swore. She looked at Tor closely, trying to see if he betrayed any signs of weakening. Then she shrugged. It was something to puzzle about later.

Before the group started for the street door, Tor pulled Gordon aside. "You're coming with us because we need you to open the gate. Just don't ask any questions, no matter what you see after we get onto the grounds."

"I don't understand," Gordon said.

"That's right," said Tor harshly. "You don't understand. And not understanding could be fatal. No questions," he repeated. "I need my granddaughter. I don't need a son-in-law."

"Anything you say," Gordon replied.

"Let's move out," Tor commanded, and led the way into the street.

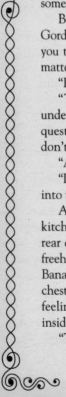

After they had gone, Fizzlewig crept out of the kitchen and looked apprehensively around him. At the rear of the room, the Balefire still glowed weakly. The freehold had not wilted under the onslaught of Gordon's Banal influence. The boggan walked over to the toy chest and ran his hands lovingly over its carved surface, feeling for the faint echo of the Glamour bottled up inside it.

"Thanks, old friend," he murmured softly.

For once Valmont raised the top of his convertible. He congratulated himself on his choice of a roomy vehicle as he watched Tor, Leigh and Rasputin climb into the back seat. Edmund shoved himself into the front seat next to Valmont. Gordon sat beside Edmund.

On the way to Presidio Heights, Tor questioned Gordon about the particulars of the hospital's wall and grounds. Gordon was relieved that his memory, trained in the accurate recall of legal minutiae, had retained a clear picture of details he had not noticed consciously at the time.

"You say a man in a uniform let you in the gate," Tor said. "Did he buzz the gate open or just unlock it?"

"There was no buzzer that I could hear," Gordon said. "He had a big key ring."

Tor nodded. "Then there's probably no electronic alarm connected to the lock, at least in the daytime."

"Are you sure it wouldn't be better to wait until dark?" Leigh asked. The reality of what they were proposing to do was beginning to sink in. She wondered what her father would do if she were caught breaking and entering.

"We have no way of knowing if their security is beefed up after hours," Tor said. "Either way is risky, but I think this way is better."

Ahead of them, they could see a tall brick wall broken only by an ornate wrought iron gate. Beyond the wall, manicured grounds led up to an imposing brick building. In front of the wall stood a small sign bearing the words "IRONWOOD HOSPITAL" in unadorned black letters.

"Here's what I want you to do," Tor said to Gordon as Valmont pulled the car to a stop in front of the gates.

"Where is everybody?" Morgan called out cheerfully as she entered the Toybox Coffee Shop. Her foray with Layla in search of mistletoe to replace the dying branch above the duke's throne had been successful, although it had been a tricky task to sneak into the throne room and complete their self-appointed mission. She hoped the new mistletoe would thrive.

She had expected that at least Tor would be waiting in the coffee shop so that she could finally tell him that she had decided to live at the palace and could now see him any time she wished. The back booth next to the group's table was empty.

"What are you doing here?"

Morgan jumped at the sound of Fizzlewig's voice. The boggan had slipped up on her unnoticed.

"Hi, Fizzlewig," she said. "Where are the others?"

"They've gone to rescue you from a mental hospital," the boggan said.

"What?" Morgan's mouth opened in astonishment. She listened as Fizzlewig recounted Gordon's visit to the Toybox. "He said they delivered you to some place in town called Ironwood Hospital," the boggan concluded. A sudden weakness seized Morgan's legs.

"My father was here?" she asked. "And he said he'd put me in a mental institution?"

"Obviously he was wrong," Fizzlewig said. "Morgan Daniels," the boggan began, his voice ominously low, "just who did your father send to the loony bin?"

Morgan had to make several attempts to get the words out, but finally found her courage.

"Princess Aliera," she said, her voice sounding little and weak. Fizzlewig paled. Morgan turned and started

the

running for the door.

"Where are you going?" Fizzlewig demanded, trying to run after her.

"I have to help them rescue the princess!" Morgan called. She bolted onto the street, nearly colliding with a figure emerging from a purple and yellow taxi.

"Georgia!" Morgan cried, her legs nearly buckling from relief. "I need a cab, quick!" she said.

"Whatever you say, ma'am," Georgia replied. "That's what I do." She held the back door open for Morgan to scramble inside, then took her place behind the wheel. "Where to?"

"The...um...Ironwood Hospital!" Morgan said, remembering Fizzlewig's words. "And step on it!"

Rasputin and Gordon climbed out of Valmont's car and approached the gate. Rasputin stifled a wave of nausea as he neared the massive iron structure. On the other side of the gate, a uniformed guard looked at the two men inquisitively. Rasputin brushed his hair back out of his eyes and smiled at the guard.

"We're the radical therapy group scheduled to tour these facilities," he informed the security officer. "You were told to expect us." He waved his hands mysteriously in front of the guard's face. Gordon looked at Rasputin dubiously, expecting the guard to back away from the gate and refuse them entry. Instead, the guard looked confused.

"I don't recall getting any message—" His voice trailed off as he frowned and scratched his head. "Forgot what I was saying," he mumbled.

Rasputin pointed frantically to the keys clipped to the guard's belt.

"Get the keys, jackass! The keys!" Edmund stuck his head out the front window and screamed at Gordon.

"The Inner Child Rehabilitation Unit, Emergency Group B," prompted Rasputin, making motions with his hand as if turning a key in a lock and glaring at Gordon.

Gordon took a deep breath, reached through the iron bars of the gate, and unclipped the ring of keys. Rasputin breathed a sigh of relief as Gordon fitted the most likely looking key into the lock. The gate clicked and began to swing open. Gordon grabbed the side nearest him and pulled.

"Well?" Rasputin demanded, looking at the guard. Looking thoroughly mystified, the guard finished opening the gate.

"Hold on," Valmont cautioned his companions. "This is not going to be pleasant." Bracing himself, he floored the accelerator and sped through the gates, screeching to a stop just beyond them. Then he got out of the car and walked back toward Gordon, Rasputin, and the befuddled security guard.

"Replace the keys," Valmont said to Gordon. Morgan's father did as he was told. Then he and Rasputin joined the others in the car while Valmont conferred briefly with the security guard. A few minutes later, Valmont returned to the car, a satisfied look on his face.

"He will not remember our arrival," Valmont said. "Nor will he realize that the gate is open."

Gordon opened his mouth to ask how Valmont could be so sure of himself, but a sharp-eyed Edmund poked him in the ribs.

"Don't ask," the redcap warned. Gordon wondered how a mere child could sound so menacing.

Valmont drove up to the brick building and parked his car at the edge of the circular drive, facing away from the hospital.

"Everybody out," barked Tor. The troll turned to

the

Edmund. "Are you sure you can conceal all of us from the people in the building?" he asked.

Edmund nodded. "They won't notice us," he said confidently.

Valmont looked around him, then inhaled as if sniffing the air. "Go around to the back," he said. "There'll be a door suitable for our purposes."

Taking the lead, Edmund marched to the rear of the building, where he paused in front of a door in the back wall. He began a series of controlled burps. Once again, Gordon looked worried. Leigh put a hand on his arm.

"Don't worry," she said, trying to sound more reassuring than she felt. Even from outside the building, Leigh felt the crushing weight of Banality within the brick walls. She concentrated her will on retaining a hold on her faerie self. She could not afford to succumb to the institutionalized disbelief enshrined within the hospital.

Edmund tried to open the door. "It's locked," he whispered, fishing in his pockets with his free hand. He let out a quiet yelp of victory as he pulled out a bent wire and shoved it into the lock. "I was afraid I'd eaten it," he mumbled. "Got it," he announced a few seconds later, and opened the door. He stepped inside and motioned for the others to follow him. As the last person in line, Leigh pulled the door shut softly behind her, trying to avoid catching the lock.

The room they entered appeared to be a patients' lounge filled with groupings of red and yellow molded plastic furniture. In one corner, three men, one of them a teenage boy with a shaved head, sat listlessly in front of a television, staring at a woman advertising a line of personal care products. Two middle-aged women played checkers at a table on the other side of the room. Near the door leading to the rest of the building, a nurse sat leafing through the pages of a magazine. She looked up briefly as the outside door opened, then went back to her reading, apparently oblivious to the arrival of six strangers.

Tor looked at Gordon and put his index finger against his lips in a gesture for silence. Then he pointed the same finger at Valmont, who nodded briefly, and walked quietly toward the middle of the room.

The eshu concentrated for a moment, trying to pierce the cold mundanity that blanketed the building's interior. Leigh felt a wave of nausea sweep over her, and found herself wondering what she was doing in a mental hospital. She looked down at her clothes, halfway expecting to see a "Volunteer" badge pinned to her breast. Someone touched her lightly on the shoulder, and she saw a sandy-haired young man standing beside her.

"Dame Eleighanara," Rasputin whispered quietly in Leigh's ear. "You need to forget you're a knight of Duke Aeon's court."

Leigh felt the unmistakable tingle of Glamour from Rasputin's touch, and she blinked her eyes, suddenly remembering what she was doing.

"Thanks," she mouthed at her companion. She looked anxiously at Tor and saw that the troll's eyes were closed. One hand clutched the axe concealed beneath his long coat.

"Please hurry, Valmont," she murmured as she concentrated on Rasputin's timely reminder.

Finally, after what seemed an eternity of listening to an inner static, Valmont began to get a sense of where he needed to go. He wiped a bead of sweat from his forehead, and walked toward the nurse. The others started to follow. Suddenly, Tor stiffened.

The harsh smell of disinfectant permeated the air. Torvald Larssen felt the walls of the veteran's hospital close in on him. He had been sent to this hellhole for treatment for something called post-traumatic stress disorder. Near him

a man in a wheelchair muttered to himself. A group of people who looked vaguely familiar but whose names he could not remember stood around him. He caught sight of his son-in-law and wondered if it was Gordon's fault that he was here, where he didn't belong. He wasn't sick. He just couldn't forget the jungle....

"No!" screamed Tor. "I'm not stayin' here!" The troll's face broke out in beads of sweat and he looked frantically around him.

"He's losing it!" Edmund yelled. "Somebody do something!" The redcap concentrated fiercely on trying to keep the others concealed from the sight of the patients and the nurse, who raised her head in response to Tor's outburst.

Valmont saw the nurse stand up and reach for a large button on the wall near the door. Almost without thought, the eshu leaped straight up into the air, one arm raised above his head as if to touch the ceiling. Using the exertion to focus his Glamour, Valmont willed the nurse's chair to slide forward, spinning wildly and slamming into the back of the nurse's knees. She sat down violently, the button untouched.

"Quick! Into the hall," Valmont ordered to the others. "Leave her to me."

Leigh grabbed Tor by the hand. Still reeling from her own brush with the omnipresent Banality of the hospital, she struggled to infuse the troll with as much of her own Glamour as she could without once again losing her own sense of her faerie nature. "Remember Morgania," she pleaded, trying to penetrate the fog which blinded the troll to his true self. "Remember your oath to Morgan!"

Tor shook his head. He stared at Leigh and slowly his face began to take on the familiar cragginess of his troll nature.

Rasputin stood by the door, one hand cupped gingerly

around the panic button. Edmund crouched next to the pooka, peering into the hall beyond the door. Valmont loomed over the nurse and flashed an elaborate pocket watch in her face, muttering to her under his breath as he swung the watch back and forth.

Leigh glanced at the patients in the lounge. The two women remained engrossed in their game. The teenager, however, looked up from the television.

"There's a bunch of freaks in here!" he informed his two companions. "Real freaks! One of 'em looks like a boulder with horns stickin' out of his head."

"That's nice," the man sitting next to him said. The other man just nodded.

"Let's go!" Leigh whispered as loudly as she dared, leading Tor into the hallway past Rasputin and Edmund. She looked over her shoulder at Gordon, standing awkwardly in the middle of the room. "Come on!" she urged him.

Gordon had to lock his jaws together to keep himself from muttering an "excuse me" to Valmont and the nurse as he passed them. The group entered a large area at the center of the building. Valmont joined them, pocketing his watch. "I think that's taken care of," the eshu said quietly.

"One of the patients saw us," Leigh said.

Valmont nodded. "I'm not surprised. Those the world calls insane often see things more clearly than most mortals." He looked at Edmund. "Are you concealing us again?"

The redcap spit into his hand and rubbed his palms together. "I hope so," he said.

"This way," Valmont said. "Let's hope nothing else goes wrong."

Ahead of them, a foyer with offices on either side led to the front door. A hallway stretched to their right, while on their left a wide staircase led to the upper floors. A pair of men in white orderly uniforms passed uncomfortably close to the group. Leigh held her breath until the orderlies entered one of the rooms opening onto the hall.

"I guess it's working," Edmund whispered.

Valmont led the others up the stairs. At the second-floor landing, a door with a safety-glass window blocked their way to the rooms which lay beyond. Leigh pointed to the stairs that continued upward to the third floor and looked questioningly at Valmont. The eshu shook his head and motioned toward the closed door. He reached into his vest pocket and withdrew three small brightly colored stones, which he carefully arranged in front of the door. Taking Edmund's hand, he motioned for the others to join hands. Then he walked through, pulling his companions behind him.

Gordon hesitated, obviously disturbed by the sight of Valmont and the others passing through a solid door as if it were not there.

Behind him, Leigh whispered, "Close your eyes. It'll be easier." She shuddered as she gave Morgan's father a shove. Gordon closed his eyes and walked through what felt like an open doorway.

The corridor beyond the door was empty and lined with rooms on both sides. Valmont dropped the others' hands and hurried down the hallway, seeming to know his way around. Gordon could hear moans coming from behind the doors, and his nose itched from the harsh smells of medicine, urine and disinfectant. Rasputin looked pale. Leigh could see the pooka's nostrils dilate with his rapid, shallow breaths. She reached out and touched the tip of one of his elongated ears, trying to reinforce his own Glamour with some of her own dwindling reserves. It was becoming more difficult to keep from falling into the sinkhole of Banality. If they stayed here too long, they might all be lost.

Valmont stopped abruptly before a door halfway down the hall. "She's in there," he mouthed silently. Placing a hand on the doorknob, he tested the door. It creaked slightly and swung open.

Gordon rushed past Valmont and inside the room, where a little girl lay strapped to a cot-like bed, snoring in drug-induced slumber. Gordon stared at her, shocked at the change that had come over his daughter in just a few days. Then he looked more closely and saw the traces of pale blond at the roots of her black hair.

He rounded on Valmont. "That's not Morgan," he said. "You've got the wrong room!" Valmont ignored Gordon, looking past him at the girl on the bed. Leigh inched forward into the room and peered over Valmont's shoulder.

"It's Aliera!" she gasped, her voice echoing through the hallway behind her. Morgan's cryptic statements of a few days ago suddenly became all too clear. "They switched places," she said, not caring that the words came out at a volume that destroyed all pretense of secrecy.

"Who's Aliera?" Gordon asked. "Where's Morgan?"

"Hey!" a strange voice sounded behind them. "What are you people doing up here?" A large, red-haired orderly stood blocking the doorway to Aliera's room. Without waiting for a reply, he reached for a pager at his waist.

"Stop him!" Leigh cried, realizing that whatever trick Edmund had used to conceal their presence had ceased to function.

"Hello, handsome," Rasputin stepped forward into the orderly's path. "What football team do you play for?" The orderly glared at Rasputin in disgust and attempted to push the pooka aside.

Tor roared and reached inside his trenchcoat. To Gordon's horror, his father-in-law pulled out a massive axe and charged the guard. Rasputin rolled out of the troll's path, making a yanking motion with his hand as he tumbled backward into the room. The pager slipped out of the orderly's grasp just as Tor, shifting the grip on his weapon to a handhold nearer the blade, drove the butt of the reversed weapon into the man's stomach. The orderly staggered back a step, shaken but not out of the fight.

"I need backup, stat!" The man yelled, slamming his hand against the wall behind him. Too late, Tor saw the button — identical to the one by the lounge door. He braced himself for the sound of an alarm. Nothing happened.

"Silent alarm!" Tor warned. "They'll be coming in force any minute. Move it!"

Leigh ran toward the princess and started furiously ripping away the straps that held her down. Her fingers fumbled at the sturdy lashings. Then she remembered the stone in her pouch. Willing herself to remain calm, she retrieved the gem and held it to each strap in turn, watching with grim satisfaction as they fell away from Aliera's comatose body. Rasputin recovered from his controlled tumble and scooped the princess up in his arms.

Valmont raised an approving eyebrow at her. "Keep that out," he said. "We might still need it." The eshu looked around the room suddenly. "Where's Edmund?" he asked.

"Get the hell out of here!" Tor commanded, as the orderly barreled headfirst into him, driving the troll into a wall. "I'll find Edmund when I'm done with this piece of trash." Valmont hurried Leigh and Rasputin out of the room, taking advantage of the path that had opened up before them.

"You get out too!" Tor growled at Gordon. "This isn't your fight."

Gordon shook his head. "It is now," he heard himself say. Searching the room frantically, he spotted a pitcher of water sitting on small shelf built into the wall. He dumped the contents down the orderly's back. The shock caused him to jerk backward, giving the troll enough time to place another blow with the axe handle. He hit the orderly squarely on the jaw, stepping aside just as the large man tumbled forward, unconscious. From down the hall, pounding footsteps announced the arrival of reinforcements.

Breathing heavily, Tor flattened himself against the wall beside the door. With one hand, he motioned Gordon to do the same on the door's other side. Realizing that there was no other way out of the situation, Gordon obeyed his father-in-law's orders.

"On my signal," the troll commanded.

Carrying the princess, Rasputin reached the top of the stairs just ahead of Valmont and Leigh.

"All's clear!" he cried frantically as he saw the pair of white-uniformed men barreling up the stairway toward him.

"Can you get Rasputin and Aliera out of here?" Leigh asked Valmont. The eshu looked at the oncoming orderlies and pursed his lips.

"I shall try," he said. "What about you?"

Leigh's face hardened as she took the measure of the opposition. A rush of adrenaline coursed through her body. "I haven't been taking karate for nothing," she said grimly. Breathing deeply, Leigh balanced herself on the balls of her feet, willing herself into a state of relaxed attention.

Valmont grabbed Rasputin by one arm. "Hold onto the princess," he said and leaped forward over the heads of the orderlies. The men paused, mouths agape, as the trio sailed above and beyond them, landing unhurt at the bottom of the stairs. Leigh saw their indecision and seized the advantage. One leg flashed out, the side of her foot landing solidly on the shoulder of her nearest target. The orderly lost his balance and toppled down the stairs. His partner charged forward, throwing himself at Leigh in an attempt to bear her to the floor.

Leigh fell backward, seizing the man's arm and pulling him past her. She heard his body slam into the corridor wall behind her. Without stopping to see if he would recover enough to follow, she regained her feet and hurtled down the stairs.

"Look!" called Morgan. "The gate's open." She fidgeted impatiently in the front seat. "Hurry! Go on through!"

"Hey," Georgia snapped. "It's not my fault I had to look the place up in the bloody phone book. I've never been here before."

"Neither have I," said Morgan. "Remember?"

On the way over, she had told Georgia what she and Aliera had done. "I wouldn't go through my childling years again for anything," had been the nocker's only comment.

The cabbie caught sight of the iron gates. "I'm not taking my car through those," she said. She swerved the cab and aimed it at the brick wall beyond the gate.

"Up," she muttered, "and over!" Morgan squealed as the cab landed on the lawn inside the walls of the hospital grounds. Georgia steered the car back onto the path.

"Go around to the side door," Morgan directed.

"I thought you'd never been here before," Georgia said. "How do you know there'll be a side door?"

"I just do," Morgan said. "There has to be."

Georgia braked to a stop at the side of the building. "You're right," she said, as Morgan opened the door and hurried out of the cab. Georgia followed her. "You're not going in there alone," she said.

Morgan ran to the door and tried to open it. It wouldn't budge.

"I could have told you it was locked," said Georgia, pulling some tools from her shoulder bag as she joined the childling at the door. A few seconds later, she stepped back and turned the knob. Morgan ran inside the building just as a white-coated young man emerged from a room a few feet away. He stared at Morgan and frowned.

"Miss Daniels," he said sternly. "What are you doing out of bed? All patients are confined to their rooms during a general alarm," he began, but stopped himself as he caught sight of the female cab driver standing behind the child.

"I'm her doctor," he said to Georgia. "Did she call you?" The nocker grinned mischievously up at the doctor and nodded.

"Don't let her leave," the doctor ordered. He reached toward Morgan. The childling ducked under his outstretched arm.

"Quick!" Morgan screamed. "Give him something!"

Georgia glanced at Morgan, momentarily puzzled.

"You have to enchant him!" Morgan dodged the doctor's second attempt to grab her.

Georgia pulled a ring of twisted wire from one of her fingers and shoved it at the doctor's outstretched hand. "Hold this," she said. "I made it for you." The man's hand closed involuntarily around the ring as Georgia tried to infect the mortal with some of her own faerie Glamour.

"Okay," Georgia said to Morgan. "I hope he's enchanted. Now what?"

Morgan crossed her fingers and concentrated on

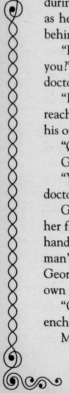

forcing the doctor to see her true self. Her body began to glow and Georgia felt herself engulfed by the diminutive sidhe's majestic presence. The doctor frowned as Morgan drew herself up, assuming the court posture she had learned from Lady Alyssa. Slowly, the doctor's face began to drain of color, his jaws working furiously as he saw a vision of power that his mind tried to tell him, unsuccessfully, could not exist in the world he knew.

"Get out of my way!" Morgan said, pitching her voice as low as possible. The doctor stepped meekly aside.

"Shit!" Georgia said softly. "It worked!"

Just then, Morgan caught sight of Valmont and Rasputin at the foot of the stairs. Rasputin carried Aliera in his arms. Leigh was running down the stairs towards them. Morgan dashed down the hallway toward them.

"They've got her!" she called to Georgia.

Leigh and Valmont turned at the sound of Morgan's voice. "Yes, we have the princess," Leigh said, harshness coloring her voice. Then she stopped, struck by Morgan's compelling aura.

"Where's my father?" Morgan said, her eyes wide with excitement and fear. "And where's Grandpa?"

"They're still upstairs," Leigh said. "We can't find Edmund, but we need to get Aliera out of here before anyone else tries to stop us." She looked pointedly at the unconscious orderly at the foot of the stairs. "Help me drag him into a corner somewhere," she said to Valmont.

"I'll look for Edmund," Morgan said and headed up the stairs. Georgia trailed behind her, leading the unresisting doctor by the hand.

"You go on. I'll wait for Morgan," Georgia said as she watched Leigh and Valmont drag the orderly into a room marked "Men."

"The car's out front," said Valmont as he and Leigh returned to the stairway. Leigh nodded. Holding the glowing gem in front of her, she ran for the front door.

It opened as the stone touched it. Valmont, Leigh and Rasputin raced for the car. Leigh pulled the back door open for Rasputin and the princess. When they were all inside, Valmont sped down the drive and through the open gate.

"How is she?" Leigh asked, turning around in the front seat to look at Rasputin and Aliera. Tears streaming down his cheeks, Rasputin ignored her question. Pressing his face close to Aliera's ear, he whispered poetry to her all the way back to the Toybox.

Halfway up the stairs, Morgan encountered Tor and her father on their way down. Both of them looked battered. Her father was breathing heavily. Without stopping, Tor scooped Morgan up with one hand. Morgan hugged him briefly, avoiding her father's eyes.

"We've got to get out of here fast," Tor said, carrying Morgan down the stairs.

"I said I'd find Edmund," she said, struggling in her grandfather's powerful arms. "We can't leave without him."

"Who's looking for me?" a familiar voice called from the bottom of the stairs. "Guess what I've been—"

Tor glared at the redcap. "I don't wanna know where you've been or what you've been up to," he roared. "Get your scaly fanny out the front door now! There's a general alarm in the building."

"No there's not!" Edmund said hotly. "I took care of that."

"My cab's around the side," Georgia said, standing near the bottom of the stairs still clutching her white-coated companion. "I'll go pull it around front. What do I do with him?" She indicated the doctor.

"Leave him here," Morgan said. Georgia ran out the open front door.

Gordon stopped at the foot of the stairs. "The papers," he said hoarsely. "We've got to get back the commitment papers — and her records — or else they'll take her right back!"

"Put me down, Grandpa," Morgan said, her voice wavering between a request and a soft command. Tor set the childling on the floor. Morgan walked over to the doctor and took him by the hand, smiling up at him.

"Take us to the office," she said. "The one where they keep the patients' files."

Wordlessly, the doctor led the group to a room just inside the front door. "Tell them it's all right," Morgan urged.

Gordon watched through a filter of numb confusion as the doctor brusquely informed the hospital's secretary that he needed to pull some files.

A few minutes later, Gordon held in his hands both the file containing Morgan's records and the hospital's copy of her commitment papers.

"We can leave," Morgan announced.

"You forgot something," Edmund said, still rankling from Tor's rebuke. Clucking like a chicken, he strutted into the office.

"We were never here," he announced to the two mortals who waited inside. "You don't remember seeing or hearing anything unusual today."

He joined the others in the hall. "Now we can leave," he said, and led the way through the front door to Georgia's waiting cab. "By the way," he said defiantly, as they piled into the purple and yellow taxi, "while you guys were getting the princess, I was eating their security system." He pulled a film cartridge from his pocket and bit off a large chunk from its corner.

Followed by Leigh and Valmont, Rasputin rushed into the Toybox cradling Aliera in his arms. Fizzlewig took one look at the pooka and his burden and started shoving chairs together.

"No," said Valmont, heading straight for the toy chest. "There's enough Glamour inside this to wake the dead."

"What a terrible thought," Rasputin said, his voice strained. Leigh placed the stone atop the puzzle-lock on the lid of the steamer trunk. The top of the chest began to glow as the pieces of the puzzle moved of their own accord, forming a picture of battling armies. Leigh snatched back the gem just as the lid popped open. Leaning over, she looked at the collection of toys that lay inside the chest. A toy soldier's eyes blinked open.

Smiling in spite of herself, Leigh shook her head. "At ease, soldier," she said. "This is a mercy mission."

Tor and the others entered the coffee shop just as Rasputin was about to lay the princess's sleeping body atop the pile of toys.

"Wait!" Morgan called and ran to the chest. She leaned over it and began furiously pushing toys aside, digging deep into the pile of dormant chimerae until her hand closed on the object she sought. Pulling the figure of a sleeping cat from the chest, she looked at Rasputin. "You can put her down now," she said. When Rasputin laid his small burden across the toys, Morgan placed the cat on Aliera's chest and wrapped the princess' limp hands around it protectively. "It's the chest's guardian," she said.

Fizzlewig appeared amid the group with a tray of steaming brownies. The boggan walked over to Gordon and held the tray up to him.

t h e

"Take one," he said.

Gordon shook his head, wondering why anyone would want to put a little girl into a dusty old steamer trunk. "I'm not hungry," he said. "Tell me, why—"

"Eat a brownie," Tor roared. "Then you can ask all the questions you want."

Afraid to disobey, Gordon picked up a brownie and bit into it. He was surprised at how good it tasted, and quickly consumed the remainder of his piece. He looked around him as the room and the people in it suddenly came into focus.

Tor had a chair ready to catch his son-in-law as Gordon's legs gave way in shock.

"She's coming around," Valmont announced from his place beside the toy chest. Opening her eyes, Aliera sat up and stared at the sparkling objects that surrounded her and supported her. Morgan carefully slipped the cat from the princess' hands and placed it back inside the chest. Aliera clapped her hands in delight.

"Toys!" she exclaimed happily.

Clearing his throat, Gordon began asking the first of a long list of questions.

chapter

fifteen

Edmund kicked viciously at the pyramid of beer cans he had collected over the last few weeks. Since the raid on the mental hospital, the redcap had moved six times. The wrecking crew finally arrived to complete the razing of the abandoned house he had occupied, and until last week he had found nothing suitable for more than temporary digs. Of course, he thought, for him living space was always temporary.

He hoped that his current shelter, a deserted church on the fringes of the Tenderloin district, would see him through the rainy months that passed for winter in California. The belfry, partially boarded over and lacking a bell, proved ideal for looking out over the squalid rows of buildings that constituted his domain, and the cellar afforded protection from the storms and heavy fog that were increasingly prevalent as the season progressed.

"If I were a noble like Morgan," Edmund said, "I could make this place into a real freehold." The redcap looked about him, finding it easy to imagine the changes a Balefire might bring to the ruined building. It was certainly old enough, he thought, to respond to an infusion of Glamour.

"I'd make you my chief adviser," the childling informed the chimeric clown that stood, arms folded over his ample girth, watching as the last of the beer cans rolled to a stop against the belfry wall.

"I don't understand it," Edmund complained, picking up a can and crushing it before taking a thoughtful bite out of its aluminum carapace. "She gets away with everything! She runs away from home, rooks the duke's snotty heir into taking her place and gets the princess locked away in a loony bin. Then she shows up at the tail end of our rescue mission, hugs her old fart of a grandfather, puts a dumb toy cat in the princess' lap and acts like she's saved the world."

Edmund paused to take another bite from the can. "Too bad you can't eat," he told Mr. Dumpy. "This is pretty tasty...less filling too."

The clown nodded. Edmund returned to the topic of his rant.

"As if that weren't enough," he said, "her father gets enchanted and everyone spills their guts to him about all of us! The duke would puke on his throne if he knew about that. But does anyone tell him?"

Mr. Dumpy shook his head, then looked at Edmund as if waiting for confirmation.

"Naw! Instead, they enchant Morgan's mother, too! So now Morgan's got this happy family all bending over backwards to give her anything she wants. She gets to live at home and go slumming with her kithain friends any time she likes so long as Leigh or one of her other friends picks her up and brings her home."

Edmund snorted and hurled the rest of his can at the wall opposite him. "Right!" he exclaimed in disgust. "Baroness Mugwort is perfectly free to run all over the city and get in the way of dragon fights and battles with wizards, but she has to have an escort to see that she gets home safe and sound. It makes me want to vomit!"

Then the redcap brightened. "Hey!" he said to his chimeric confessor. "You want to come with me to the Shadow Court's Samhain bash? I could go as a clown and everyone would think we were twins."

Mr. Dumpy looked doubtful.

"Yeah, you're probably right," Edmund said. "Everyone would also notice that you were a refugee from the toy chest. I bet if you were Morgan's, they'd let her keep you. You'll just have to stay in my pocket. I'll be a clown anyway. Did you know the Shadow Court is holding their party at the duke's palace this year? That should be a trip and a half. I've never been to the palace! The closest I've ever been to court has been that stupid farce of Raputin's. He told me I made a great Sir Cummerbund!"

Edmund stood up and peered between the boards that kept the wind from whistling through the belfry. "It's nearly dark," he said. "If we want to make the party early, we'd better get going."

As if on cue, Mr. Dumpy obligingly shrank to toy size. Edmund scooped up the painted clown and stuffed him in his pocket. Picking up another can for a snack on the way to the Samhain Revels, he descended the rickety wooden stairs that led from the belfry into the church's deserted sanctuary.

The carnival atmosphere of Halloween in San Francisco cheered him considerably as he made his way through the winding streets to the ducal residence. Halfway there, he heard the clarion call, summoning the kithain of the city to an evening of mayhem and misrule. It would be his kind of party.

The sound of the clarion caught Rasputin putting the finishing touches on his costume. Pulling the black eyepatch over his left eye, he surveyed himself in the mirror. "Black Jack O'Hare," he said, "Lord of the Pirate Pookas!" He shrugged. "It'll have to do," he murmured.

His latest happening had exhausted most of his physical and mental energies. Instead of bringing about the influx of Glamour he had hoped to derive from an evening of spontaneous poetry and organic music — the burp-along chorus had been truly inspired — he had returned to his apartment only to feel the Glamour drain from him as soon as he stepped inside.

He sighed, smoothed his ears, and hoisted his bag of tricks onto his shoulder. Switching his eyepatch from his left to his right eye, he hurried toward Nob Hill.

The Samhain Revels were in full swing when Leigh arrived with Morgan at the duke's palace. Since their awakening to the reality of their daughter's nature, Morgan's parents had ceased to interfere in the childling's affairs aside from their understandable concern for her safety. Gordon, in particular, had proven surprisingly adaptable. His confrontation with the harsh environs of Ironwood Hospital had sparked in him an almost missionary zeal as a campaigner for legal rights for mental patients. Gordon had terminated the services of Morgan's psychologist, demanding her records of Morgan's sessions and threatening the doctor with a malpractice suit. Leigh suspected that Mr. Daniels had found a way to exert similar pressure on the hospital, for so far there had been no visible repercussions from the group's timely rescue of Aliera.

Leigh clasped Morgan's hand tightly as they approached the ducal palace, its once pristine grounds already showing evidence of Unseelie abandon. A crowd of childling redcaps dashed across her path, hot in pursuit of a terrified lapdog who had chosen the wrong moment to wander through the neighborhood. Unsightly ruts in the manicured lawns led to a row of motorcycles parked haphazardly beneath a stand of cypress.

Although the sun had set over an hour earlier, multicolored chimeric lanterns placed among the trees and atop the palace flooded the freehold with light, illuminating the growing chaos that was ripping away at the estate's grandeur. Leigh shook her head in dismay.

"There's Grandpa!" Morgan exclaimed and pulled her hand from Leigh's grasp to run toward Tor. The childling had insisted on bedecking herself in a witch costume — in keeping with House Eiluned's reputation as masters of sorcery — for the Samhain celebration. Leigh had to admit that Morgan made a fetching witch-child. In keeping with her status as a knight, Leigh's own costume, a white, loose-fitting medieval style gown modeled on Waterhouse's painting of the Lady of Shallott, was more decorous.

Joining Morgan and Tor, Leigh gave the troll's carnival attire an approving glance. Tor was decked out in a splendid suit of polished battle armor, his only concession to costuming a horned Viking helmet which transformed the troll into a figure from Norse legend. Next to him stood Fizzlewig, looking decidedly uncomfortable in his knight's armor and domino mask.

Leigh greeted them formally, then smiled at Fizzlewig. "I'm glad you came," she said.

Fizzlewig grumbled. "Word got round that the duke's people needed all the support they could get, so here I am."

Leigh nodded gravely. The duke's decision to host the Unseelie festival had spread by word of mouth throughout Goldengate and Oakhold, but a second communication had gone out from Lady Alyssa to all Seelie kithain, nobles and commoners alike, begging for their attendance at the festival.

"Have you seen Valmont or Rasputin?" Leigh asked.

Tor nodded his head in the direction of a small cluster of kithain standing near a long buffet table set up on the lawn. Leigh recognized Valmont, resplendent in a genie costume complete with swirls of chimeric fog about his slippered feet, and Count Elias, who had donned the garb of a Turkish pasha for the celebration. "Who's the guy with the mohawk?" Leigh asked.

"That's Blade," a loud childish voice informed her. Leigh looked down at the garishly painted clown who bore Edmund's unmistakable imprint.

"He's the one who nearly wasted Valmont with the iron dagger!" the redcap informed Leigh. "At least that's what they say on the streets," he said smugly.

"They seem awfully chummy right now," Leigh observed, catching Valmont's eye and nodding to him. A few seconds later, the eshu broke away from Elias and Blade and strolled toward Leigh.

"I don't think Rasputin's here tonight," a rabbit-eared pirate wearing an eyepatch in the middle of his forehead like a third eye said mournfully.

"Hi, Rasputin!" said Morgan. The pooka bowed to the childling. "Repulsed, as usual," he mumbled, kissing her hand.

"Are we all here?" Leigh asked, taking a head count. The six oathmates, followed by Fizzlewig, left the cacophonous outdoor gathering and entered the duke's palace. Once inside the grand entry hall, the group made their way toward Lady Alyssa and Sir Cumulus, who huddled forlornly amid a small gathering of Seelie nobles near the foot of the grand staircase.

Leigh gave way to Morgan's senior rank as a baroness and watched as the childling executed a sprightly curtsey to the duke's advisers. When Morgan had finished, Leigh saluted Lady Alyssa and Sir Cumulus, then stood aside while Sir Charles Fizzlewig gave his formal greetings to the duke's chamberlain and herald. Lady Alyssa smiled distractedly at the boggan knight.

"You have been too long from our company," she said.

Fizzlewig mumbled something about pressing freehold business and too little help in the kitchens.

After Valmont made his obeisance to the noble pair, the eshu turned and introduced Tor, Rasputin and, finally, Edmund. He held his breath as the greetings transpired without any mishaps.

Leigh chatted with Alyssa and Cumulus for a few minutes about the quality of the food at the party and the difficulty in pleasing the wide variety of palettes present. Then she steered Fizzlewig into a conversation with Sir Cumulus about swordplay and signaled for her companions to follow her and Morgan farther into the palace. Princess Aliera, a gossamer-winged faerie princess in hundreds of pink and white ruffles, stood outside the library waiting for them. Beside her, a slim eshu childling dressed in a close-fitting leopard-spotted body suit with glittering whiskers drawn on her cheeks motioned them to approach.

Morgan and Aliera embraced like sisters. The princess had recovered from her close call with Banality except for a slight aging of her mortal seeming, making her look nearer Morgan's eleven years. Apparently no one at court had noticed.

"What's this secret meeting bit?" Edmund demanded. "I got your message," he said to Leigh, "about getting together for some important hush-hush business tonight. So what's going on?"

"You, sir, are impertinent," the eshu childling spoke up, startling Edmund, who had not expected such a rebuke from another commoner. "My name is Layla," she informed the redcap, "and you must be the renowned Edmund, eater-of-many-things." She gave Edmund a scintillating grin that made the childling blush beneath his clownface.

"Does this have anything to do with the rumors that have been circulating about the duke?" Valmont asked quietly.

"What rumors?" Tor asked.

"It is being noised about that Duke Aeon will pronounce himself the new Prince of the Shadow Court for the coming half-year and will bring the freehold with him into the Unseelie camp."

"That was obvious," Rasputin said. Leigh looked at Valmont in unfeigned shock.

"When is this supposed to take place?" she asked the eshu. "And aren't you the current prince? This isn't your doing, is it?" Suddenly she felt as if she did not know Valmont at all.

Valmont shook his head. "I would rather not discuss my lack of information about the doings of the Shadow Court," he said. "At any rate, my reign, — such as it is — will be over at midnight, when the new prince is crowned."

"That's a little under two hours from now," Leigh said.

Princess Aliera stamped her foot, setting off a jingle of soft bells about her ankles that caught everyone's attention. Then the princess nodded to Morgan.

"It's about the harp," Morgan said. "Maybe it's about the other thing, too," she added as an afterthought.

She took the group into the library. Layla shut the door behind them.

"What harp?" asked Edmund.

Morgan told her friends about her brief stay in Princess Aliera's rooms at the palace and about the eerie music she had heard coming from the duke's chambers late at night.

"Layla is the one who actually saw the harp," Morgan said. "She told Aliera about it, and Aliera told me."

The princess nodded. "I miss the duke," she said. "I haven't seen him in ages, and I think it's because of the harp."

"What harp?" Edmund repeated, wondering if it was just that girls were dense or if he had missed something everyone else had gotten.

Layla described her foray into the secret passage outside the duke's rooms and how she had dared to peek through the spy hole in the wall. "I saw him with my own eyes, and this is not a pooka's truth I am speaking." She covered her mouth in embarrassment as she heard Rasputin's miffed "harumph."

"I shall never forget that slight to my kithain," the pooka mumbled. "Let me stop you from explaining things."

Layla continued. "In his room there is an ebony harp which plays itself, such unpleasant music. The duke sits at his desk filling pages and pages of paper with writing. I think he has done nothing else for some time."

"I've never heard any legends of cursed harps," Rasputin said. "We should leave it alone since it's obviously doing the duke no harm."

"That's what this meeting is all about," Morgan said emphatically. "We're going to get rid of the harp."

"Surely you're not talking about invading the duke's chambers," Rasputin muttered.

"Cool!" said Edmund. "Where's this passage?"

Tor's bulk would not fit through the narrow passage.

"Why don't you and I go round to the duke's rooms and just ask to see him?" Leigh suggested. The thought of sneaking up on her liege, however critical the situation, did not sit easily with her.

"I never broke my oath," Eleighanara said softly as her punishment was announced before the Seelie lords and ladies of Arcadia.

"That you narrowly avoided forswearing your allegiance is the reason we have chosen this form of punishment for

you," the silver-voiced faerie lord said, heartbreak turning his violet eyes to deepest indigo. "Through your travails in the mortal world, your headstrong spirit will be broken and reformed. You have a great purpose to fulfill in your new home beyond the Dreaming, but you must come to that purpose with a suppleness of will and a strength of temperament that are still lacking in your nature."

"You sentence me to eternal exile," she cried.

"We sentence you to your destiny," came the cold response.

Leigh shuddered in the sudden chill that seemed to settle around her.

Unaware of Leigh's momentary vision, Tor grunted his agreement to her suggestion. Together they watched as their friends, led by Layla, disappeared through a false bookshelf in the library. Princess Aliera remained behind.

"I'll come with you to provide a distraction," she said to Leigh and Tor.

Sir Cumulus stood like a sentry at the foot of the stairs. "We want to see the duke," Tor growled. "It's important."

"I'm afraid his Grace is not receiving this evening," Sir Cumulus said. "He is expected to make an official pronouncement later. Perhaps at that time—"

Princess Aliera screamed, her shrill voice echoing through the cavernous front hall. She ran furiously toward the front door of the palace. Like a ball shot from a cannon, Sir Cumulus drew his sword and rushed after her.

Leigh and Tor looked at one another.

"So much for subtlety," Leigh murmured. The pair climbed the staircase to Aeon's chambers.

Inside the secret passage, Layla pointed to a small hole in the wall. Standing on tiptoe, she could barely press her eye against the opening. Valmont took his turn spying on the duke. Then Edmund insisted on being held up so that he, too, could look. "That's a harp, all right," he said softly, for once remembering the difference between a whisper and a shriek. "The duke looks like a goth biker," he added approvingly.

After everyone had taken turns at the spy hole, Layla placed her palm in a small depression in the wall. A panel slid aside, allowing entry into the ducal suite.

In her darkened room, the lady sensed the presence of intruders outside the chambers where her harp's companion instrument lay. Frantically, she began playing a tune intended to drive the duke over the edge into the full fae madness known as Bedlam. She must not fail.

The duke's personal guard, a pair of trolls armed with halberds, stopped Leigh and Tor at the door to Aeon's chambers. Leigh and Tor could hear anguished music coming from beyond the door.

"The Duke has given orders that we are to admit no one," one of the trolls said.

"Not even in a matter of utmost urgency?" Leigh asked. Briefly she contemplated attempting to awe them with her own faerie grandeur. As if reading her thoughts, Tor shook his head. "Won't work on them," he said. "They're doing their job."

Leigh nodded at the duke's guards and turned as if to go. Using Tor's body as a screen, she slipped the emerald stone from her waistband and lunged toward the door. With a loud groan, the massive door swung open behind the trolls. Tor drew his axe and held it above his head.

"I call challenge on both of you in this place and at this time!" he bellowed.

Seizing her opportunity, Leigh dove between the trolls and plunged into the duke's sitting room.

Aeon was jerked from his tortured reverie by the

sudden clamor that surrounded him. The door to his chambers burst open and a figure dressed in a white flowing robe flung herself past his guards into the room. Outside the doorway, Aeon saw his troll sentinels engaged in a furious, though one-sided, combat with another troll who parried their attacks with a long-handled battle axe wielded in quarterstaff style.

Aeon rose from his writing desk and confronted the intruder.

"How dare you disturb me!" the duke thundered, staring at the red-haired woman. Through the fog that clouded his perceptions, he recognized Dame Eleighanara, and his face grew cold and harsh.

Leigh knelt before the duke, an imploring look on her face.

"Forgive me, your Grace," she began.

"I do not forgive you!" Aeon cried. His form began to radiate with noble power. "I gave orders that no one who honored me should disturb the sanctity of my private chambers. Do you renege upon your vow?"

Behind Aeon, a door in the wall opened up and Edmund toppled into the duke's rooms. Aeon turned at the noise and saw Valmont, Rasputin and Baroness Morgania emerge from the hidden passage.

"Am I beset on all sides by traitors?" Aeon's voice was a cry of outrage and despair. He was in the fullness of his faerie glory.

"Leave me!" he ordered.

Leigh despaired as she realized that no one in the room could withstand the duke's Glamour-enforced command. As if unseen hands were dragging her from the room, Leigh stumbled to her feet and backed toward the door.

Edmund turned and ran for the door in the wall, only to find Layla standing outside blocking his passage.

"Out of my way," the redcap yelled. Layla grinned

toybox

and used both hands to shove him back into the room. "Edmund the all-consumer is not so easily dissuaded," she said.

Struggling to resist the duke's command, Rasputin held his breath and let fly a wooden juggler's club. Valmont ran past him for the front door and launched himself at one of Tor's opponents. Morgan squeezed her locket protectively and tried to make herself approach the duke. It felt like walking through molasses.

"Missed!" Rasputin cried triumphantly as his missile struck Aeon in the forehead, dropping the duke to the floor and dissipating his awesome presence.

"The harp!" cried Morgan, once again able to move freely. She and Edmund reached the instrument at the same time. Morgan looked at the redcap frantically.

"What do we do?" she whispered. Edmund looked at her and grinned.

"Don't eat it!" Morgan screamed. "It might kill you!"

Edmund hesitated. The thought of what might happen if he ingested a cursed faerie treasure had never occurred to him. He looked around for some other implement of destruction.

He spied the candle beginning to gutter on the duke's writing desk. "Get some paper," he called to Morgan. He grabbed the candle while Morgan began snatching up armfuls of crumpled sheet-music to pile around the harp.

Leigh and Rasputin joined the battle in the hallway outside the duke's door. Tor was on one knee, desperately fending off blow after blow from Aeon's guards. Leigh stepped in to even the odds, grabbing one guard's weapon near the blade and pulling it downward in an attempt to wrest it from his grasp. Her weight dragged the halberd nearly to the floor, but the troll held on gamely. Rasputin began a singsong chant and mimed pulling at the legs of one of the guards. The troll stumbled and fell forward, helped in his tumble by a lightning-fast jerk from Valmont.

Edmund shoved the lit candle against the dry parchment, fanning it until the paper burst into flames. After scrounging in his pockets, he pulled out a disposable lighter.

"I don't smoke, anyway," he said, tossing it into the flames. "Better back up," he said to Morgan.

The explosion turned the center of the duke's room into a bonfire. Morgan screamed and ran to Aeon's crumpled body, then began tugging the duke away from the conflagration. "Help me!"

"Can't you do anything by yourself?" Edmund scoffed, and went to Morgan's aid.

"Let me help, too," he heard Layla's voice say, and he moved to make room for her to grab one of Aeon's feet. The three childlings slowly dragged Aeon toward the door.

The harp seemed to scream and writhe as the flames consumed it. Echoing its cries of pain, Aeon groaned and then shrieked in agony. The childlings watched in horrified fascination as convulsions wracked the duke's body, while beyond him, ebony colored harp strings snapped and buckled in their death throes. Suddenly, a black, oily smoke seemed to rise from the flames and streak through the air for the curtained window opening onto the second-floor balcony at the rear of the palace. A final scream filled the chamber, followed by a silence broken only by the sounds of battle outside the duke's door.

"The duke's been hurt!" Morgan yelled. Aeon's guards broke off their battle at her cry and rushed into the room. Leigh helped Tor to his feet and looked at him anxiously.

"Why didn't you fight back?" she asked.

Tor shook his head. "It would have been wrong to

attack the duke's sworn bodyguard," he muttered.

Morgan leaned over the duke and kissed his forehead while she let healing Glamour flow from her to Aeon. "Valmont?" Morgan looked at the eshu, who hurried to her side. Following Morgan's lead, he pressed his lips against the forehead of the duke and added his own healing energies to those of the childling. The duke groaned softly, his eyes slowly opening to stare up at Morgan's heart-shaped face. His face softened and he gave her a brilliant smile.

"Baroness Morgania," he said, his voice light and filled with gentleness. "To what do I owe the honor of this fair awakening?"

Leigh leaned into Tor and nearly wept with relief. Rasputin slipped into the room and, ripping down one of the black curtains from the window, smothered the fire.

The lady of shadows pulled her flaming fingers from the strings and howled in pain, breaking the connection between her harp and its dying sister. Shaking with anger and fear, she stared in horror at her blistered hands. "I have failed my lord," Glynnis whispered, and huddled in her scented rooms, awaiting the wrath to come.

In the aftermath of the Samhain Court, the quiet time known as Crepusc, when revelry and mirth are past and, some say, wisdom and arcane secrets wait at the doorway for admittance, a small company of kithain gathered in the duke's ruined chambers. In the center of Aeon's sitting room a scorched spot marked the place where the harp had been.

Aeon sat in his chair, the only seat in the near-empty room, while Leigh, Valmont and Rasputin made themselves as comfortable as they could on the floor. Tor stood with Sir Cumulus in the doorway. Lady Alyssa allowed herself the liberty of leaning just a little on the duke's writing desk. Aliera sat on Aeon's lap, and Morgan did her best to imitate Alyssa's stance, although the desk was too high for her. Finally, she gave in and hoisted herself up to sit atop the desk. Edmund and Layla sat on the window ledge, their backs to a sky that was just beginning to show signs of light.

Outside, the revelers had taken their party elsewhere, most of them blissfully unaware of what had nearly transpired within the palace. Valmont supposed that another Prince of Shadows had been selected. He wondered if this one would be kept in the dark about the real doings of the Unseelie kithain, as he had so carefully been.

Aeon listened as the oathmates recounted with mixed feelings of pride and embarrassment all that had happened since Leigh's tumultuous knighting. When asked, Leigh handed the emerald gem to the duke, who turned it over and over in his slender fingers before returning it to Leigh.

"I can only tell you that it is, as you have already determined, a powerful faerie treasure," the duke said. "I think that it is also very, very old."

Lady Alyssa straightened suddenly and reached for a ponderous ring of keys she wore at her belt. "If your Grace will pardon my absence for a moment?" she asked.

"That I will not do," the duke replied, "until I have had a chance to beg your forgiveness for the burdens I have so callously and thanklessly laid upon your shoulders. Both you and Sir Cumulus, my dear companions, have never swerved in your steadfast devotion to me. I am in your debt now and for all time."

Alyssa's face turned bright pink and Cumulus lowered his head and coughed softly in embarrassed pleasure.

"Now, dear Lady Alyssa," the duke said, "I give you leave to go, yet I hope for your swift return."

By tacit agreement, no one mentioned Aliera's disastrous foray into the mundane world except for Valmont, who made a vague allusion to an improvement in Morgan's home situation which would allow her to spend more time in kithain society. Aeon accepted the eshu's statement without probing into the particulars behind it.

"So Malacar has finally fled the fief," Aeon remarked. "Good riddance, if in truth he has left these lands...."

"The wording of your pronouncement upon him was quite explicit," Leigh said. "I could feel it bind him as I spoke your words."

Aeon nodded.

"You and Baroness Morgania have discharged your duties faithfully," he said. Turning his head to encompass the other oathmates in his next statement, he continued. "All of you have labored to execute my commands without direction or support. Such service demands a suitable reward."

"Way cool!" Edmund called from the window.

"Though each of you may claim some suitable reward from among the ducal treasures, if you wish, you might prefer my promise of assistance."

"I want a real sword!" Edmund cried.

"I shall ask Sir Cumulus to find you a weapon of a weight and size befitting to you." Aeon looked toward his herald. "Perhaps a short sword or a battle knife could be found for this aspiring warrior?" Sir Cumulus bowed to Aeon and motioned to Edmund to follow him from the ducal chambers.

"A favor is the last thing I would want, your Grace," said Rasputin. Aeon looked puzzled for a moment, until Aliera whispered something in his ear. The duke looked at the pooka and nodded gravely.

"When the time comes, I shall endeavor to fulfill my understanding of any reasonable request you may make of me."

"I'd like to ask a favor, too, your Grace," Morgan said, her heart suddenly in her throat. Aeon extended his hand to the tiny Baroness, who slid from her perch atop his desk and came to stand by the duke's side.

"No wondrous bauble for you, Baroness?" the duke asked chidingly. Morgan shook her head.

"I would like to ask for your forgiveness for anything I might have done in the past which would, if you knew of it, arouse your anger."

Leigh held her breath and stared at Morgan, thankful that Edmund was not in the room.

Aeon threw back his head and laughed delightedly. "A splendid request if ever I heard one," he said. "Are you sure you do not wish to include future misdeeds in your accounting?"

"No, your Grace," Morgan said, her voice firm and clear.

"You have my forgiveness and my pardon for any such iniquities," he said. "That was easily done."

Tor cleared his throat self-consciously. "Your Grace," he rumbled, "I've got my own treasure, but I wouldn't mind it if you could see your way clear to granting Sir Fizzlewig outright custody of that old toy chest that caused us all so much trouble. He's holding it in trust for Baroness Zoe, his liege, but she might just want to take it away from him and put it someplace safer." Tor paused and coughed, unused to stringing together so many words at once.

"He loves that chest, and what happened wasn't anybody's fault—"

"Enough!" Aeon held up his hand. "You argue your friend's case with eloquence. I shall speak with the baroness and make certain that the chest is duly awarded to Sir Fizzlewig without delay."

"Look!" Edmund exclaimed, marching into the room ahead of Sir Cumulus. The redcap brandished a child-sized sword in his hands. The weapon was finely made and mimicked a noble's sword in everything except for size. "It's not just chimerical either!" he exclaimed, giving Morgan a superior look.

"It was my own sword from my childling days," Sir Cumulus muttered. "But the first thing you must learn, youngling," Cumulus said sternly, as Edmund nearly caught him with a backstroke, "is never to brandish a weapon in the presence of your duke."

"Oops," Edmund said, sticking the sword in his belt and returning to his place beside Layla at the window.

Aeon turned next to Valmont. The eshu bowed low before he spoke. "Your Grace," Valmont said, "There is a strange kithain who has lately made his presence known in the fief...."

"Yeah!" said Edmund. "He's got this severe armor and this glowing blue hand...."

Rasputin's dream came back to him. "He's not one of the Dauntain," he said quickly.

"As my friend has opined," Valmont continued as though Rasputin's outburst was not news to him, "he may be dangerous to the safety of the kithain in your fief."

"I will instruct my knights to make every effort to locate this kithain and, if he should prove as dangerous as you indicate, see to his removal from my lands. But what of something for yourself?" Aeon asked.

"If you wish me to make a more personal request," Valmont said, "I shall beg your leave to defer it to a time when one suggests itself to me."

Aeon nodded to the eshu. "As you have spoken," he said. Last, he turned to Leigh.

As Leigh was about to claim the same right of deferral as Valmont, Lady Alyssa returned to the duke's chambers, bearing with her a heavy tome.

"Your Grace," she said, "here is something that may concern us all." She laid the book on the duke's desk and opened it to a page marked by a red silk ribbon.

"This is a copy of the legends of True Thomas," she said.

"True who?" Edmund asked.

"Thomas the Rhymer," Valmont said, "also known as Grand Bard of the Fae. Those of my kithain revere him as one of the great storytellers of the Dreaming; others may honor him for their own reasons."

"In this particular volume," Alyssa said, "which is, unfortunately incomplete, he writes of a great feud that occurred during the time of the Shattering, a war between brothers that took place during the closing of the last gate to Arcadia."

"Silver's Gate," Aeon said suddenly. "That much of the tale is known to me." He turned to the others. "Its location has been lost for ages, covered by the mists which bar us all from congress with the realm of the Dreaming."

"The story also mentions gemstones, one of which he refers to as the Keystone or the Eye of Opening. According to him, that stone — which matches the stone in Dame Eleighanara's possession — can open anything it touches."

"We knew that," Edmund whispered loudly. Layla shushed him, her eyes wide with fascination.

"Malacar was trying to use the stone in Golden Gate Park," said Morgan suddenly. "Maybe..." she hesitated, not daring to speak the thought that was in all of their minds.

"Silver's Gate couldn't possibly be anywhere in Golden Gate Park," Rasputin said.

"I would like to make my request to your Grace," Leigh said, suddenly. As she spoke, an eerie sense of other eyes, unseen eyes, watching her made her shiver.

"Please," Aeon said. A strange look crossed his face and he stared intently at the Fiona knight.

Leigh stood before the duke. "I would like to undertake a further quest for you," she said. "For all of us," she amended. "I would like to attempt to seek this lost gate and, with your permission, reopen the path to the Dreaming."

Morgan gasped. Everyone was silent as Duke Aeon rose from his chair and approached Leigh. "Before all here, and on behalf of all the kithain under my care, I charge you and your companions—"

"—oathmates," Morgan whispered softly, then stopped her mouth with a hand.

"—oathmates," Aeon repeated, "to find and open Silver's Gate."

When he returned to his church home sometime after dawn had risen, Edmund stared for a long time at his sword before carefully tucking it away under the blanket he used as a bed. Then he cursed.

"I should have asked the duke for Mr. Dumpy," he said bitterly. He reached in his pocket and drew out the miniature clown. "I guess I'll just have to keep you hidden," he told the figure. Then he had a consoling thought. "He probably wouldn't have let me keep you, anyway." A look of sympathy seemed to pass over the clown's tiny face.

In the early morning, the imprisoned prince sent forth a pair of dreams. The first, to the fearful, fallen Lady Glynnis, contained explicit instructions for a new task, one filled with a sense of urgency. The second dream was a message to Eleighanara, newly found and eagerly awaited. It contained only a phrase but it, too, was filled with the same command for haste.

Leigh awoke suddenly from a restless, dream-filled sleep. "Go to the place of eternal flowers," she said as if the words had been placed in her mind. "There lies the gateway to undying powers." She wrote the words down on a scrap of paper so that she would be certain not to forget them, then fell back into a dreamless slumber.

chapter

sixteen

Bevin Murdoch got by on looks and charm — and a few skills he preferred to keep under wraps. A high school drop-out from Los Angeles, he had left home the day after his sixteenth birthday, confident that he could sell his angular physique and death-angel face to the first talent scout he ran into. Two years later, although he wasn't famous or rich, he was getting by.

Moving to San Francisco, where the climate was milder and the competition less severe, had been a brilliant idea. Although there were fewer opportunities for commercial modeling than L.A. had to offer, the ones that existed came to him as often as not. Jeans and shirts were his specialty, but he also did shoes, jewelry, cologne, and anything else an advertiser wanted to pay bucks for a pretty face and a good body to wear, hold or fondle.

His latest gig, gotten just yesterday, when he had almost run out of mad money, intrigued him. Almost as much as the lady who had hired him for the shooting. "Wear leather," she had said, "lots of it. And velvet, if you can find it. Black would be a good color for you."

Bevin snorted as he tossed back his long, fashionably shagged black hair and applied just a touch of kohl to accent his dark eyes, making them look even darker. She wanted him to meet her just before midnight at the Conservatory of Flowers, where, she said, she wanted to photograph him amid the jungle-like foliage. She wouldn't give him any particulars about what he would be selling, but she assured him that it was nothing that would embarrass his reputation in the industry.

She was also adamant about one other thing. "Don't wear any jewelry," she said. "Not even a belt buckle. Wear a sash or a rope or something." He had wondered how he could wear leather without studs, but finally found a pair of fitted black leather pants and high boots that met her requirements. He pulled a flowing velvet poet's shirt over his head and cinched it at the waist with a black silk braided rope. On impulse, he found some ravens' feathers in his collection of "things to put in one's hair," and stuck them in a braid down one side of his face.

He posed in front of the full-length mirror that dominated his one-room walk-up in the Castro district.

"Not bad," he said to himself. Wondering if the lady would be available after the gig, he left his apartment and headed for Golden Gate Park, whistling and strutting all the way.

Leigh arrived with Morgan at the Toybox just before dark. Tor was waiting for them, his axe resting on the table near the back of the coffee shop. Although he was more or less reconciled with his son-in-law and thus able to visit with his daughter Alicia and with Morgan, the troll steadfastly refused their offer to move in with them. Morgan did her best to ensure that they remained enchanted, and therefore amenable to her suggestions, but Tor was afraid that even the normal amounts of Banality associated with daily life in the nuclear family would prove too much for him.

A few minutes later, Edmund and Valmont entered the coffee shop. Just as they were about to greet their companions, Rasputin dashed through the door, slamming it shut behind him. Winded, the pooka slumped into his chair at their table.

"What's wrong?" Morgan asked.

"Nothing," Rasputin said. "I was not followed here, I'm certain of that."

"Who followed you?" Valmont asked. "Was it our dark knight?"

Rasputin nodded his head. "I think so," he said.

"Great!" grumbled Tor. "If it wasn't him, who was it?"

Rasputin shook his head, helpless to answer. He had woken up late in the afternoon feeling uneasy. As he dressed to meet his companions, he got the distinct sense that someone was with him in the small apartment. Telling himself that he was only suffering from post-revelry, pre-second-quest nerves, the pooka had continued his preparations. It was when he reached under the bed for a juggling ball that had strayed from his shoulder sack that he felt something brush past his arm. His hand closed around the ball, and he jerked his arm away from the dark underside of his bed. He thought he heard a hissing response to his movement. Thoroughly spooked, he had grabbed up his bag and fled the apartment. Now, thinking back, he couldn't remember whether he had locked the door behind him.

"I got it!" cried Edmund. "Is it animal, vegetable or mineral?" The redcap beamed at his own cleverness.

Rasputin shook his head again. Edmund repeated his question, breaking it down into its three components. To each of them, Rasputin gave the same helpless nod.

Finally he looked at them. "I've had the most wonderful dreams lately," he said softly. "But everyone knows that dreams never come true in the physical world..."

"I believe Rasputin is trying, in his own circuitous fashion, to tell us that he has given birth to a chimera of some sort and that it has now chosen this time in his life to make its presence known." Valmont stood behind Rasputin and, feeling the tense muscles in the pooka's back, began to massage them.

"So are we gonna go comb Golden Gate park in search of this silver gate or not?" Edmund asked.

"We have to decide exactly where we're going to start searching," said Leigh. "After all, Malacar was obviously in the wrong place."

Edmund groaned. He got up from the table and began walking around the coffee shop, presently empty except for his oathmates and Fizzlewig. He sort of missed the childling gang he used to run with, but they had given up on him when he suddenly found more important things to do. Now he was stuck with a bunch of Seelie wimps who did some really cool things but took forever to get around to doing them. As he shuffled around the room, he shoved his hands in his pockets, hoping to turn up something that would occupy his time. His right fist closed on a squishy tube he had found in a dumpster behind a hardware store.

He looked around him for something to do with its contents. He caught sight of Morgan, with her back to him, sitting primly at the table, looking like a queen holding court. Her long black hair hung in a single braid down her back. Casually she flipped it over the back of the chair. Grinning to himself, Edmund pulled out the tube of superglue and inched his way toward the table.

"Malacar was in the Japanese Tea Garden for a reason," Valmont said. "The place must have something in common with the gate's location or he would never have attempted the ritual of opening — which is what the circle must have been all about — in that place."

"I thought you said Malacar was looking for treasure," Morgan said.

Valmont shook his head. "That's the problem with picking up rumors," the eshu replied. "The eshu believe that rumors were invented by pookas," he smiled down at Rasputin, hoping to elicit a response from his melancholy companion.

Rasputin looked up and gave Valmont a half-hearted smile, but said nothing.

"At any rate," the eshu continued, "Malacar may have given it out that he was searching for faerie treasures, or he may have truly believed that he was opening up a lost freehold in which such treasures were stored. It's likely we will never know. What we do know is that something led him to the Japanese Tea Garden."

Leigh's heart thudded. Frantically, she fished in her belt pouch for the scrap of paper she had tucked in it before leaving for the Toybox. Finding it, she read the words written upon it.

"Go to the place of eternal flowers," she intoned. "There lies the gateway to undying powers." The others looked at her with blank faces. "I dreamed those words this morning," she said.

"Eternal flowers," Valmont echoed, sighing. "I suppose it would be too much to ask for a less cryptic pronouncement from beyond...."

"There aren't any flowers in Golden Gate Park," mumbled Rasputin.

Morgan jumped as something lurched against the back of her chair. She turned around and saw Edmund falling to his knees.

"Sorry," the redcap said, "I tripped!" He picked himself up and rubbed at one kneecap.

"What's that in your hair?" Leigh asked Morgan, putting her hand to the childling's braid. "It's sticky," she said, trying to release her grip on Morgan's hair. "I can't free my hand."

Valmont leaned over Morgan and peered at her braid. Then he looked down at Edmund.

"Were you holding anything in your hand when you tripped?" the eshu asked the redcap.

Edmund felt around on the floor. His hand closed around the tube he had let drop in his "fall." He handed it to Valmont wordlessly.

"What is it?" said Leigh, still struggling to extricate her fingers from Morgan's hair without hurting the childling.

"Superglue," Valmont replied.

Morgan started to cry. "Get it out of my hair," she sobbed.

"Best thing you can do is cut it." Fizzlewig approached the table, a pair of scissors clutched in his hands.

"Gosh, I'm sorry, Morgan," Edmund said, trying his best to sound convincing.

"No you're not, and you know it!" Morgan retorted hotly, her face screwed into a grimace of anger and despair. "I hate you, Edmund! I hate you, I hate you, I hate you."

"Morgan!" Tor's voice was sharp. "You don't hate anybody. It's not in you, or it shouldn't be."

"Stop telling me what to do!" Morgan cried, unable to control the fury she felt.

Tor looked at Morgan. "You're my granddaughter," the troll said slowly. "So long as that remains true, I will tell you what you need to hear."

Morgan's eyes widened in surprise. As quickly as it had come to her, her towering rage departed under her grandfather's stern admonishment.

"Edmund!" Leigh exclaimed. "How could you do something like that?"

"Please," said Rasputin woefully. "We need to fight. It's good that we solidify our group identity with bonds of hatred and anger!"

"Rasputin's right," said Valmont. The eshu looked at Morgan. "I'm terribly sorry for my friend Edmund's behavior. I have no proof that it was anything other than accidental, however, and you must accept his apology at face value."

Morgan looked up at Fizzlewig, tears still in her eyes. "Isn't there anything else you can do?" she pleaded with the boggan.

Fizzlewig shook his head sadly. "'Fraid not, missy," he said gently. "Best get it over with."

Morgan nodded glumly. The boggan grasped Morgan's hair just above her braid and, centering the scissors, closed them firmly.

"Sounds like a guillotine!" said Edmund, then ducked his head as the others glowered at him. "Well, it does," he muttered.

The braid came off in Fizzlewig's hand. Giving it a swift yank, he freed Leigh's hand. She yelped with pain and glared at the raw patches on the inside of her fingers. Then she looked at Fizzlewig, determination on her face.

"Don't go away," she said to the boggan. She reached behind her and gathered her own luxurious red hair at the back of her neck.

"Cut it," she ordered Fizzlewig, her eyes fixed on Edmund as she spoke.

The boggan looked at her, incredulous. Then he looked at Morgan, who was shaking out her ear-length hair and running her fingers through it tremulously.

"Whatever you want," he said, and repeated his single cut, this time with Leigh's hair in his hands.

Leigh shook her head from side to side. "I kind of like it," she said to Morgan. Rasputin leaned over and picked up several strands of red and black hair and stuffed them into his shoulder bag.

"Now, get on about your business and get out of here so I can clean the place up," Fizzlewig growled, trudging back toward the bar.

"Where were we?" Tor asked, trying to piece together the remnants of the conversation Edmund's escapade had interrupted.

"We were talking about flowers," said Valmont.

"Eternal flowers," Leigh corrected him. "Where would you go to find eternal flowers?"

"Not a museum," Rasputin offered.

"I don't think so," Leigh said. "Paintings — even paintings of flowers — aren't eternal."

"What's an eternal flower?" Edmund asked, trying to fit himself back into the scheme of things.

"Mistletoe," Morgan said abruptly. "The duke's mistletoe."

"I don't know," began Valmont, then stopped as he saw the faraway look on Morgan's face.

"Mistletoe is the symbol of a ruler's eternal power," said Leigh. "She could be right."

"I know I'm right," said Morgan. "And I know where there's some mistletoe!"

"Yeah," said Edmund. "Above the duke's throne. Everybody knows that."

"No," Morgan insisted. "I told you Layla and I replaced the duke's mistletoe with some we found... didn't I?"

"No," Leigh said. "You didn't tell us a lot of things."

Morgan looked abashed. "I meant to," she said. "I really did. But anyway, we found some mistletoe in Golden Gate Park — in the Conservatory of Flowers!"

Edmund jumped up from his seat. "Let's haul our butts down there then," he cried.

Leigh shook her head, straining to hear a voice that seemed to resonate within her. "Midnight," she proclaimed. "We have to go there at midnight."

"This is getting spooky," Edmund said. "How do you know that?"

Valmont placed a hand on the redcap's shoulder.

"Sometimes things come from the Dreaming to those who are willing to listen," the eshu said.

This time, his strength was such that he could direct Glynnis and her ensorcelled companion to the place where he needed them to be. In the possession of one who was meant to use it, the Keystone — or the Stone of Opening — radiated enough power for him to use some of its excess as a beacon to call his procuror and his liberator to the place of his remaking. Hunger filled him, hunger for a life that consisted of more than an eternity of waiting. Locked within his cage, he dreamed of tasting the Glamour and the Banality of the mortal world. They were both within his grasp, and he knew how best to make use of them. Unlike his Seelie cousins, he did not fear Banality's icy cold. It was a force that could be harnessed, and he had spent a lifetime learning its secrets. For that knowledge, and for his ambitions, he had been punished by the rulers of Arcadia. But the time of his captivity was nearly over.

For the first time since his imprisonment, he allowed himself to speak the syllables of his rightful name, the name by which he would be known by those who would come to serve him. Yrtalien of House Ailil. He felt his power grow as he mouthed the name again, this time adding to it his chosen epithet. Yrtalien, the Forsworn Prince.

Clutching her grandfather's hand, Morgan led the group through Golden Gate Park to the graceful, white-domed Conservatory of Flowers, where she and Layla had gone in search of mistletoe. Filled with people by day, at night the vast expanse of green that was San Francisco's pride took on a lonely grandeur. On their way through the park, they passed a few benches occupied by some homeless sleepers. Tor shook his head sadly, remembering the nights when he, too, had been driven to find refuge in the Park.

Behind Morgan and Tor walked Leigh and Edmund. The redcap had declined Leigh's offer of a hand, preferring both hands free to practice with his new sword. Rasputin trailed after Edmund, nervously looking over his shoulder and starting at every rustling noise he heard. Valmont paced a little behind Rasputin, hoping that the pooka would take some comfort from his presence as a rear guard.

Leigh mulled over the preparations they had made. It had not been difficult for them to find rose petals, and a trip to a jeweler friend of Valmont's had procured enough silver powder for them to make a circle. She had debated asking Fizzlewig for one of the creatures from the box, but blanched at the idea of a sacrifice, even a chimeric one. Somehow, she felt that Malacar's use of the bride had been a misunderstanding. Once again, she regretted letting the satyr go before extracting from him the exact specifications of the ritual he had attempted.

"There it is," Morgan whispered excitedly as they neared the Conservatory. "We don't need to go inside at all," she said. "The mistletoe was growing on the oak trees in the gardens behind the building."

"Good," Leigh called softly up to her. "I don't relish the thought of another attempted B&E."

The group skirted the building and headed for a cluster of oak trees. Leigh felt heat at her waist and looked down.

"You're glowing!" Edmund pointed at the pouch containing the gem.

"Trust the stone," Valmont said. "The gate may act as a homing beacon for it."

Leigh pulled the stone from its pouch and held it tightly in her fingers.

Soon they were gathered before a stand of blue and California oak trees. Morgan pointed upward through the branches at some pale berries tangled in the leaves. "There's the mistletoe," she said.

The gem throbbed in Leigh's hand. "Here," she said. "We make the circle here."

Within the Glamour of her concealment, Glynnis watched as the group of kithain made their way to the spot beside the oaks. She smiled to herself and placed a protective arm on the handsome youth who stood, slack-faced, at her side, his mind devoid of memory and his will subsumed in her faerie grandeur. "When you see the light," she whispered to him, implanting a single thought in his vacant consciousness, "go forward. In the light, you will meet your destiny." Smiling with anticipation, she waited.

Valmont sprinkled the powdered silver according to Leigh's direction. Morgan followed after the eshu, strewing rose petals in his wake.

Edmund stood next to Tor, watching the others and hoping for a chance to use his new weapon.

Rasputin thought he heard something rustle in the trees above his head.

It had kept its distance, drawn to its creator, yet feeling a greater source of power calling to it. Now it experienced an irresistible urge. Loosening its grip from the mistletoe-wrapped branches, it dropped to the ground, seeking its fulfillment.

Leigh held the brilliantly glowing green stone in front of her and took a deep breath. Standing behind her, the others watched her walk toward the circle. Just then Rasputin screamed as something fell from the trees and wrapped itself around his arm.

Edmund whooped and ran toward Rasputin, swinging his sword wildly in front of him. "I've got it!" he yelled. Morgan shrieked in response to Rasputin's outcry and rushed toward the pooka, Tor right behind her. Valmont saw the general convergence on Rasputin and glanced at Leigh, torn between the urge to help his pooka friend and the need to ensure Leigh's safety.

Unable to stop herself, Leigh barely heard the commotion behind her. The stone was pulling her toward the circle's center.

"How can you keep us apart!" she cried out when she heard the entirety of the punishment meted out to her and her fallen prince.

"How can we afford to allow you to remain together?" her judge's voice rejoined. *"The prince of House Ailil is far too dangerous to be granted freedom in either this world or the mortal realm. That we do not excise him from the Dreaming, that we leave him his life, is mercy enough."*

"You have imprisoned my heart!" she moaned in despair.

"We have freed you for your true destiny."

"You cannot keep me from him forever," she said in a voice filled with bravado.

"We shall most certainly try."

"They cannot keep me from you forever," Leigh murmured, as she held the stone resolutely before her, following its inexorable direction.

Edmund's first cut at the creature missed; his second glanced off Rasputin. "I'm trying!" he called. "Don't die on me before I can kill it!"

Tor shoved Edmund aside and, throwing down his axe, wrapped both hands around the snake-like creature with the belt-buckle face. Roaring, he pulled the chimeric nightmare away from Rasputin. Holding it at arm's length he struggled to contain the hissing, writhing monster.

An ethereal glow began to fill the circle, bathing Leigh in its otherworldly light. The gem seemed to struggle, trying to leap from her hand. Leigh clutched it tighter. Valmont watched her as she reached the center of the brightness. A rich vibration filled the air around them, building in intensity and pitch until it crossed the threshold from music to agony. Then the light and noise fused into a new sensation, neither sight nor sound, but something greater than either. Time seemed to stop.

"Something's wrong," Valmont called. "I can see the gate, but it's not opening! Something else is needed!"

"The snake, Grandpa!" Morgan cried. "Throw it in the circle!"

Before Tor could move, Rasputin lunged toward the captive monster. Screaming, he grabbed the chimera by the tail. Concentrating all his will, he looked at Tor.

"Let go!" he yelled. Tor released his grip, startled by the pooka's vehemence.

Rasputin whirled around in a circle and released the creature at the peak of his swing.

"I am not Raphael!" he howled. He dropped to his knees in the grass, shivering uncontrollably.

The chimera landed in front of Leigh and the circle of light exploded, releasing a surge of Glamour with a crash of soundless thunder. Leigh fell backward into Valmont's arms just before he lost his balance, over-whelmed by the splendor of the portal now gaping open before them. Morgan grabbed her grandfather around the waist and stared, wide-eyed. On Tor's other side, Edmund dropped his sword and sat down abruptly.

"Go now!" Lady Glynnis commanded from the shadows which hid her from view, shoving Bevin Murdoch toward the circle of light.

Freed from his prison halfway between Arcadia and the mortal world, Yrtalien stepped through the portal, his ageless body suffused with pent-up Glamour. A cold, icy pain stabbed through him, as though an iron sword had pierced his heart. He screamed as his unprotected faerie essence began to wither in the grip of the world's Banality. Casting about blindly, he felt his hands connect with the body of a young man. His orders to Lady Glynnis had been specific, and she appeared to have selected a fitting vessel to house his faerie self. Unlike others who had passed from Arcadia into the mortal world, he could not afford the luxury of implanting his spirit in an unborn child. Relief flooded him as he forced himself inside the tendered cloak of human flesh, consigning Bevin Murdoch's mortal soul to some unknown destination and severing its connection with his body.

Yrtalien, the Forsworn Prince, looked at the world around him through mortal eyes, marking the faces and forms of his accidental liberators. He took a step toward the red-haired woman whose mortal body concealed the spirit of one he had loved in Arcadia and felt his body tremble with weakness. Realizing his vulnerability in his newfound mortal guise, he looked down upon Eleighanara with something akin to resignation.

"When I am stronger," he whispered in a voice only she could hear, "I will call you to me."

The Unseelie prince sensed the nearby presence of Lady Glynnis, his accomplice and his strongest ally. Staggering from the circle toward her, he collapsed into her waiting arms. Whispering a poem of journeying, the lady of the shadows and her long-awaited prince vanished into the night.

With a sound reminiscent of a sigh, the portal faded away, plunging Leigh and the others momentarily into darkness.

"What was that?" Edmund asked.

"I don't think it was Arcadia," Valmont said, struggling to his feet and pulling Leigh after him.

"Someone came out of the portal," Morgan whispered.

"I don't see any portal," Edmund complained.

"I saw him," Morgan insisted. "He looked beautiful and terrifying. He was shining so brightly I had to close my eyes. When I opened them, he had changed. He seemed more like—" The childling paused, struggling to describe what she had seen.

"More like a mortal," Valmont said. "There was a second man, a human, waiting for him in the circle." The eshu's voice was still and cold. "Your shining figure clothed himself in the body of that other man."

"Like an eviction, or what?" Edmund asked.

"More like murder," Tor said quietly. "There was a woman in the shadows beyond the circle," the troll added. "I think she spirited the newcomer away."

"Yrtalien," said Leigh, certain of the truth in her words. "His name is Yrtalien."

"Do you know him?" Edmund asked.

Leigh shook her head. "No," she said quickly. "Not anymore," she added in a whisper, more to herself than in answer to Edmund's question.

Leigh looked around her, then back at the now empty circle. Rasputin crept slowly to the place where the light had been and peered carefully at the grass at his feet.

"The beast is gone," Valmont reassured the pooka. "It vanished when the gate opened."

"What have we done?" Leigh asked softly, but in her heart she knew the answer. She had taken the first step on a journey that had been marked out for her in the Dreaming.

"I'm sure it's nothing we need concern ourselves

over," said Rasputin.

"Is that it?" demanded Edmund. "Does this mean our quest is over?"

"Oh no," Morgan replied, her voice filled with certainty and trepidation. "That wasn't Silver's Gate at all. I think our quest has only just begun."

Cyprian Ryder struggled to remember why he was on a plane bound for the east coast. He had vague memories of wandering down Haight Street, following some urge that had to do with the ache in his hand. Some figures stepped into his path and...for a moment he thought he remembered the glint of swords. He had tried to defend himself, but they were more than he could handle and they overwhelmed him. He had awoken on the plane.

He shook his head and summoned a stewardess to bring him a drink to ease the dryness in his throat. His left hand throbbed with pain. Looking down at the blue discoloration in the center of his palm, he felt the stirring of a faint memory fighting to overcome the fog within his mind. Sooner or later, he knew, he would remember everything. There was something he had to do, someone he had to find. All he needed was time and rest, and everything would come to light.

He sipped his drink and stared out the window into the night, letting the plane's hum lull him to sleep. A word stuck in his mind just before he surrendered to slumber. The word was a name — Chevalier. He willed himself to remember the strange word. It meant nothing to him now, but it was a place to start.

biography

A native of Appalachia, Jackie Cassada has spent most of her life (with the exception of a ten-year sojourn in Boston) in the Blue Ridge Mountains. An avid reader, she majored in English in college with a specialty in Victorian literature. Her discovery of role-playing games in 1978 resulted in rediscovering a talent for "let's pretend" and an appreciation for the art of oral storytelling.

She has been the science fiction columnist for *Library Journal* since 1984. In 1993, she began working as a freelance writer for White Wolf's **Wraith: The Oblivion** and other games in the **Storyteller** ™ system, and her short stories have appeared in White Wolf's fiction collections **Death and Damnation, Truth Until Paradox, City of Darkness: Unseen,** and **The Splendour Falls.**

Besides writing, she has played in several rock, folk rock and traditional folk bands, worked as a "techie" for local college and community theatres, and collaborated on the musical score for an adaptation of **Pinocchio** for children's theatre. She currently works as a member of the administrative support staff for the Asheville-Buncombe Library System.

She shares a house in Asheville, North Carolina with a long-time companion and five demanding cats. **The Toybox** is her first novel.

you've read the book | now live the adventure with the **immortal eyes: the toybox** sourcebook.

The **immortal eyes: the toybox** sourcebook is the perfect companion to this novel. Every important changeling citizen, along with every freehold in san Francisco, is lavishly expanded upon with details not revealed in the novel. Designed as a story guide for the **changeling: the dreaming** storytelling game, **immortal eyes: the toybox** sourcebook is a must-read for anyone who has come to know the fae of san Francisco.